The Red Gene

Rosalind Beale

Published by New Generation Publishing in 2014

Copyright © Rosalind Beale 2014

First Edition

The author asserts the moral right under the Copyright, Designs and Patents Act 1988 to be identified as the author of this work.

This novel is a work of fiction. Names and characters are a product of the author's imagination and any resemblance to actual persons, living or dead, is entirely coincidental.

All Rights reserved. No part of this publication may be reproduced, stored in a retrieval system or transmitted, in any form or by any means without the prior consent of the author, nor be otherwise circulated in any form of binding or cover other than that which it is published and without a similar condition being imposed on the subsequent purchaser.

www.newgeneration-publishing.com

To Tiffany, with love, for all her help and encouragement

Chapter 1

It was the fringe of autumn yet the sun retained enough of its summer heat to warm Bethany's back as she pedalled vigorously along the leafy suburban roads of North Oxford. She cycled with purpose, oblivious of drawing an admiring glance from a passer-by as he appreciated the rhythmic movement of her slender athletic legs and the bobbing of her titian-red curls. She seemed the essence of a happy and healthy eighteen-year-old, revelling in her youth and without a care in the world.

But little is as it seems.

Beth was troubled. That morning, before leaving the confines of the comfortable Edwardian house where she lived with her parents Desmond and Prudence Burnett, Beth had rowed with her mother and now she was furious with herself for letting her quick temper get the better of her.

Beth's anger often flared no matter how hard she tried to keep it in check. Afterwards she was generally full of regrets and was quick to apologise but this morning the row had made her late for work and she had left the house without making peace with her mother. Beth recognised she would spend an uncomfortable day knowing that her apology would have to wait until the evening when the spontaneity would be lost. Her remorse would, as always, be accepted by Prudence with grace and equanimity but all the same Beth wished she hadn't put it off.

Prudence and Beth differed in all respects. Prudence was a quietly self-assured woman, having grown up the only child in an affluent household where she had been encouraged in all her endeavours. She was petite with pale translucent skin, thick dark wavy hair and deep blue eyes that proclaimed her Irish roots. Beth on the other hand stood out from the crowd, not only for her lanky five foot ten but also because of her mop of bright red curls. At school she had rarely been teased about the colour of her hair. This was partly due to her size but mainly because friends and acquaintances soon became aware that she was extremely adept at quelling those trying to tease with a few well chosen words. Afterwards she often wished she had treated the situation with disdain but somehow her annoyance always got the upper hand.

This morning, apart from her frustration at her inability to keep her temper under wraps, Beth had been disturbed by a remark made by her mother in the heat of the argument. She had raced down the stairs in a tight fitting short skirt that she had recently bought and had been looking forward to wearing. She had dived into the kitchen to bid her mother a hasty goodbye before dashing off to her job at The Flower Basket, a local florist's shop. Prudence had turned from stacking the dishes ready for the daily help's arrival and a frown had puckered the smooth skin of her forehead.

'What's that you're wearing?'

'It's the new skirt I bought on Saturday.' Beth twirled hurriedly. 'Like it?'

'I like the colour but it's much too short, it's well above your knees.'

'Oh Mum it's nineteen sixty-five, everyone is wearing their skirts this length now.'

Prudence hated to be called mum, preferring the formality of mother, but she let it pass this time in order not to detract from the matter of Beth's skirt.

'So they might be but not everyone rides a bicycle to work. That skirt will show an indecent amount of thigh when you're pedalling and what Molly will say having her assistant dressed like that at work I dread to think.'

'Mum, why do you have to be so old fashioned? I'm only eighteen. I don't want to dress like a frumpy old woman. I bought it with my own money and I'm going to wear it whether you approve or not.' Beth turned to leave, bright spots of anger glowing on her cheeks.

'Bethany!' Her mother's sharp voice caused her to turn. 'I object to being referred to as a frumpy old woman …'

'I didn't mean...' Beth was cut short as her mother continued.

'And I don't like 'mum' as you well know. Now while you're living here your father and I expect you to behave in a manner that befits the daughter of a well regarded city solicitor. I don't want people who know us seeing you riding through the city on your bicycle showing your suspenders like some brazen hussy from the depths of Cowley.'

Beth saw red. 'That's all you think about isn't it? What other people think. It's all you care about.' She gasped for breath before yelling, 'Mother you're a snob.'

Prudence's pale cheeks reddened. 'Your temper matches that red hair of yours and where that came from I'll never know. Not from me or your father that's for sure. Now go upstairs and change into something more suitable.' Her small frame turned and Beth was left staring at her mother's rigid back. Prudence's remark concerning the unknown legacy of her red hair and temper took the wind out of her sails and she was left temporarily speechless.

Angry and confused she slammed out of the kitchen and took the stairs two at a time to her room on the top floor where she changed into a skirt that was just a few inches longer than the offending one. Beth reckoned that she had made a sufficient gesture towards her mother's idea of decency. She knew that her employer Molly was broad minded and didn't mind what she wore to work, so long as it was clean. Her clothes were covered by a large green apron when she was in the shop so no one noticed what she was wearing anyway.

Beth rode swiftly and with determination. She wished she had fought her corner in a more measured way and without resorting to shouting at her mother. But the thing that troubled her most was the remark her mother had let drop about the colour of her hair. For some time now Beth had vaguely wondered about her red hair and from whom she had inherited it. Her father Desmond was of average height and, at forty-five with a sedentary job, was beginning to look a little portly. Beth more than matched his height but that was where the similarity ended. His brown hair was neatly cut with a parting on one side and already showed a sprinkling of grey. He was a quiet, serious man with a gentle sense of humour who loved his passionate daughter deeply but did not show his affection in an overly demonstrative way. Her mother was slim but short, reaching only five foot two in her stocking feet. Her dark hair was thick and wavy, quite unlike Beth's mop of titian curls, and she had a quiet poise that was rarely ruffled. Beth thought it strange that she had nothing in common physically or in temperament with either parent. Pedalling hard, she searched her mind for relations that had the slightest hint of red in their hair, but she drew a blank.

Deep in thought and with her head down Beth didn't see the other cyclist hurtle out of a side turning and therefore took no avoiding action. Their handlebars locked together and they struggled unsuccessfully to keep upright. Beth quickly lost her balance and fell with both bicycles on top of her. The other cyclist managed to jump clear.

Chapter 2

'Damn it, oh hell!' He dragged the bicycles off Beth, disentangled them and dumped them on the pavement. Beth sat up slowly and rubbed her knee. The young man squatted beside her. 'I'm so sorry. Are you alright?'

'You idiot, I should think you are sorry. Didn't you see me? Don't you know you have to stop at a junction? And no I'm not alright, I'm hurt and my stockings are ruined.' Beth examined her bleeding knee and the gaping hole in her stocking.

'I'm so sorry.'

'So you said but it's a bit late for regrets, the harm's done now. Didn't you see me?'

'I did see you and I tried to stop but it appears I have no brakes. Here let me help you up.'

'It's ok I can manage.' Beth shrugged off the outstretched helping hand and struggled to her feet. She winced as she put her foot to the ground.

'It's not ok. You're hurt and it's my fault.' The young man took Beth's arm and firmly guided her onto the pavement where she leaned against a garden wall.

'You're too right it's your fault. Whatever possessed you to ride a bicycle with no brakes?'

'I'm not used to bikes. I thought it was alright. I've just obtained it from the police pound. They've got heaps of bikes down there, mostly dumped by ex-students and so they're pleased to get rid of any they can. My name's Rupert by the way.' He held out his hand. 'But all my friends call me Bear.'

The hand was once again ignored but the corner of Beth's mouth twitched. Really boys did give each other weird nicknames.

'They've no right to sell you a bicycle with no brakes,' she said indignantly.

'The constable didn't sell it. When he saw which one I had picked out he said I could have it but that I must get it checked out. I didn't realise that the brakes were completely shot.' Bear paused and looked searchingly at Beth. Despite her challenging attitude, which he conceded was somewhat justified, he liked what he saw. It was his first term at Oxford as a medical student; he knew he was going to have to work hard but he intended to play hard too. He favoured Beth with a disarming smile. 'And your name is?'

Beth dusted the road grit from her hands onto her skirt before replying.

'Bethany,' she muttered, without returning his smile. She bent to examine her bicycle. 'My lovely Pashley! It better not be damaged.'

'Your what?'

'Pashley – it's the make of my bicycle – it's a Pashley Princess. It's less than a year old. I got it for my eighteenth.'

Bear smiled at the idea of a bike being named Princess. The smile deepened when he realised to his satisfaction that he had found out Beth's age.

'Your bike looks alright but you can't ride it with that cut leg and there's no way I'm going to ride this old thing.' He kicked his bike as it lay on its side on the pavement and a wheel spun squeakily. 'Now we had better work out what's to be done. I was going to check out my lodgings in Summertown but I guess that's not on the agenda now.' He paused and ran his hand through his fine fair hair. 'Do you live far from here Beth?'

'My name's Beth*any* and no, not far, but I'm not going home I'm on my way to work.'

'Isn't it a bit late for going *to* work?' Bear looked pointedly at his watch.

Hostility radiated from Beth as she raised her chin defiantly but she managed to swallow a sharp reply. 'I was held up at home.'

'Oh dear and now I'm making you later than ever. Where would work be?'

Beth stared suspiciously. 'Why do you need to know

that?'

'I'm not being nosey; I'm just trying to help.' Bear sighed patiently. 'It was my fault you're hurt so I'm happy to see you safely to work.'

'I'm glad you're happy about it.' Beth dabbed at the blood trickling down her leg and pulled at the ever-enlarging hole in the knee of her stocking.

'That's not what I meant and you know it.' Bear spoke more brusquely than he had intended. Really this girl was making a great deal of a cut knee and a bump on her forehead. But on the other hand she was gorgeous looking and it hadn't been her fault so he conceded she was entitled to be a bit angry. 'If you can possibly tell me where you work and it's not too much for you to walk, I'll push the bikes. Or would you rather I got you a taxi?'

'There's no need for a taxi, I can manage to walk thank you.' Beth retrieved her bicycle and turned it around. 'Actually I think I will go back home and get cleaned up. I can't really turn up at work like this.'

'Ok, that's a good move.' Bear took hold of the handlebars of both bikes and nodded for Beth to lead the way. He seemed relaxed as he walked, pushing a bicycle on either side. Every so often Beth stopped to dab at the trickle of blood from the cut on her knee. 'You ok?'

Beth nodded but said nothing. After a few minutes of silent walking she took a sidelong glance at the young man beside her. He was considerably taller than her and slim with fine fair hair that flopped over his forehead. His hands on the bicycle handle bars were capable-looking with long slender fingers. She liked what she saw and now that she felt calmer, she wished that she had been more polite. Bear felt her eyes on him.

'What do you do for a job... or shouldn't I ask?' he grinned.

Beth bristled slightly at his teasing tone. 'I don't make a habit of giving every strange man I meet my personal details,' she retorted snappishly. Oh dear, why did she have to be so offhand? She bit her lip.

'And very wise too.'

Bear's easy-going nature was infectious and Beth smiled inwardly but, unusually for her, she could not think of anything to say to rescue the situation and so she remained silent.

On their arrival at the house Beth led the way round to the side door.

'Thanks, I can manage now. Please put my bicycle in the shed over there.'

'Are you sure you'll be ok…?' Bear began.

'I'll be fine, there's a first aid kit in the bathroom and my mother's quite good at patching my knees. I've been riding a bicycle since I was ten and it's not the first time I've come off.' The ghost of a smile lit Beth's face and Bear thought how attractive she was. As he reluctantly turned away she called out. 'Thanks for your help. If you want to get your bicycle fixed there's a very good repair shop on Walton Street. Tell Joe I sent you, he's a friend of mine, he'll do a good job for you.'

Inside the house was ominously quiet. Beth called out a greeting but there was no reply. She looked in the hall cupboard to find that her mother's everyday navy jacket was missing. That means she's probably gone to the shops in Summertown, Beth thought. Oh well, she would just have to look after herself.

Annoyingly the first aid kit was not in its usual place and Beth couldn't think where else to look for it, so she did the best she could to remove the road dirt with a wet flannel before going upstairs to remove her torn stockings and muddy skirt. At least I wasn't wearing the new one, she thought, as she changed into a pair of dark blue pleated linen shorts that obviated the need for stockings. The cut on her knee was quite painful and continued to bleed so she decided to walk to work, dropping her bicycle off at Joe's on the way to get it checked for damage.

Chapter 3

Beth entered the florist's shop where she worked via a narrow dark workroom at the rear. At the sound of the back door closing a tall thin woman of indeterminate age appeared through an archway that linked the shop with the workroom. She had a mass of wiry steel-grey hair pulled back into an untidy bun and wore an all-enveloping apron of a heavy green cotton fabric. In her hand she brandished a broom.

'You decided to come in then?'

Beth grinned inwardly. All Molly needs is a tall pointy black hat to complete the disguise, she thought as she reached for her matching apron from the hook behind the door. She knew that Molly's attempts at sarcasm were never ill-meant and that behind her forbidding exterior lived a gentle soul.

Beth moved into the light.

'Oh my lord what have you been up to?' Molly stared at the burgeoning lump on Beth's temple and the blood congealing from the cut on her knee.

'It's nothing much. I fell off my bicycle that's all. Sorry I'm late.'

'You should have gone home.'

'I did, but my mother was out and I couldn't find the first aid box so I just washed off the mud and came straight here. I couldn't leave you to do the orders on your own as well as serve in the shop.' Beth took a breath and slumped onto her work stool. She realised that she didn't feel as well as she made out. She felt cold and more than a little shivery.

Molly gave a wry smile. She had managed for years on her own but nevertheless she was touched by Beth's remark.

Beth had worked for Molly for the best part of two years, first as a Saturday girl and then for longer hours in the school holidays. Initially her parents had been solidly against the idea of her working, particularly in a shop, albeit a florists. The idea of a flower shop slightly alleviated the problem as far as Beth's mother was concerned as she considered it as somewhat up-market but she still had serious reservations about her only daughter working as a shop assistant. Beth's parents had insisted that they could provide her with everything she needed; there was no need for her to earn pocket money. But in the face of her persistent pleas they had finally given in, thinking she would soon tire of the work. But Beth hadn't taken it on for the money. She had a strong creative urge and she loved flowers, so to be able to combine the two gave her enormous satisfaction. Her parents had ultimately resigned themselves to their only child working on Saturdays in a shop. She was the apple of her father's eye and generally got her own way fairly easily.

That was – until the day Beth had announced that she was not going to apply for university.

At first they hadn't taken her seriously but, following a worried call from her careers mistress at the High School, who had been given the same message from Beth, they had realised that their strong-willed daughter meant business. Alternatives had been suggested: teacher training college, nursing, secretarial college… but Beth had shaken her copper curls at all of them. This time her parents had not given way without a fight.

Her mother had been distraught at the constant arguments and her father had been deeply concerned. As a well-educated and liberal-minded man he wanted his moderately clever daughter to have a career and had always presumed that she would attend university, not Oxford or Cambridge perhaps, but at least one of the better red-bricks. 'It's nineteen sixty-four,' he had told her, 'not eighteen sixty-four. Girl's these days need a career, the days of relying on marrying a rich man to keep you in a comfortable manner are past.' This had made Beth smile inwardly. While her father was reasonably well paid for his work as a solicitor, she was aware that their very comfortable house on the Woodstock Road had come as part of her mother's inheritance. However, she had said nothing of this knowledge. She merely reiterated that her chosen career was that of working for Molly Watson in the flower shop. As a sop to their aspirations, she had promised she would attend courses and if possible obtain some qualifications.

'With what end in view?' her father had asked.

'To run my own florist business,' she had happily told them.

The debate had lasted several weeks, with the school backing up Beth's parents in their arguments. Eventually Beth's father had visited Molly Watson in her flat above the flower shop, and had asked her to talk Bethany out of her obsessive desire to work permanently in the shop. That evening he had returned and, following a short but heated discussion with his wife behind the closed door of his study—Beth could hear the firm rise and fall of his voice from her position in the passage—he had summoned Beth and informed her that they would give their blessing to her working at the flower shop for one year. If, in that time, she had gained some useful qualifications and was able to demonstrate a viable career path for herself, they would allow her to stay on. If not, she was to attend the private Secretarial College on St. Giles.

Beth had been astounded at her father's capitulation. She knew Molly Watson had something to do with it but was not going to probe how it had come about. It was sufficient that she had achieved her aim. She had given her father a hug and then twirled her mother around the small room, bumping into the furniture as she went. "Bethany!" her mother had protested, tucking a stray wisp of her soft dark hair behind her ear. But Beth had known from her mother's slightly flushed face that she was not totally displeased. Prudence outwardly supported her husband's views but, not having followed further education herself, she failed to understand why he thought it so important for a girl to have a career. She considered a more important feminine role was to support a husband in his career.

The following Saturday, when Beth had turned up for work at The Flower Basket, Molly had given her a lecture on the value of hard work and commitment. She had then told Beth that there was a permanent job for her at the shop when she left school if she wanted it and if she was serious in her desire to be a florist.

'It's not just a matter of serving in the shop. There's a lot more to running a business than that and much of it is solid hard work, as you will learn,' she had told her. Beth had flung her arms round Molly but had been gently pushed away. 'There's no need for that, I'm your employer not your maiden aunt,' a flushed-faced Molly had stated but in a softer tone had added, 'however, as we're going to be spending a lot of time together you can drop the Mrs. Watson and call me Molly.'

Beth's chalice of pleasure had been full to overflowing. She had put school happily behind her. It wasn't that she hadn't enjoyed her schooldays; it was simply that she had been ready to embark on the next stage of her life and was glad it was of her own choosing.

***

Now Beth faced her broom-toting employer with equilibrium.

'You'd better bathe that nasty cut and put some antiseptic on incase there's dirt in it. There's a first aid box in the cloakroom cupboard. I'll shut up shop and put the kettle on while you're doing it.' Molly propped the broom against the shop wall and crossed the floor to lock the front door.

'We can't shut yet, it's not lunchtime.'

'M'dear, you're in no fit state to serve customers. You'd frighten the best of them away appearing with blood trickling down your leg and a dirty great bruise on your face, not to mention the state of your hair.' Beth put a hand up to the tangled mass of curls. She had been in such a hurry that she hadn't thought to wield a hairbrush. 'And I've had quite enough for this morning,' Molly continued decisively, 'so be a good girl and go and get cleaned up.'

Over hot sweet tea Molly looked thoughtfully at her young assistant. 'Now what possessed you to fall off your bike? It's not like you.'

Beth smiled. The tea was making her feel much better.

'Well actually I didn't fall off.' Molly raised an eyebrow. 'I was knocked off by this rather gorgeous bloke who came hurtling out of a side turning on his bicycle and sent me flying.'

'And does this "gorgeous bloke" have a name?'

'Bear.'

Molly looked flabbergasted. 'What sort of a name do you call that?' she asked in disbelief.

Beth smiled. 'His real name is Rupert but all his friends call him Bear and I think it suits him, he's …'

'Furry?' Molly chortled at her own joke and Beth could not suppress a grin.

'He's extremely handsome.' Beth smiled at the recollection of Bear's firm touch and remembered how his blond hair flopped disarmingly over his forehead. 'I was very rude to him,' she sighed.

'Why am I not surprised?' Molly rolled her eyes in Beth's direction. She was well aware of Beth's short fuse that went with the colour of her hair.

'Well it was his fault, and I told him so, but actually if I'd been paying a bit more attention I might have been able to avoid a collision,' Beth added contritely.

'What was so important that you weren't concentrating on the road, or would you rather not tell me?' Molly never liked to pry into other peoples' concerns but was always ready to lend a sympathetic ear when required.

Beth took a few mouthfuls of tea and Molly waited patiently. Beth looked down and with a thoughtful finger traced an imaginary pattern on the workbench. Eventually she spoke.

'I was thinking about my mother.'

'And?' Molly prompted.

'We had an awful row this morning and she put this idea in my mind about me being different.'

'And how are you different from us ordinary mortals?' Molly laughed.

'My hair for a start.' Beth pushed an edgy hand through her titian curls making them stick out from her head.

'My dear girl, you're not the only person with red hair.' Molly's voice took on an impatient air.

'It's not red,' Beth snapped.

'Well carrot or ginger or copper or whatever you want to call it. It's all the same to me. No point in being touchy about it. And anyway it's beautiful and, as I said, you're not the only one with red hair.'

Beth, slightly appeased by Molly's compliment, continued.

'I know there are plenty of people around with red hair but none of them are in my family,' she paused, looking at Molly to assess the effect of her words, 'and I've been wondering who I take after, but as far as I know there's no one in the family with hair like mine,' she repeated.

Molly was puzzled. 'There has to be someone, somewhere among your ancestors.'

'Well there isn't and there could be another …explanation.'

'And what might that be?'

Beth hesitated. The idea she was about to share with Molly had only recently occurred to her and she still wasn't sure whether she was being ridiculously fanciful or not. She decided to continue and see what Molly made of it.

'The reason I'm the only person with red hair in my family is because … ' she took a deep breath '… I'm adopted'

'What!' Molly banged her empty mug down with some force. 'That is the most absurd suggestion I've heard in a long time, just as though your parents would have left you in ignorance of such a thing.' She shook her head in

14

disbelief, certain that not telling a child it was adopted could not have happened.

Beth was taken back by the vehemence and conviction of Molly's reply.

'I didn't really mean it – it was a kind of joke remark.' Beth's downcast face moved Molly.

'Some joke!' Molly's voice softened. 'Ask your parents about red-heads in the family. There's bound to be at least one somewhere and that knowledge will settle your worries.'

Beth nodded miserably. She didn't have Molly's conviction but at least it was worth a try. Now that the idea had taken root she desperately needed to find an answer.

Chapter 4

Prudence sat at the kitchen table, an untouched cup of tea in front of her. Her day had been most unsatisfactory. First there had been the awful row with Bethany which had upset her more than she would admit. Then Mrs. Taylor, her cleaning lady, hadn't turned up, so after she had visited the local shops she had spent the day tidying an already neat house. She had scrubbed the spotless kitchen table, flapped a cloth around the dust-less surfaces in the living rooms and plumped up a row of fat cushions on the velvet covered three-piece suite. Upstairs she made the beds and smoothed the immaculate satin bedspread in her and Desmond's room and tweaked the chintz curtains in the guest rooms before refolding the towels in the rose-pink bathroom. Flitting aimlessly from one chore to another, her mind kept reverting to Bethany's outburst that morning and she wished she hadn't let her daughter leave the house in such a bad mood. She loved Bethany dearly but sometimes she couldn't help wishing she had born a more placid child. Perhaps if Bethany had not been their only child things would have been better, but somehow Prudence doubted that siblings would have made much difference to Bethany's nature.

Her husband Desmond arrived home to find Prudence gazing thoughtfully at the cup of tea in front of her. He dropped a light kiss on top of her head and she looked up with a weak smile.

'You're early.'

'Got to go out again – meeting at the Rotary Club about the firework show we're putting on in the South Parks.'

'But that's weeks away.'

'Yes, but it takes quite a lot of planning and it's not a good idea to leave these things until the last minute.' Prudence nodded and Desmond continued. 'Haven't got time for supper before I leave so I'll have something on a tray when I get back, but I could do with a cup of tea.' He inclined his head towards Prudence's cup. She got up hurriedly.

'This is cold, I'll make some fresh.' Prudence bustled about making a fresh pot and laying a tea tray with clean cups and a plate of biscuits. She put the tray down with a sigh and began to pour.

Desmond looked at her thoughtfully. 'Anything the matter Prue?' Prudence didn't approve of shortening peoples' names and Desmond was the only person she allowed to call her Prue. Secretly she liked the way he pronounced the shortening, it made her feel special.

'It's Bethany,' she told him with a sigh. 'She got in a temper this morning when I told her to change her skirt.'

'Why did you do that?'

'Because the one she was wearing was far too short to wear riding a bicycle.'

Desmond helped himself to a biscuit and drank his tea thoughtfully. 'Perhaps it's time we let Bethany make her own decisions, she is after all nearly nineteen.'

'But I couldn't let her go out making a spectacle of herself like that!' Prudence was indignant.

Desmond patted her hand. 'Maybe, if left alone to try riding her bicycle in a very short skirt, she might have come to the right decision and returned home to change it for something more appropriate,' he gently suggested. Prudence lowered her eyes and traced her finger round the rim of her cup. Looking back at her husband she nodded.

'I think maybe you're right. I do treat her like a child still. I forget that's she's grown up and needs to think for herself.'

Desmond squeezed the hand he covered with his own. 'At her age you were already married and had a child on the way.'

Prudence smiled and a faint flush touched her cheeks. 'So I was, but things have changed. At the end of the war there seemed a greater urgency to get on with life. These days girls don't seem to want to get married so soon. Bethany doesn't even have a boyfriend at the moment.'

'And a good thing too. Girls should have a career and pursue their independence. There's plenty of time for marriage after that.' Desmond drained his cup and stood up. 'This won't get the work done. I'll be back about nine.' He gave Prudence's hand a final squeeze and left the room.

Beth parked her bicycle in the shed next to a large black one belonging to her father. It was little used these days. Since his acceptance of a partnership in the firm of Jenks, Jenks and Sparks and the advent of the shiny new Morris Oxford, the old bicycle had become obsolete and rusted its days away in the open shed. Beth's was the only other bicycle there. Her mother refused to own one. She either walked to her Oxford destinations or, if a little too far for walking, she took a taxi. For destinations outside Oxford, such as London for shopping and the hairdressers, she took the train.

Beth let herself in through the back door and hurried the few steps along a dark passage to the kitchen door. The kitchen was large and light due to tall French windows at the far end that opened out onto a paved terrace overlooking the rear walled garden. In her grandparents day it had been the dining room but with the demise of a cook and maid Prudence had decided that she didn't like the idea of the kitchen being in the basement and had it moved lock stock and barrel to the former dining room. The morning room became the dining room and the basement was converted into an informal sitting room. Her bedroom apart, the basement was the room Beth loved the most.

On Beth's entrance Prudence looked up but kept stirring the pan in front of her. Over her pencil slim skirt she wore a sprigged apron with a tiny bib that did little to protect the silk blouse beneath. There was a slight tension between mother and daughter as both remembered their parting of that morning. Beth bent to place a kiss on her mother's lightly powdered cheek and her mother slid her free arm round Bethany's waist, giving it a squeeze before releasing it to turn her concentration back to the progress of her sauce.

'Sorry about this morning,' Beth whispered in her mother's ear. Prudence smiled her acceptance of the apology and gave Beth another brief hug.

'I'm sorry too Bethany, we shouldn't have shouted at each other like that.' Apologies made, the tension eased. 'Good day darling?'

'Mmm...' Beth stretched her arms above her head and yawned. 'I got knocked off my bicycle.'

Prudence dropped her spoon into the saucepan and gave her daughter her full attention. 'My dear, whatever happened? Are you much hurt?'

'Nothing much, just a scratch on my knee and a bump on my forehead.'

Prudence looked her daughter up and down. 'It doesn't look like nothing much to me. Sit down and let me take a proper look.' Prudence removed the remains of a large stained sticking plaster from Beth's knee and examined the cut. 'It's quite deep. Stay there while I get a dressing. 'A few minutes later the cut was bathed and covered with a soft white dressing and arnica had been applied to the bruising on Beth's temple. 'There, you'll do.' Prudence closed the lid of the first aid box in her matter-of-fact way. 'Now I must get back to the sauce otherwise it'll be full of lumps. Why don't you pop up and get washed and changed while I finish off? Your father's home but he has to go out again in a few minutes – just called to pick up some papers for the Rotary club meeting – so he'll have his supper on a tray in the study later. I thought, as it's only the two of us this evening, we might for once eat in here, that is if you don't mind.'

''Course not – nice and cosy in the kitchen.' Beth was pleased; she wished they ate supper in the kitchen more often, but her mother was a stickler for formality and so the mahogany dining table saw regular use.

Upstairs Beth kicked off her shoes, then unbuttoned her shorts and let them slide to the floor in a heap of navy pleated linen. Her blouse followed and lay where if fell to one side of the shorts. She crossed in her underwear to the washbasin in the far corner of the room. While the basin slowly filled she studied her face in the mirror, searching for some small feature that would link her physically to her mother. But there was nothing. Not a single thing to say: "hey, look, this is my smile and it's just like my mother's" or for others to comment – "she's definitely got your eyes Prudence". From the top of her thick auburn curls to the tips of her size six feet on the end of her long athletic legs she was the antithesis of her petite, dark-haired, blue-eyed mother. Beth looked down and wrestled quickly with the tap as water began to pour down the overflow.

Having washed and relegated her cast off clothes to the linen basket, Beth surveyed the contents of her wardrobe for something comfortable to wear. Her dresses were in uniformly plain green, blue or neutral fabrics. Not a yellow, red or pink among them. When they searched the dress shops for a new purchase her mother always commented – "we must take into consideration the colour of your hair my dear". And Beth always agreed – she felt it better to save her arguments for more important matters – but how she longed to make a bit of a statement now and then with what she wore. A slim-fitting mini dress in shocking pink was what she desired. It would add panache to her otherwise dull wardrobe and might even divert attention from her hair. Beth unhooked a pale blue dress with a full gathered skirt and built-in petticoat. One day I think I'll get married in shocking pink for the pleasure of seeing the horror on my mother's face as I glide up the aisle, she thought and a spontaneous giggle surfaced.

Beth laid the dress on the bed and sat down beside it. Her mind slid back to the question of her uncharacteristic temper and accompanying flaming hair. Despite having outwardly dismissed the idea of her being adopted she couldn't banish the thought from her mind. Beth knew that she had a very well developed imagination and so she was determined to keep her concerns in check. She stretched out, tucked her hands beneath her head and thought about the possibility of a family member past or present who had the same colouring as her.

The tinkling of the dinner bell roused her. Punctuality at mealtimes had been instilled into Beth since childhood. With practiced haste she stepped into the blue dress, pushed her arms into the sleeves and swiftly raised the zip. She brushed her hair vigorously and fastened it back into a short ponytail. Snatching up a matching cardigan, she hurtled headlong down the two flights of stairs, only slowing when she reached the hallway.

Beth had a healthy appetite and Prudence was a very good cook. She gained pleasure from seeing others enjoy the food she prepared. They ate in silence for a few minutes then Prudence enquired into the details of Beth's accident. Beth gave her the briefest of details but Prudence was not going to be put off.

'You should speak to your father about it,' she advised, 'there's a possibility that you could sue that young man for damages to yourself and your bicycle. That Pashley was very expensive you know and you've had it less than a year.'

'Mum!' Beth glared. 'I've no intention of suing anyone. It was mainly his fault but if I had been paying more attention I might have been able to avoid him.'

Prudence hated being called mum. She shrugged, realising that she was telling Bethany what to do again. 'I just thought...you don't have to say you weren't paying attention.'

'Mum. He was a student, probably penniless, and I was very rude to him at the time and he was very nice looking...' Beth tailed off remembering his smile and blond hair that flopped into his eyes. She wished she had been nicer to him. 'So I'm not going to sue, alright?'

There was that "mum" again. Prudence decided that she would tackle Bethany about it. She appreciated that she was too old to call her mummy and would suggest once more that she used "mother" instead. But Prudence realised that this was not an opportune moment to bring up the subject. She was familiar with her daughter's manner when she was set on a particular course of action. She knew of old that no amount of advice would persuade her once she had made her mind up and so she cast around for another topic of conversation.

'I see you've put your hair up.'

'Yes I've been practicing so that I can wear it like this for work. It's getting longer and it won't get in the way so much fastened back.' Beth reached up and ran the short pony tail through her hand. She rather liked her new hairstyle.

'I suppose it will be better tied back when you're busy but it seems a shame to hide such lovely curls especially when the colour of your hair is so special.'

Beth was astounded; her mother rarely voiced complements. But this was the opening she needed. To give herself a moment to think she cleared their empty plates. Returning quickly to her seat she leaned across the table and laid a hand lightly on her mother's wrist.

'Where does my hair colour come from? You say it's unusual but there must be someone in the family with hair like mine. Yours is very dark and Daddy's is brown so I must have inherited it from someone else... a grandparent perhaps. I remember granny and grandpa both having white hair but maybe one was ginger originally?'

Prudence frowned. She had wondered the same thing when Beth's fair baby down had developed its signature red glow. As there hadn't been an obvious answer to the question she had put it out of her mind until recently.

'Well, there are no redheads in my family. I remember my mother having dark hair and my father was dark also and Aunt Helen, my father's sister, had light brown hair. As you know there are no aunts and uncles on my mother's side as she was an only child like me.' Prudence saw Bethany's disappointment and added, 'but I suppose there could be someone of my grandparents' time that I'm unaware of.'

'What about Daddy's family?

'As far as I know they all have dark or light brown hair but you'll have to ask your father – he might know of someone.' Prudence regarded her downhearted daughter. 'Is it very important to you to know who you take after?'

Beth nodded. The idea that she might be adopted had taken hold again and it gave her a marked sense of foreboding. 'I would just like to know, that's all,' she told her mother.

'Well ask your father when he gets in, he shouldn't be long. And I must get on.' Prudence hurriedly cleared the last of the dishes and stacked them next to the sink. 'Would you be a dear and wash the dishes for me? If I stop to do them I'll be late for my bridge evening. I could leave them for Mrs. Taylor to do when she comes in the morning but I always think it looks rather slovenly to leave out washing up from the previous day.'

Beth didn't mind. There wasn't much washing up and anyway it was a mindless task that gave her the opportunity to think. By the time she had stowed the last dish she knew what she was going to do. Somewhere in her father's study there was a photograph album. Beth thought it was just possible that the album held the answer she needed.

Chapter 5

After a short search of the shelves Beth found what she wanted. The album was covered in brown leather-cloth and to hold the pages in place it was looped through with had a length of faded gold cord ending in a pair of frayed tassels. She settled down in her father's armchair and opened the book. Immediately her heart sank. All of the photographs of her father's generation and before were black and white! Why hadn't she thought of that? They were not going to be much help in pinpointing the colour of someone's hair. Despite this major setback Bethany decided to look carefully at each picture just incase there was the slightest hint of anything other than blond, brown or black.

Each photograph was held in place on its grey card page by four white corners and under each was written the names of the occupants. There were several pictures of her grandparents, some in middle age and some later. They were no help. They were greying in the former and snowy white in the latter. Photographs of her father's brother and sister were equally unhelpful. Her uncle obviously had dark hair like her father and her aunt's was really quite light. Probably mouse-brown Beth conjectured but maybe … She gently eased the photograph of her aunt out from its restraining corners and took it over to the table lamp where she held it under the light to examine it more carefully.

'Bethany what are you doing in here?'

Beth spun round at the sound of her father's voice and dropped the photograph. She had been so engrossed that she hadn't heard him come home.

Desmond Burnett was a serious man. As a solicitor he dealt with his clients efficiently, politely, if necessary firmly, but always with respect. He treated his daughter in much the same way. Despite the fact that at times her outbursts disconcerted him, he loved her dearly, although he did not show it in a demonstrative way.

'Sorry, I was just looking at the photos in the old album.' Beth bent to retrieve the fallen picture and attempted to slot it back into the restraining corners, but replacing it was infinitely more difficult than taking it out.

'Here, let me do that.' Her father deftly repositioned the photograph. 'What made you decide to look at the album, you haven't done that since you were a small girl?'

'Err…I was interested…' Beth couldn't decide whether or not to confide in her father. He was a kindly man and Beth was very fond of him but she had never been in the habit of sharing confidences with him.

'Interested in what Bethany?' Her father was waiting for a reply.

'Interested in finding out who I take after with this red hair of mine.' There, she'd said it.

'Whom, Bethany.'

'Pardon.'

'*Whom* I take after…'

'Oh, yes, sorry.' Beth began to wish she hadn't spoken.

'Well looking at black and white photographs won't be much help will it?' He smiled benignly.

'I know, I just thought there might be some clue.'

'And was there?' Beth shook her head. 'Perhaps I can help. Come on sit down at my desk and we'll look together and I'll tell you what I know.'

They settled down side by side and Beth felt contentment steal over her. It was agreeable sharing time with her father.

'I was looking at the photo of your sister, Aunt Anne.'

Desmond shook his head. 'She wasn't red-haired. Her hair was a light brown before she went grey. My brother was dark-haired like me and neither of my parents were red-heads. No, we need to look further back than my generation.' He turned the pages back to those showing his grandparents. 'Unfortunately I only remember my grandparents with grey hair. My grandfather had steely grey hair so it was very unlikely that his hair had been red.

I suppose my grandmother's hair could have been but when I knew her she had quite a sallow skin, not the pale complexion that usually accompanies red hair.'

Beth sagged as her father turned over a page. This was getting her nowhere. 'Who are the children in this picture?' She pointed to a boy of about eleven holding a baby on his knee with a small girl standing by his side.

'The little girl standing is my mother, your grandmother, the boy is her brother, Uncle John, and the baby is her sister, Aunt Edith. They would be your Great Uncle and Great Aunt.'

'Did any of them have red hair?'

'Your grandmother as I've already mentioned did not and I'm pretty sure Uncle John was dark-haired but I can't be sure about Aunt Edith.'

'Why not?'

'I only remember seeing her once. She was much younger than the other two and married an Australian. My parents went to the wedding but I was too young to attend. She and her new husband came to visit us shortly afterwards and the next thing I heard was that they had gone to live in Australia.' Beth listened with mounting impatience.

'That's very interesting Daddy but did she have red hair?'

Beth's father scratched his ear. 'My dear I really couldn't say.'

'Why ever not?'

'I was only about six years old when she left. A child of that age doesn't notice such things. Had her hair been bright ginger I might have remembered but if it was a beautiful rich auburn like yours it's quite possible that it wouldn't have registered.'

Beth slumped in her chair. No result. It looked as though she would never know how she came to have copper-coloured curls. Desmond picked up on her disappointment.

'I'm sorry Bethany. It's obviously quite important to

you?' Beth nodded and pulled a face.

'If Granddad and Grandmama were still alive I could ask them but it's too late for that now.'

'Indeed.' Beth's father looked grave.

'Is Great Aunt Edith still alive?'

'As far as I know she is. We haven't heard from them for a while but a couple of Christmases ago we received a card and ...wait a sec... if I remember rightly, there was a photograph.' Beth's heart skipped. Maybe they were getting somewhere at last. 'Now where would I have put it?' Desmond handed Beth the album and began to search absently through some of his desk drawers. Beth meanwhile leafed through the remaining pages.

'It's here Daddy, in the back of the album.' Beth picked up a faded envelope bearing an Australian stamp and withdrew a Christmas card and a coloured photograph.

'Must have put it in there intending to stick the photo in the album later. Let's have a look at it.'

Their two heads touched as they craned to examine the picture. It showed an elderly couple seated on a veranda each holding a drink which they lifted towards the camera in a toast. The man wore flannels and an open-necked shirt and the woman wore a flowery dress in a bright shade of pink. To Beth's enormous disappointment her Great Aunt Edith had a halo of blue-rinsed curls.

'Not much help there then.' Her father replaced the photograph and closed the album. 'Of course I should have thought – Aunt Edith must be well into her seventies by now.'

Beth gave a disappointed sigh as she replaced the album on the bookshelf.

I know who I am – Bethany Burnett – and that's good enough for me she told herself firmly. She glanced at her father taking some papers out of his briefcase and arranging them neatly on his desk. He was a kindly man and Beth was very fond of him, as she was of her mother. How could she upset her lovely caring parents by suggesting that she thought she might not be their natural daughter? She pushed the idea to the back of her mind and was determined that it should stay there. Of course they would have told her if she had been adopted. But the doubt niggled in the back of her mind and refused to be rationalised. How could she stop this nagging uncertainty and find out for sure? It was then that the answer came to her; the names of her birth parents would be on her her birth certificate! She had never actually seen her birth certificate, there had not been an occasion when she needed to, but now it was imperative that she did. Why hadn't she thought of that before? Beth was elated at having solved the problem, but then came the panic – what if it confirmed her worst fears? And what reason would she give her parents for wanting to see the certificate? She could hardly say she wanted to be sure she wasn't adopted.

'Mum's left your supper on a tray. Would you like me to get it for you?'

Desmond looked up and smiled at his beautiful daughter. 'That would be very kind of you Bethany. Thank you.'

As she carried the tray to her father's study Beth thought about Bear who had knocked her off her bicycle and wished she had been nicer to him. Why do I have to be so snappy with people? My mother and father are not like that, why do I have to have such a quick temper? And that thought strengthened her resolve to find a way of checking her birth certificate; after all it was clear she did not take after either parent and she needed to know why.

Chapter 6

Beth hummed cheerfully, if a little tunelessly, as she bowled along enjoying the afternoon sunshine and the fresh breeze that had sprung up. Her thoughts were firmly fixed on her encounter with Bear. She wished she'd found out more about him and wondered if there was a possibility of bumping into him again. Not literally of course, she remembered the collision with a shudder. At least, apart from a few tiny scratches, her bicycle was undamaged and she wondered if he had been successful in getting his repaired. It was this thought that led to the germ of an idea. Perhaps if Bear had called in at the bicycle repair shop she had recommended, Joe, the owner, might have a name and address for him. He wouldn't give it to her willingly of course but she reckoned she would be able to persuade him to part with it eventually. But what would she do with the information if, by a lucky chance, she did come by it? She couldn't turn up on his doorstep with a "Hi how are you?" particularly after she'd been so rude to him. Oh well she'd think of something.

Ahead of Beth a girl walked with her shoulders bent to counteract the weight of a bulging canvas bag slung over her shoulder. She was slender with a fair bob that lifted with the breeze but it was the apparent weight of the bag that caught Beth's eye. As Beth approached, two young women walking abreast were about to pass the girl from the opposite direction and Beth was astounded to see that they bumped her forcefully as they went by. No word of apology was spoken and indeed, the two smiled at each other as they went on their way. The girl had tried to take avoiding action, resulting in her bag slipping from her shoulder and landing on the pavement with a thud. There was no grass verge on this road and the pavement adjoining the small front gardens of the terraced houses was narrow. The contents of the bag, mostly books and papers, cascaded across the pavement and into the gutter.

The girl bent to retrieve the books and looked up with dismay as a light breeze fluttered the papers further along the road and out of her reach. Beth pressed the pedals down with more urgency and stopped a little further on. She propped her bicycle against the curb and snatched up a handful of papers. The rest she chased along the gutter until she had gathered them all.

'Sorry they're a bit muddy.' Beth handed the papers to the girl who stuffed them hurriedly into her bag.

'Thank you so much; I would have been desperate if I'd lost that lot.' The girl gave Beth a bright smile and began to refill her bag with the pile of books at her feet.

'Here, let me help.'

'Thanks again.' The girl heaved the heavily loaded bag into her arms and nodded a goodbye to Beth.

'Hey, you can't manage that lot like that!'

'Looks like I'm going to have to. The strap's broken so it's the only way I'm going to get them home.'

'Let me help.' Beth looked at the struggling girl and saw frustration in her eyes. 'Here, put them in my bicycle basket and you may as well put the bag on top there's no way you're going to carry it with that broken strap. I'm Beth by the way'.

The girl hesitated for a thoughtful moment. 'Katie,' she said with a smile as she began to pile her belongings into the bicycle basket.

'Come on I'll walk you home. Where do you live?'

'Jericho, Juxon Street, but please…if it's out of your way ….'

Beth shook her head. 'It's not out of my way. I work at The Flower Basket just round the corner on Walton Street, we're practically neighbours.' The girl nodded but made no further comment.

Beth hauled the heavily-laden bicycle onto the pavement and proceeded towards Walton Street with a subdued Katie by her side. She stole a fleeting look at the girl walking quietly beside her. She can only be a year or two older than me Beth thought and yet strangely she felt protective towards her, as she might to someone younger. Why had those two pushed past her like that? Did the girl know them? Beth was convinced that they had barged into her on purpose, so why had they picked on this particular girl? Bethany knew what it was to stand out from the crowd, although in her case it had not resulted in bullying or even much teasing. She had been blessed with a strong physique and, when the need arose, a powerful temper. She shot a friendly smile in Katie's direction and received a flicker of a smile in return. They walked in silence for a while until Beth felt the need to find some answers.

'What was that all about?' Katie shrugged and looked away, thrusting her hands deep into her jacket pockets. Beth persisted. 'It looked to me as though those two pushed you on purpose? Do you know them?' There was a long pause as they waited to cross into Walton Street. 'Come on, you can tell me.' Beth was concerned that the incident she had witnessed was not an isolated occurrence. Katie peeped from under her untidy fringe. Her straight fair bob swayed gently as she walked. After a sideways glance in Beth's direction, she spoke softly so that Beth had to bend her head to catch the words.

'It's nothing really.'

'Didn't look like nothing to me. They shouldn't get away with behaviour like that.' A sigh escaped Katie's lips as she straightened her shoulders but she remained silent. Beth halted. 'Katie, you really need to talk about this. If you know those two there has to be a reason why they barged into you like that. We don't know each other, we're strangers. What harm can it do to share a problem with a stranger?'

Katie took a long look at Beth, as though weighing up her potential as a confidante and then quietly she began to speak. 'They barged into me because they remembered me from school.'

'Why...' Bethany prompted, sure that there was more to this than it appeared.

Katie shrugged. 'They were in the same class as me at

the High School and they were bullies.'

'What did they do?'

'Well it seems trivial now…' Katie paused and Beth nodded encouragement. 'They used to slam doors in my face and they'd call me Miss Clever Clogs in a sneering kind of way and whenever I spoke in class they would make a hissing noise. It was difficult for the teacher to know who was doing it so they got away with it most of the time.' She paused and scrutinised Beth's face, trying to assess the impact of her words.

'Why did they do that?'

Katie looked embarrassed. 'It could be because I'm reasonably good at exams and I quite enjoy school work. I was on a scholarship you see. There was no way my parents could afford the fees but my primary school teacher persuaded them to let me sit for a scholarship and I was lucky enough to pass.'

'Goodness, you must be pretty clever then.'

'Not really. I just enjoy learning new things and I find it easy to remember stuff. Anyway, because I was on a scholarship I was expected to work hard and the school was keen to get as many girls as possible into university so everyone was expected to work towards that end…'

'Don't I know it!' Beth's sudden and heartfelt interjection caused Katie eyes to widen. 'I was at the High too. I only left in July and the head was not at all pleased when I refused to try for university, neither were my parents – but that's another story.'

'I thought I recognised you. Didn't you play netball for the first team?'

'Fancy you remembering me out of that group!' Beth grinned.

'It's your hair, it makes you stand out.'

'Oh, and here's me thinking it was my excellent ball skills and goal scoring that caught your eye.'

Katie blushed. 'I didn't mean…'

'It's ok, only joking!' Beth shot a reassuring grin. 'My hair has a lot to answer for, I couldn't get away with anything at school. I stood out like a sore thumb.' The smile faded. 'But we were talking about your problems not mine. Tell me more, maybe I can help.'

Katie smiled. It was good to talk to this friendly attractive girl. 'Well I sat for the Oxford entrance and passed and now I'm in my third year at St Hilda's studying maths. Those two girls didn't do much work and got into trouble for that and eventually for bullying and they were asked to leave at the end of the fifth form. Unfortunately they still recognise me but luckily I rarely cross paths with them. This afternoon was an isolated incident.'

At the low wooden gate that guarded the short path to the front door of the white-painted terraced house Katie held out her arms for her belongings. Beth helped carry the books to the front doorstep and an attractive smile illuminated the girl's pale face.

'Thank you for helping with my books, it was very kind of you. Mum will be home from work now, will you come in and have a cup of tea?' Beth smiled at the formality of Katie's invitation and wished that she could accept.

'Sorry, would love to but I must get back to the shop and help Molly with the clearing up before we close. I'm late already... she'll be wondering what has happened to me.' Beth turned her bicycle and hopped onto the saddle with a cheery wave for her new friend. She cycled swiftly back towards Walton Street with the dawning realisation that she had been away from the shop for a considerable length of time.

The Flower Basket was situated on the corner of Walton Street and a narrow side street. Beth was concerned to see that the pavement in front of the green-painted façade was empty. The customary row of buckets containing bunched flowers had already been taken inside. She took a quick look at her wristwatch. Three-fifteen. No that couldn't possibly be right. She raised it to her ear. Silence. Once again she had forgotten to wind the wretched thing up! Well, if the flower buckets had been moved into the shop, it must be much later than she thought. With mounting concern, Bethany hurried round the side of the building past Molly's little Austin van parked on the side street and hastily parked her bicycle in the back yard. She entered breathlessly through the rear door into the dark workroom. She could hear the rasp of Molly's broom as she vigorously swept up the debris from the shop floor.

'Hi Molly, sorry I'm late.'

Molly ceased her sweeping. 'You going to make a habit of taking the afternoon off when I send you out on a delivery?'

'So sorry Molly. The lady in Summertown loved the posy you made up for her.' Molly's frown softened. 'But she wanted to tell me all about her grandson who had sent the flowers. She sounded so proud of him I felt I had to stop and listen, but I did politely refuse the cup of tea she offered. Then on my way back there was this girl and some people barged past her and the strap broke on her bag and she spilled all her books and I had to help…'

'Alright, alright, save me the sordid details. Here, the shop floor needs sweeping then you can give me a hand tidying up in here.' Molly's smile belied the harshness of her words as she passed the broom to an eager Beth.

Half an hour later the shop was ready for the following day's trade and the workroom was scrubbed and neat.

'Now,' Molly untied the long ties of her apron, 'don't forget tomorrow is Saturday and the wholesaler will be here early, so make sure you arrive in good time. I've got a lot of early deliveries to make so it's imperative that you're here to take in the order…and don't forget to check it, it's not beyond that no-good delivery man to sell us short. Don't trust anyone in business, that's my motto, then you won't get diddled.' Beth smiled widely. She loved it when Molly went off on one of her rants. 'It's no laughing matter m'girl,' Molly continued but Beth could see the hint of a smile pulling at her mouth. 'And for goodness sake wind your watch up when you go to bed tonight and no stopping on the way to sort out other people's problems.'

'But Molly, the poor girl was distressed I had to help her.'

Molly's brown eyes twinkled. Deep down she approved of Bethany's soft heart. 'How about you tell me about it over a cup of tea? That is if you've got the time.'

'I've always got time for a cup with you,' Beth answered happily, hanging up her apron next to Molly's and, picking up her cardigan, she followed Molly upstairs to her little flat.

The flat was simply furnished, not with old-fashioned clutter or with the brash modern teak and ebonised furniture that was fast becoming popular, but rather with a few simple traditional pieces nicely arranged. The soft furnishings were subtle and muted. No lip service was paid here to contemporary designs in orange, lime green or purple. Instead bold accents of colour were provided by a pair of eye-catching flower arrangements placed on matching highly polished occasional tables.

Bethany settled herself in a small dark blue wing chair, one of a pair that stood either side of the fireplace, and surveyed the room. She loved its simplicity and subtle colours of greys and blues. It was a comfortable space, there were soft cushions to snuggle into and the cream painted fireplace had been fitted with a gas fire that flickered a warm glow into the room. Molly entered with a tea tray that she carefully lowered onto a table between them.

'Tell me about your good deed for today,' she demanded as she carefully poured two cups and offered a plate of biscuits to Beth. So Beth related how she had helped Katie home with her load of books. Molly tut-tutted throughout the discourse, shaking her head over her tea cup.

'Why ever do they behave like that? No doubt got everything money could buy, sent to a posh school, and yet they have to be mean and nasty. She sounds like a nice enough girl though,' she commented when Beth had finished.

'Because she's different, that's why,' Beth retorted with feeling. 'She's clever and works hard and doesn't come from a privileged background like theirs.' Molly looked up sharply, startled at Beth's passionate response. 'I know what it's like to be different,' Beth continued in a quieter tone. Her worries, particularly those associated with her red hair, were taking up more and more of her quiet thinking time but now didn't feel like the right time to air them.

She finished her tea. 'See you tomorrow Molly. Thanks for the tea.'

Molly looked thoughtful as she cleared away the tea things. That girl has got something on her mind, she thought, and the sooner she deals with it the better.

Chapter 7

Beth absently swept up the debris of stalks and leaves left from the arrangement she had just completed and tipped the bits into the bin. Her mind was not on her work this afternoon, her thoughts were increasingly with Bear. She nursed the hope that he might find a way of getting in touch with her. The more she thought about him the more attractive the memory of him became. She wished wholeheartedly that she had not been so angry after the bicycle accident and had been friendlier when he had walked her home, and why for goodness' sake hadn't she told him where she worked? Not for the first time Beth regretted her quick temper but what could she do about it? The more she tried to curb it the worse it seemed to get.

It was while Beth brooded over her problems that an idea occurred to her. Why not write to Aunt Edith in Australia; the aunt in the photo who just might have had red hair when she was younger? She could ask her if she had the temper that was universally linked to red hair and if so how had she managed it. If the photo was anything to go by it appeared that Aunt Edith was happily married and had been so for many years so she must have got to grips with it somehow. It was a bit cheeky but what had she to lose? The worse that could happen was that Aunt Edith didn't reply. Beth's mind was made up. She would write that evening as soon as she got home but she wouldn't mention the letter to her parents, they might not like the idea.

Beth continued to daydream about Bear making contact and asking her out, he knew where she lived after all, perhaps he would call round one evening? When she had collected her bicycle from Joe's repair shop she had described Bear but Joe had said gruffly that no one of that sort had called at the shop. So now there was little else she could do but wait and hope. Up until now she had been content to socialise with a group of her old school friends but since meeting Bear she felt differently. She remembered his long slender fingers on the handlebars of her bicycle and butterflies careered around in her stomach.

Molly bustled into the shop at the precise moment that Beth gave vent to a huge yawn.

'You getting to bed early enough?' she enquired with a smirk and Beth coloured. 'It's alright,' Molly picked some small pieces of greenery out of Beth's hair, 'you've worked hard today m'dear and it's time for a tea break. I'll make it today then you can sit down in the workroom and make up the rest of the bouquets that have been ordered while I mind the shop.'

Beth smiled her thanks and settled happily to her allotted tasks. She loved making up the orders and tried hard to make sure that each one gave out a suitable message. Her first order was destined for the maternity hospital and the proud father was going to collect it on his way to visit his wife and new baby girl later that afternoon. She was engrossed in perfecting the basket arrangement containing a posy of pink rosebuds, white chrysanthemums and gypsophila, when she heard a man's voice in the shop.

'Could you make up a bouquet for me please?'

'When did you want it for?' That was Molly's voice.

'This afternoon if possible.'

'Well we are quite busy but we could possibly manage one more if it's kept reasonably simple. What did you want in the bouquet?'

'I'm not sure ... don't know much about flowers I'm afraid – I just want something superb for a extraordinary girl.'

'Perhaps I can make some suggestions. We've some lovely roses in this week or maybe freesias would be more appropriate?' The voices became indistinct as Molly moved across the shop to point out some of the blooms available and Beth stopped listening to concentrate on putting the finishing touches of pink and white ribbons on the new baby's basket of flowers.

Molly came into the workroom with a fresh order form in her hand. 'We've got a bit of a rushed job on here. The customer doesn't want the bouquet to be delivered, he's calling back in half an hour to collect it so we need to get a move on.'

'Oh, shame, we won't know who the recipient is then.' Beth particularly liked getting out on her bicycle to make local deliveries. She enjoyed seeing the pleasure that the thought behind an arrangement of flowers invariably brought.

'Well actually I do know who they're for.' Beth placed the finished pink and white posy basket on the shelf and looked at Molly expectantly. Molly's lips twitched. 'Perhaps I shouldn't divulge a confidence.'

'Oh Molly, come on I'm sure he didn't tell you in confidence. He sounded young. Is it for his girlfriend? Maybe he's going to propose to her this evening.'

'You have an over-developed sense of the dramatic young lady. No, he's delivering them himself tomorrow morning ...' Molly grinned widely.

'To whom ... Molly what's so funny?'

'He's giving them to a very pretty girl called Bethany. Apparently he had the misfortune to knock her off her bicycle and the flowers are by way of an apology.'

'What?' Beth's green eyes opened wide.

'I believe you heard what I said.' Molly smirked.

Beth flushed. 'There are other girls called Bethany. They must be for someone else.'

'With red-gold curls, a lovely smile and a Pashley Princess bicycle?' Molly shook her head.

'But Molly I don't want flowers. I don't want to see him again.' Beth blushed, partly because she hadn't expected this, and partly because she knew in her heart that she was not telling the truth.

'Why ever not? He looked a very personable young man to me.'

Beth looked down. 'I was very rude to him when he bumped into me.'

'Well this will give you the opportunity to apologise. Now hop off that stool and mind the shop while I make up the order. You can hardly be expected to make your own bouquet that would spoil the surprise.' Molly was already collecting together flowers, greenery, florist tape, cellophane wrapping and ribbon. 'And Beth ... make sure you are out of sight when he returns, it wouldn't do to spoil his surprise!'

***

'Beth if you're coming to church with me you will need to hurry up. The service starts in ten minutes.' Prudence glanced up the stairs to where Beth stood on the half landing.

'Actually I think…'

'Oh of course your poor knee and all those bruises.' Prudence slipped her arms into a grey tailored jacket. 'Yes, you'd better stay at home and rest.' She fixed a small rose-pink feathered hat in place above her immaculate French pleat and viewed the effect in the hall mirror with a turn of her head. 'I've prepared the vegetables and the joint is in so there's nothing for you to do except check on it a few times and baste it. Oh, and would you take your father a cup of coffee? He's reading the papers in his study.' Prudence picked up her matching gloves and crocodile-skin handbag, glanced at her wristwatch and swiftly opened the front door. With a brief wave towards her daughter she was gone.

Beth descended the stairs into the hall where a faint reminder of her mother's perfume lingered. She quite often accompanied her mother to church but today she wanted to be at home when Bear arrived with the flowers. Despite what she had said to Molly, now that she had got used to the idea, the thought of seeing him again sent pleasurable shivers up her spine. She tried to picture what he looked like but it wasn't easy; she had been quite shaken by the sudden fall from her bicycle and had not registered his looks in any detail. She did remember however that he was taller than her and slim and that he had straight fair hair that flopped over his forehead. His voice she did recall. His speech was clear and clipped, posh some would call it, with a slight accent that she couldn't quite place.

She had no idea what time he planned on arriving so what to do in the meantime? She looked at the meat in the Aga which was sizzling away nicely, made a pot of coffee and took a cup into her father.'

He took the coffee with a smile. 'Not at church this morning?'

Beth shook her head. 'Feel a bit stiff and sore.'

'Of course, the bicycle accident. What you need is a comfortable chair and a good book.'

'That's an idea. Any suggestions?'

'Take your pick.' Desmond waved his arm in the direction of the crammed bookcase. Beth did a quick scan of the shelves, selected a collection of short stories entitled "The Ghosts of Oxford", thanked her father, who had already returned to the perusal of his Sunday newspaper, and made her way to the snug basement sitting room from where she would hear anyone approaching the house.

She began the story of Dorcas, a puritan maid who died of a broken heart due to her unrequited love for a young Cavalier. It is said, Beth read, that Dorcas haunts Magpie Lane off the High Street. Beth was unmoved by the descriptions of the various hauntings. They didn't make her spine tingle or the hair on the back of her neck stand up. She was not afraid of ghosts and the stories bored her. Luckily further reading was interrupted by a loud knocking on the front door, followed by a persistent finger on the bell. Beth's pulse quickened as she took the basement steps two at a time. At the top she paused and took a breath before crossing the hallway. It wouldn't do to look too eager. She could see the outline of a tall man through the door's stained glass panel and guessed it was Bear. The butterflies returned but this time they felt like large furry moths. She swung the door open and feigned surprise.

'Oh … it's you.'

Bear's right hand remained raised near the bell; his left by his side clutched the bouquet which Molly had carefully assembled.

'I didn't know whether to knock or ring so I did both.' He grinned and Beth felt weak at the sight of his very attractive smile that showed a row of perfectly even teeth.

'Well you certainly made enough noise.' Beth swallowed the laughter that welled up and her short ponytail bobbed a she spoke.

Bear took stock of the girl before him. The bruise on her forehead had spread around her left eye and the bandage on her knee had been replaced with a large pink sticking plaster. She looked as though she had been in a playground brawl. Bear was confused. This girl was obviously much younger than he remembered. He had had the idea that she had said she was eighteen but perhaps he'd been mistaken. She was staring at him, waiting for him to say something, and he noticed the unusual green of her eyes. She looked from his face to the flowers in his hand and back again. He pulled himself together.

'Here, these are for you to say sorry for knocking you off your bike and I hope you're feeling better.' He held out the flowers with another captivating smile and Beth took them with hands that felt clammy. Bear was relieved that the anger he had witnessed on the day of the accident seemed to have left her.

'Thank you, they're lovely.' Beth's eyes sparkled and she buried her face behind the stiff cellophane wrapping paper so that Bear would not see her amusement.

'I got them from a small florist's near the bicycle repair shop that you told me about. I called in while Joe was fixing my brakes. He's made a really good job of them, I can stop on a sixpence now, and he said that my bike is quite a good model.'

'Good … and the flower shop, how was that?'

'Fine. At first I thought the woman behind the counter

was quite scary but she turned out to be very helpful. She took my order, even though she was very busy, which was kind of her.'

Beth grinned. 'Her bark is worse than her bite. She *is* a very kind person.'

'You know her then?'

Beth stifled a giggle and nodded furiously. 'I work for her.' In an effort to contain the laughter that threatened to well up she clasped the flowers tightly making the cellophane wrapping crackle.

Bear stared. 'You work for her,' he repeated. 'But you weren't in the shop when I called.'

'I was in the back room making up some orders.'

'So you knew I was going to bring you flowers?' Beth nodded and her laughter rippled around the porch. 'You've been leading me on, you ...' Bear couldn't help it, Beth's laughter was infectious, he smiled widely and joined in. The thing that pleased him most was the realisation that, as she was at work, Bethany must be at least sixteen and his recollection of her saying she was eighteen was probably correct. 'Sorry you had to make up your own bouquet,' he remarked.

'I didn't. Molly insisted on doing it so as not to spoil the surprise.'

'Some surprise!' Bear observed ruefully.

'It doesn't matter they're lovely and thank you. I'm sorry I was grumpy.' Beth grinned, 'I must have looked a sight with dirt on my face and bloody knees.'

'You did rather.' Beth opened her mouth to protest then, just in time, it dawned on her that Bear was joking and they both dissolved into more laughter.

Prudence was surprised to see her daughter at the door holding a large bunch of flowers and laughing with the delivery man. Bear turned at the sound of her footsteps on the gravel and she took in his new-looking tweed jacket, striped silk tie and long but tidy hair. Surprisingly well dressed for a delivery man, she thought. Her gaze shifted to Beth and one delicate eyebrow arched imperceptibly.

'Mum.' Prudence cringed inwardly at the word; she really must tackle Bethany on the subject. 'This is the person who knocked me off my bicycle. He brought me these flowers to say sorry.'

'How very thoughtful,' Prudence looked again at Bear and revised her initial summing up of the young man. She held out a gloved hand, 'Mr...?'

'My name's Rupert, but please call me Bear, everyone does. Prudence's eyes widened at the unexpectedness of the name but she quickly regained her equilibrium. She formed a half smile to acknowledge his friendliness, but she was not in the habit of shortening names or calling people by nicknames, bizarre or otherwise She did however like they way he spoke.

'Rupert, thank you for checking up on Bethany. As you can see she's still a bit fragile but nothing that won't mend quite quickly.'

Bear favoured Prudence with one of his most charming smiles, kept especially for mothers. 'I'm so glad,' he told her with a slight bow in her direction.

Prudence didn't usually make hasty judgments concerning people but she immediately liked this attractive young man.

'Bethany you shouldn't keep Rupert standing on the doorstep. Why haven't you asked him in?' Prudence nodded toward Bear, stepped inside and began to remove her gloves and hat in front of the hall mirror.

I would have if I could have got a word in sideways, Beth thought ruefully as she moved aside and motioned Bear to enter.

'Actually I can't stop.' Beth felt a pang of disappointment as Bear took a step back from the door and reached for his bike that was propped up against the porch. 'I'm meeting a friend from college for lunch so I must get back.'

'You're a student then?'

'Yes, first year medical student for my sins.' Bear turned his bike and Beth noticed that the ends of his trousers were tucked into a pair of brightly coloured striped socks.

'You should get some bicycle clips,' she remarked, in an effort to prolong the conversation. But apart from this observation she could think of nothing more to say.

Bear grinned. 'Yes, I must look a fool like this.' He raised a foot in Beth's direction.

'You do rather,' Beth attempted to keep the smile from her lips but the surprised look on Bear's face had her giggling uncontrollably.

'Touché,' he grinned, looking back at Beth as he swung onto the saddle. 'Would you care to come to tea with me this afternoon?' The question was thrown lightly over his shoulder so that Beth almost missed it.

'Pardon?'

'Tea,' he repeated. 'Four o'clock at the tearooms on the High. To make up for our accident.'

'It was no accident. It was entirely your fault.' Beth bristled.

Bear shrugged. 'So it was.' He pushed off and pedalled away down the short drive.

'I'd love to come!' Beth called out and hoped that he had heard her.

Chapter 8

Mondays at the Flower Basket were generally quiet but today was an exception. There were several large table displays to make up for the conference room at the Randolph Hotel and four wreaths for a funeral, including a complicated one where the deceased's name was to be spelt out in flowers. Molly and Beth both set to work in the back room, keeping alert for the ringing of the shop doorbell.

Lunchtime arrived surprisingly quickly, by which time the hotel flowers were ready for delivery. Molly slid off her stool and stretched her stiff muscles.

'Pop the kettle on Bethany. We'll take a break now and have our sandwiches while it's quiet.' No sooner had she spoken than the shop bell rang out its message and Molly with a resigned shrug turned to serve the newly arrived customer.

'I'll go Molly, you get your lunch.' Beth darted past Molly and confronted the smartly suited young woman in the shop. 'Can I help you?'

'I certainly hope so.' The woman looked pointedly at her watch. 'I need some flowers to take on a hospital visit later today but I have to be quick. I'm on a short break now but I have to return to work immediately. My job is very important and I can't be spared for very long.' Beth wondered what on earth this young woman did for a living that was so important, she couldn't be more than twenty-five, but she decided not to ask. She had the feeling that the woman was rather hoping that she would inquire but because of her brusque attitude Beth didn't feel like giving her the opportunity to explain.

'Of course. Now who are the flowers for?' Beth practiced her best "difficult customer" smile.

'I don't see why you need that information.' The customer's vividly painted nails beat a noisy tattoo on the counter.

'It's because of the choice of flowers and type of arrangement,' Beth patiently explained. 'What is suitable for an elderly lady perhaps would not be right to celebrate the birth of a baby.'

'I see ...well they're for my mother – who is not elderly.'

'Right. Roses would be nice. They always go down well. A bunch of these beautiful red ones would be six shillings.'

'How much?' The woman clutched her handbag tightly.

'What about some pretty yellow chrysanthemums? I always think they're cheerful flowers and they don't cost so much.' Beth felt hunger pangs and wished the woman would make up her mind.

'They look cheap, might as well give a bunch of daisies.'

Beth almost said there's nothing wrong with daisies, but thought better of it. The woman cast her grey-shadowed eyed around the banked selection of blooms. 'That's it!' she pointed to a small container of pink carnations. 'Those will do nicely.'

'Would you like something else with them?' Beth had never been a fan of carnations on their own.

'Certainly not, they're perfect as they are. Now would you please hurry up and wrap them, I really must get back to work.'

Beth flopped onto her stool in the back room with a heartfelt sigh.

'Difficult customer?' Molly passed her a mug of tea with a sympathetic smile.

'Well not so much difficult as uncaring. I do like people to take time in choosing flowers, it's so important to get it right especially when you're buying them as a gift.' Molly nodded as her brisk fingers cleared the work surface ready for the next assignment. Beth unwrapped her sandwiches and admired the hotel arrangements as she ate. She loved the unusual colour combination of the blooms which were in rich autumnal shades of orange and purple against a background of dark greenery. It had been her choice and she was pleased at how well it had worked.

Molly watched her. 'I wasn't sure about the colours at the start but I'm impressed with how well they work together. You certainly have a talent for spotting the unusual.' Beth glowed. Molly was sparing with praise so it was all the more pleasing when it came. 'By the way how are you getting on with that young man of yours, Bear was it you called him?'

Beth jumped at the unexpected remark. She had been so engrossed in her work that she hadn't thought about Bear all morning. She cleared her sandwich wrapping with a tiny sigh that did not go unnoticed.

'He's not my young man thank you Molly.'

'So what's the problem then? You've got a face as long as a trail of ivy all of a sudden.'

Beth was glad of the opportunity for a chat and she knew that whatever she told Molly it would go no further. 'After he gave me the flowers we went for tea at that cafe on the High.'

'And?'

'It was fine. We chatted and had a lot to talk about'

'So?'

'Bear mentioned in the conversation that he hoped I'd show him around Oxford in the week before lectures start.'

'Well what's wrong with that?' Molly cleared their mugs a trifle impatiently.

'Nothing except that he didn't mention it again and it's been over a week and I haven't heard from him since so I don't think he really meant it, it was just something to say.'

'He didn't strike me as the kind of person to go back on his word, he seemed pretty keen.' Molly moved the hotel arrangements onto a nearby table and began replacing them with the materials needed for the funeral wreaths. 'I expect something cropped up, he'll be in touch before long you see.' Beth nodded but she did not have Molly's confidence. If Bear had been serious why hadn't he made a definite arrangement when they said goodbye and why hadn't she heard from him since?

The afternoon customers were few and the funeral order and a bouquet for the New Theatre were completed in good time. Beth helped Molly stow the funeral wreaths carefully in the back of her small green van and, for the umpteenth time, assured Molly that she would be quite alright minding the shop on her own while Molly made the deliveries.

Beth returned to the peace of the shop. She breathed in the heady perfume of the blooms; some sweet, some subtle, some strong. The aromas worked their magic and she felt calm and content. She looked up from tidying the counter and smiled a greeting as the shop door bell tinkled and two women entered.

'We would like a quote for wedding flowers.' The older of the two placed her polished green crocodile-style handbag on the counter and finger by finger removed her matching kid gloves. Tight permed curls, in an unlikely shade of yellow, encircled a small felt hat speared by a long thin feather in the same vibrant green as her gloves. Bethany glanced from her to the younger woman, whom she presumed was the daughter and bride-to-be. The girl alternately fiddled with the buttons on her cherry-red jacket and pulled at her very short black skirt. She shot Bethany a provoking glance.

'Of course but first I'll need some details of what you require.' Beth reached for a pad and pencil.

'A bouquet for my daughter, two bridesmaids' posies …'

'No mum, four bridesmaids.'

'Deirdre we agreed on…'

'No we didn't. I want four. Sally, Mimi, Hilda and Jen.' Beth's pencil remained poised above the pad.

'You can't possibly have Hilda, she's far too …'

'That's what I want and if I can't have what I want the wedding's off.' The girl turned as if to leave.

'Well maybe, we'll see.' The mother turned back to Beth, 'a corsage for me and four buttonholes for the men.' Beth made a quick note and turned to the bride.

'What would you like in your bouquet?'

'Roses I suppose.' The girl shrugged and her mother intervened.

'Yes, white roses and possibly white freesias for their scent.'

'No mum, red roses. I want red roses.' The mother frowned and her fingers silently drummed on the counter.

'A bride should be all in white to signify purity, it's traditional, so red roses would not be appropriate Deirdre.'

'Well I'm not pure so I'll have red roses thank you very much.'

Two bright pink spots highlighted the older woman's face. 'Deirdre,' a warning tone had entered her voice, 'I am having apricot flowers in my corsage so red roses in your bouquet would clash horribly, apart from being unsuitable.' Deirdre opened her mouth to reply and Beth thought it was time to intervene.

'Perhaps if you both settled for apricot. It's a very versatile colour, there are varieties of roses in the most beautiful pale apricot shades and some in deep vibrant, almost orange colours. That way your daughter could have the pale ones, which would merge beautifully with white chrysanthemums and cream freesias, and you could have the deeper shade and because they are of the same tone they won't clash.' Beth took a breath and surveyed the two faces hopefully.

'Thank you, we'll settle for apricot.'

'Only if I can have the orange ones.'

'We'll decide that later.' The mother turned from her pouting daughter and continued, 'the bridesmaids' posies will be pink and white chrysanthemums.'

'Ugh, I hate pink.' Deirdre's latest remark was ignored. She raised her voice a few decibels. 'I hate pink.'

'What colour does the groom like?' Beth tried to inject a more positive note into the proceedings.

'Him? I dunno, never asked him. He'll have whatever I decide.' Poor chap Beth thought but she did not voice her feelings.

'If you leave me your details I'll work out a quote for you and send it by post tomorrow. When is the wedding to be?'

'Next month.' The mother fitted her plump fingers carefully into the green gloves and picked up her bag.

'No mum, December. I want a proper winter wedding so as I can wear a fur-lined red velvet cloak with a hood.'

'Deirdre we cannot wait that long.' She turned from her daughter. 'The name's Wills, 14, Albermarle Street,' she told Beth and with that she left the shop followed by her sullen daughter.

Beth drew breath. She felt sorry for the groom being embroiled in those frightful argumentative wedding arrangements. She had heard that some girls became obsessed with getting married and turned into monsters when they finally had a wedding to plan. Maybe, she thought, that's why some men fight shy of committing themselves to a serious relationship. The memory of how she had chatted non stop with Bear over several cups of tea came into her mind. He had seemed interested but perhaps her forwardness had frightened him off and given him second thoughts about meeting up with her again.

The back door banged shut and a tired and frustrated Molly entered the shop from the work room.

'We missed the New Theatre's flowers when we loaded the van. They were left in the back.' She waved a large bouquet in Beth's direction. 'Now I'll have to go out again. It's a pity you can't drive m'girl you could do some of the deliveries for me then.'

'I could go on my bicycle but I think the bouquet is a bit too big for the basket.'

'No, we can't chance it falling out. I'll just have to go out again.'

Beth considered the options. She quite liked the idea of some fresh air and a break from customers. 'Why don't I walk to the theatre with them? It's really not far and I could do with the fresh air.' She looked expectantly at Molly.

'If you're sure...'

Beth quickly shed her apron, took the bouquet and was out of the shop door with a wave before Molly had time to change her mind. Not that there was much chance of that; Molly had had a difficult time with the maitre d'hôtel at the Randolf Hotel who had kept changing his mind over the position of the flower arrangements and now she was ready to take the weight off her feet. She pulled out a stool from under the counter, sat down and reflected on the idea of Beth sharing some of the driving. She had voiced it on the spur of the moment, but the more she pondered the notion, the more it seemed a good idea.

Beth pushed open the heavy glass doors and entered the gloom of the theatre foyer. As it was Monday there was no matinee so the place was silent and apparently deserted. She approached a set of double doors and entered the main auditorium at the back of the stalls. The theatre smelt of stale cigarette smoke with a sickly overtone of popcorn. Beth wrinkled her nose and retreated to the foyer where she spotted a brass bell on the box office counter. She banged it furiously and was relieved to hear footsteps on the stairs to her right. A girl in a maroon uniform appeared.

'Delivery from the Flower Basket.' Beth waited for the girl to sign the delivery note and then escaped thankfully to the fresh air of Baumont Street. She turned right and crossed the road towards St.Giles. She knew this route would take a little longer but it was a more interesting walk. As she approached the Ashmolean museum three people descended the wide steps. Their arms were linked and they laughed as they took the steps at speed. In the centre was an attractive girl with long dark hair that streamed behind her. On her right arm a young man laughed as he pulled her along. Linked on her left was Bear. As Beth watched, the girl raised her face to Bear and he smiled down at her.

Beth's insides lurched. At any moment Bear might turn round and see her behind him. He would think she was following him. She swiftly turned on her heel and retraced her steps the way she had come. Now she knew why he hadn't been in touch about meeting her next week; he had another girlfriend. And from what Beth had seen she was exceedingly pretty.

On reaching The Flower Basket Beth picked up her apron from the counter and tied it firmly in place. Her heart was still beating quickly due in part to the unpleasant surprise of seeing Bear smiling down at a very pretty girl and in part to the speed at which she had returned to the security of the shop. Molly glanced at Beth's flushed face.

'You ok?'

'Yes fine.' Beth turned away and pretended to rearrange a selection of flowers.

'Well it's been unusually busy for a Monday and you've worked hard. It's almost closing time, so I suggest you get yourself off home now and see if that boy of yours has been in touch.'

Beth thought she already knew the answer to that but didn't say anything. She would be glad to stop work early so she nodded and smiled at Molly. As she once again removed her apron the shop door flew open, its bell tinkling madly.

'Thank goodness, I thought you might be closed.' Katie smiled a greeting.

Molly stepped forward. 'I'll deal with this lady, you get off home.'

'It's ok Molly, Katie's a friend of mine. She's the person who dropped her books in the road, you remember, when I was late back.'

'Pleased to meet you Katie.' Molly turned to Beth. 'I'll leave you to serve Katie then and when you've finished you can lock up for me and get off home.'

'Thanks Molly.' Beth turned to Katie. 'It's nice to see you again. What can I get you?'

'I need some flowers for my mum. It's her birthday today and we're having a family tea party for her.'

Beth made a few suggestions and Katie finally chose a large pot of deep purple African violets. 'Mum will love those,' she enthused, 'and they'll last much longer than a bunch of flowers.' While Beth encircled the pot in gift wrap Katie looked thoughtful. 'Why don't you come to tea with us, Mum would love to meet you?'

'Oh I couldn't do that, you said yourself it was a family party.'

'Of course you can. Mum was put out that you didn't come in to say hello last time. She was wanting to meet you after you had been so kind to help me home with that pile of books. If I tell her you refused to come again she'll be even more upset.'

Beth considered the offer. Molly had said she could leave early, her mother wouldn't be expecting her home for some time, she liked Katie and it would be good to talk to someone near her age. Since leaving school many of Beth's friends had left Oxford to study or train for a career. They would be back in the holidays but in the meantime she missed their company. Also it would help to take her mind off Bear and the girl with the flowing dark hair.

She passed Katie the gift-wrapped pot of violets. 'Thank you, I'd love to come.'

Chapter 9

Katie opened the front door of the white painted terraced house on Juxon Street and the rich sweet smell of baking assailed their nostrils.

'Mmm … smells like fruit cake.' Beth suddenly felt very hungry.

Katie grinned. 'My mum makes the best cakes in the world, especially fruit cake. I offered to come home early and bake a cake for her birthday but she said she would bake her own as I should get on with my work. I'm quite glad she did, mine wouldn't have been a patch on hers.'

At the end of a narrow passageway Katie opened a door that led into an overcrowded kitchen. Despite its slightly chaotic appearance it was warm and welcoming and was presided over by a plump woman in a flowered overall. Her blond hair was fine and fastened up high into a bunch by a multi coloured silk scarf, from which a few strands had escaped and trailed down her neck. She turned as the girls entered and a beaming smile lit up her features. Beth could see immediately the strong resemblance between Katie and her mother, despite the difference in their size.

'Mum, this is Beth – she gave me a hand with my books the other day.'

The older woman stepped forward and gave Beth a warm hug and then stood back and took stock of her.

'What a bonny girl! And you hair, what a gorgeous colour.'

Beth was taken aback. Her mother never hugged strangers or anyone else for that matter, apart from very close family members, and then the hug was perfunctory rather than affectionate. Nor did she make "personal remarks" about peoples' appearance, not even nice comments.

Beth touched her hair self conscientiously. 'Mrs…err…' too late she realised she didn't know Katie's surname. 'I do hope you don't mind me coming on your birthday.'

'Mind, why ever should I mind? The more the merrier I say and, as you're a friend of Katie's, you're more than welcome to drop in any time. And please call me Elsie, everyone does. I was christened Elisabeth but Elsie does for me.' She turned towards her daughter. 'Go and say hello to your Dad and tell him tea will be served in ten minutes, so he'd better stop what he's doing and get cleaned up.'

'Usual place?'

'Yes down in the shed making some contraption or other.' Elsie's smile softened as she spoke of her husband. 'Now look at me, still in my pinny.' She quickly shed her wrap-around overall and bundled it into a drawer. 'Beth, perhaps you would help set the table while Katie fetches Jack from the garden.'

Beth was pleased to be busy it made her feel a part of this welcoming family. She arranged plates and tea cups on the scrubbed kitchen table and all the time Elsie kept up a constant flow of chat.

'Where do you work m'dear, Katie did tell me but I forget what she said?' She filled a large whistling kettle and set it on the stove.

'The Flower Basket on Walton Street, do you know it?'

Elsie nodded and her two chins worked busily. 'Course I do. Run by that nice Molly Watson, such a pleasant woman. She's run that shop for as long as I can remember. Great pity she was left alone like that.'

Beth, startled, put the sugar bowl down heavily and a couple of sugar lumps bounced out. 'Like what?' she asked, hastily scooping up the lumps and returning them to the bowl.

'You don't know then? Well perhaps it's not for me to say … ah, here are Katie and Jack so as soon as Thomas arrives we can sit down to tea.'

Beth wanted to question Elsie further about Molly – what had she meant by "left like that"? But the moment had passed and Katie was introducing her father. He was a tall man who stooped slightly, as tall people often do. Beth thought he looked quite old, well considerably older than her father at least. His sandy hair was pale and greying at the temples and when he shook hands she could feel the roughness of his palms. He crossed to the sink to wash his hands. When he had done so, he looked around, without success, for a towel.

'Towel needed!' he boomed so that Beth jumped. Elsie opened a drawer in the overloaded dresser, took out a faded blue hand towel and, to Beth's amazement, she tossed it across the table to her waiting spouse. He caught it deftly and with a laughing, 'thanks love', dried his hands and tossed it neatly back to his wife's waiting hands. She then hung it swiftly on a hook next to the dresser and continued buttering thick slices of bread. Katie watched Beth's startled reaction.

'You'll get used to my mum and dad, they're always larking about like a couple of kids.' She regarded her parents with affection.

Elsie looked up at the kitchen clock. 'Now where has that boy got to?'

'Mum, Tom's not a boy anymore, at twenty-four he's a man.'

'He'll always be a boy to me no matter what his age, same as you'll always be a girl, despite the fact that you've now turned twenty-one.' Elsie placed a large fruit cake and a heaped plate of bread and butter on the table and began to pour the tea. 'We'll start and the boy can have what's left,' she announced with a twinkle.

No sooner had she put the teapot down than her son breezed into the room. He was as tall as his father, maybe even a little taller, with broad shoulders and slim hips. But the thing about him that caught Beth's eye was his hair. Tight ginger curls, cut close to his head, spread back from a smiling face. He went straight over to his mother and bent to kiss a rosy cheek. 'Happy birthday mum!' He produced a small package from his pocket. 'It's not much but I hope you'll like it.'

'You shouldn't have, but I'm glad you did.' Elsie tore off the paper to reveal a brooch in the form of a bunch of flowers. The petals were set with stones of various bright colours and the stems glistened with diamantes. 'It's beautiful Thomas, thank you.' She returned his kiss before pinning the brooch onto her ample chest. 'Now sit down and eat before it gets cold.' Her family laughed at her suggesting that bread and cake could get any colder than they already were.

Thomas looked enquiringly across the table at his sister. Katie caught his gaze.

'Oh sorry Tom, this is Bethany, a friend of mine.' Beth's mouth was full with bread and jam so she smiled a greeting.

'Hi. Bethany ... love the hair.' Tom indicated Beth's copper curls with a wave of the hand and Beth's cheeks turned pink. Never before had her hair been so much remarked upon as by this happy and united family.

'Beth please,' she managed to say through a mouthful of crusty bread and raspberry jam. 'All my friends call me Beth.'

Tea progressed with a constant flow of conversation into which Beth was drawn. It became apparent to her that both Katie and Tom lived at home. In her first two years at college Katie had lived in halls of residence but due to lack of sufficient university accommodation in this, her final year, she had returned to live at home. Tom talked cars with his father and described in detail a Sunbeam Rapier sports that had come into the garage that morning. Elsie explained to Beth that Tom worked as a mechanic in a local garage that specialised in the repair and maintenance of sports cars and that her husband Jack worked on the assembly line at the MG works in Abingdon. She went on to say that Jack was on the night shift this week which explained his presence at the tea table.

Elsie stood up to cut her birthday cake and Katie passed the first slice to Beth. 'How do you like working at The Flower Basket?' she asked.

'I love it.' Beth's eyes sparkled. 'Every day is different. You never know who is going to walk into the shop and I love working with Molly she's so kind and patient.'

'And do you still live at home like my two?' Elsie asked.

Beth grinned. 'Yes, I only left school this year so there's no way I could branch out on my own yet, even if I wanted to.'

'And where would home be?'

'The Woodstock Road.'

'Oh, not so far from here then,' Elsie exclaimed.

Talk of home brought Beth to earth with a bump. She glanced at her watch and looked up in concern. 'I'm so sorry but I'm afraid I'll have to go. I didn't tell my mother I was going out to tea and she'll be expecting me home for supper. She'll be wondering what's happened to me.'

'That's alright m'dear. It's been lovely to meet you and I hope you'll come again soon.' Elsie glanced out of the window. 'It's dark now so Thomas will walk you home.'

Beth pushed back her chair. 'There's really no need. I've got my bicycle and it has a dynamo and lights. I'll be quite alright.'

'It's no trouble.' Tom also stood up and squeezed his way round the table to stand by Beth. 'Can't have a little thing like you walking the streets round here in the dark on her own.' Beth glanced to see if he was teasing. She had never been called a "little thing" even as a young child. But Tom's face was impassive, not the glimmer of a smile touched his lips. He's not referring to my size but to my age, Beth thought. He thinks I'm a child still. The thought bothered her but there was nothing much she could do about it. She smiled goodbye to Elsie and Jack, waved at Katie and collected her coat from a peg in the passage.

Beth and Tom walked silently along Walton Street and continued into Kingston Road. Tom had taken charge of Beth's bike, pushing it along the gutter with one hand so that he walked on the outside of the pavement with Beth safely tucked in on the inside. Tom regarded the quiet girl beside him. She was stunning looking, and that hair! He wanted to run his hand over those bouncing curls. She looks about sixteen, maybe seventeen, he thought. If she's seventeen that makes a difference in our ages of seven years he calculated. Too much, pity she's not a few years older.

'How long have you worked at Molly's shop?' he asked.

'Full time, since the summer. Before that I worked on Saturdays and sometimes in the school holidays.'

'Didn't you want to stay on at school and then go away to college somewhere? I thought that was what most girls wanted to do these days.'

'I'm not most girls,' Beth replied somewhat sharply. 'And I did stay on at school and, for your information, I got quite good grades in my A levels.'

'Sorry Beth I didn't mean to judge you, I was just interested that's all, and to tell you the truth I was wondering how old you were.'

Tom's frank reply took the wind out of Beth's sails and her irritation vanished. 'I'm eighteen – nineteen in December,' she replied more calmly. Tom nodded. That was better than he had thought but still an enormous gap of five years.

'Tell me about the flower shop,' he commanded. Beth needed no more prompting and she happily chatted about her love of flowers and her ambition to eventually run her own floristry business. She poured out all her future aspirations as she had never done before and Tom listened intently.

'You're quite some girl,' he remarked eventually, 'but where does marriage and a family come into your plans?'

Normally she would have bristled at being asked such a personal question but, coming from Tom it seemed alright. 'Not for years and years. I haven't really thought much about that side of things yet,' Beth replied candidly.

'Well I hope your business venture is a great success,' Tom told her seriously, holding back the sigh that threatened to escape. Pity, too young and too career minded he thought with an inward shrug.

'And what about your work?' Beth inquired.

'What about it?'

'Your mother said you worked in a garage that specialises in looking after sports cars.'

'It's not very interesting, I'm a car mechanic that's all.'

'Well I think it's interesting,' Beth told him with a winning smile that melted his reserve so Tom told her how, on leaving school at sixteen, he had joined his father at the MG works in Abingdon and had worked for several years on the line making MGB sports cars. Beth nodded and Tom felt encouraged to continue. 'Then I got talking to a chap over a pint in the Royal Oak on Woodstock Road. He had started up a car repair garage not far from there and he specialised in sports cars. Naturally I was interested and told him that I helped to build MGs in Abingdon. Well the upshot of the conversation was that his mechanic had left unexpectedly, he couldn't manage the work on his own and he offered me the job. I jumped at the opportunity. Initially I was taken on for a probationary period of twelve months but since then I've worked for Rob for five successful years.'

'That's brilliant,' Beth smiled. 'Will you go on working there or have you greater plans?'

Tom looked at Beth pensively. This young lady has ambitions, he mused, and she expects others to be the same, well I'll show her. 'I hope to work with Rob for a very long time,' he told her. 'He's offered me a partnership in the business and I'm saving hard to be able to buy my share. Of course it is more risky than being paid a wage but the satisfaction and rewards will be much greater.'

'I think that's marvellous,' Beth clapped her hands. 'And what are your plans for a wife and family?' she asked with a gleam in her eye. Tom opened his mouth to speak but instead roared with laughter.

'Like you, I haven't made those sorts of plans yet.'

They rounded the corner into Beth's road and she stopped by her gate. Tom looked askance at the imposing Edwardian house. She's out of my league he thought resignedly.

Beth held out a gloved hand. 'Thank you so much for walking me home.'

'No trouble I enjoyed our little chat.' Tom ignored the outstretched hand, instead he raised his in a farewell gesture. As he did so a call made them both turn sharply.

'Beth!'

Bear was cycling rapidly towards them.

'It seems you're wanted. I'd better be off.' Tom raised his hand once more, turned and briskly walked away.

Bear pulled up with a squeal of brake blocks on metal. Beth, to her surprise, realised she hadn't thought about Bear for some hours. But now he was here in front of her his good looks and smile of greeting caused her heart to flutter.

Bear's eyes followed Tom's retreating back. 'Who was that?'

'Tom,' Beth replied without additional explanation.

Bear's eyes narrowed but, glancing at Beth's face, he decided not to pursue the matter immediately.

Despite the fluttering in her stomach, Beth regarded Bear with a frown.

'What do you want?' she asked brusquely, pushing her bicycle through the front gate. Bear dismounted and followed her, a puzzled look in his eyes.

'I came to talk to you about our arrangement for this week.'

'What arrangement?' Beth was determined to make things as difficult as possible.

'You said you would show me around Oxford.'

'Oh did I? I must have forgotten.' Beth lied. 'Anyway I presumed you had got better things to do with your time.'

Bear felt annoyed. What was Beth playing at? Last week she seemed more than happy to spend time with him, now she was being totally offhand.

'Why did you presume that?'

Beth hesitated. She was not one to beat about the bush, better to come right out with it. 'You seemed to be enjoying yourself with your girlfriend this afternoon. Did you enjoy your visit to the Ashmolean?'

Bear's eyes widened. So that was it, Beth had seen him with Camilla and had presumed that she was his girlfriend. Well she can think again he thought. There's no way I'm going to be tied down to one girl just yet. He reacted quickly.

'You shouldn't jump to conclusions Beth,' he said quietly. 'If you had looked carefully you would have seen there was another person with us. Peter's Camilla's boyfriend, not me.'

Beth felt the colour rise in her cheeks. She had seen the other boy but she had ignored his presence and had jumped to a hasty assumption. She viewed Bear's smiling face with remorse. Why did she have to be so quick to berate others and think the worst? She should have known there was a rational explanation.

'Sorry Bear I thought…'

'I know what you thought and it was quite wrong.' Bear grinned now that he had the upper hand. 'I came here to tell you that I won't be free to spend time with you this week…' Beth sighed deeply. I deserve this she thought sadly. Should have kept my temper in check, I've really messed up my chances with Bear now. 'It's Freshers Week,' he continued, 'and there are so many activities laid on for us first year students that it looks as though I won't have a moment to spare, I'm sorry.'

'It's ok I understand. Thanks for taking the trouble to let me know.' Beth moved dejectedly towards the house.

'Wait Beth I haven't finished!' Bear reached out and grabbed her coat sleeve. 'There's a disco dance laid on in college on Friday night and I would like you to come.'

Beth stared at Bear. Had she heard correctly?

'Friday?'

'Well?' Bear tapped the handlebars of his bike

impatiently. He wasn't used to girls keeping him waiting.

Beth pulled herself together. 'Yes that would be great, I'd love to come, but now I really must go I'm very late home and my supper will be spoiled.'

Bear stared at Beth's retreating back. He was used to girls falling at his feet if he so much as clicked his fingers, but this one, she was different, a little strange even but fantastic looking and therefore well worth an extra effort he decided.

Chapter 10

'You're in a good mood,' Molly remarked next morning as Beth hummed her way round the shop. 'You heard from your young man then?'

Beth nodded happily. 'He called round yesterday evening and he's asked me to a disco dance on Friday.' Her face fell, 'the trouble is…'

'You're always worrying your head about something.' Molly interjected. 'What is it now?'

'I've nothing suitable to wear.'

'You must have, you told me yourself that your mother is always buying you dresses.'

'She is, but they're all fussy and feminine and not at all suitable. I'd look like an old fashioned freak wearing any of them to a disco.'

'So what is the younger generation wearing these days, as if I didn't know?' Molly grinned.

'It's not funny Molly,' Beth frowned, 'I'm serious. I can't go to the disco wearing anything in my wardrobe. I'll just have to make up an excuse and tell Bear I can't go.'

'Don't be daft. Can't you ask your mother to buy you something new?'

'She wouldn't buy the sort of dress I want.'

'Why ever not?'

'Because it needs to have a short skirt, at least above the knees, and you remember the row we had over me wearing a skirt of that length. I know she wouldn't agree to it.'

Molly frowned. She was of the opinion that young people should, within reason, be allowed to express themselves in what they wore. She thought Beth was much too old for her mother to still be laying down the law over her clothes. But what could she do about it?

The shop bell heralded a customer. The woman was dressed in a tight-fitting black costume with a large gold plated brooch in the shape of a bow pinned to her ample bosom.

Molly stepped forward. 'Good morning Mrs. Wills, what can I do for you?'

The woman looked towards Beth. 'I'd like the young lady to serve me. I dealt with her last time I was in and she was very helpful.

Molly shrugged slightly. 'Beth, a customer for you,' she called before disappearing into the back room.

Mrs. Wills had returned with some last minute alterations to her wedding flowers order.

'Your daughter not with you today,' Beth inquired with a touch of relief.

'No, she's decided to let me organise the flowers, too many cooks and all that. Any anyway she's in a tizzy over the dresses at the moment, and then there's the hurdle of the reception to cross.' Mrs. Wills gave a heartfelt sigh and the feathers on the wide brim of her black straw nodded in sympathy. Beth thought she looked as though she should be arranging a funeral rather than a wedding.

She produced a dog-eared piece of paper from her patient-look handbag and passed it across the counter. Beth ran her eye down the list.

'I see you've decided on roses, carnations and freesias. That's a nice combination.' Beth could be very diplomatic when she needed to be.

'I thought so,' Mrs. Wills managed a smile. 'The bridesmaids' posies though will be a couple of rosebuds and some small chrysanthemums, seeing as there will be four of them,' she added, rolling her eyes.

'Of course but perhaps we should make it three rosebuds to balance the arrangement and would you like me to bind the stems with ribbon?'

Mrs. Wills was about to shake her head but an impatient customer behind her broke in.

'That's a good idea it'll make a bunch of chrysanths look worth a lot more.'

Mrs. Wills glared down her nose at the unwarranted interruption.

'As I was about to say, that would be very nice thank you.'

'Delivery on Saturday 6th November before ten still alright?'

Mrs. Wills nodded, gathered her bag and gloves and left the shop with a hunted look in her eyes.

Bethany attended to the impatient customer who, now she was being served, seemed to have all the time in the world. While the woman tried mixing various combinations of flowers together, a man with a little girl entered noisily. Bethany shot them a friendly smile of greeting but her customer frowned at the disturbance to her deliberations. She finally made her choices and left the shop with an irritated look at the two who were sniffing flowers and exclaiming at the beauty of everything they saw.

'Hello, how can I help?'

'We need some flowers for my wife…'

'Mummy's got a new baby,' the little girl twirled around excitedly. 'We're going to the hospital this afternoon to see them.'

'How lovely. Girl or boy?' Bethany aimed this last remark at the father.

'Little boy. Seven pounds ten. They say he just like me. I can't see it myself but there you are, must be something in it if the nurses can see a likeness.' The man's face glowed with pride.

'We want really pretty flowers for Mummy like those.' The little girl pointed to some large white lilies.

'Don't think they are quite right poppet. We'll let this nice lady choose something for us, she'll have a good idea what will be right.'

Bethany smiled as she put together a selection of flowers in shades of white and blue and tied them with a large satin bow. What a lovely man she thought and how lucky to have a baby son that looks just like him.

This last thought reminded her of the fact that she didn't look anything like either of her parents and the need to see her birth certificate once again surfaced. The pleasure in serving such a likeable customer faded slightly as her worries returned. When they left the shop she forced a smile as she returned the little girl's wave but it quickly faded into a frown. She couldn't just ask outright to look at her birth certificate, she needed a plausible reason but at the present time she was unable to think of one.

Beth consulted her watch, one o'clock, time for lunch. She turned the notice on the door to "closed" and repaired to the back room. To her surprise there was no sign of Molly. She had expected to find her putting the kettle on. Then she heard creaking on the floor above in Molly's flat. Beth unwrapped her lunch and wondered what Molly was doing upstairs. She soon found out when Molly puffed into the work room carrying a large dusty suitcase.

'You going away Molly?' Beth grinned.

'Ha, ha, chance would be a fine thing,' Molly retorted, looking pleased with herself.

She blew the dust off the surface of the case, making Beth choke on her sandwich, and pressed the brass catches so that they sprang open. By now Beth was thoroughly intrigued and leant over Molly's shoulder to see what the case held. A layer of yellowed tissue paper was hastily removed. Underneath lay some fabric, subtly patterned in peacock shades of green and blue. Molly lifted it up and shook it out. In her hands hung a shift dress, sleeveless with a square neck and a fringe round the hem.

'What a beautiful dress,' Beth exclaimed feeling the softness of the fabric. 'Where did it come from?'

'It's mine. I wore it many years ago when I was in my twenties. Goodness knows why I've kept it all these years, must be getting soft in my old age.' Molly held the dress against herself and Beth could see that Molly had been very slim when she was young.

'I know why you kept it.'

Molly raised an eyebrow. 'Oh yes?'

'Because it's absolutely beautiful and at heart you are a softy, despite the fact that you pretend not to be.'

Molly coloured. Beth was nearer to the truth than she liked to admit. 'Well I thought, with a bit of alteration, it might solve your problem of what to wear at the disco on Friday. We could take off the fringe and shorten it a bit.'

'You would really lend me your beautiful dress?'

'That's what I said wasn't it?' Molly replied gruffly.

'Oh Molly!'

Without hesitation Molly took up a pair of scissors from the workbench and snipped off the emerald green fringe. 'Now try it on while the shop's closed and we'll see what it looks like,' she commanded. Beth did as she was bid and the shift snaked over her hips as though it had been made for her, but it finished up just below her knees. Molly stood back. 'Oh dear, too long. Wait here.' She appeared a few minutes later carrying a small blue tin of pins and without another word she knelt at Beth's feet and was busily pinning up the hem. 'There, perfect! Now come upstairs and have a look.'

Beth twirled in front of Molly's dressing table mirror. The dress was indeed perfect. The colour complemented her hair and made her eyes shine like emeralds. Its simple style was young looking but also gave Beth an air of sophistication. She would stand out from the crowd.

She turned a glowing face to Molly. 'How did you know what length to make it?'

'I may be old but that doesn't mean I don't notice what's going on around me,' Molly replied. 'Now I take it that the dress will do?'

'Do? It's the best dress I've ever had and it's just what I need for the disco.' Beth turned and flung her arms round Molly's neck.

'No need for that.' A flushed-faced Molly hastily detached Beth's arms. 'You've work to do. Don't think you're getting off that lightly. What are your sewing skills like?'

Molly closed the shop promptly at five and in the quiet of her flat she taught Bethany how to neatly hem the dress. She watched as Beth bent to her task and by the time she had finished shortening the dress Molly had made up her mind.

'Beth how would you feel about learning to drive so that you can help out with the deliveries?'

Beth was shocked, she hadn't expected this, but she knew right away what her answer would be. 'I would love to be able to drive,' she told Molly. 'And if it meant I could help you by driving the van then that's a good as reason as any to learn.'

'Well you must talk to your parents about it before you do anything and make sure that they are happy with the idea.'

'But I'm nearly nineteen, I should be able to decide for myself.' Beth was indignant.

'That's as maybe, but it's much better to get your parents on board, with a little gentle persuasion if necessary, rather than face them with a fait accompli which might cause antagonism.'

'Oh Molly, you're so clever and wise. I wish I was calm like you. I always seem to charge into situations without thinking and then get angry when things go wrong.'

That evening Beth was unusually quiet at the supper table. She listened in silence as her parents compared notes on the relative happenings of their days and pondered how to raise the question of learning to drive without alienating them. No good ideas came to mind so, in a brief lull in the conversation, she broke in.

'Molly thinks it would be a good thing if I learned to drive.' Two sets of cutlery were lowered and two astonished pairs of eyes met hers. Oh dear that was not very tactful she realised.

'Why do you need to drive? You don't have a car and anyway I can give you a lift whenever you need one,' her father was brisk with his reply. 'And what business is it of Molly Watson's I'd like to know.' He spoke uncharacteristically sharply.

'My dear the roads are so busy I think it would be a

good idea for you to wait until you're a little older.' Prudence spoke gently and with genuine concern but Beth had made up her mind.

'It's Molly's business because she needs me to be able to help out with the deliveries and that means being able to drive the van. I've got to learn sometime and they say that people make better drivers when they learn young.'

'I very much doubt that, and Molly Watson has no right to go behind our backs suggesting you should learn to drive.' Desmond was on his high horse and Beth could see that she needed to step carefully if he was to be persuaded to climb down.

'It wasn't quite like that Dad. Molly hurt her ankle badly the other day and yet she still had to drive to make the deliveries. She suggested that I should learn to drive to help out on the odd occasions when she was not able to, providing I got your agreement first.'

'Well Desmond that's…'

Desmond Burnett shot a warning glance towards his wife. He would have the final say on this matter.

'I don't want you careering about in some van Bethany before you have considerable experience on the road. They're dangerous places nowadays and Oxford is particularly busy, especially in term time with those irresponsible students riding about madly on their bicycles without a thought for anyone.' Beth opened her mouth to protest but then remembered that one of those irresponsible undergraduates had recently knocked her off her bicycle, so she rapidly closed it again. 'When the time comes you will need to have proper driving lessons and plenty of practice before you take your test and in the meanwhile you will need to organise a provisional driving licence.'

'Does that mean you agree then?' An astounded Beth could hardly believe what she heard.

'All in good time, but in the meantime there's no harm in being prepared. You could get a provisional driving licence.' Her father picked up his knife and fork and continued with his dinner. Beth knew that was her father's way of backing down and she had won the major part of the battle. Once she had her licence it wouldn't be difficult to bring forward the driving lessons. She gave her mother a beaming smile and Prudence nodded in response.

Bethany waited until both parents had finished eating. 'How do I go about obtaining a provisional licence?' she asked.

'Fill in a form. They have them at the main post offices. Then show proof of age and pay the required amount. The licence will be sent to you here.' Desmond dismissed the subject and attacked his pudding.

Proof of age – Bethany's heart performed a little skip – that means my birth certificate she thought, but she decided to say no more for the time being.

***

Beth shivered as she unfastened her bicycle from the post in the bike shed. The October sun was bright but the morning bore an autumn chill and she pulled her jacket closer. How to approach her mother over the question of her birth certificate?

'Strike while the iron's hot.' A voice in her head told her.

'Yes,' Bethany agreed, 'no point in waiting.'

She hurriedly returned to the house. Her mother turned sharply at the sound of the back door being flung open.

'Forgotten something?'

Beth shook her head. 'It's colder than I thought so I'm going to wear my coat instead of this jacket.' She paused. 'I'm going to ask Molly to let me off a few minutes early at lunch time so that I can get to the post office before it closes… I thought I would start the ball rolling with the provisional driving licence… could you possibly get my birth certificate for me while I change my jacket?' She spoke as nonchalantly as she could and looked at her mother hopefully.

Prudence bent to pick up some of the ironing that had slipped from the neat pile she was holding. When she straightened up her cheeks were pink with exertion.

'Sorry my dear I can't do that.'

'Why not?' Bethany's heart skipped at her mother's refusal.

'Because I don't know where it is.' Prudence rubbed her forehead as though she had the beginnings of a headache. 'Your father looks after all of our important papers and I'm not sure where he keeps them.'

'But you must know. How can you not know where they are? What if you needed something in a hurry?' Beth raised her voice in agitation. 'It's not right that you don't have control of your own personal papers and I should have access to mine.'

'Bethany please...' Prudence was upset by her daughter's outburst. 'I trust your father to look after our wellbeing and I'm quite sure he has all of our important papers filed safely. If there was an emergency I'm certain he would be able to produce them quickly enough.' Prudence's normally pale complexion had taken on a rosy hue.

'That's all very well but what if something happened to Dad? Where would we be then? Don't you have any idea where they might be?'

'Bethany there's no need to shout. No I don't know where they are kept. And this is not an emergency. You don't need your birth certificate in a hurry and if you did I'm sure your father would produce it for you immediately.'

'But he's not here and I want it now. I intend to apply for my driving licence today.' Bethany's anger fed on the thwarting of her plans and an underlying fear of what the real reason might be for her mother's reluctance to produce the certificate. Unwanted thoughts rushed through her mind. Was her mother playing for time so that she could talk to Bethany's father about how to prepare Bethany for the news of her adoption?

'Well?' Beth faced her mother defiantly, almost accusing her of delaying tactics.

'It's no use looking like that Bethany. This is not an emergency so you can ask your father for your certificate when he gets home. And I suggest you ask with a great deal more politeness than you have shown me.' Beth was not one to give up easily, she opened her mouth to speak but her mother quickly intervened. 'Now I really must get on and you'd better hurry otherwise you'll be late for work.' With that she continued on her way to the airing cupboard without a backward glance at a worried Beth. Her rigid back conveyed the message that Beth had overstepped the mark once again and this time by a very long way.

Despite the lack of her birth certificate, Beth decided to continue with her plan to visit the post office in Summertown at lunch time and obtain the necessary driving licence form. At least I can get it all filled in ready to send off as soon as I get my birth certificate from Dad she thought.

She pondered that morning's altercation with her mother and regretted that she had handled things so badly, she would apologise as soon as she got home. But her mother's refusal to produce the certificate and her reason for not doing so still bothered Beth. Why had her mother seemed so anxious?

Chapter 11

Beth was pleased Molly had given her the afternoon off, it would be a change to do some baking with her mother, always a pleasant task. And more importantly it would provide a chance to apologise for this morning's outburst. She turned smartly onto Woodstock Road and noticed with surprise that an ambulance was parked with its rear doors open not far from her house. She pressed the pedals down more firmly and as she drew closer she could see two ambulance men carrying a stretcher bearing a prone figure covered with a red blanket. The horror of the situation suddenly hit her. The ambulance was actually right outside her house and the person on the stretcher was her mother! Beth did not remember pedalling the remaining distance. She threw her bicycle onto the pavement at the same time that her father emerged from the house. Beth flew up the gravel drive and flung her arms round him. She could feel the trembling of his body.

'What's happened?'

Desmond patted her back then held her at arm's length. His face was pale and drawn. 'Your mother's had a nasty fall on the stairs.' He ran his hand through his hair. 'I kept telling her not to wear those high heels in the house but she didn't listen.' He shook his head vigorously as though to remove the thought of Prudence catching her heel and falling headlong down the steep flight of stairs at the top of the house. 'I phoned to say that I was on my way home for lunch and there was no reply, which I thought was very strange. I think she might have tripped and fallen on her way to answer the phone.'

'How bad is she?'

'It's quite serious. I found her unconscious on the landing when I got back from town and she felt very cold, so I think she must have been like that for some time. I phoned for the ambulance …' He looked up as one of the ambulance crew called out that they were ready to leave.

'And now I really must go with your mother to the hospital.' Desmond gently pushed his daughter away and stepped towards the ambulance where the attendant holding the rear door open was waving impatiently for him join them but Beth ran after him and grabbed hold of his jacket.

'Let me go with her,' she wailed. 'It all my fault that she fell.'

'Bethany, don't be melodramatic, you need to be strong for your mother. It's better that you stay here. I'll ring you as soon as there's any news. And if your mother needs anything from home you'll be on hand to pack what she needs and bring it in.' With that the back doors were closed firmly behind him and the ambulance sped away leaving Beth alone on the pavement, dazed and shaken. She watched as the clanging vehicle disappeared round the corner on its way to the Radcliffe Infirmary. At least the hospital was very close and her mother would receive good care once she was there. In the ensuing silence Beth felt a cold breeze eddy around her and she began to shiver convulsively. She picked up her bicycle, propped it against the porch and went inside.

Beth pulled her thick coat tightly round her. The house felt cold and she was shivering too much to want to take it off. She went into the kitchen. Everything was spotless and tidy. No baking dishes or ingredients stood ready on the scrubbed table and Beth's eyes hurt with unshed tears. Why, oh why, had she left in such a temper this morning? Now her prepared apology was unsaid and what was going to happen to her mother? Perhaps she would never have the opportunity to tell her mother how sorry she was and how much she loved her. Silent sobs convulsed Beth's body and she grasped the edge of the table for support until they passed. If it wasn't for the stupid idea that had taken hold that Prudence and Desmond were not her natural parents none of this would have happened she told herself. That of course was irrational, but Beth was not thinking straight and blamed herself for her mother's accident. She kicked out at the table leg but even that uncharacteristic act of aggression didn't relieve her misery. She made a determined pact with herself that she would forget her obsession with being adopted and not make any more fuss over her missing birth certificate, of course Prudence was her real mother, she knew it in her heart.

Beth couldn't tolerate looking at the empty kitchen any longer. It was her mother's domain and now she wasn't here to fill it with her warmth and personality. Beth wandered upstairs to the sanctuary of her bedroom. At the bottom of the steep flight of stairs that led to the top floor and her room lay the crumpled eiderdown that belonged on her parents' bed. Her father had obviously used it to keep her mother warm until the ambulance crew arrived. Near it lay one of Prudence's shoes. Beth looked for the other one. It rested on the stairs with the heel broken. With a strangled sob Beth gathered up the eiderdown and replaced it neatly on her parents' bed, but she left the shoes where they were. She couldn't bear to touch them.

Beth didn't want to look at her mother's shoe on the stair so she retraced her steps and went into the sitting room and from there into the drawing room and then into her father's study. Every room was silent and their untouched neatness seemed to reproach Beth for her thoughtless behaviour. The only untidiness was in her father's study where his briefcase was uncharacteristically lying on the floor with papers spilling out of it onto the grey Wilton carpet. The telephone extension was pulled forward to the edge of his desk and Bethany realised that this was where her father had phoned for the ambulance. Tears threatened to spill over once more as she imagined the horror her father must have gone through on finding her mother unconscious. She looked at the phone and willed it to ring with good news of her mother but it stubbornly remained silent.

Beth slumped into her father's chair, rested her elbows on his desk and put her head in her hands. She needed someone to talk to. Molly was the first person she thought of but Beth could hardly expect her stop work for a chat when she was in sole charge of the shop. Her closest friends had left for their respective colleges and the rest of her old school friends were away studying or travelling. For the first time she regretted staying in Oxford and choosing to go straight out to work from school; it was so much more difficult for her to make new friends than if she had been at college. She thought about Bear but she didn't have a number for him and anyway she had only known him for a very short time, she could hardly burden him with traumatic family matters. There was old Mrs. Elliston who lived across the road. She was a sympathetic person with whom Beth had chatted since she was a little girl. Over the years she had taken the place of a grandmother in Beth's life. Beth felt sure that the old lady would be glad to help and her hand reached out to the telephone. She lifted the handset slightly off its rest and could faintly hear the purr of the dialling tone. What was she thinking of? While she was talking on the phone her father might be trying to contact her with important news. She let the receiver drop sharply into its cradle and rose stiffly from her father's chair.

Back in the cold kitchen Bethany's mind was in turmoil. What if the fall left her mother permanently disabled? What if she had brain damage? And worst of all, what if she didn't recover and died? Bethany's stomach clenched as she remembered the many occasions when she had been less than helpful, sometimes short tempered and, like this morning, downright bad tempered towards her mother. The thought that she might never get the chance to make up for these shortcomings wrapped her in a cloak of despair. Without thinking what she was doing Bethany put the kettle on and made a pot of tea. Her eyes focused on the pretty china teapot and she reached for the handle and began to pour tea into a matching cup. The phone shrilled, the teapot went down with a bang, catching the freshly filled cup and knocking it across the kitchen table.

Bethany tried to hurry towards the telephone in the hall but it felt as though her legs would only move in slow motion. The short distance seemed to take forever and she was certain the thing would stop ringing before she got to it. Thankfully she grabbed the receiver before that happened.

'Yes?'

'Oh Bethany, sorry to bother you on your afternoon off but I can't find the reel of wide pink ribbon anywhere. Any idea where it might be? Only I've got to make up a birthday bouquet this afternoon and the client has specifically ordered pink ribbon.' Molly's voice came clearly down the line. Bethany tried to speak but no words came. 'Beth?' Molly called. 'Beth, are you there?'

'Yes,' the reply came out half croak, half sob.

'Is something the matter m'dear?' Molly's concerned tone was all Bethany needed. Tears flowed and sobs erupted as she began to describe her mother's accident. 'Beth!' Molly's firm voice broke through Bethany's incoherent outburst. 'Please stop crying, take a deep breath and start again. I haven't been able to make sense of a word you've said.'

Beth pulled a tissue from the box on the hall table, blew her nose and obediently began again, more clearly this time. Molly listened silently until Beth had finished.

'Now I want you to listen carefully Beth. Your mother's not the first person to fall down and bang her head and in the great majority of cases they make a full recovery quite quickly, so we should think about what is most likely to happen and plan for that. After a bang on the head and a brief spell of unconsciousness …'

'How do we know it was brief, she might have been lying there for hours,' Beth wailed.

'That's most improbable and what did I say about thinking positively?' Molly's voice became firmer. 'Your mother will, in all likelihood, be kept in hospital for a day or two so she will need things from home. Go upstairs, find an overnight bag and pack it for her. Nightie, bed-jacket, dressing-gown, slippers, toothbrush, soap, flannel, cologne, hairbrush and anything else you can think of. Now have you got all that?'

Beth nodded slowly, 'I think so.'

'Good, now you get on with packing so that it's ready for when you father phones from the hospital.'

The mention of her father caused Beth to slam the phone down abruptly. She had been so engrossed in pouring out her fears to Molly that she had momentarily forgotten that her father would be phoning. What if he had been trying to get through while she was occupying the phone? Beth hovered in the hall for a short while. She remembered Molly's instructions but was unwilling to move too far from the phone. She glared at it, willing it to ring, but it stubbornly remained silent and she reluctantly climbed the stairs to her parent's room with a heavy tread.

The bag was packed and Beth placed it near the front door ready for a quick getaway should it be needed. She paced the hall floor, past the small table holding the phone and back again. Why hadn't her father phoned? What was taking so long? Surely her mother must have regained consciousness by now? Her legs started to shake and the incessant questions patrolling her brain made her feel quite dizzy. She slumped uncomfortably onto a hard kitchen chair and wondered what to do to make the time pass more quickly. There was the mess of spilt tea on the table that needed clearing but she didn't have the energy to rise and find a cloth. She doodled a trail in the cold tea and wallowed in self recrimination until a persistent ringing on the front door bell sharply interrupted her lethargy.

Her heart pounded and her whole body started to tremble uncontrollably as she made her way fearfully out of the kitchen. Why was her father back so soon? And why was he ringing to be let in? Perhaps he left in such a hurry that he didn't pick up his keys, but if that was the case he would come in through the back door surely? And then the worst thought of all hit her, it must be bad news that he couldn't tell her over the phone.

Chapter 12

Molly stood in the porch holding a bouquet.

Beth's face crumpled. 'I thought you were my father.'

Molly gently took hold of Beth's arm, guided her inside and closed the door quietly behind them. She laid the flowers on the hall table and put her arms around Beth's sagging shoulders and patted her back as she would have done to comfort a small child. After a moment Beth raised her head and straightened her back.

'Sorry Molly I wasn't expecting you. I thought it was my father with bad news but I'm really glad you're here.'

Molly gathered up the flowers. 'Come on m'dear we need to stand these in water so that they are fresh when you visit your mother.' Beth nodded and led the way into the kitchen. It was good to have someone to take charge.

Five minutes later the flowers were standing in a jug of water, the table had been cleaned and Molly was pouring out fresh sweet tea into delicate china cups. She had asked Bethany for mugs but Bethany had told her with a faint smile that her mother did not entertain the idea of mugs, so china cups had to suffice. The biscuit barrel had been unearthed and put in the centre of the table.

'Now drink your tea and tell me exactly what has happened,' Molly ordered.

Bethany sipped her tea, felt a little better, slipped her coat onto the back of her chair and began. She told Molly about her row with her mother over her missing birth certificate and ended with how she had come home after lunch to find her unconscious mother being loaded into an ambulance.

Molly picked out a garibaldi biscuit from a cut glass biscuit barrel and dunked it thoughtfully into her tea. 'Bethany, mothers and daughters have rows from time to time, it's natural, goodness knows I had enough differences with my mother when I was your age, but it has nothing to do with your mother's accident. You mustn't blame yourself for her fall.' Bethany unthinkingly reached for a biscuit. 'Perhaps you're right, but I haven't been able to tell her how sorry I am and,' Bethany caught her breath, 'I may not be able to tell her.'

'No good will come of thinking like that.' Molly patted Bethany's hand.

'But Dad said he would phone as soon as there was any news, and he still hasn't rung.' Bethany rubbed her temples in an attempt to relieve the tension.

'That's not at all surprising,' Molly pushed a second cup of tea with two biscuits in the saucer in Beth's direction. 'These things take time and your father hasn't been gone all that long. On admission at the hospital your mother will have been examined to ascertain the extent of her injuries. Then she will have been seen by specialist doctors and possibly had some x-rays taken and tests done. Then there would be admission procedures to go through and assessments and nurses observations to be undertaken.' Molly had never been into hospital but she had a good imagination and, to calm Beth's agitation at not having heard from her father, she made the list of things to be done as long as she could. 'So it's unlikely that your father has anything concrete to report just yet. Come on eat up. You don't want to be weak and watery when he does phone now do you?'

Beth shook her head and glanced at her wristwatch. Three o'clock. A sudden and disturbing thought entered her head.

'Molly … the shop?'

'Take that worried look off your face m'dear I haven't closed early.' A mischievous grin twitched the corners of Molly's mouth upwards. 'I've got a new assistant.'

Beth's eyes opened wide and Molly laughed.

'Don't worry m'dear, it's only a temporary arrangement she won't take your place if that's what you're bothered about. That little friend of yours, the one who you helped carry her books, came to the shop after lunch. She wanted to talk to you so I told her what had

happened to your mother and she offered to mind the shop while I came to see you. I wasn't sure about letting her take over but she said she had a free afternoon with no lectures and she seems a steady sort of girl and anyway there wasn't much of an alternative so there we are …'
Molly began to wash the tea things in the big white pot sink.

'Molly, I'm sorry to have given you so much trouble but I'm sure Katie will manage ok.'

'I expect she will but I can't leave her on her own for too long so we need to spend this time usefully. Your father will probably be home soon and will need something to eat so let's do what you and your mother had planned and do some baking.'

With the oven on the kitchen warmed up and Bethany happily rummaged in cupboards for the various ingredients that Molly requested. Before long Molly was mixing up a rich fruit cake and Bethany was kneading the dough for a batch of cheese scones when the phone rang loud and urgently. Beth dropped the dough onto the board, started towards the door then stopped, examined her dough-encrusted hands and turned back towards the big pot sink.

Molly flapped in her direction. 'Go on, go on, no time for that, a bit of flour on the phone won't do any harm.'

Beth returned to the kitchen with two bright spots of colour on her cheeks. She faced Molly silently and absently wiped her sticky palms down either side of her skirt.

Molly closed the oven door sharply and straightened up. 'Well?'

'She's awake and they think she's going to be alright.'

Molly opened her arms wide and Bethany flew into them. This time the tears flowed noisily and Molly waited patiently until the sobs of relief subsided and Beth looked up with a tear-stained smile.

'Dad's going to stay another hour or two with her then he's coming home. He says there's no point in me going tonight as she needs to rest and sleep but it will be alright for me to go first thing in the morning. She's in a private room now so I can visit anytime.' Beth stopped for breath.

'Now what did I tell you? Everything's going to be fine.'

'Dad says there are no broken bones but her ankle is badly sprained so she'll be unable to walk for a while and they want to keep her in hospital for twenty-four hours under observation because of the head injury, but providing there are no adverse effects they will let her home tomorrow or Friday.'

'That's really good news.' Molly untied the tea towel she had used as a makeshift apron and hung it over the back of a chair. 'Come on, get a move on with those scones, your Dad is going to need food when he gets back.'

Beth grinned and used her pent up energy to roll out the dough and stamp out a good batch of scones.

'The cake will need about an hour or so, just prod it with a skewer to see if it's done in the middle, and now I really must go and see how your friend Katie is managing on her own.' Molly buttoned her coat. 'I'm leaving the washing up for you to do. You will need something to keep you occupied while you're waiting for your Dad to arrive,' she added with a smirk.

'Thank you so much for coming Molly, I don't know what I'd have done without you.' Bethany bent to give Molly a hug but she moved smartly to one side.

'Oh no you don't young lady. You might not mind being covered in flour and dough but I'd rather remain clean if you don't mind, I've got customers to deal with.'

Beth grinned. Molly was back to normal and she felt as though an enormous weight had been lifted.

Beth hummed as she washed up. When everything was safely stowed away she scrubbed the kitchen table and swept the floor. A surge of energy had her looking round to see what else needed doing. She set a tray for her father with plates ready to receive the scones and cake. She removed the golden-topped scones from the oven and put them to cool. She skewered the cake but it was still sticky in the middle so she left it for a while longer. A glance around the kitchen for inspiration gave her the idea of putting a pot of flowers in the centre of the table. There were some pretty chrysanthemums in the garden that would brighten the kitchen admirably. She was busy arranging the flowers in a bowl when the click of the front door closing alerted her to her father's arrival.

'Dad!' Beth flew into the hall and into her father's arms. Desmond Burnett was not generally a demonstrative man but today he held his daughter tightly before releasing her in order to remove his coat. 'You're back early. Is mum really alright?'

Desmond nodded. 'I wouldn't have told you she was if that hadn't been the case,' he replied seriously. 'As for being back early, the doctor politely recommended that I return home. While I was sitting by her side she was inclined to try and talk and they want her to get as much rest as possible so they've turned the lights down in her room and suggested that I leave her to rest. The nurses are doing a good job, they're checking on her constantly, and they will telephone if there is any adverse change in her condition.' Beth took his coat and hung it on the hallstand. She thought her father looked drawn and tired. His dark eyes fixed on her face. 'Your mother has had a lucky escape, it could have been a lot worse, but she is going to need looking after for some while and will need plenty of rest.'

'I can do that, I'll look after her.' Bethany beamed at her father.

'I know you will when you're here Bethany but you have work to go to …'

'I'll take time off work for a week or two, I know Molly won't mind.'

'No Bethany that won't be necessary, it wouldn't be fair on Mrs. Watson to stay off work for a prolonged period. I'll get Mrs. Taylor to come in every day while we are at work and I'll ask her if she would do some cooking.

I'm sure she won't object if I make it worth her while. In fact I'll telephone her now while it's in my mind.'

Bethany put the kettle on, took the cake out of the oven and buttered some scones while her father talked to Mrs. Taylor. He came into the kitchen looking slightly happier.

'That's that organised. Mrs. Taylor is pleased to do the extra hours and some cooking for as long as we need her. My goodness you have been busy.' Bethany looked up from pouring the tea.

'It's not all my own work,' she confided, 'Molly called and she organised the baking to give me something to do while I was waiting to hear from you and so that you would have something to eat when you got back.'

'Well I'm very grateful to Mrs. Watson, she's a good sort, you're lucky to have such a thoughtful employer.' Desmond sat down and accepted the cup Bethany passed across the table. She followed it with a plate of scones and freshly sliced fruit cake. Desmond took a scone but rested it in his saucer. He looked across at Beth. 'Bethany there's something I need to talk to you about before you go to visit your mother.' Desmond looked so serious that Beth's heart started to beat at what felt like twice its normal speed. There's something he hasn't told me about Mum's injuries, she panicked. Her hands felt clammy as she twisted them together.

'What is it?' she whispered.

'When your mother came round she kept mumbling something about a certificate. I told her not to worry about it but I could see she was intent on telling me something.'

Beth felt the colour rise in her cheeks. 'I know what she was trying to say …'

Desmond raised his hand. 'Let me finish please. Eventually she was sufficiently alert to tell me that you wanted your birth certificate and you were angry because she hadn't been able to give it to you. She was upset and so to calm her down I told her I would deal with it as soon as I possibly could.'

Beth put her hands to her burning cheeks. 'Sorry Dad I

was horribly grumpy this morning and I did shout at Mum, I'm so sorry.' Unbidden tears trickled down her cheeks.

'Dry your eyes Bethany there's no lasting harm done. It is simply that I don't want your mother to worry about anything at the moment. I want her rested and calm so that she makes a rapid recovery so I don't want you to mention the birth certificate when you go to visit her and if she brings the subject up tell her that I've seen to it.' Beth nodded vigorously.

'Sorry Dad, it doesn't matter about the certificate, I'll never mention it again.'

Desmond smiled. 'There's no need for such extreme measures. I understood that you wanted it so that you could apply for your driving licence.' Beth nodded again and Desmond regarded her seriously. 'I keep all of our important papers in a safety deposit box at work. I'll look out your papers and bring them home tomorrow.' Desmond took a bite of his scone. 'The more I think about you learning to drive the more I think it would be a good idea, especially now that your mother will be off her feet for a while. It would help her out to have someone other than me to drive her occasionally.'

Beth smiled and passed her father a slice of cake. He had mentioned her 'papers' and she wondered what else he could possibly have apart from her birth certificate but just at the moment she had other things to worry about.

Desmond rose from the table. 'If you don't mind Bethany I've got some work in my study that requires my attention. It shouldn't take too long and then …' His words were interrupted by the ringing of the doorbell. 'I'm up I'll go,' he said as he made his way towards the hall. Beth heard voices in the hallway. 'A friend of yours I believe.'

'Katie!' Beth beamed at the slight fair girl who followed her father into the kitchen.

'I do hope you don't mind, only Molly gave me your address and she said she thought you could probably do with some company.'

'Of course I don't mind, I'm so pleased to see you.'

'One good turn deserves another.'

Beth hugged her friend then helped her off with her coat. 'Sit down and have some tea.'

Katie asked after Beth's mother and Beth described in detail the terrible day she had endured so far. She told Katie how she had shouted at her mother and then had blamed herself for her mother's accident. 'It's this quick temper of mine. Sometimes I find it so difficult to keep calm words just burst out of me before I have time to think about the consequences. It's this red hair of mine, everyone says it goes with a terrible temper.'

'That's moonshine. A temper is just a matter of learning to take a deep breath and counting to ten before you speak, it's got nothing to do with your beautiful hair.'

'Sometimes I don't like it at all and wish it was ordinary and inconspicuous.'

'You shouldn't say that. I think it's fantastic and so does Tom.'

'Does he really?' Katie nodded and Beth felt inordinately pleased.

Katie changed the subject. 'How's it going with that boyfriend of yours?'

Beth was surprised at the question she was sure she hadn't told Katie about Bear, then she remembered that Tom had been with her when Bear had turned up on Monday evening. Tom must have told Katie.

'It's going fine. He's taking me to a disco dance at his college on Friday night.' Beth's face fell. 'But I don't think I'll be able to go now that mum's hurt. She'll need me at home. Dad has Rotary Club meetings on Friday evenings and he wouldn't want to miss that.'

'Oh that's a shame, you ought to go.' Katie looked thoughtful. 'How would it be if I came and looked after your mother until your dad gets home?'

Beth brightened. 'Would you really? That would be marvellous but I'll have to check with mum first to make sure she doesn't mind.' Then another thought struck Beth. 'Don't you want to go out, it's a Friday night after all.'

Katie looked at Beth solemnly as though weighing up what to tell her. Eventually she said. 'I don't have a boyfriend at the moment, if that's what you mean.' Beth was surprised at Katie's remark. 'I occasionally get asked out but nothing serious ever comes of it.' She laughed but there was a brittle tone to her humour. 'Probably too choosey, or maybe it's because I always put work first,' she added.

Beth didn't know quite how to reply to Katie's admission so she changed the subject.'I'm getting a provisional licence so that I can learn to drive. Do you drive?'

Katie shook her head. 'No need. Haven't got a car and not likely to get one for years to come so I've never bothered. Tom drives though. He had to learn so that he could drive the garage's breakdown truck and now he's got an ancient sports car that he spends every spare minute lovingly restoring. He says it's almost ready for its first test run.'

Beth listened to Katie talking about her brother. They obviously had a good relationship. 'I wish I had brothers and sisters,' she said wistfully.

Katie laughed. 'It's not all roses. We used to fight all the time when we were younger.'

'I would like to have a sister so that we could discuss fashions and make up and boyfriends.' Beth remarked longingly.

'You wouldn't like it when she borrowed your make up and stole your boyfriends!' Katie laughed.

'Perhaps not, but it would be nice to have a girl near my age to confide in occasionally.'

Katie nodded. 'I know what you mean.' She paused. 'I had a sister once.' Beth sat up straight. Katie had certainly caught her attention with that unexpected remark.

'Once?'

Katie nodded a trifle sadly. 'I never knew her. She died soon after she was born and I was only two at the time so I don't remember her at all. If she was alive I suppose she would be about your age.'

'Oh, how sad.' Beth blinked back the tears that prickled beneath her eyelids. She wasn't prone to easy tears but this sad story on top of her traumatic day made her feel weepy. 'Your poor mother, it must have been terrible for her to loose a child.'

'I suppose so, but she's never made much fuss about it. I suppose when something like that happens you count your blessings, she already had two healthy children after all. The baby's buried at St. Luke's and mum lays flowers there every so often. I expect the pot of violets I bought for her birthday will end up there eventually.' Katie looked at Beth's stricken face. 'Come on we're getting morbid. Tell me what you're going to wear for the disco on Friday.'

Prudence was discharged from hospital the next day, non the worse for her fall apart from a sprained ankle and a few bruises. Beth had been given the day off work and she had charged from room to room making sure everything was neat and tidy for her mother's return. Finally she laid a tea tray and took it into the drawing room where she had lit a welcoming fire in the large marble fireplace. Prudence hobbled in on crutches with Desmond at her elbow. She lowered herself gingerly into an armchair and passed her crutches to Beth's waiting hands. Beth bent over her mother and, afraid a hug might hurt her, she squeezed her hands.

'Mum I'm *so* sorry.'

'Bethany you have nothing to be sorry about. The accident was entirely my own fault. If I hadn't been stupidly wearing those high heels to do the housework the fall would not have happened. In future I'll wear carpet slippers in the house despite the fact that they'll make me look like a ninety year old granny! Now who's going to pour the tea?' Beth and Desmond smiled with relief at Prudence's attempt at humour. It meant that she was on the mend and the topic of her accident was closed.

After tea Desmond left the room, returning with a large foolscap envelope which he passed to Beth. On the front a printed label stated: BETHANY MARGARET BURNETT – Private and confidential.

'The papers you wanted I think.'

Beth's heart skipped as she took the envelope and slowly lifted the flap. What was she going to find? She knew it contained her birth certificate, because that was what she'd asked for, but what were all these other papers? Adoption papers perhaps? The thought made her feel giddy. With a shaking hand she pulled out a sheaf of papers, watched intently by her father and mother.

On top lay a buff folder with BIRTH CERTIFICATE emblazoned across the front. Beth reached inside and pulled out a stiff cream paper neatly folded into three. She slowly opened it out and read the words with disbelief.

Chapter 13

Her full name was Bethany Margaret Prudence Burnett. Her father was Desmond Richard Burnett and her mother was Prudence Mary Helen Burnett. At the time of her birth her parents were resident at Flat 1, Grove Street, Oxford and she was born on October 23rd 1945 at St. Mary's Maternity Home, St. Mary's Road, Oxford. The cursive copperplate handwriting swam before Beth's eyes as she re-read its message carefully. Over the last few days she had almost convinced herself of her adoption and now that she had proof that she was truly Desmond's and Prudence's daughter she could hardly believe what she saw. She looked up.

'The handwriting's lovely isn't it?' Prudence observed.

Beth nodded. 'It's beautiful,' she whispered.

'Now Bethany, take care of it, it's the only one you've got and it's not easy to replace a lost birth certificate. And if you wish, when you've finished with it, I could put it in safe keeping again.' Desmond regarded his daughter seriously. 'As for all the other papers, you can do with them as you like but I should put them somewhere out of harm's way if I were you.'

Bethany had forgotten about the rest of the papers but now she spread them out on her lap. There were: swimming certificates, ballet dancing certificates, piano exam results, a pile of school reports, and most important of all, her O and A level certificates. There was not a single adoption paper to be seen! Beth clutched the papers to her chest and stood up.

'Thank you so much for keeping these safe for me,' she said, leaving the room before her parents saw her tears of relief.

In her room Beth spread out the papers on the bed. Before her lay her life so far, from her birth, through the highlights of her achievements at school, to this summer when her A level results arrived after she had left school and started work for Molly Watson at The Flower Basket. She read the contents of the birth certificate once more before folding it carefully and replacing in its envelope. Well that's one thing decided, I'm definitely not adopted, she told herself. But it still didn't explain her unusual hair and quick temper. It didn't seem so important to Beth now but still she would like to know how she had inherited such outstanding colouring. Perhaps a reply from Aunt Edith would solve that one.

Downstairs Prudence looked at Desmond, a worried frown creasing her forehead. 'I'm concerned about Bethany – she's not been herself lately.'

'In what way?'

'Well...she's been very short tempered for a start.'

Desmond smiled reassuringly. 'That's nothing new Prue, she's never been one to hide her feelings and has always been quick to snap.'

'Yes I know, but she was getting better but just lately she's regressed. Take her latest outburst over the birth certificate. She was really angry and it's not as though she needed it urgently, you said she should wait a bit before taking driving lessons.'

Desmond stirred his tea slowly. 'Mmm... she does seem worried about something. I hope everything is going alright at work. I still think she shouldn't have rushed into that job at the flower shop.' Prudence nodded her agreement. 'Perhaps it would help if she did learn to drive.' Desmond looked thoughtful. 'Having to cope with other road users might teach her a little more patience and it would be useful for you to have someone to drive you when I'm busy.' Desmond drank his tea and put his cup down firmly on the tea tray. 'I'll arrange some lessons as soon as her licence comes through.'

Prudence shifted uncomfortably in her chair. 'That's kind of you, I'm sure she'll appreciate it.'

'I hope so. We should try to treat her as an adult, she is after all nearly nineteen. In the meantime my main concern is looking after you so that you get better quickly.'

***

Friday at the Flower Basket was even busier than normal. Beth was run off her feet serving in the shop and helping Molly make up a large numbers of orders for the weekend.

'Business is booming m'girl,' Molly yelled happily from the workroom. 'Should be able to afford new overalls at this rate.'

'Oh Molly you are funny.' Beth loved Molly's dry humour. She was feeling pretty cheerful herself. This evening she would see Bear again and she couldn't wait.

During the afternoon the constant stream of customers kept Beth so busy that she was surprised when five o'clock came round. Thoughts of the approaching disco rushed into her head and excitement bubbled inside her.

'Time you went home,' Molly announced.

'But it's not half past yet.'

'I can tell the time, I'm not in my dotage yet, and I can do without an assistant who has a look in her eye that says she would rather be elsewhere. You get off home, I can lock up.'

Beth didn't need telling twice. 'Oh Molly thanks, you're a dear.'

Molly smiled and for once did not have a quick answer. 'Don't you be late home now, you've got work in the morning, and then you can tell me all about it,' she added to soften the apparent harshness of her previous remark.

Beth's excitement rose as she pulled on her coat and hurriedly wheeled her bicycle from the shed in the yard at the back of the shop. Cycling along Kingston Road she spotted a familiar figure in the distance. She put on a spurt and drew up alongside.

'Katie, hi.'

'Hello Beth, I wasn't expecting to see you for another half hour. Thought I'd get to your house early incase Mrs. Taylor has already left and your mum needs anything.'

'Molly let me off early.'

'She's such a kind person. My mum says she's the salt

of the earth,' Katie remarked.

Beth agreed and the two walked the short distance to Beth's home indulging in quiet chatter.

***

Beth shivered. The evening had an autumn chill to it and the promise of a frost later hung in the air. She had brushed her hair vigorously into a short pony tail that was a froth of tight curls and had secured it tightly with an emerald green band. She was pleased with the result but it didn't keep her neck warm in the way that her loose hair did. The fabric of Molly's altered dress was thin and it ended well above her knees and, despite the fact that she wore some of the new pantyhose which were warmer than stockings, Beth felt the evening chill and wished that Bear would hurry up. She waited where they had arranged to meet on New Inn Hall Street. She hadn't intended to be early, it didn't do to look too eager, but in her excitement she had rushed and now here she was five minutes before the allotted time.

Ten minutes later Bear still hadn't arrived and Beth shivered with irritation as much as the cold. A steady stream of students passed her and entered through the heavy wooden gates next to where she stood. Some ignored her as they laughed and joked with their companions but others weighed her up, wondering if she was good for a date. One even stopped, smiled and opened his mouth to speak but was deterred from making further advances by the look of anger on Beth's face. A further ten minutes saw Beth fuming at being left standing in the cold. Five more minutes, Beth thought, then I'm leaving.

She was about to do just that when Bear came running towards her, coat flapping and blond hair flopping up and down as he ran. Beth was ready to let vent to her anger but at the sight of him running towards her waving madly her fury subsided a little. Bear wrapped his arms round her and kissed her neck. He was wearing a thin cream polo-neck sweater tucked into belted trousers that sat neatly on his hips. He smelt of aftershave and Beth's resolve dissolved.

'So sorry I'm late. Got caught up with an old friend. Couldn't just dump him. Have you been here long?' Beth shook her head. Only thirty flipping minutes, her inner voice said, but unusually Beth remained silent. Bear's charisma had her in its spell and she gave him a beaming smile. He looked approvingly at the expanse of nylon-clad legs that showed below her jacket and putting an arm round Beth's shoulders he propelled her through the tall wooden gates. 'Come on you must be frozen, let's get inside.'

They crossed a cobbled courtyard and Bear guided Beth through a narrow archway that gave onto a flight of well-worn steps leading down into the darkness below. As they descended Beth could feel, rather than hear, the music rising from the space below, as the base beat vibrated through her body.

On entering the large vaulted cellar Beth's ears were assaulted by the noise. Raised voices fought with one another to make themselves heard over the sound of the music and the atmosphere was already thick with cigarette smoke. Bear took Beth's hand and towed her behind him as he skirted the crowd. He led the way to some trestle tables set up as a makeshift bar. 'What will you have?' he shouted. Beth didn't know what to choose. At home she drank infrequently, just an occasional glass of wine with a special meal, and now she was bewildered by the array of bottles on offer. She didn't attempt to make herself heard but instead waved her hand towards a bottle of cider. That should be safe enough. 'Good choice.' Bear uncapped the bottle and handed it to her with a grin before doing the same for himself. 'Cheers!' He raised his bottle to his lips. For a split second Beth waited for a glass to be produced but then realised that none was forthcoming, so did the same.

At the far end of the room the disc jockey worked away unceasingly behind his console, changing discs, announcing titles, making light banter, and occasionally pressing buttons to change the colours of the flashing lights that bounced off the stone walls. A few couples danced in the space marked off for dancing in front of his equipment but most were busy trying to talk with their friends. 'It's going to get hot in here. Let's dump your jacket over there.' Bear pointed to some upright wooden chairs that had been placed either side of the entrance. Beth slid her arms out of her jacket and felt Bear's eyes on her. 'Nice dress,' he commented, 'and nice legs to go with it.' Beth flushed with pleasure and held out her hand to Bear but he didn't take it, his attention was caught by a girl that had materialised by their side. A girl that Beth remembered having seen on the steps of the Ashmolean Museum with Bear and another boy.

'Hi Bear, I was wondering where you'd got to,' she shouted, flicking back her sleek dark hair.

'Got held up,' he replied shortly. 'Where's Peter?'

'How should I know, he'll be around somewhere.' The girl shrugged and glanced at Beth with a question mark in her eyes.

Tom saw the question. 'This is Bethany. Bethany … Camilla.'

'Hi, please call me Beth.'

The girl looked hard at Beth for a moment or two. 'Ok, Beth.' She turned immediately to Bear. 'Want to dance?' Bear looked at Beth as if asking her if she minded. She shrugged and took the almost empty bottle that he held out to her. Camilla took Bear's hand and they made their way to the dance floor area leaving Beth holding two bottles of cider. She wished she knew someone other than Bear then at least she would have someone to talk to. She felt decidedly conspicuous and took a few steps back until she was leaning against the wall.

A tall boy with dark greased hair that curled over the collar of his open neck shirt glanced at Beth as he passed. He took a second look over his shoulder and stepped back until he was level with her once more. 'Hello carrot-top …

divine dress ... care to dance?' Beth was so shaken by his form of address that her usual quick tongue deserted her.

She held up the two bottles. 'No thanks, I'm waiting for someone,' was the best she could do.

The boy raised his prominent shoulders to his ears and spread out his hands. 'Please yourself.' He disappeared into the melee and Beth breathed a sigh of relief. She hadn't liked the look of him at all. Her relief however was short lived. On straightening up from depositing the sticky bottles on the floor she was confronted by a cheerful looking fellow with a smooth round baby face and glasses.

Would you care to dance?' he asked politely. Beth weighed up her options. There was no sign of Bear, she was tired of standing on her own, and this chap was at least polite, so dancing with him was preferable she decided to being a permanent wallflower. Also Bear was on the dance floor with Camilla and hopefully he would see her and come to her rescue.

They made their way with difficulty through the chattering crowd to the dance area. Many more couples were now dancing and the floor was crowded. As she danced Beth peered in all directions for a glimpse of Bear but there was no sign of him. We must have passed in the crowd Beth thought with rising panic. Bear would be back where he left her and would be wondering where she was, and here she was stuck on the dance floor with baby-face. The record seemed to last for an age. Beth danced mechanically and as soon as the music paused she made her excuses and left the dance floor. The boy she was dancing with was so surprised at her sudden departure that he made no attempt to follow.

Back at her spot by the wall the two bottles remained where she'd left them but of Bear there was no sign. Beth was at a loss. Should she remain here or go in search of Bear? The decision was taken from her as a good looking boy approached.

'Sorry, I'm not dancing, I'm waiting for my boyfriend,' she told him firmly before he had a chance to speak. He appeared unmoved by Beth's blunt outburst.

'Now let me guess By your appearance I would say you're waiting for Bear.' A cheerful smile lit his face.

Beth stared, 'How did you know that?'

'Bear has described his latest conquest and you fit the bill exactly. How many girls are there in this cellar with fantastic auburn hair and legs to die for?' Beth blushed. 'I'm Peter,' he continued holding out his hand, 'an old friend of Bear's, we were at school together.'

'I'm Bethany but everyone calls me Beth, and you must be Camilla's boyfriend.'

Peter stared hard at Beth for a split second. 'Not so as you'd notice,' he replied with a grimace. 'She seems to prefer Bear at the moment.'

Beth was confused. 'But...?'

Peter interrupted her. 'Here they are now.'

Bear and Camilla were laughing as they descended the cellar steps, both holding a bottle.

'Bear where have you been, I've been looking for you?' Beth could not keep a note of reproach from her voice.

'I might ask you the same. I came back here when our dance finished and you were nowhere to be found. Camilla thought you might have gone outside for some fresh air so we went up to the courtyard to look for you.' Bear took a mouthful from his bottle and Beth relaxed a little.

'Well you've found her now and I think it's time I danced with my girlfriend.' Peter guided a startled Camilla towards the dance floor with a smile for Beth and a backward glance at Bear.

Bear put his arm round Beth's waist and gave it a squeeze. 'Sorry I deserted you. Let's make up for lost time. I need a drink then I'll dance with the most beautiful girl here.'

Beth forgave Bear immediately. They danced. Bear fetched more cider. They danced some more and Bear, leaning against the bar with a fresh bottle in his hand, introduced her to some of his friends.

'Come on beautiful, let's dance.' Bear set down his now empty bottle on the bar and took Beth's hand. Beth was beginning to feel a bit nauseous, she wasn't used to strong cider or cigarette smoke. She glanced at her watch.

'Bear it's turned eleven, I must go.'

Bear turned an incredulous face to her. 'You mean you're leaving before the end?'

Beth nodded. 'Sorry Bear but I need to be up early. I've got work tomorrow.'

'But this goes on until one, you can't leave this early.'

Beth had had enough. Her feet hurt, the cider was much stronger than she had realised and the smoke was making her fell a little sick. She just wanted to go home. Bear's fury showed on his face. 'Well I suppose I'll have to see you home.' His face brightened. 'I don't suppose you came on your bike?' he asked hopefully. Beth sadly shook her head.

'You don't need to walk me home. I can manage. You stay here and enjoy the rest of the evening.'

'Oh yes, and if anything happened to you I'd be the one to get the blame. Come on, get your coat.' Bear walked ahead of her up the stone steps and Beth followed despondently.

The sudden cold air after the closeness of the cellar had the effect of making Bear feel drunk, not unpleasantly so, but drunk nevertheless. He cupped his hand around Beth's elbow and swiftly guided her through the market square, past the Ashmolean and onto St. Giles. Beth had difficulty walking so quickly in her new sling-back high heels and had to stop a few times, hopping first on one leg and then the other to reposition the straps round the backs of her heels. She could feel Bear's impatience as he waited for her to continue. If only he would walk a little more slowly, Beth thought, but she knew he was eager to return to the disco so she said nothing. They walked in silence along the broad thoroughfare of St. Giles. Bear glanced at his watch and his mood improved – perhaps if they were quick he could get back to the disco in time for a bit more fun. He glanced at Beth's serious face.

'Cheer up, it's not as bad as all that.' He put his arm around her shoulders. 'Sorry I was grumpy. I didn't realise you had to work on a Saturday.'

Bear's apology cheered Beth and she snuggled into his arm. 'I'm sorry I didn't mean to spoil your evening.'

Bear grinned. 'You haven't.' He pulled her closer and Beth could smell the cider on his breath.

Without warning Bear turned sharp left into a narrow darkened street and put Beth's back against the wall of a small shop. He was slightly unsteady and leaned heavily against her. 'Show me how sorry you are,' he muttered as her pressed his lips hard against hers. Beth squealed, the move was so unexpected and not entirely to her liking. Bear's lips were hurting hers and she was finding it difficult to breathe. But her discomfort was nothing to that which she felt as Bear's hand travelled up her thigh. The soft fabric of her dress slid up easily and Bear's fingers were pulling at the waistband of her tights. Beth summoned all of her strength to raise her hands to his chest and with an enormous effort she pushed Bear off balance. He staggered and caught hold of Beth's shoulder to steady himself.

'What the hell?' Bear let go but a second later lurched towards her.

'Get off me. Don't touch me. How dare you do such a thing in the street?' Beth radiated anger.

'But I thought …' Bear swayed, he had difficulty standing and needed someone to lean on.

'Whatever you thought it was wrong. Now go back to your disco. I am quite capable of walking the rest of the way home.' Beth pulled away and ran toward the lights of the main road and headed for home.

'Beth wait! I didn't mean to upset you. Beth please …' floated on the cold air behind her. She looked over her shoulder. Bear was stumbling out of the side road. She quickened her steps.

Chapter 14

Beth was glad the road was well lit with wide pavements. She passed a restaurant where, through the dimly lit windows, she could see waiters wiping tables and stacking chairs. One of them looked up and gave her a cheery wave. The pounding in her chest slowed and she felt a little better. Further along she came to the stone wall that bounded the Radcliffe Infirmary where her mother had been taken after her fall. Was that only a few days ago? To Beth it seemed like an age.

The pavement here was wide and deserted, a few cars passed but there were no other pedestrians. On the other side of the wide road the last of the drinkers were spilling out from the Royal Oak onto the pavement. Beth quickened her pace; she did not want to get mixed up with any more drunks. As she hurried along the shouts of the revellers grew fainter but another sound grew louder and it caused her concern. Behind her Beth could hear heavy hurrying footsteps. A furtive glance over her shoulder told her that a man was gaining on her quite quickly. He wore dark trousers and a bulky donkey jacket and a thick scarf obscured the lower half of his face. His hands were casually placed in his jacket pockets but his walk was purposeful. He's probably in a hurry to get home too, she thought, but nonetheless she quickened her pace.

Despite her extra spurt, Beth was aware that the person behind her was quite close; she could hear his breathing as well as his footsteps. She considered crossing the road before he reached her, but the pavement on the other side was overhung with trees and dark shadows lurked beneath them. She paused at the kerb, unsure of what course to take, and a hand was placed on her shoulder.

'Bethany!'

The voice was faintly familiar. Beth turned and relief flooded through her. Katie's brother Tom smiled a greeting.

'Oh… Tom… it's you!'

'Sorry if I frightened you. I wasn't sure it was you until I got up close and I didn't want to accost some unknown woman at this time of night. And talking of the time, what are you doing out so late on your own? Beth opened her mouth but Tom continued, 'ok, don't answer that. It's none of my business.'

'I've been to a disco and I'm on my way home.'

Tom frowned. 'Why isn't that boyfriend of yours taking you home?'

'He was,' Beth replied hurriedly, 'but when we got to the end of St. Giles I told him I'd be alright on my own. This is a main road with cars passing after all.'

'That maybe so but if anything happened to you on the pavement passing cars would probably not even notice at night, let alone stop.' Tom looked thoughtful. 'A little thing like you should not walk out alone after dark.' Beth was inclined to agree with him, not about the little thing bit but about the inadvisability of being alone late at night. Her crestfallen face moved him. 'Come on, I'll walk you to your door.' Without another word he took Beth's hand and tucked it into the crook of his arm. Beth saw no reason to protest she liked this quiet man, he was reliable and she felt safe with him. They set off at a brisk pace, Beth matching her tread to Tom's long strides.

Despite the brisk walk Beth shivered, the promised cold snap had definitely arrived, and she held the neck of her jacket closed with her free hand. Tom stopped.

'Here, you're cold.' He unwound the grey knitted scarf he was wearing and held it out. She was startled by his sudden action and made no immediate effort to take the offered scarf. With one continuous movement Tom gently wound the scarf around Beth's neck, tucked the ends into the top of her jacket, linked her arm with his and set off once more.

'Thanks.' Beth snuggled into the scarf's warm woolliness and felt happy for the first time that evening.

After a few minutes of walking in silence Tom

enquired, 'how's life at The Flower Basket?'

Beth needed little prompting to talk about her work and regaled Tom with anecdotes about the most colourful customers. 'And,' she told him proudly, 'I'm learning to drive so that I can take the van and help Molly with the deliveries.'

'Good for you, everyone should know how to drive. Who's teaching you?'

'My dad knows someone who has just started up a driving school so he's going to ask him to take me on. The lessons will have to be on Sundays or my half day so it's going to take some time before I'm ready for my test.'

'Well, if it's any help, I'll take you out in my car for some practice.'

Beth remembered that Katie had told her Tom had an old car. She hoped it wasn't too old and rickety otherwise her father might have something to say about her going out in it and she really wanted to have some driving practice with Tom, he was so kind and calm she was sure he would be a good instructor.

'Thank you that would be great,' she told him with a smile. Tom's heart leapt. He was glad he had thought of a way of seeing more of this delightful girl. But then the difference in their ages and the fact that she had a boyfriend dampened his mood and he sighed inwardly.

That night Beth was restless and wakeful. She lay on her back going over the events of the evening in her mind. She pictured Bear's smile and recalled the sound of his voice and she was moved, but the memories of his disappearance with Camilla during the disco and his drunken behaviour on the way home chased each other round her brain until she felt like screaming. She turned on her side and tried to blank her mind so that she could sleep but the ticking of the small clock on her bedside table marked the passing of time and kept her awake. Strange, Beth thought, how I never notice the ticking in the daytime but at night it fills the room loudly enough to keep me awake. She changed her position yet again and thought about Katie's brother Tom. He was kind and protective just as she imagined a big brother should be. She smiled as she remembered snuggling into his warm scarf and then she fell asleep.

***

Beth woke to a grey outlook. She peered out between the bedroom curtains and shivered in her thin pyjamas. The sky outside was as grim as her mood. She dressed quickly in a dark green woollen skirt and reached for a warm sweater. Why had she allowed herself to like Bear? She might have known that an undergraduate wouldn't be interested in a girl who worked in a flower shop. Why had she let his smile and a pretty bunch of flowers seduce her into thinking he might want to see her again? She pulled the dull brown sweater over her head and vigorously brushed her ruffled curls into some semblance of order. A gust of wind splattered a flurry of raindrops noisily onto the window. Beth looked disconsolately towards the wet glass. The bright sun of the last few days was not going to shine today.

Prudence turned from the Aga. Her pale complexion was faintly flushed with the heat from the cooker but her soft dark hair retained its customary neat French pleat.

'Good morning darling. Porridge or cereal?' Beth slid onto her chair and put her elbows on the table. Prudence gave her daughter a frown to signify her disapproval of the elbows.

'Just toast please I'm not feeling very hungry.'

'Oh my dear, are you sickening for something?' Prudence swept a cool hand across Beth's forehead.

'Mum, of course I'm not sickening for something, I'm grown up and I've had all the childish illnesses. I'm just not hungry that's all.' Prudence knew of old that arguing with her daughter was pointless. She placed a full toast rack on the table and followed it with a plate of scrambled eggs and bacon. Beth poured herself a cup of tea and spread marmalade sparingly on a neat triangle of toast. She stretched a hand towards the post that her father had placed next to his plate. Maybe there would be a positive response to the letter she had sent to great Aunt Edith in Australia and she would not have to worry about being the only red head in the family.

'Anything for me?' she asked hopefully. Her father peered around his newspaper and Prudence sighed. Reading at the table was another habit that she disliked but in the interest of harmony she had let it pass and now it was Desmond's daily modus operandi at the weekend breakfast table. He did however respect her wishes when it came to the dinner table.

'Not unless you're interested in the electricity bill or taking out a subscription to a rather boring magazine,' he replied dryly. 'Were you expecting something?' he added more kindly.

'No, just wondered that's all.' Beth lied and unthinkingly attacked the bacon and scrambled eggs that Prudence had placed before her. Her mind raced through the possibilities of a note from Bear. She recalled that moment when she had seen Bear and the dark-haired Camilla laughing together on the cellar steps. He didn't want to see her again, he had other fish to fry that was the truth of the matter. Did she mind after his drunken groping on the way home? The memory of the incident made her angry and she convinced herself that she was better off without him.

***

Beth shook the rain off her yellow plastic cycle cape and draped it over the sink in the work room. Molly silently passed her a rough towel and Beth vigorously towelled her hair until it surrounded her head in a mass of damp copper-coloured curls.

'Beastly day,' she commented. Molly nodded her agreement.

Saturday at The Flower Basket was unremarkable. Beth was tired from her late night and was not inclined to chatter. Molly, as always, picked up on Beth's mood and remained quiet. She refrained from asking whether Beth had enjoyed the disco as she feared from Beth's silent demeanour that the answer would be no.

At the end of the working day Molly locked the shop. 'If you finish clearing up the workroom I'll go upstairs and put the kettle on then, if you feel like it, you could join me for a quick cuppa.' She hoped Beth would be more forthcoming in the comfort of her flat. Beth nodded her assent and continued sweeping. She had almost finished when a frantic knocking on the shop door interrupted her contemplation of the workroom floor. She felt irritated by the disturbance but shrugged and continued with her task. Molly appeared at the workroom door agitated and out of breath from rushing down the flight of stairs from her flat. The banging continued.

'Can't you hear that racket?' she asked more sharply than usual.

'Yes but we're closed.' Beth was equally annoyed.

'I know that m'girl but it could be something important. Folk don't hammer like that for nothing.' Beth made no move to investigate the banging on the shop door. 'Alright I'll go.' Molly thumped her way past an unrepentant Beth and into the darkened shop. Beth heard the bolts being drawn back and voices, Molly's and a man's.

'It's your young man.' Molly announced as she returned to the workroom. Bear hovered behind Molly in the darkness. 'I'll leave you two to it,' she said bluntly.

Chapter 15

Bear had spent an uneasy Saturday nursing a foul hangover and recalling the events of the previous evening. In his present almost-sober state he wished he had handled things differently. When he came up to Oxford he knew that as a medical student he would have plenty of hard work ahead of him but he intended to balance this with an equal amount of socialising. A serious girlfriend was out of the question, he needed to be free of ties for several years to come, and anyway girls were attracted to him so why stick with just one when he could take his pick and have several on the go at once? He liked Camilla. With her long sleek hair and generous curves in all the right places, she was easy on the eye and he sensed that she was out for a good time with no strings attached too. She had enrolled at a private secretarial college and lived with several other would-be secretaries from the same college in a hall of residence in North Oxford, not far from his digs in Summertown. She was only going to be at the college for a year so that would be an easy way out if he had had enough of her by then. But in the meantime, best of all, her wealthy father had provided her with a nippy sports car so they would be able to get out of Oxford when the mood took them.

Yes, Camilla was a good start, but then there was Bethany. Beth intrigued Bear. She was fantastic looking and didn't seem to be aware of the fact. He liked the way that she turned heads and he wanted this stunning red head to be his property. She was naive but that was part of her charm and she would soon grow up if he had anything to do with it. The trouble was Beth worked full time and this meant that she was only available at weekends. On reflection, that could work in his favour, it would leave weekdays free for fun with Camilla. Not a bad outcome. But, he pondered, how to make things right with Beth? He had been the recipient of her quick temper on two occasions now. Would she forgive as quickly as she raged? Somehow Bear thought not, so how was he going to get round her? It was also a question of his pride, there was no way he was going to be cast off by a girl no matter how beautiful, he was the one who did the dumping. The problem irritated his brain and aggravated his headache, so he shelved it and went into town for a lunchtime hair of the dog.

Peter was in the pub and greeted Bear with a shout. 'You look dreadful. Better do something about it before tonight or the girls will look elsewhere.'

'Ha, ha, very funny,' Bear replied with a sardonic smile as he downed a pint of black and tan.

'What's making you so cheerful then, as if I didn't know?'

'If you know so much then why ask?' Bear's irritation increased with his friend's banter.

'I know you didn't see her home. If you had you wouldn't have been back at the disco so soon. What happened? She dump you?'

'Of course not you moron,' Bear's annoyance with Peter increased as he came close to the mark. 'We had a slight disagreement that's all.'

'Ho, ho, and now you've got to eat humble pie to get her back.' Peter gave the student sitting opposite a knowing wink. 'You'll have to go on bended knees to please that one,' he continued. He was enjoying the situation. He and Bear had been friends since school and this was the first time he had seen Bear in a quandary over a girl.

Bear looked at Peter with near hatred in his eyes. Damn it, Peter was right, he would have to grovel to Beth. But was she worth it? He considered this conundrum as he thoughtfully drank his next pint.

***

Beth leaned on her broom and Bear saw the chilling glitter

in her green eyes.

'Well, you've managed to gain entry now what do you want? And you'd better make it snappy Molly will be back in a minute and I've got things to do.' Every fibre in her body was taught as she faced Bear. He was undeniably the most handsome man she'd ever met but at this moment she was boiling with fury. She averted her eyes, she was not going to let his good looks influence her resolve.

Bear felt stronger when Beth looked away. She's unsure of herself he thought.

'Beth I'm so sorry about last night,' he began.

'Yes I'm sorry too but probably not in quite the same way,' Beth retorted.

Bear tried another tack. 'Beth please, please don't be angry…'

'What do you expect me to be, thankful? You go off to dance with darling Camilla and then desert me for half the evening. Luckily for you that nice Peter came to talk to me otherwise I'd have walked out sooner. Then you didn't want to walk me home and to cap it all …'

'Ok, ok, you have every right to be angry with me, but that kiss …'

'Kiss you call it! Was that what it was? You could have fooled me.'

'Beth honestly, you're so beautiful and attractive I just meant to kiss you goodnight, the rest of it happened because I was drunk and I'm very, very sorry it did.'

'You didn't need to get as drunk as that.'

'I know and I didn't intend to but that Diamond White cider is far stronger than I realised. I had no intention of getting drunk you must believe me. I'll never touch the stuff again.'

Beth did not answer immediately. Bear's explanation had a grain of truth. She had felt quite light headed after only one bottle of cider. Should she believe this handsome boy or follow her previous instincts and refuse to have anything more to do with him? Bear took her silence as a sign of her capitulation and pressed home his point.

'Beth it won't happen again I promise. Now let's be friends and start again. Peter and I and a few others will be in the Kings Arms this evening why don't you join us?' He held out a friendly hand. Beth was torn. Despite his drunken behaviour the night before she still found him incredibly attractive. Should she give their relationship another chance? Slowly she extended her hand. Bear took it and pulled her towards him but Beth put the broom between them.

'There's just one thing I have to say to you Bear. If you ever treat me like a street girl again you'll regret it.'

Bear nodded seriously. He had learned his lesson, as far as Beth was concerned anyway. 'Will you come tonight?' he asked contritely.

'I'm not sure, there's something I have to do after work and my parents are expecting me home for dinner.'

'Well come after dinner, we'll be there all evening so it doesn't matter what time you turn up.'

'I might,' Beth conceded. She wasn't going to make things that easy for Bear this time.

Beth fastened her coat, called out goodbye to Molly and picked up Tom's grey woollen scarf. She intended to make a short detour via the garage on her way home in order to return it to him. She was very grateful that he had come to her rescue last night and she was not sure that she had thanked him properly. Returning the scarf would provide an opportunity for her to do just that. She wound the scarf found her neck. Might as well keep warm on the ride to Tom's garage she told herself and anyway it reminded her of Tom's kind smile and it smelt, not unpleasantly, of oil and grease.

She found the garage quite easily. Tom had pointed out the entrance on their walk home yesterday night and Beth was not surprised that she hadn't noticed it before. The garage was positioned behind a row of tall terraced houses on the Woodstock Road and could not be seen from the road. Access was gained through an archway between two of the houses over which the red letters on a small enamelled sign spelt out neatly: *Hurst's Garage – Sports cars a specialty.* Beth crossed under the archway and along the wide passage between two of the houses. She found herself on an area of hard standing on which several cars were neatly lined up. As she crossed the yard to the large wooden building on the far side, Beth could not help noticing a small dark green MG sports car parked alongside the others. The car was stylish but old fashioned with a small folding windscreen and running boards down either side of the elegant body. From its design it was obviously quite old and yet it looked as though it had just driven out of the factory. Beth thought it was the smartest little car she had set eyes on.

The double doors of the garage were propped open with worn tyres. Beth peered inside and waited a moment for her eyes to become accustomed to the gloom. At the far end another MG stood over an inspection pit, this was a newer model in royal blue. A wire-covered lamp was clamped on a stand nearby so that it shone onto the underside of the car. The place was silent and apparently deserted and Beth felt a pang of disappointment. Obviously she was too late and Tom had already gone home. Why hadn't she thought of that possibility?

'Bugger!' The exclamation followed a sharp clang as something metal hit the bottom of the inspection pit and an oily face, followed by a pair of greasy dungarees, heaved out from under the car. A look of astonishment mingled with the grease and grime on Tom's face as he saw Beth silhouetted in the doorway.

'Whatever brings you here?' he called crossing the garage with long strides.

'Sorry to disturb you when you're working. I came to say thank you for rescuing me last night and I brought your scarf back.' Beth unwound the scarf and held it out.

'You didn't need to do that, it was a pleasure to see you home and you're not disturbing me I was about to take a break, I need a smoke.' Outside Tom stretched and breathed deeply before reaching into an inside pocket for his cigarettes. He shook one out from a small hole in the top of the packet, put it between his lips and, cupping his hands around it, he lit it with a safety lighter that he had picked up from a workbench on his way out. Beth watched and noticed the neatness of his ginger hair as it curled back and away from his face. Tom inhaled deeply then blew out a stream of smoke through which he contemplated Beth. Her turning up at the garage was an unexpected surprise but a very pleasant one for all that. Beth watched Tom quietly. She didn't feel the need to chatter. He was a calm sort of person and she felt relaxed in his company. He was almost like the big brother that she had never had.

'I thought you might have finished for the day,' she observed.

'No such luck, but this is the last one today so, when it's fixed I'll be off home.' Tom wanted to say more but couldn't quite find the right words.

'That's one good thing about my job we always close on time.' Beth smiled.

'So you're on your way home now?'

Beth nodded and looked across at the small green MG. 'I like that car,' she remarked.

A wide smile creased Tom's face. 'So do I. It's a nineteen forty-six MG TC. Cars of that era didn't changed much from the pre-war thirties roadsters, unlike the MGBs and Midgets being made today which are a completely different kettle of fish.'

'It's the same age as me but it looks brand new, it's incredible.'

'That's because it's undergone complete restoration, right down to its new British Racing Green paintwork.'

'It's lovely,' Beth observed.

And so are you, Tom wanted to tell her but instead he said, 'glad you like it.'

'Well I must be getting home.' Beth once more offered the scarf to Tom and this time he took it and hung it over his shoulder. He ground out his cigarette firmly under his heel and looked at Beth.

'Beth, I'm nearly done here. Would you like to wait in the garage while I finish off. You could make yourself a cup of tea in the back room if you like and then we could go and get some fish and chips, there's a very good fish restaurant on Walton Street.' Tom watched Beth's face for her reaction to his suggestion.

Her face lit up with pleasure then fell as quickly. Tom's hopes fell almost as fast.

'Oh Tom that would be lovely but I'm expected home for supper and then I've promised to meet some friends immediately afterwards in Oxford so I really need to get a move on.' She paused. 'Why don't you join us, we'll be in the Kings Arms, we could do fish and chips another day?' Tom shook his head despondently.

'Better not. Thanks for the offer but I'm not sure how long this job is going to take. Some other time then.' Tom turned back to the garage as Beth mounted her bicycle and didn't see her cheery wave as she pedalled away. He held the scarf to his face. It smelt of her fragrance.

Chapter 16

Beth ate her supper quickly, refused dessert and asked to be excused from the table.

'Going out?' Prudence enquired as Beth pushed back her chair and stood up. Beth nodded, eager to get going, it was already eight o'clock and it would take her another half an hour to get changed and cycle to Broad Street.

'Anyone we know?' Prudence tossed the question lightly, deliberately not looking directly at Beth.

'Bear.' Beth took a step backwards towards the door.

'Bear?' Prudence screwed up her face in distaste. 'Do you mean Rupert, that nice medical student who brought you flowers?'

'That's the one.' Beth prepared to make a dash for the door.

Desmond accepted his dessert from Prudence. 'Hope he's reliable, this young man.'

Beth smiled. Reliable wasn't quite the word she would have used to describe Bear. 'He's very nice,' she commented as she left the room.

Upstairs Beth hurriedly replaced her working clothes with a newly purchased pink sweater and black mini skirt. Usually she changed before supper but today she hadn't wanted another confrontation with her mother over the length of her skirt. She decided not to wear her hair in a ponytail, instead she brushed it vigorously, swept one side back and secured it with a tortoiseshell clip that had once belonged to her grandmother. Looking in the mirror she was satisfied that it made her appear more sophisticated.

She clattered down the two flights of stairs, past the dining room where she could hear the murmur of her parents' voices and out through the side door. She stopped at the bicycle shed and wheeled out her Pashley. There was no way she was going to be walking home alone tonight!

The Kings Arms was a favourite haunt of undergrads

and as such it was plainly furnished with rough wooden floorboards and a diverse assortment of tables and chairs. Beth hesitated in the doorway; she didn't like going into pubs on her own and hoped that Bear would be visible from the door so that she could go straight to him. Unfortunately that wasn't the case. Every table was full and the bar was crowded but of Bear and his friends there was no sign. Beth felt annoyance rising. Why hadn't they bothered to tell her the arrangement was off? The thought of refusing fish and chips with Tom added to her frustration. Her anger at being stood up overcame her reluctance to enter a pub on her own. She was not going home to spend a lonely boring Saturday evening on her own. Beth raised her chin, shook her copper curls and walked purposefully to the bar. She immediately caught the eye of a young barman.

'An orange juice please,' she demanded with more assurance than she felt. She was aware of sidelong glances from some of the bar drinkers and it made her uncomfortable. To counteract them she gave the nearest one a long haughty stare which only caused the instigator to take a greater interest. He moved closer as the young barman poured Beth her drink.

'You Beth?' The barman held onto the glass of orange juice and looked at Beth seriously. Beth froze, her hand extended to receive the glass. She didn't know this young man from Adam and yet he knew her name.

'So, what if I am?' She didn't want to admit to it outright. The smirking student next to her listened intently.

'A chap came in earlier and said that if a stunning red head came in later by the name of Beth, I was to tell her they were in the snug. Since you're the only red head in tonight and you're as he described, stunning, I'm giving you the message.' Beth blushed and the barman grinned at her as he pushed her drink across the counter.

'Where's the snug?' she asked. The barman indicated with a thumb over his shoulder and then moved to serve a noisy crowd at the far end of the bar.

'I'll show you Beth.' The leery student moved even closer. Beth pulled herself up to her full height. There was no way she was going to be picked up in a grubby student pub.

'Do I know you? Or perhaps you are a friend of my boyfriend Bear?'

The smile faded and the youth shrugged. 'Please yourself Miss High and Mighty.'

Beth found her way to a passage behind the bar. On one side a heavily varnished door stood open and Beth peered into the room beyond. The small space held a sagging leather sofa, a couple armchairs that had seen better days and some scuffed occasional tables laden with ash trays and glasses. The air smelt of stale beer and was thick with smoke from cigarettes, augmented by that from a spitting log fire struggling to give warmth in a tiny blackened grate. Bear was sitting on the sofa with his back to the door. His arm stretched along its back and his long fingers tapped rhythmically on Camilla's shoulder.

Peter was the first to see Beth hovering in the open door.

'Hi Beth!' This was accompanied by interested murmurs from other members of the room and a wolf whistle from the depths of an armchair in the far corner. Bear leaped to his feet.

'Shut up you lot, she's mine.' He gave Beth a perfunctory kiss on the cheek to cement her position as his girlfriend and led her to the sofa. 'Shift up.' The words, accompanied by a wave of the hand, indicated to Camilla her place in the pecking order. Bear sat down, Beth on one side of him and Camilla on the other. How much better could life get he thought?

'You came,' he stated. Beth smiled at the unnecessary nature of this remark.

'Well I'm here aren't I?' Bear put his arm along the sofa back and let his hand settle on her shoulder.

'You haven't got a drink. What would you like?'

Beth remembered the orange juice she had left on the

bar. 'I ordered an orange juice at the bar but I forgot to pick it up,' she told him.

'Orange juice? Don't you want something stronger than that, it's Saturday night for heavens sake?'

Beth gave Bear a sideways look that said more than words could, and he remembered his promise about drinking too much.

'Ok, ok, orange juice it is then.'

Peter was standing near the door. 'I'll get it. Anyone for a top up?' Several hands went up, glasses were quickly drained and Peter gathered up the empties. He returned sometime later with a tray of foaming beers and a glass of fruit juice topped with ice and a small paper parasol for Beth. He handed it to her with a flourish. Beth smiled her thanks. She warmed to Peter, he was easy going and cheerful. Camilla on the other hand was sulking. She sat with her back half turned to Bear and Beth and brooded over her gin and tonic.

The conversation turned to university matters. Descriptions of newly met tutors and lecturers were bandied about with anecdotes of the students' first encounters with same. Eventually a young man with long hair and wearing a collarless jacket asked Camilla which college she attended.

'St. Giles Secretarial College,' she informed him in a dismissive way.

'And what lessons do you learn there?' he enquired with more than a little sarcasm.

'To marry the boss and not get involved with people like you.' Camilla smiled, knowing he would have no reply to that statement. She was right, the student coloured and turned to his neighbour with an aside that Camilla did not wish to hear.

'Are you at the secretarial college too?' Beth realised that the question was being put to her.

'Goodness no,' she replied, and then realised that the tone of her voice could anger Camilla further. 'It's a very good college but being a secretary is not for me.'

'What do you do then?'

Bear shifted uncomfortably in his seat. 'I work in a florist's shop,' Beth told the room with a smile. There were a few raised eyebrows but Beth had the attention of those around her. She was never happier than when talking about her work. She explained the intricacies of ordering blooms, the pleasure they brought to the recipients, how flowers lifted interiors from ordinary to exceptional, and how flowers raised the spirits of everyone even if they didn't recognise why. She told her, now interested, audience that flowers had a meaning all their own, sadly now little remembered, and could convey a message to a loved one without a word being spoken. By now Bear had relaxed and Beth had everyone's attention.

'I love what I do and one day I intend to run my own business. There's a lot of money to be made in flowers,' she added for the money-minded contingent in her audience. There was silence in the smoke-laden room as Beth finished, and then from the depths of a frayed armchair came an admiring handclap. This was taken up by others and Beth glowed in their praise. Bear looked at her in admiration. She had the attention of all of his friends and he could sense that they were impressed by Beth's spiel. His arm tightened around her shoulders and he planted a kiss on her forehead.

The remainder of the evening passed in a haze of drinking and chat and Beth was surprised when the bell announced last orders. A clear, brisk night with a myriad of stars shining in a blue-black sky met them as they laughingly jostled onto the pavement. Bear held Beth close to him with a protective arm about her shoulders. Camilla turned from a conversation with Peter.

Want a lift Bear?' she called, walking towards a shiny red MGB parked a few yards along the road.

Bear hesitated for a nanosecond. 'Sorry, I've got to see Beth safely home.'

'You don't need to Bear I've brought my bicycle. I've got a dynamo and lights, I'll be quite safe on that.'

Bear hesitated once more. 'Are you sure?'

'Absolutely.'

Bear bent and kissed her. 'See you soon. Will be in touch,' His parting words echoed in Beth's head as he shouted 'hey, Camilla, change of plan …' Bear hopped over the car door and settled himself in the passenger seat of the red MG. Camilla let out the clutch and accelerated in a cloud of road dust.

Beth crossed the road to where she had left her bicycle chained to the railings surrounding the new Bodleian Library. She crouched and her cold hands fumbled with the lock.

'Here, let me help.' Peter bent beside her and undid the lock. I'll walk with you if you would like,' he said diffidently. Beth straightened up and regarded the young man before her. She felt sorry for him. He was supposed to be Camilla's boyfriend and yet somehow he always seemed to be in Bear's shadow.

'Do you mind Bear going off with Camilla like that? she asked.

'Why should I mind?'

'I thought Camilla was your girlfriend.'

Peter gave a dry laugh. 'She's my girlfriend when it suits Bear, otherwise she's his property.' Beth frowned.

'What do you mean by that?'

Peter paused and regarded Beth's concerned face with sympathy. 'Beth I'm sorry to be the bringer of bad news. You're a lovely girl and I don't want to see you hurt but you need to know that Bear likes to have a posse of girls around him. Girls are attracted to him like bees to a honey pot and he can take his pick. If you don't want to be one of Bear's conquests then I suggest you get out now.'

Beth was astounded at Peter's words. Was there some truth in what he had said, or was it sour grapes because Camilla seemed more interested in Bear than him?

She wheeled her bicycle into the road. 'Thanks for the advice Peter, I'll think about it and thanks for offering to see me home but there's no need, I'll be perfectly safe on my bicycle.' She waved to Peter as she mounted her bicycle but there was no answering wave as he stood, hands in pockets, on the edge of the pavement staring after her retreating back.

Chapter 17

Shoes in hand Beth crept silently up the stairs. It was nearly midnight and she did not want to disturb her parents. She need not have bothered, she had forgotten about the loose floor board on the first floor landing. It noisily announced her progress to her room and a second later a thin pencil of light at the base of her parents' bedroom door was extinguished. Damn it, she thought, they've been listening for my return, no one would think I'm nearly nineteen.

Beth woke in a darken bedroom. She stretched and lazily reached for her watch. To her surprise it was eight-thirty. Must be a foul day to be this dark she thought and a glance outside confirmed her assumption. Dark clouds scudded across a grey sky, propelled by a lively wind. Beth shivered and jumped back into the warmth of her bed and pulled the satin-covered eiderdown up to her chin.

She'd had a disturbed night with thoughts of Bear uppermost in her sleepless mind. It was to those thoughts that she now returned. Beth had enjoyed last evening at the Kings Arms, Bear had been attentive and his friends seemed to like her. They had listened to her description of her work at The Flower Basket and no one had belittled her choice of career. Peter was her problem. She had liked him at first but his remarks at the end of the evening had unsettled her. Were they based on jealousy of Bear or was there truth in his claim that Bear had a string of girlfriends including Camilla? Beth sighed, she was strongly attracted to Bear and didn't want to believe Peter's insinuations but he had sewn a seed of doubt. Why couldn't Bear be honest with her, she wasn't a child after all?

Prudence gave Beth a brief nod as she entered the kitchen.

'I've just cleared the breakfast things,' she remarked flatly. 'If you're hungry there's cereal in the cupboard.'

'No chance of scrambled eggs?' Beth asked hopefully.

Prudence looked pointedly at the clock. 'If you hadn't got in so late you might have been up in time for a cooked breakfast. As it is I've got other things to get on with this morning.'

'Cereal will be fine.' Beth reached for a bowl and placed it down firmly on the table. She would really have liked scrambled eggs but realised that Prudence was not prepared to cook for late comers. 'How do you know I was late home?' Beth asked with her mouth full of crunchy cornflakes.

'You weren't exactly quiet.'

'It wasn't me that was noisy it was that dratted loose floor board you should get it fixed.' Beth felt aggrieved. She had tried to be quiet so as not to wake them but they hadn't been asleep anyway – their light had been on until they heard her come home. In her usual fashion she waded straight in. 'You don't need to wait up for me. I'm a big girl now not a child.'

'That's not the point Bethany. Anything could happen to you late at night and we worry about you ...'

'Well don't, there's no need.'

Prudence was not going to let Bethany get the upper hand. 'Your father noticed that you had gone out on your bicycle which meant you would be cycling alone late at night, that's not a very wise thing to do.'

Beth banged her spoon down and milk splattered across the kitchen table. 'There you go, checking up on me and treating me like a child!'

'Bethany there's no need for that behaviour.'

'There you go again mum, speaking to me as though I'm eight not eighteen.' Beth pushed back her chair and flounced out of the room. Prudence watched her daughter go in exasperation. She wished wholeheartedly that Bethany would learn to curb her temper tantrums. Beth stormed up to her room wishing that everyone, Bear included, would stop treating her like a child.

The house was silent. Prudence had left for church, without asking Beth if she wished to accompany her, and her father was reading the Sunday papers in the seclusion of his study. Beth went down to the basement sitting room. Her parents didn't use the room a great deal and normally Beth enjoyed relaxing in its slightly worn comfort. She could be untidy there without it mattering too much. She especially liked it in the winter months when the worn armchairs and sofa beckoned in their creased linen covers and a fire crackled and spat in the grate. But this morning the fire hadn't been lit and the wind rattled the loose fitting window. Beth switched on a small electric fire and pulled it close to her chair. She picked up one of her mother's magazines from a side table and leafed idly through its pages. It was full of household hints, knitting patterns and facetious short stories. Why did her mother bother with such rubbish she thought? Beth tossed the magazine back onto the pile and moved across to the window. She craned her neck to look up the light-well at the world beyond. The wind had died a little but still gusted, bringing with it squalls of light rain. It was not a good day to venture outside but Beth felt the need for fresh air and a brisk walk. She hoped it would lighten her mood.

Outside Beth fastened the toggles of her duffle coat and hastily tucked her hair into the shelter of its hood. Where to go? Port Meadow was one of her favourite walks but it was perhaps a little too far on such a day and its open spaces would provide little shelter from the wind. Instead she opted for the canal path and, hands in pockets, she set off in that direction.

Beth walked briskly until she reached the path and then had to take a more measured pace. The ground here was muddy from the rain and the path was narrow and overgrown in places but at least it was sheltered from the worst of the squalls. She walked steadily, enjoying the solitude, few people had ventured out on a wet Sunday. Her thoughts returned to Bear. She pictured his smile that crinkled the corners of his blue eyes and his blond hair that flopped attractively onto his forehead, and her insides did a flip that was not at all unpleasant but it was quickly followed by a sense of despondency. She didn't want to be just a casual friend that he picked up and then dropped as it suited him, she wanted more than that. She wanted Bear exclusively, but how to be sure of him? Her mood deepened as she recalled her quarrel with Prudence that morning. She knew that her mother had only been concerned for her safety, so why did she have to be so snappy?

Her thoughts were interrupted by a short gust of wind that flipped her hood back and ruffled her copper curls. Beth stopped and impatiently pulled it back into place. It was then that she noticed a couple ahead of her on the path. They huddled together under a large golfing umbrella so that Beth only saw the lower half of their backs. The man held the umbrella low over the woman who was considerably shorter than him and his free arm protectively encircled her waist. They walked slowly and it was obvious that they were deep in conversation. Beth did not want to catch up with the couple. The path was narrow and she would have to acknowledge them and squeeze past and Beth was in no mood to talk to anyone, so she slowed her steps further, keeping them in sight so that she did not gain on them.

A short while later the couple stopped and the man passed the umbrella handle to the young woman. He kissed her quickly then ducked out from underneath and, turning up his collar against the weather, he began to jog back along the path towards Beth. As he passed her he pulled his collar up further so that his face was partially covered and turned his head away. Despite this Beth noticed that he wore a neatly trimmed dark moustache and beard. The woman watched him go and then she too began to walk back the way she had come. Beth didn't look at the woman as she passed, wanting only to be on her own again with her thoughts. But this was not to be. Her name was called out sharply and she turned to see Katie holding the striped umbrella.

'Beth I didn't recognise you straight away with your

hair tucked inside that hood.' Beth was still struggling to find words when Katie pulled her under the protection of the umbrella. She seemed nervous and more than a little agitated. 'I didn't expect to see anyone down here on such a foul day.'

'I could say the same,' Beth remarked, surprise in her voice. Katie had clearly told her that she didn't have a boyfriend and yet here she was walking with a man, and not just any man, one that kissed her when he said goodbye. 'That man …' Beth trailed off not knowing how to proceed. Katie fixed her with an intent stare.

'Beth before I tell you who that was I need you to promise to keep a very important secret.' Beth's eyes opened wide. What could Katie possibly be about to tell her that was so confidential? She nodded her assent. 'Nobody must know about this, not even my parents, the only person I've told is Tom and now you.' Katie turned, took Beth's arm and propelled her gently along the canal path. 'The man you saw is called Nathan. We met two years ago when I first attended university. A few weeks into that first term we both realised that we were strongly attracted to each other and we have been seeing each other ever since.'

'So what's the secret, is he married or something?' Beth was intrigued. This was a side of Katie she had not imagined.

Katie grinned. 'No nothing as terrible as that,' her smile faded, 'but bad enough, at least for the time being.'

'Well?' Beth could hardly bear the suspense.

'You promised?' Katie looked apprehensive and Beth nodded vigorously. 'He's not a student as you might imagine, he's…' once more Katie looked at Beth for reassurance before she continued, 'he's my maths tutor.'

Beth was surprised, she hadn't expected this. 'Is that so bad?' she laughed.

'Yes. Dons are not allowed to have a romantic relationship with any of the students in their care. If it were known that Nathan and I are seeing each other and have been for the past two years he would lose his position and would find it difficult to get a post at another university.'

'How ridiculous!' Beth was astounded.

'Ridiculous it might be but it's a fact, so now you know why our meetings have to be secret and away from prying eyes.'

'You poor thing, having to meet up like that.'

'Not so much of the poor thing we love each other which makes us rich.' Katie informed a melancholy looking Beth. 'It has been hard at times,' she continued, 'but in a few months I'll be finished here. I plan to work for my accountancy exams with a firm in London and Nathan is going to apply for a post at London University, then we'll be able to see each other openly. We plan to marry next summer so I've that to look forward to.' Katie's eyes sparkled and Beth, although more than a little pleased for her friend, couldn't help feeling a bit envious. Why couldn't her life be as well-planned as Katie's?

Katie regarded Beth's downcast face with concern. 'Well, now you've heard my news, how about you tell me what's making you so miserable?'

Beth did not need prompting. The need to unburden her worries was great and she regaled Katie with the events surrounding her blossoming romance with Bear. Katie listened attentively and with a grave face.

When Beth paused for breath she asked, 'Beth how much do you like Bear?'

'Well, I haven't known him for very long but I find him very attractive and he gives me butterflies whenever he looks at me.'

Katie frowned. 'Beth there's attractive looks and attractive natures. It seems to me you are attracted by his looks but what about how he behaves towards you?'

Beth blushed. Katie had hit the nail on the head. She wasn't quite sure she knew enough about Bear yet and some of his behaviour bothered her. She told Katie about Bear and Camilla and recounted what Peter had said. 'I think Peter is making some things up because Camilla prefers Bear to him,' Beth said optimistically.

'If you want my opinion,' Katie said, without pausing to ascertain whether Beth did or not, 'you'll take things carefully and slowly. If it turns out that Bear is like Peter says and he has a string of girlfriends that he picks up and drops on a whim, then I should end your relationship as soon as you are certain, otherwise you're going to get hurt. On the other hand Bear might have realised that you are special, in which case his behaviour towards you should be as attractive as his looks.'

Beth listened carefully to Katie's words of wisdom. She thought she understood what Katie was getting at and made up her mind to give Bear the benefit of the doubt and see how things turned out. She sighed. Why did life have to be so complicated?

Katie was aware that she hadn't cheered Beth up entirely. 'Come on, what else is bugging you, you can tell auntie Katie.'

Beth looked surprised. 'Is it that obvious?'

Katie nodded. 'Come on, out with it.'

'It's my temper,' Beth said quietly. 'I had another monstrous argument with my mother this morning about getting in late. She treats me like a child still, but instead of calmly putting my side of things I behave like a child and shout and bang out of the room.'

'Oh dear.' Katie patted her arm but Beth was not to be consoled.

'It's this wretched hair of mine,' she wailed, pushing back her hood and running an impatient hand through her curls. 'Why was I born with red hair and a temper.'

Katie looked serious. 'Now listen to me Beth. You were born with red hair but *not* a temper. The two things do not go hand in hand, it's an old wives tale. Look at Tom for instance. He's got red hair but he's nearly always calm and, although he can get angry when it's justified, he never gets in a rage. You just have to learn how to control your anger,' she told Beth bluntly. Katie peered out from underneath the bright umbrella. 'Oh look, silly us walking along under this umbrella when the rain has stopped and the sun is attempting to shine.' Beth hadn't noticed the change in the weather but now she looked up she could see patches of blue sky between the scudding clouds and she felt cheerful for the first time that day. Beth thought about Tom and smiled. Katie was right he was the most relaxed and kindly person she knew.

Chapter 18

Late September's promise of an Indian summer had faded into oblivion as winds blew gales and yet more rain in from the west. Summer had faded into a dim memory and winter had taken a strangle hold of autumn. All this week Beth had struggled against the high winds and blustery showers on her way to work. This morning she had dressed appropriately in navy trousers and a thick green Guernsey and had tied her hair back firmly to prevent the wind from whipping it across her face. Where had the misty, moisty days of autumn gone with their bright skies and crisp leaves, she wondered as she took her place at the breakfast table?

'You look nice.' Prudence smiled at her sensibly clad daughter. Strangely she didn't object to Bethany wearing trousers for work. Probably because they make me look young, Beth thought nastily, but she managed to keep her thoughts to herself and greeted her mother with a bright smile. She was learning, thanks in part to Katie's sensible advice. 'What have you got planned for your birthday tomorrow?' Prudence asked brightly.

'Bear's taking me to the cinema.' Beth helped herself to honey and spread it thickly onto her toast.

'That's nice.' Prudence regarded her reticent daughter. 'No party then?'

'He's taking me to the evening showing so there's no time for a party.'

'I thought Molly had given you the afternoon off. Why don't you go to the matinee, then you could invite some friends back here in the evening for a bit of a party?'

'She has given me the afternoon off but it's too late to invite people now and anyway I thought I'd go into town this afternoon and look for something nice to wear.'

Prudence was about to comment that Bethany had plenty of nice dresses but bit back the words. She didn't want to antagonise her daughter again, particularly as she and Desmond had a surprise in store for Bethany and she wanted nothing to spoil the occasion.

The ping of the toast popping up was accompanied by the rattle of the letterbox in the hall as the morning post was delivered. Desmond put down his paper and made to rise but Beth was already on her feet. In the hall she gathered up the post and rifled through it on her way back to the kitchen. There were a couple of brown envelopes addressed to her father, a stiff cream envelope for her mother and underneath a postcard for Beth. She had hoped for something from Aunt Edith in Australia but perhaps it was too soon to expect a reply from so far away. She quickly turned the postcard over and scanned the message. It read:

Beth, so sorry will have to postpone Saturday's visit to cinema. Wretched tutor had landed me with a load of work! Will be in touch, love Bear.

Beth frowned and re-read the message a couple of times. Why did Bear have to complete his work at the weekend surely it could wait until Monday? Now her birthday was utterly spoiled. Seeing her coat hanging on a peg in the hall, she thrust the card into the pocket. She did not want her parents questioning her about it. Back in the kitchen she slapped the rest of the post onto the table and resumed her seat heavily.

'Everything alright Bethany?' A concerned Prudence enquired.

Beth buttered her second piece of toast vigorously, 'Fine thanks.'

Desmond looked up from his paper and saw the scowl on Beth's face. He reached into an inside pocket of his jacket and produced a small brown envelope. 'Here's something to cheer you up,' he said as he pushed it across the table. I'm not in need of cheering up Beth nearly retorted but she managed to swallow the words and accepted the envelope with as good a grace as she could muster. 'I was given some complementary tickets for the firework display in South Parks that I've helped to organise and I thought you might like to take some of your friends. It's not until the week after next but it should be a good show.' Beth peered into the envelope. Four brightly coloured tickets nestled inside.

'Thanks, that's great, I'll think who I can ask. It should be good fun.' Beth smiled, despite her disappointment at not seeing Bear at the weekend and at the thought of her spoiled birthday. Desmond, satisfied he'd done his bit to cheer up his daughter, returned to his newspaper.

As she set off for work Beth put the tickets into her coat pocket alongside the card from Bear. She intended to ask Katie and perhaps Tom if they would like to go and the other ticket she would keep for Bear.

Friday at The Flower Basket was, as usual, very busy. There were orders to complete for the weekend and a steady stream of customers. Molly was run off her feet with deliveries and much of the morning Beth was left to manage the shop alone. It was during one of these periods that Katie's mother Elsie popped in.

'Hello …err… Elsie, lovely to see you.' Beth was not used to calling a friend's mother by her first name.

'Likewise Beth. We haven't seen you since my birthday. It's high time you paid us another visit. Jack was saying only last night what a lovely girl you were and it's so good to see Katie enjoying the company of someone nearer her age. She doesn't bring home many friends her work seems to take up so much of her time.'

Beth smiled inwardly, she knew what else occupied Katie's time but she hugged the secret to herself she did not intend to divulge Katie's secret, not even to Elsie. She would learn about it all in good time and would be glad for her daughter.

'I was planning to call round this evening after work,' Beth told her. 'I've got some tickets for a firework display and I thought Katie might like to come.'

'That's very kind of you. I can't speak for Katie so you come round and see how she's fixed. Now, I came in for a pot plant what would you recommend?'

'That depends on what the plant is for and where it will be kept,' Beth told her.

Elsie looked slightly taken aback at Beth's statement. 'Err ... something suitable for outside you know, on an outside window sill or something like that.'

'We have some beautiful dahlias in pots but they don't like the cold nights. You're better off with chrysanthemums at this time of the year. If you put them in a fairly sheltered spot they'll go on flowering for weeks.'

'Chrysanthemums it is then.' Elsie took out her purse. 'What colours have you got?'

'Yellow, bronze or deep red.' Beth indicated the pots on the far side of the shop.

Elsie rubbed her nose. 'I don't suppose you have any pink ones? They're for a little girl.'

'Wait a moment we might have a pot in the workroom. I was using some pink chrysanths for a bridesmaid posy and I think there was a pot of pink ones left.'

Beth returned carrying a potted plant covered in tiny pink blooms.

Elsie's face lit up. 'They're just perfect, so tiny and dainty. Thank you so much for finding them for me.'

'Can we deliver them?' Beth enquired.

'Thanks for the offer m'dear but I need to deliver them myself.' Elsie delved into her purse and paid what she owed.

'I hope she likes them,' Beth smiled.

Elsie stared at Beth.

'The little girl ...' Beth prompted.

'Oh, yes of course.' Elsie clutched the plant to her chest and waved a hasty goodbye as she left the shop.

Molly parked the small Austin van alongside the back entrance to the shop. She admired the elegant lettering on the side of the vehicle. "The Flower Basket" it proclaimed in cream-coloured lettering that stood out nicely against the van's dark green paintwork. When she had purchased the van the lettering had been a huge extra expense but now she was glad she had gone that extra mile. Where ever she went it advertised the business and she was sure that a great deal of sales had come her way because of it. Also being able to deliver customers orders had brought in a lot more business. The biggest drawback was in the amount of work deliveries entailed. It was tiring climbing in and out of the vehicle and lifting awkward and heavy arrangements in and out of the rear doors. Molly felt the stiffness in her bones and knew she needed some help.

'Busy morning?' she asked, entering the shop.

'You could say that again,' Beth wiped her hands down her green apron. 'I haven't had a moment to myself. 'Fraid I haven't finished the other bridesmaid posy. I'll do it at lunch time.'

'We'll have our lunch first before we do anything else.' Molly moved to the shop door and purposefully turned the sign to read "closed".

In the back room the two relaxed over tea and sandwiches both deep in thought. Molly was the first to break the silence.

'How are the driving lessons coming along?'

Beth looked up from her contemplation of Bear's cancellation of their date, glad of something else to think about. 'They're going fine. My instructor says I'm a natural.'

'Does he indeed?' Molly smirked, she didn't believe in self promotion. 'I expect he says that to all the young ladies he has to teach.'

Beth was not put off. 'Maybe, but he did say that ten lessons should be enough before I take my test and I've had two already,' she beamed confidently.

Molly did a quick calculation. 'So if you carry on like this you should be ready to take your test by the end of November?'

Beth nodded. 'Should be, especially as Tom had offered to take me out in his car for extra practice.'

'Tom? I thought his name was Bear.'

'No, Bear doesn't have a car. Tom is Katie's brother

and he's got an old car and he's happy for me to practice driving it.'

'Sounds like a nice young man, letting you drive his car.'

'He is nice but he's not that young.'

'Well how old then?'

Beth's lips moved as she calculated. 'He must be about twenty-four or five.'

'Not young! If twenty-four's not young, what does that make me then?' Molly squeaked in mock horror. 'I must be in my dotage and about to be put out to grass.'

'Oh Molly I didn't mean it like that. You're not old. What I meant was that Tom is very grown up. He left school at sixteen and has worked ever since and he's very calm and steady and he refers to me as a little thing.' Beth paused. 'He's kind and he treats me like a little sister.'

Molly raised an eyebrow. 'You like this Tom I gather?'

'Yes, he's lovely. He walked me home after the disco and he leant me his scarf because I shivered. I wish I had an older brother like him.'

Molly frowned. 'You're confusing me again. I thought you went to the disco with your student friend.'

'I did.' Beth looked apprehensive, guessing what Molly's next question would be.

'Then why didn't he see you home?'

'Because I had to leave before the end. It went on 'til one and I told him I would be perfectly safe on my own.' Beth improvised. 'And then I met Tom and he insisted on walking home with me.'

'I should think so, leaving you on your own like that late at night, what ever was the boy thinking of?'

Molly remained thoughtful. 'Are you going out with that Bear tonight?'

Beth was not expecting this question and looked sharply at Molly's face but it gave nothing away. 'I was, but he has a lot of work to do at the moment so we're not seeing a lot of each other.'

'Things cooling off a bit are they?'

'No!' Beth retorted sharply, but ...'

'But?' Molly repeated. She had a way of listening that encouraged Beth to talk.

'I'm not sure about him.' There, she'd said it.

'Not sure in what way?' Molly asked. So Beth told Molly of her fears that Bear didn't really care about her and was just out for a good time with any nice looking girl he met. Molly listened attentively then fixed Beth with her soft brown eyes.

'Don't be too quick to judge him Beth but on the other hand don't get involved with someone you don't trust completely just because he's the only one about at the moment. Remember you're a very pretty girl and there are plenty more nice men out there. If Bear's not the one for you, and I'm inclined to think he's not from what you've told me, someone else will come along who fits the bill.'

'I wish I could believe that,' Beth moaned. 'Look at me I'm nineteen tomorrow and Bear's the first real boyfriend I've had.'

'All the more reason not to take him too seriously. Look around, there's a big wide world out there.'

Beth put the lid on her sandwich box and considered Molly's wise words. Molly wasn't married, despite the fact that she called herself Mrs. Watson, and she had no family that Beth knew of so how was it that she was so perceptive? She looked at Molly thoughtfully.

'I know what you're thinking m'girl. You're thinking what does that old woman know about love and men, she's not even married.'

Beth was horrified. 'I wasn't thinking any such thing and you're not old.' She hurriedly cleared their empty mugs to cover her embarrassment. 'But ...'

'Go on, out with it.'

'Well ... I did wonder how you could give such good advice when you haven't been married, which isn't the same thing at all.'

Molly regarded Beth through narrowed eyes. 'One day m'girl I'll tell you how I know so much about such things but it's a very long story so it'll have to wait for another time.'

'Oh Molly please!' Beth was intrigued. Molly had never mentioned her private life before and Beth was consumed with curiosity.

'No time now, there's work to be done.' Molly dismissed the subject and Beth knew better than to insist. Molly got up creakily from her stool. 'And while we're on the subject of my age, I'm touched that you don't think of me as old but these joints of mine are telling me a different story and I'll be very glad when you've passed your driving test. Are you still happy to help with the van deliveries?'

'Of course, that's the sole reason I'm learning.' Beth's eager face gave Molly great satisfaction. This young lady was turning out just as she had hoped and one day she might fulfil a plan that had taken shape in Molly's mind.

Chapter 19

Molly closed the shop promptly at five and Beth donned her coat ready for a chilly ride home. It was then that she felt the tickets in her pocket and remembered that she had planned to go round to Katie's to see if she would like to go to the firework display. She was greeted at the door of the small white-painted house by a smiling Elsie.

'Katie's just got in, she's in the kitchen, go on through.'

Beth noticed that the pot of pink chrysanthemums she had sold to Elsie earlier had not been delivered but was sitting on the windowsill behind the sink. She looked away and made no comment.

'I'm taking them round tomorrow,' Elsie stated, seeing where Beth's eyes had strayed. 'Now you girls will have a lot to talk about so don't mind me I'll get on with making us a nice cup of tea.'

'Well actually we met quite recently on the can …' Beth bit her lip as she realised she was about to get into deep water and Katie gave her a furious frown. Luckily Elsie was filling the kettle and, with the noise of the running water, appeared not to have heard Beth's remark.

'Sorry,' Beth mouthed while Elsie's back was turned then hastily pulled the tickets out of her pocket. 'My dad's given me these tickets for the bonfire display at South Parks and I wondered if you would like to come with me?'

'That sounds like fun. When is it?'

'It's actually going to be held on bonfire night November the fifth. It's lucky it falls on a Friday this year which is convenient.'

'Great, I'd love to come.'

'I've got several tickets, do you think Tom would like one?'

'Couldn't say what his plans are you'll have to ask him but I wouldn't be surprised if he agreed. It would do him good, he doesn't get out half enough.'

'Will he be home soon?'

Elsie chuckled. 'Chance would be a fine thing. All that boy does is work, work, work. No, we'll be lucky if we see him before nine o'clock.'

'Why does he have to work so late?' Beth was concerned, she occasionally stayed late when they had a rushed job on at The Flower Basket but no one should have to work late every night.

'He's got some idea about saving up so that he can buy into the business, hardly spends a penny if he can help it.' Elsie saw Beth's look of surprise 'Don't get me wrong,' she continued hurriedly, 'he pays generously for his keep and he's good with remembering birthdays.' Beth thought back to the pretty brooch Tom had bought his mother for her birthday. 'But,' Elsie continued in defence of her son, 'he spends next to nothing on himself, it doesn't seem right at his age not to enjoy life a bit.'

'Mum he's doing the right thing,' Katie insisted. 'This is his opportunity to make something of his life and if he doesn't grasp it now the chance might never come again.'

'Perhaps you're right,' Elsie conceded, 'but I still wish he got out more and had a girlfriend or two.'

Beth finished her tea and stood up. 'Perhaps you could ask him if he would like to come with us to the fireworks?'

Elsie looked thoughtful. 'Why don't you ask him yourself?' Beth's eyes opened wide at Elsie's rather blunt remark. 'I don't mean to be rude,' Elsie continued, 'but you could do me a big favour.' Beth waited for further enlightenment. 'Tom was in such a hurry to leave this morning that he left his food behind. If I know him he won't have had a morsel to eat since breakfast time. I was going to walk round to the garage with it but, if you've got time to go on your way home I'd be very grateful and you could ask him about the fireworks at the same time.'

'Of course I'll take his food. Poor thing not having anything to eat all day.' Beth was horrified at the idea. She loved her food and the thought of going all day without any filled her with dismay. Also she liked the idea of going to the garage again and seeing Tom.

Elsie reached down a battered cream and green painted tin from the dresser. 'Here wait a minute while I put in a slice of fruit cake, he'll need more than is in here if he's going to be really late.' She handed the filled tin to Beth who couldn't suppress a giggle. On the pale green lid was painted *Thomas Reilly – KEEP OUT* and a faded transfer of a fire-breathing dragon. Elsie smiled too. 'I know, silly isn't it, but he's had that tin ever since he took packed lunches to school and he won't let me throw it away.'

Beth propped her bicycle against the side wall of the garage. To her surprise the small green sports car was still parked in the same spot on the forecourt. Must need a lot of repairs to be here this long she thought as she approached the heavy double doors. Inside Tom was at the far end of the garage bent under the bonnet of a flame red MGB.

'Hi!' Beth called loudly so that Tom would hear her.

Tom jerked up and banged his head. 'I thought I told you …' He broke off when he saw that it was Beth. 'Oh, sorry Beth I thought it was someone else.'

'Who did you think it was?'

'The dreadful female who owns this car,' he growled.

'Goodness, you are in a bad mood. Katie tells me you never get cross, so it must be lack of food. Here I've brought your supper.' Beth held out the tin with a smile and an answering smile creased Tom's face.

'Thanks Beth, you're an angel, just what I need.' Beth mimed polishing her halo as Tom wiped his hands on an oily rag. 'Come on we'll go into the office. I'll make a brew, I'm sure you could do with a cup. While Tom collected mugs and milk together he opened the lid and began demolishing the large slice of fruit cake that Elsie had placed on top.

'You should eat the savouries first and keep the sweet things for after,' Beth admonished him playfully.

Tom flipped at her with the oily rag. 'Don't tell me what to do young Beth, if you were as hungry as I am you wouldn't care what order you ate your food in. Now what brings you here, apart from bringing sustenance to a poor workman?'

'Do I have to have a reason to visit a poor workman in his greasy garage?' she asked coyly.

'No, you are welcome anytime, unlike the lady who persuaded me to take her car for repair without any warning and then expects it to be done immediately.'

'You should have refused to take it.'

Tom's mouth was full of pork pie so he shook his head vigorously. 'Can't turn business away Beth. Rob and I need to build up a good client base and turning away customers is not an option,' he replied eventually.

'Well, if it's so important, why are you slaving away on your own? Where is this Rob?'

'He's delivering vehicles back to their owners, it's an important part of the service we offer. Rob's the front man, he brings in much of our business and he also does most of the paper work, which suits me. I'm the mechanic and make sure the repair jobs are done well so that customers return to us year on year. We complement each other, that's what running a successful business is all about, being part of a team.' Beth listened intently. She could learn a lot from Tom.

'Oh God, here she comes and her car's not yet ready.' Tom tossed his half-eaten pie back into the tin. Beth looked through the office window into the garage beyond. A girl was silhouetted in the entrance. She glanced around before stepping hesitantly inside and it was then that Beth recognised her. Camilla was looking round the deserted garage for a sign of Tom. She stood in the middle of the empty space wearing a low cut white blouse adorned with frills around the neck and sleeves. Beth noticed how the buttons strained across her barely concealed bust. Her red skirt was short and tight and matched almost exactly the red of her car. She flicked her long dark hair back over her shoulders.

'Anyone around?' she called piercingly.

'Oh no!' Beth moved away from the window. 'I know

that girl and I'd rather she didn't see me, I don't want to talk to her.'

Tom raised an eyebrow but made no comment. 'I'll get rid of her if I can. I told her the car would take at least two hours. Can't think why she's come back so soon. Help yourself to tea, there's sugar in the packet over there though I don't expect you take it you're sweet enough already.'

Tom's last remark surprised and pleased Beth, despite the fact that it had been said in jest, she took it as a compliment. She smiled as she moved closer to the open office door so that she could hear what he said to Camilla without being seen.

'Your car's not ready yet I'm afraid. I did say it would take at least two hours.'

'I can see that. What exactly is wrong with it, or haven't you discovered that yet?'

Tom ignored her contemptuous tone. 'I know exactly what is wrong with it and it's going to take a bit longer to fix it.'

'Well, what is the matter with it?'

'I've checked the shoes and drums on the back and they're fine, the brake pads on the front discs are a bit worn but there's plenty of life left in them, shouldn't need replacing before the Spring, unless you do a lot of unnecessarily hard breaking. No, the reason you found the brakes spongy was that you're losing brake fluid. It's a hydraulic system and the seals on your master cylinder have failed.'

'Spare me the lecture.' Camilla frowned. 'All I want is to know is, can you fix it and if so how long will it take?'

'Of course I can fix it. It will involve new seals, refilling the cylinder and then bleeding the brakes. It's a relatively straightforward procedure and should take about three quarters of an hour.'

Camilla looked relieved. 'Well I hope you're right. I need the car tomorrow, I'm taking my boyfriend up to London for the weekend. We're going to a show in the evening and the tickets are already paid for.' Poor Peter, Beth thought, being stuck with her all weekend.

'I can assure you it will be ready. Now if you'll excuse me I need to finish my supper before I get back to work.'

Camilla looked Tom up and down. 'If it's going to be ready within an hour I might as well wait here.'

Tom shrugged. 'Please yourself. I'm afraid there's nowhere for you to sit down.'

'I'm ok standing.' Camilla regarded Tom's tall supple figure thoughtfully as he returned to the office. She found his loose workman's overalls a turn on, especially when she thought about what they covered up. Could be quite entertaining watching him work, she thought.

Safely inside the office Tom resumed his interrupted supper and accepted the mug of tea Beth held out to him. ''Fraid she wasn't that easy to get rid of,' he declared quietly.

'Oh well do you mind if I stay here until she's gone?' Beth whispered.

'You stay as long as you want. Now if you'll excuse me I'd better go and see to milady's vehicle.'

Tom reached the door and then let out a shout that was so forceful that it nearly made Beth fall off her stool. 'Put that out – now!'

Beth glanced through the doorway to see Camilla's equally startled face. The cigarette she had just lit still dangled between her lips.

'Did you hear what I said? Can't you read?' Tom pointed angrily to the NO SMOKING notice. 'There's petrol fumes in here, you could blow us all to kingdom come.'

Camilla slowly removed the cigarette from between her lips with her brightly painted fingers and stared at Tom who was now striding towards her. 'Oh really, you don't need to be so melodramatic.'

'I most certainly do.' Before Camilla had realised what was happening Tom removed the cigarette from her unsuspecting fingers and crushed it vigorously with the heel of his shoe.'

'Hey …'

Before she could say more Tom continued. 'I think it would be better if you waited at home for your car. If you give me your address I'll deliver it as soon as it's finished.' Camilla opened her mouth to protest but Tom intervened. 'I need to take it for a test run to make quite sure that the brakes are safe so I can deliver it at the same time.'

Camilla saw the determination on Tom's face and capitulated. Pity, she had looked forward to watching this good-looking man working and perhaps chatting to him while he fixed her car. She turned with a flounce and strode from the garage as fast as her stiletto heels allowed.

As soon as Camilla was out of sight Beth emerged from the office with a grin as wide as the Cheshire cat in Alice in Wonderland. 'You certainly told her where to go.'

Tom matched her smile. 'Silly bitch. Don't usually speak to women like that but she was so bloody condescending and what she did was incredibly dangerous.'

'Well, I'd better be going.' Beth got as far as the door when she remembered the tickets. Tom was bent under the bonnet of the MG. 'Tom, I forgot, would you like to come to a firework display on bonfire night?' she called loudly. For the second time that day Tom banged his head as he straightened up suddenly at the sound of her voice. He regarded her seriously and rubbed his head. Oh dear, that's twice, Beth thought. He won't want to come she guessed, disappointed.

'I'd like nothing better.' Tom raised a hand before resuming his work.

Chapter 20

Saturday dawned bright but blustery. After a busy morning at The Flower Basket Beth wheeled her bicycle out of the back yard only to find that her back tyre was a flat as the proverbial pancake. Resignedly she wheeled it down the road to Joe's repair shop. Joe was in the middle of a job but he promised to have her bike ready by the middle of the afternoon so Beth pulled her coat close against the sharp wind and set off for home on foot. She had planned on going to the shops to look for something new to wear but now that Bear had cancelled their date there didn't seem much point. Some birthday this turned out to be she thought sadly. She could have asked some friends around for the evening but it was too late now, they would all have made other arrangements on a Saturday night.

Despite the cold wind Beth didn't hurry; she enjoyed the feel of the sun on her face it was such a change after all the rain they had been having recently. She sauntered along past St. Luke's Catholic church and looked up at the large statue of Mary that stood under a wooden shelter next to the notice board by the entrance. Beth stopped and admired the subtle browns and blues of her robe and veil and the look of serenity on the gentle plaster face. Beth wished she had an inner composure like that rather than the passion that so often welled up inside her. Beth wasn't a great church-goer, she sometimes went with her mother to St. Andrew's to keep her company but in general she didn't bother too much about religious matters and she had never been inside a catholic church. She wondered if was as pretty inside as the statue that graced its gateway.

Without further ado she pushed open the gate and wandered up the stone path to the black hinged wooden doors. To her surprise they were slightly ajar and so Beth pushed them a little further open and went in.

She paused, waiting for her eyes to adjust to the dim interior, before proceeding along the aisle. The inside of the church was a disappointment. There were many statues of varying sizes but none attracted Beth like the one outside and the rows of pillars were in an orangey- brown shade of marble that Beth found unpleasant. She was about to leave when she noticed a sole figure kneeling in an empty pew. Despite the ringing of Beth's shoes on the tiled floor the figure had not looked up to see who else had entered the church and was obviously deep in prayer. Beth turned and walked as quietly as possible in the echoing church back the way she had come. To her horror her whispered name followed her down the aisle and she felt a prickling sensation down her spine. She did not look back and quickened her steps.

'Bethany!' This time the voice was louder and sounded more human. Beth dared to glance over her shoulder. Elsie was hurrying behind her clutching the pot of pink chrysanthemums to her chest. 'Beth it is you! I thought that hair could only belong to you.' Elsie caught up with her. 'What are you doing here? You don't usually worship at St. Luke's do you?'

Beth shook her head. 'I could ask you the same thing,' she replied with a relieved smile.

'Ah …' Elsie returned the smile and paused as though she was considering something. She resumed, 'I was asking God to bless these flowers. They're the ones I bought from your shop yesterday.'

'I recognised them, but why do they need blessing?' Beth asked puzzled.

'Because they're for a very special person,' Elsie replied seriously. She regarded Beth speculatively for a moment or two. 'Do you have a few minutes Beth or are you in a rush to get home?'

Beth hadn't had her lunch but it seemed rude to refuse Elsie, she was such a kind person. 'No I'm not in a hurry.'

Elsie took Beth's arm and led her outside to a small graveyard containing an assortment of old tumbled-down stone gravestones that were so worn by the wind and rain that most of the names carved on them had long since become unreadable. Elsie hurried past them on the narrow gravelled path and rounded the side of the church and Beth followed. The graves here were newer and many of the head stones were in coloured marble. Fresh and fading flowers adorned the spaces in front of some headstones but a few graves were overgrown and unkempt. Beth noticed that quite a few of the flowers were plastic, made to withstand the weather and not needing to be replaced that often, and she shuddered. Elsie led the way to a part of the churchyard where the gravestones were smaller and closer together. Beth paused to read the inscription on one and to her horror it dawned on her that these tiny stones all marked the burial place of a child. When she looked up Elsie ahead of her was carefully removing some faded flowers from a small grave with a tiny white marble headstone over which hovered a carved angel. She replaced the dead flowers with the pot of pink chrysanthemums and then bowed her head. Beth felt awkward, not knowing quite what to do so she stood quietly behind Elsie. After a moment Elsie raised her head and turned to Beth. Her eyes were moist.

'Today is a special day,' she said gently. 'I don't usually bother others with my loss of a child but seeing you in the church like that and as you took so much trouble over the flowers and I didn't feel at the time I could tell you what they were for, I thought you might like to know their purpose.'

'Why is today so special?' Beth whispered.

'Read the inscription,' Elsie instructed.

Beth crouched to decipher the message. It read:

Angelica Reilly
Born 23 October 1946
Died 24 October 1946
Baby daughter of Elisabeth & Jack
And sister for Thomas & Katie
Sadly missed but in the care of the angels

Beth straightened up and tried to swallow the lump in her throat. She put her arms round Elsie and buried her face in her neck. Elsie patted her shoulder then gently held her at arm's length.

'It's so sad, you loosing a baby like that.' Beth dragged the back of her hand across her eyes.

'It's not the loss of the baby I grieve it's the loss of her future. To see her growing up, learning the ways of the world, and turning into a beautiful woman, that's the loss I grieve for.' Elsie spoke so softly that Beth strained to hear her words.

'Didn't you think of having another child?' Beth asked.

'Another child would have been just that, another child, to love and care for. Well-meaning folk often suggest it as a cure for grief but it would not have taken Angelica's place or lessened my sorrow.' Elsie smiled tenderly. 'If she had survived it would have been her nineteenth birthday today. So you see I felt the need to mark the occasion. I don't make a fuss of it to Tom and Katie. They never knew their little sister so it's not right to bother them with her death. But thank you for letting me share it with you Beth, I hope you don't mind.'

'Elsie I'm so glad you did and now I've got a surprise for you.'

'What's that m'dear?'

'It's my birthday today and I'm nineteen.'

Elsie stared. 'So that means …'

'Yes, I was also born on the twenty-third of October nineteen forty-six.'

'Well what a coincidence that is!' Elsie paused on the narrow gravel path that ran between the grassy mounds and stared hard at Beth. 'How lovely that you share a birthday with my Angelica,' she beamed. The information seemed to have cheered her up but when the two reached the church gate she regarded Beth seriously. 'Can I ask you something Beth?' she enquired earnestly. Beth nodded. 'I have some very precious things. As you have a link to Angelica so to speak, I don't suppose I could show them to you?'

'Of course you could.' Once again Beth didn't feel she could refuse Elsie's request. 'I'll tell you what, I have go to back to Walton Street this afternoon to collect my bicycle from Joe's. How would it be if I called round then?'

'That would be perfect. Jack and Tom are at work and Katie's gone out to meet a friend so we needn't bother them with it. We can have a nice cup of tea and I can show you Angelica's things.'

Beth nodded. She had a good idea which friend Katie had gone to see and she felt happy for her, which was more than she felt about Elsie's baby things. Keeping mementoes of a dead baby was to her mind a morbid thing to do.

At home Beth found a cold lunch left for her under a cover on the kitchen table. Of her mother there was no sign, which was unusual, so Beth put her lunch on a tray and took it down to the basement sitting room. After she had eaten Beth picked up a novel that she was half way through. She tried to get back into the plot but memories of Elsie's face when she told Beth about her dead baby kept floating before her eyes. She was happy to put down the book when a light tap on the door heralded the entrance of her mother, carrying a beribboned parcel.

'I thought you must have gone straight to the shops so I left your lunch in the kitchen.'

'Yes thank you I found it.' Beth pointed to the empty tray.

'Oh good. And did you find something nice at the shops?'

'I didn't bother in the end.'

'Why not? I thought you wanted to get something special to wear when you go out with Rupert tonight.'

'I did but we're not going out after all. Bear's got too much work to do.'

'Oh my dear, what a shame, and on your birthday too.' Beth nodded and sighed but made no reply. What more could she say on the subject anyway? 'Well perhaps this will cheer you up a bit. There wasn't time to give it to you this morning you were in such a rush to get to work.' Prudence held out the parcel.

Beth undid the carefully tied satin ribbon and unfolded the pretty wrapping paper and a layer of tissue to reveal a powder-blue cashmere jumper.

'Thank you it's lovely.' She obediently kissed Prudence's offered cheek.

'That's not all.' Prudence's normal calm exterior was highlighted with excitement and Beth wondered what else was to come. Prudence sat down on the linen-covered sofa next to Beth and regarded her daughter.

'Bethany,' she began hesitantly. 'I'm aware that you and I have had our differences over the years …'

'I'm sorry, I've got such a temper,' Beth broke in.

Prudence patted her hand. 'It's not entirely your fault Bethany. I am also to blame. I have persisted in treating you like a child when in fact you are now a young adult, and that must have angered you at times.' Beth was speechless. This was a turn up for the books. 'Your father and I have discussed the matter and, if you are agreeable, we would like to mark the occasion of your nineteenth birthday with a rather special present.' Beth's eyes widened. Whatever could be coming?

Prudence straightened her shoulders. 'We would like you to have this room as your very own sitting room. Your father and I rarely use it and we know how much you enjoy being down here, so it could be your own private space where you could entertain your friends without having to refer to your father or myself. We would still like you to eat with us when you're on your own but other than that you would be free to come and go as you like. Beth was momentarily lost for words, she could hardly believe what she was hearing. She flung her arms round her mother. 'You could do up the room to suit,' Prudence continued. 'I'll arrange for the decorator to call and you can tell him what you would like. And perhaps some new curtains and covers wouldn't go amiss.'

At last Beth found her voice. 'Mum it's the best birthday present ever. Thank you so much.' Prudence ignored the "mum", now was not the time to protest. 'I met Elsie, Katie's mother, on my way home and she invited me for a cup of tea this afternoon. If Katie's there maybe I'll ask her round this evening and we could have supper together down here.' Beth's eyes shone. There was another reason Katie might like the seclusion of a friend's basement sitting room and Beth was ready to help if she could.

Prudence was happy with her decision to stop treating Bethany as a child. This first overture on her behalf had been a resounding success and she was glad she had listened to Desmond's advice.

Despite the fact that her birthday date with Bear had been cancelled, Beth felt cheerful as she walked to Juxton Street to have tea with Elsie. It's a bit macabre keeping a dead baby's things Beth thought but if it makes Elsie happy what did it matter?

Her knock on the door was answered by flushed-faced Elsie with wisps of fine hair escaping the confines of their hairpins. 'Been baking m'dear so that we can have cake with our tea.' Beth breathed in the comforting aroma of warm cake as she entered the familiar kitchen. As before, it was chaotic with every shelf crammed with pretty porcelain and kitchen gadgets. Elsie hastily removed a pile of papers and magazines from a chair so that Beth could sit down. She flipped a tea towel over the flour strewn table and cut thick slices of moist chocolate cake which she placed next to two mugs of steaming tea. 'How's your birthday so far?' she asked Beth between mouthfuls of cake.

Beth recounted to Elsie the news of her parents' special gift. 'What a thoughtful present,' Elsie commented. 'You're a very lucky girl, I wish I could give my two a sitting room of their own but this little house won't run to that I'm afraid. I particularly worry about Tom,' she continued, 'he really needs a place of his own at his age.' Elsie stood up. 'Would you mind clearing the table m'dear?'

Beth did as she was bid and Elsie left the room, returning a few moments later bearing a cardboard box held together with green garden twine. Beth noticed that the box was decorated with sprigs of holly and bore a picture of Christmas crackers on the lid. She watched fascinated as Elsie struggled with the knots, carefully removed the lid and folded back a layer of yellowed tissue paper. She wondered what relics she was going to see and hoped it wouldn't take too long.

The first thing to be lovingly lifted out was a neatly folded lacy shawl. Elsie shook it out and refolded it into a triangle as though she was about to wrap a baby in it. 'I knitted it specially for the new baby, the one I had for Tom and Katie had become yellowed and matted with constant washing in our hard water so I decided the little-un would have new.' She held the soft wrap to her cheek for a second before hurriedly putting it down and reaching inside the box. A small parcel of tiny clothes appeared next, all in white. A nightdress edged in lace with delicate white embroidery on the yolk, a crochet matinee jacket, a matching bonnet and a miniature pair of fabric shoes fastened with pearl buttons were laid proudly on the table.

'They're beautiful,' Beth exclaimed. 'Did you make them yourself?'

Elsie nodded proudly. ' I love to do a bit of sewing, don't always get the time now, and baby clothes are so satisfying to make, they take no time at all.' She held up the tiny nightgown. 'I always like newborns dressed in white,' Elsie remarked. 'Pink and blue's not appropriate when you don't know if it's going to be a girl or boy and I think yellow is a most unflattering colour to dress a tiny baby in.'

Beth was fascinated by the shoes. She gingerly picked them up. 'They're so small,' she exclaimed.

Elsie took the shoes from Beth and held them in the

palm of her hand, saying nothing. Suddenly she gathered up the clothes and began to wrap them up. 'You must think I'm daft keeping these things all these years.'

'Of course I don't think you're daft. I think I'd have done the same.' Beth stroked the soft shawl. 'Is this all you kept?'

'Everything else went to the nun's charity box but I felt the need to keep a few things.' Elsie paused, 'Beth ... grieving is a very lonely business, especially when it's for a child who only survived for a matter of hours. Everyone's sorry at first but then they want to get on with life and forget. The mother is often left silently grieving on her own. That is what happened to me. I couldn't share my grief and so, instead of fading, it grew over the years. Now, today you were there when I needed someone and you have been kind and thoughtful so for the first time I've shared my grief and already the load has lightened. Thank you Beth.'

Beth was lost for words. She felt tears prickle behind her eyelids and hoped she wasn't going to cry. She reached across the table and took Elsie's hand. 'I'm glad I could help,' she managed gruffly.

Elsie folded the shawl and replaced it in the box. 'There is just one more thing but I wasn't going to show it to you,' she added hesitantly. 'Would you mind?' Beth shook her head, she was intrigued, what else could Elsie have to show her? Elsie reached underneath the baby clothes and withdrew a small oval photo frame. She passed it across to Beth. The baby in the photograph was wearing a nightdress similar to the one in Elsie's box. Her eyes were closed and she looked peaceful. Beth stared at the picture for a while, fascinated by the tiny features. Then she raised her eyes questioningly to Elsie. 'One of the nurses had a camera. While we were waiting for the priest to come she asked me if I'd like her to take a photo of Angelica. It was clear to everyone that she was unlikely to survive, her heart was failing fast, so I agreed.' She pointed to the picture in Beth's hand. 'That came a couple of weeks later when I was at a very low ebb and it helped me get through a difficult time.'

'Why don't you put it up?'

'It didn't seem appropriate and I didn't want to upset the children or Jack.'

'Well I think you should put it on the shelf.' Beth indicated a dresser shelf where several photos of Tom and Katie as children were displayed. She stood and placed it next to them and Elsie made no attempt to remove it.

'Perhaps you're right.' She closed the box and left the photograph on the shelf.

They were finishing washing the tea things when Katie blew in on a gust of cold air. 'You've just missed tea,' Elsie exclaimed as Katie kissed her cheek, 'but sit yourself down I can soon make another pot.'

Katie turned her attention to Beth. 'I didn't expect to see you here.'

'Beth and I have been having a nice chat.'

'What about, or shouldn't I ask?'

Beth looked to Elsie for guidance. 'We talked about your little sister.' Elsie told her bravely.

'Oh yes, the baby that died. You did tell me about her when I was old enough to understand but I shouldn't have thought there was much more to talk about.'

Beth looked to Elsie for reassurance and received a nod. 'There's a photo of her there.' Beth pointed to the dresser shelf.

'Where?' Katie followed Beth's finger and, leaping to her feet, snatched the photo down. 'Why haven't you shown us this before?' she demanded staring at her mother.

Elsie sighed. 'I'm sorry Katie I probably should have done, I didn't want to upset you.'

'I wouldn't have been upset. Children accept these things more easily than you think.' Katie looked from the photo to Beth and back again. 'But I am feeling upset now, seeing my little sister for the first time after all these years.'

Chapter 21

Cycling was not allowed in the University Parks but Beth was not concerned by the rule; she was quite content to walk. She dismounted at the gate and continued on foot, following the path towards the river. On one side ornamental trees shaded the grass while opposite green acres of playing fields stretched into the distance.

Ahead of her she could see a group of young men casually kicking a football to and fro from one to the other. As she drew nearer she recognised one or two faces. They were the students that had been in the snug of the King's Arms that Saturday when she had met Bear there. Not wanting to get involved with them, she turned her head and pretended she hadn't noticed them. To her dismay her name floated across the grass from the group and she looked more carefully to see who was calling her. If it was that long-haired individual in the collarless jacket she decided she would ignore the call. To her surprise she saw Peter waving and beckoning to her. Beth sighed and waved in return, she had better find out what he wanted. She turned her bicycle and pushed it over the rough grass to where he stood on the edge of the group. The casual game of football had stopped and they stood around, interested in this turn of events.

'Hello Peter didn't expect to see you here,' she greeted him.

Peter startled her by kissing her on the cheek before he replied. 'Why not may I ask? I do live in Oxford you know.'

'It's just that you're back earlier that I expected. I thought you were going for the whole weekend.'

Peter looked puzzled. 'Back from where?'

'London.'

'What made you think I was going to London for the weekend?'

It was Beth's turn to be perplexed. 'I overheard Camilla

say she was going to a show in London with you.'

Peter's bewilderment cleared to be replaced by awkwardness. 'Not me sweetie.' He gave the others a fierce look and they shuffled away to resume kicking their ball. One or two of them looked back over their shoulders and grinned knowingly at Beth.

'Then who?'

Peter regarded her questioning face. This was not good news for her but it could be his chance. 'Where do you think Bear is?' he asked her.

'Finishing off all the work his tutor gave him I imagine,' Beth replied quickly. 'But what has that got to do with anything?'

Peter couldn't help himself, he gave a shout of laughter. 'Is that what the devil told you?'

Beth began to feel sick as the realisation of what lay behind Peter's words sank in. 'Do you mean it was Bear who went to London with Camilla for the weekend?'

Peter nodded slowly and decisively. 'I thought you knew.'

Beth shook her head, fighting back tears of anger. 'I've been a fool,' she muttered looking down at the ground so that Peter wouldn't see the tears in her eyes.

'Look, Bear's the one that's a fool, upsetting a girl like you. But I did warn you he's out for a good time with any pretty girl that takes his fancy. I'm only sorry a nice girl like you had to get involved.' Peter reached out a hand but Beth moved back before he could touch her. She was too angry to accept sympathy. 'How about we meet up for a drink this evening and I'll try to cheer you up?'

Beth shook her head. 'Thanks Peter but I'm off men at the moment. Some other time perhaps.' She turned her bicycle and set off back the way she had come without a backward glance. She felt humiliated. Those students must all have known about Tom and Camilla. What an idiot she had been.

Back at The Flower basket Beth threw herself into her work. She served in the shop, took the orders for bouquets, floral tributes and commercial floral decorations, ordered the blooms they needed from the wholesaler and tended the shop flowers so that they always looked fresh and attractive. When there was a lull in these activities she swept the floor, cleaned the shop window glass and tidied the work room shelves. Never before had The Flower Basket looked so tidy. Molly watched Beth's activities with a measure of apprehension. Beth hadn't confided in her but she knew that she was working off a deep set anger and needed to be kept occupied. Molly said nothing but kept her eye on the situation incase Beth should need her. Beth was glad she had her job to concentrate on. When she was busy she was able to relegate thoughts of Bear's duplicity to the back of her mind. When she did think about him it was not sadness but anger that coursed through her veins.

Lately Prudence too had recognised that something was wrong with her daughter but did not want to pry. Beth would tell her in her own good time.

'It's Saturday,' she mentioned brightly at the breakfast table, 'If you've no other plans why don't you invite that friend of yours, Katie isn't it? I could make something suitable for supper that you could take down to your room on trays.' Beth looked up from the cereal she was pushing around her bowl. That wasn't a bad idea. A girly chat with Katie appealed to her and might just lift her spirits.

'Thanks mum, that's a good idea I might do that. I'll see if Katie's free.'

'Well if you do want supper for yourself and Katie let me know when you get in from work so that I can prepare something nice for the two of you.' Prudence was happy she had suggested something that pleased Bethany.

That evening after work Beth went straight down to her sitting room to tidy up and make it presentable for Katie's arrival. She was looking forward to showing off her newly acquired space to her friend and hummed tunelessly as she went about her tasks. Following a light tap, Prudence popped her head round the door.

'There's a visitor for you Beth. Didn't you hear the bell?'

Goodness Katie's early thought Beth, I haven't even finished the tidying yet. She hastily plumped cushions as Prudence continued. 'Shall I tell him to come on down?'

'Him?'

'Yes, it's that nice medical student, Rupert, who brought you flowers.'

Beth's stomach did a flip. She faced her mother. 'He's not nice and I do not want to see him so please ask him to leave!'

Prudence was bewildered. 'But Bethany that's rather impolite when he's come round especially to see you.'

'I don't care. I don't want to see him and that's that.' Beth put on her mulish face and Prudence knew she was beaten. She turned to return to the front door but met Bear on his way down the stairs behind her. She barred his way. 'I'm sorry Rupert but for some reason, known best to herself, Bethany refuses to see you.'

'It's alright Mrs. Burnett, I only want a quick word.' Bear quickly squeezed past an embarrassed Prudence and faced a furious Beth in the doorway.

'Didn't you hear what my mother just said – I – do – not – want – to – see – you.'

'Please Beth I owe you an explanation.'

'Of what? The fact that you lied to me and went to London with Camilla instead of taking me out on my birthday? As far as I'm concerned there's nothing to explain, what you did is perfectly clear, now will you please leave, I'm expecting a guest any minute.'

Bear took hold of her arm but Beth shook him off. 'Beth please let me in I really do have something important to say to you.'

Beth was about to reiterate her refusal to listen to anything Bear had to say but a glimpse of Prudence lingering at the top of the stairs and listening to their conversation changed her mind. She pulled a surprised Bear inside and slammed the door shut.

Beth faced Bear, colour blazing in her cheeks. 'Now what have you got to say that's so important, and make it quick, I can only spare you a few minutes.'

'Beth I've been an idiot and all I can do is apologise.'

'Right on the first count, wrong on the second,' Beth retorted. 'It's too late for regrets Bear, you lied to me and that can't be undone.'

Bear felt panic rising. This was proving more difficult than he had imagined. 'Beth I'm sorry I listened to Camilla. She can be very persuasive. All we did was take in a show, nothing happened, I stayed at my parents' house in Fulham.'

'Why should I believe you? You've already lied to me.'

'Because I've finished with Camilla. I've told her I won't be seeing her again. It's you I want Beth.'

'Well I don't want you Bear. I have never been more certain of anything in my life. I am not prepared to be a plaything for you to pick up when you feel like it and discard when something else takes your eye.' Beth crossed the room and held the door open. 'Please leave.'

'Beth …'

'Now!'

When Bear had reluctantly climbed the stairs Beth sat down on the sofa and started to shake with laughter but gradually her mirth turned to tears and she cried bitterly until the hiccoughs started. The combination of the cathartic tears and having dealt decisively with Bear relieved her stress and by the time Katie arrived she felt a great deal happier. She greeted Katie with a hug but Katie took one look at Beth's red-rimmed eyes.

'What's the matter Beth? Has something dreadful happened?'

'No, not dreadful, and now that I've got used to the idea I don't even mind very much.' Katie waited for Beth to explain. 'I've told Bear I don't want to see him again.'

Katie sat down and patted the seat next to her. 'Come on, tell me all about it.

Chapter 22

The next morning Beth woke with a headache. Despite having dealt satisfactorily with Bear, the stress of the previous week had caught up with her and she felt terrible. She turned over and was just about to try and go back to sleep when she remembered it was Sunday and she had a driving lesson at ten. Struggling out of bed she found a pain killer in her handbag and hastily swallowed it with water from the small basin in her bedroom.

Prudence was worried when she saw Beth's pallor and the dark smudges under her eyes. 'Are you sure you want to go for your driving lesson this morning?' she asked gently.

Beth nodded. She was feeling better following a strong coffee and some warm toast and honey. 'I'll be alright,' she told her mother, 'just a bit tired that's all.' Prudence let it pass. She knew better than argue with her strong-minded daughter.

Because Prudence didn't press her, and together with the fact that she owed her mother an explanation for her outburst the previous evening when Bear had turned up unexpectedly, Beth felt inclined to confide in her mother. She gave Prudence a potted version of Bear's behaviour and told her that she did not intend to see him again.

Prudence was horrified. 'You poor darling, you should have told us. Your father would have had a strong word with that young man.'

Beth smiled inwardly. She was glad things had not come to that. How embarrassing that would have been!

Beth's driving lesson was uneventful. When she pulled up outside her house the instructor patted her knee. 'You're doing very well my dear, just try to remember to be in the correct gear at all times and do some work on the Highway Code before next time.' He heaved his bulk out of the passenger seat and Beth was glad the lesson was over. She didn't like his over familiar manner. He might be a friend of her father's but that didn't give him the right to pat her knee like that. She would be glad when she had passed her test. The sooner the better she decided.

Prudence heard her come in and popped out of the kitchen. 'There's a note for you on the hall table. He called with it personally but I told him you were out.'

'Oh hell, what did he want this time?'

'There's no need to swear Bethany and it wasn't Rupert it was some man with oily hands and dirt-engrained finger nails.'

'Tom!' Beth cried in delight.

'Yes, I believe that was his name.' Prudence put on her most disapproving face. 'Who is this Tom? A workman of some kind I presume, and how do you happen to be on his mailing list?'

'He's Katie's brother!' Beth threw over her shoulder as she rushed to the hall to gather up Tom's note. The message was brief and to the point: *Going for a drive – want to come for some practice? If so will pick you up at midday. Might buy you lunch if you're good! Tom.*

Beth consulted her watch. Less than an hour! She rushed upstairs and emptied her wardrobe. Why did she have nothing to wear? After trying on various items and discarding them, she eventually settled for her warm navy trousers and teamed them with her pale blue birthday jumper. She tied a green and blue silk scarf casually round her neck and slung an emerald green jacket over her shoulders to completed her outfit. After a twirl in front of her full length mirror Beth was satisfied with her appearance and went downstairs to wait for Tom.

In the hall Prudence surveyed her beautiful daughter. 'Going out darling?' she asked nonchalantly.

'Yes, Tom's taking me for some driving practice and he's going to buy me lunch.'

'He has a car then, this Tom?'

Beth nodded. She didn't want to get into a conversation on the age of the vehicle. She knew from what Katie had told her that it was quite old and didn't want her parents to veto the idea of driving practice with Tom. Luckily the sound of a car drawing up outside precluded further discussion and Beth hurriedly kissed her mother before rushing off.

Outside to Beth's enormous surprise Tom was climbing out of the little green MG sports car she had seen at his garage. He held the passenger door open for her.

'Should you be using this car?' she asked as she lowered herself into the passenger seat.

'Why not?' Tom smiled, climbing in beside her.

'Because the owner might object.'

'He doesn't mind.'

'How do you know that?'

'Because he's sitting right next to you.'

It took a few moments for Tom's words to sink in. 'You mean it's yours?' Beth was disbelieving. Tom nodded with a gratified smile.

'Didn't look like this when I got it. It's taken me two years of hard work in my spare time to return it to its original condition.' Tom let out the clutch and they roared down the road.

Beth sat back, let the cold air blow away her stress, and enjoyed the exhilaration of riding in an open sports car. After a silence she asked, 'where are we going?'

'A few miles outside Oxford,' Tom told her. 'Boars Hill, know it?'

'I've heard of it but I don't think I've ever actually been there,' Beth admitted.

'There's a nice country pub there where we could get some lunch.'

'Oh, you're going to feed me then?' Beth grinned.

'It's the least I can do after a ministering angel brought me food last week when I was dying of starvation.' Beth giggled. Tom was so easy to be with. 'And there are some very quiet lanes,' he continued, 'where you can have a go at driving this little gem.' Tom patted the steering wheel affectionately.

Beyond the city bypass Tom accelerated and Beth

removed her scarf, folded it into a triangle and covered her hair with it, crossing it under her chin and tying it securely at the back of her neck. Tom glanced at her profile. 'Nice,' he remarked and that simple word made Beth glow with pleasure.

They parked at The Fox pub next to a new Triumph Spitfire. Beth regarded it thoughtfully. 'What do you think?' Tom asked.

'I like its lines but it's nowhere near as good as yours.'

'Tom patted the bonnet of the MG. That's my girl!' he remarked happily.

Beth wasn't sure whether he was referring to her or the car.

The interior of the black and white timbered pub was dark but welcoming. Their footsteps rang on the worn stone flags as they made their way to stand in front of a large stone fireplace which housed a glowing log fire. They rubbed their cold hands and held them out to the warmth of the fire. A rotund barman came out from behind the bar wiping his hands on a cloth tucked into the waistband of his baggy trousers.

'What can I get you two young people?' he asked pleasantly.

'Lunch I hope,' Tom remarked with an answering smile.

'Certainly. We don't have a big choice of menu but what we have is good home-cooked fare. I can do you a roast beef Sunday lunch, how would that be?'

Tom glanced at Bethany to ascertain that it was to her liking.

'Perfect.'

The barman puffed his way up a few steps to a mezzanine level, beckoning Beth and Tom to follow. With a flourish of his cloth he indicated three scrubbed tables set for lunch. Beth chose the table nearest the window. It overlooked a wooden balcony and a steep overgrown garden beyond. The barman pulled out Beth's chair for her, dusted it down assiduously and, with a small inclination of his head, he motioned her to sit. Beth grinned at Tom and he smiled back. She felt a little like a child pretending to be grown up.

'Can I fetch you both a drink while you're waiting for your dinners?'

Beth hesitated and looked to Tom for help and he nodded. She coloured slightly. 'I'd like to try a gin and tonic,' she asked more loudly than she had intended.

'And a very good choice too if I may say so.' The barman took Tom's order for a beer and backed away leaving them grinning at each other across the table.

'He makes me feel like a naughty schoolgirl,' Beth whispered.

Tom leaned across the table. 'You look like a naughty schoolgirl,' he whispered back. 'I'm surprised the barman served you at all.'

Beth opened her mouth to protest but seeing the smile on Tom's face she thought better of it. 'Tom don't tease,' she laughed.

Tom sipped his beer pensively. He hadn't entirely been teasing. Beth looked so young with her mop of unruly curls, her cheeks tinged with colour from the wind and her green eyes sparkling as she took in everything around her. He had fallen for this beautiful girl ... but she was too young, five years his junior, she needed to have fun with people her own age. And then there was the indisputable fact that she came from a very different background, big house, private school, she wouldn't be interested in someone like him. He would have to watch his step otherwise he might lose her company altogether. The best course of action he decided was to continue to treat her like a younger sister, that way she wouldn't suspect his real feelings for her.

'To driving practice!' he smiled, raising his glass. Beth lifted her glass and touched it against Tom's with an answering smile, but a second later the smile had disappeared and she put her drink down so sharply that some of the contents slopped onto the table. Tom followed

Beth's gaze to the lower part of the pub. A young man and a girl with long sleek dark hair had just entered, letting in a gust of cold air that caused the fire to flare up. The couple didn't look up to where Tom and Beth sat but Tom knew who the young man was, he had seen him once on his bike outside Beth's house. Beth clutched the stem of her glass and turned her head away.

'Friend of yours?'

Beth looked at Tom and he saw her eyes were a soft deep green.

'He used to be,' she whispered, pressing her other hand flat on the table.

'What happened?'

Beth hesitated. 'You did!' she grinned.

Tom was stunned. Then he realised that Beth was returning his teasing of a few moments ago. He covered her hand with his and gave it a squeeze. 'I'm glad I've been useful.'

Chapter 23

In the car park Beth passed the flame-red MGB without a glance. Tom recognised it too and remembered the obnoxious girl who had brought it to his garage. He's welcome to her, he thought angrily; they deserve each other.

Tom drove to a quiet lane where he parked the car. 'Come on, that was some feast, we need to walk it off.' He opened Beth's door for her and put a helping hand under her elbow as she eased herself out of the low seat. He tucked her arm through his in what he hoped was a brotherly way and led the way back along the lane. Eventually the hedges and trees surrounding the large houses on their spacious plots were replaced by a wooden fence edging an open field. The field fell away steeply to a patchwork of yet more fields and there, in the great Thames valley below, lay Oxford. Beth leaned against the top rail of the fence and breathed deeply. Tom watched her face carefully for her reaction and was pleased with what he saw.

'It's beautiful,' she breathed. 'I can see North Oxford and Tom Tower on the entrance to Christchurch and the Radcliffe Camera and look, all those houses are Cowley and those spreading up the hill beyond are Headington. It's breathtaking I wonder why I've never been up here before?'

Tom quietly unhooked Beth's arm from his and pointed out a few more landmarks. 'It's a very famous view,' he told her, sliding his arm gently across her shoulders. 'It's thought that this vista inspired Matthew Arnold when he wrote 'The Scholar Gypsy' and his poem 'Thyrsis'. From here he described Oxford as "the dreaming spires", which is the term everyone connects with Oxford today.'

Beth turned a surprised face to Tom. 'How do you know all this?' she asked amazed.

Tom looked at her a little sadly. 'Just because I left

school at sixteen doesn't mean I didn't learn anything at in my time there,' he told her gently. 'I had an inspiring English teacher who gave me a love of poetry.'

'Sorry Tom, I didn't mean to imply you were ill educated.'

Beth's woebegone face moved Tom. He gave her a quick squeeze. 'Of course you didn't. Now, sole purpose of mission was to give you some driving practice, so come on it's time for me to sit back while you drive me around this delightful piece of Oxfordshire.'

'It will make a nice change from driving with that awful driving instructor,' Beth told him.

'What's the matter with him,' Tom smiled.

'He keeps patting my knee with his podgy hand!' Beth exclaimed.

Tom's smile changed to a frown. After a moment's thought he asked, 'would you like me to teach you Beth?'

'Would you really?'

Tom nodded. He would do anything to be near this delightful girl.

'I'll tell my father that I've found another instructor,' she told him happily.

Darkness had fallen when they drew up outside Beth's house. Beth climbed out and walked round to Tom's side of the car. She bent and gave him a light kiss on the cheek.

'Thank you for the driving practice and lunch and everything. I've had a brilliant afternoon.'

Tom didn't trust himself to return Beth's kiss in a brotherly way so he let out the clutch and floored the accelerator, leaving Beth standing on the pavement surprised at his sudden departure.

***

Tom searched the workbench for the spanner he wanted for the job he was doing on an old Wolsey that needed a complete overhaul.

'Seen the adjustable spanner?' he called.

Rob poked his head round the office door and scanned the bench.

'It's there,' he pointed to the bench

'Where exactly? I've been looking here for the past five minutes,' Tom replied irritably.

'Right next to your left hand my friend, you're almost touching it.'

Tom picked up the tool and returned to the car only to put down the spanner and walk back to the bench. Rob watched him in some concern. It wasn't like Tom to mess about when there was work to be done. Once again Tom searched through the row of tools, moving some so that they were no longer in their correct place.

Rob crossed to the bench. 'What you looking for now?'

'I need the torque wrench.'

'It's there mate, on the shelf where it's always kept.'

'Oh right, thanks.' Tom reached down the wrench and made to return to the car but Rob barred his way.

'Something the matter Tom? You're not yourself this morning, you can usually lay your hand on every single tool in this garage. If I didn't know better I'd say you were in love.'

Tom, startled, stared at Rob. Hell, the man was perceptive! What was he going to do now, admit it or deny it? He thought for a split second before replying.

'On this occasion, unlike others, you've hit the nail on the head,' he told a surprised Rob.

Rob's mouth fell open but he quickly gained his composure. 'Go on then don't keep me in suspense, who is the lucky lady? And when are the church bells going to ring?'

'That's the problem, there's no future in it, she's just a kid, years younger than me.'

'For goodness sake Tom you've got me worried, how old exactly is she?'

'No,no, she's not *that* young. She's just turned nineteen.'

Rob looked relieved. 'Phew, you had me worried there

for a minute.'

'Rob I don't want you to breathe a word of this to anyone. She's a friend of my sister and I don't want her to get any idea of how I feel about her.'

Rob looked puzzled. 'Why not? She might fancy an older man.'

'Because,' Tom banged the wrench down firmly, 'she's got a boyfriend already and looks on me as an older brother. And,' he continued vehemently, 'she has a very upper middle-class background – lives in one of those big houses on the Woodstock Road and was educated privately. When I called at the house last week her mother really looked down her nose at me.'

'Oh dear, well out of your league then. You don't think she might fancy a bit of rough?'

Tom gave Rob a withering look. 'I'm serious Rob. If I come on to her she will avoid me like the plague and I wouldn't get to see her at all. So the best thing I can do is to play the big brother for all I'm worth so that at least we get to spend some time together. At the moment I'm teaching her to drive and I don't want that to stop, right.'

'Oh dear you have got it bad old thing. You can count on me, won't breath a word, epitome of discretion that's me.' Rob took in Tom's solemn face. 'Come on, you never know, things might turn out better than you think. What's she like this girl of yours?'

'Haven't you been listening to a word I've said? She's not my girl, that's the trouble.'

'Well what's she like this girl who you would like to be yours,' Rob corrected himself.

Tom couldn't help but smile at Rob's facetious rephrasing. 'She's got the most amazing red hair ...'

'Oh of course you red heads must stick together.'

'No it's not ginger like mine, it's the colour of ... of ... burnished copper.'

'My god, this love bug has got you waxing lyrical! Perhaps you need a spell of working on a rusting old car to bring you back to earth.'

Tom grinned. Hint taken, he returned to his job on the old Wolsey.

***

Beth worked busily serving a steady stream of customers and when the shop was finally empty she went to help Molly make up the orders in the back room.

'Don't forget we have to order the flowers for Deirdre Will's wedding this week. Delivery of the bouquets is on Saturday morning early so we'll need the flowers for Friday to make up the bouquets and buttonholes in advance,' she reminded Molly.

'Don't tell me that girl is getting married in white,' Molly remarked nastily.

'Yes, her mother insisted and anyway why shouldn't she?'

'Because she's up the duff that's why.'

Beth blushed. 'You mean she's …'

'Yes expecting, in the club, pregnant, what ever you want to call it, the result's the same no matter what name you give it, a baby's on the way. Silly girl, having to care for a child at her age, she's no more than a child herself.'

'Molly it's not like you to be so condemning. At least they're getting married so she won't have to bring it up on her own.'

Molly regarded Beth's innocent face. 'Sorry Beth you're right. Shouldn't be so judgmental. Just feeling tetchy this morning.'

'Molly, what's the matter?'

'It's these knees of mine, giving me gyp they are.'

'Oh, poor you. Can I get you some liniment from the chemist at lunch time?'

'Thank you that might help but I'm thinking of a longer term solution. How are the driving lessons doing?'

'They're fine. I'm applying for my test this week. I'm not quite ready yet but there's a bit of a waiting list so Tom says I should be ok by the time my date comes up.'

'That Tom still helping out with the practice then?'

'Yes. He took me up to Boars Hill yesterday and I drove round some pretty little lanes. The views from up there are amazing.' Beth paused. 'I did hope he would be in touch to take me out on my half day, but perhaps I forgot to tell him it was tomorrow.' She brightened. 'Never mind I'll be seeing him on Friday at the fireworks so maybe we'll fix up something then.'

Molly nodded. 'Well you let me know as soon as you've passed your test and then we'll do some deliveries together so that you get the hang of things.'

'But Molly we can't do that.'

'And why not pray?'

'Because there would be no one to look after the shop if we both went out.'

'Ah ... that was the other thing I wanted to talk to you about.' Beth looked up sharply from the bouquet she was arranging. 'Since you joined me full time the shop has flourished. We're doing more than twice the business than when I was on my own, thanks to your hard work.' Beth flushed with pleasure at Molly's praise. 'I've been thinking for sometime now we should take on some help. Maybe part-time at first but later, who knows, if the business continues to thrive we might be able to take on someone full-time and that would mean you could attend a day release course and learn a lot more than I can teach you.'

'Molly, I'm sure no one knows more than you about floristry, but I did promise my father that I would try and obtain some qualifications so it would be wonderful to have the opportunity to do just that.'

'Well that's settled then. Now how about nipping off to the chemist's on Little Clarendon Street and getting me some liniment for these pesky knees of mine?'

The chemist shop was busy and Beth had to queue up for some time. At last she got what she came for and hurried out of the shop clutching the paper bag containing Molly's liniment. Outside the shop the street was exceedingly narrow and the pavement barely wide enough for two people to pass. A bicycle pulled up alongside her and the rider dismounted.

'Beth!' To her horror Bear barred her way. 'Beth I need to speak with you.'

'Well I don't need to speak to you. I thought I had made myself quite clear.'

'Beth please, hear me out.'

'You had your chance. We have nothing more to say to each other, now let me pass please I'm on my lunch break and I need to get back to work.'

A car horn beeped impatiently. Bear's bike was partially blocking the very narrow road and the car was unwilling to pass and chance scratching its shiny paintwork. Bear turned angrily at the unwanted interruption. 'You could drive an eight-wheeler lorry through there,' he shouted at the driver as he hauled his bike onto the pavement out of the way. Beth felt sorry for the woman driver being on the receiving end of Bear's anger but her attention was captured by the car's passenger and her eyes rested for a brief second on Tom before the car moved on.

Beth felt out of sorts as she hurried back to work. She wished Bear would leave her alone. But her main thoughts settled on wondering who the woman was in the car with Tom. She had looked quite young and, from the little Beth had seen, quite pretty too. Who was she and why was Tom driving out with her in the middle of the day when he should be at work? Beth realised that she knew very little about Tom other than those things he had chosen to tell her. She had presumed he didn't have a girlfriend because Elsie had said he didn't. But mothers didn't always know what their grown up children got up to did they? Take Katie for instance. She had been seeing Nathan for over two years and her mother knew nothing of it. The thought of Tom with a girlfriend made Beth feel empty. He was her friend and she surprised herself by admitting that she didn't want to share him with anyone else.

'Wait there with Katie and Nathan,' he shouted over his shoulder as her raced after the two youths who were pushing their way between groups of onlookers in order to get away from the scene. He followed them as quickly as he could but as they were smaller they found is easier to squeeze in and out of small spaces and Tom momentarily lost sight of them. When he reached the gate he saw with relief that two marshals had the boys firmly by the arms and were marching them towards the local constable who Tom knew would deal with them in an appropriate manner.

Tom turned hurriedly, he needed to check that Beth was ok, but the sight of a couple standing at the back of the crowd halted him. He was pretty sure the boy was Beth's friend Bear but he did not recognise the girl. She was tall and slim with white-blond hair piled on top of her head and she wore a belted overcoat with a fur collar that was pulled up casually around her ears. It looked expensive Tom thought. But the thing that caught his entire attention was seeing Bear's arm around the girl's waist and as Tom watched Bear pulled her towards him and kissed her briefly on the lips.

Tom retraced his steps slowly, thoughts racing through his mind. Should he tell Beth? His instinct told him he must tell her. He couldn't stand by and see her become even more involved with such a deceitful individual. Poor Beth he thought, this is going to upset her terribly. Then he had a happier thought. With Bear out of the way maybe ...

Returning to the others Tom was reassured to find that Beth wasn't hurt. She had been frightened but the damage only amounted to a few holes in her stockings.

'Where's Nathan?' he enquired when he had established that Beth was alright.

'He's gone. He thought he shouldn't stay too long incase anyone saw us and put two and two together. We're meeting up later,' Katie remarked quietly.

'At a secret location.' Tom teased with a wink.

'Something like that.' Katie rejoined with an answering

grin.

They turned their attention back to the fireworks but Tom was aware that Beth spent more time looking over her shoulder than she did enjoying the display. He realised that she was worried about more fireworks being let off behind her. Very gently he eased her so that she was standing in front of him and he was therefore protecting her back. A look of thanks from Beth lifted his heart. He placed his hands on her shoulders and stood as close as he dared. He was aware of the sweet smell of shampoo on her hair and it weakened his resolve to treat Beth as a younger sister.

A few moments later a spectacular finale of rockets lit the sky and Beth leaned back to watch their progress across the tree tops. Tom felt her against him; her curls brushed his face and he tightened his grip on her shoulders.

As the last sparks fell from the sky they made their way among the slow moving crowd to the park gates where Katie said goodbye and disappeared into the night in the opposite direction. Tom steered Beth across the road where it was slightly less crowded and they walked briskly until they were on their own. Tom pondered the problem of how and where to tell Beth about Bear and the girl in the fur coat. After walking in silence for some time Beth looked fleetingly at Tom's unsmiling face. 'You're looking very thoughtful, anything the matter?' she remarked.

'No nothing's the matter,' Tom lied, 'I was just wondering, would you like to go for a drink instead of going straight home?'

'That would be nice but don't buy me rum, I've had quite enough of that for one evening.' Beth laughed.

At Tom's suggestion they stopped at the Royal Oak. He knew it would be less busy than a city centre pub and a quiet venue was what he needed for his conversation with Beth. He settled her at a small table in a corner near a crackling fire, and returned with their drinks a few minutes

Back at The Flower Basket Molly was already serving the first customer of the afternoon so Beth settled down in the workroom to complete an order from the High School. They were having a piano recital that evening and had ordered a large floor-standing display to place near the piano and a bouquet to present to the pianist. Because it was her old school Beth was taking extra care over the arrangements. She knew the headmistress would realise they were Beth's work and she wanted to impress her. She was so engrossed in her task that she didn't hear Molly enter the room. She put the finishing touches to her work and moved them to one side with a heartfelt sigh. She wished she hadn't seen Tom in the car with that woman.

'You still brooding?' The sound of Molly's voice made Beth jump.

'Brooding?' she repeated.

'Yes, over that hair of yours.'

Beth relaxed. For a moment she thought Molly had read her mind about Tom. 'I've tried to put it out of my mind,' she told Molly truthfully. 'I now know that I'm not adopted which is the important thing and I suppose I'll never know who I take after.'

'So you're happy about it then?'

'Well, not happy exactly. I still feel more at home with Katie's family than my own. They're so friendly and cheerful and Ben's got red hair like me and, don't get me wrong, I love my parents but I just don't seem to have much in common with them, so I suppose I'm resigned to not knowing where my red hair came from rather than happy about it.' Beth took a deep breath and slid off her stool as the shop bell rang heralding a customer needing her attention.

Molly scratched her head. It didn't sound to her that Beth was entirely resigned to being the only one in her family with red hair but time would tell.

Chapter 24

Sheila dropped Tom off at the garage and he waved goodbye with a smile as she carefully drove away in her MG Midget. But as soon as she was out of sight the smile faded, he wasn't feeling as cheerful as he appeared. Seeing Beth with her boyfriend Bear on Little Clarendon Street had unsettled him. He knew about Beth going out with Bear but actually seeing the two of them together and obviously deep in conversation made him tense and irritable. How long could he go on pretending that he only felt brotherly affection for her? Perhaps it would be better if he didn't see her in future. He was already committed to going to the firework display on Friday but after that maybe it would be better if he tried to avoid contact. He had intended to offer to take her driving this week on her afternoon off but perhaps this was the time to put his decision onto practice. With a heavy heart he donned his overalls and started work on changing the oil on a rather nice Rover.

***

November Fifth dawned wet and windy. The weather matched Beth's mood. She was looking forward to seeing Katie and Tom but her sighting of Tom earlier in the week with an attractive girl by his side dampened her excitement considerably. Added to which he hadn't been in contact about her driving practice and that worried her.

Katie knocked on Beth's door at precisely six o'clock.

Beth was dismayed to see Katie alone. 'Where's Tom isn't he coming?'

'That's a nice greeting I must say!' Katie pulled a face. 'No "hello Katie lovely to see you" just, where's Tom?'

'Sorry Katie, of course it's lovely to see you.'

The two girls hugged and Katie resumed her usual cheerful disposition. 'Only joking. I called at the garage on my way but Tom was finishing off a job on a Mercedes so I thought I'd come on ahead for a bit of a girly chat. He'll be here in half an hour which will give us plenty of time to walk to South Parks for seven.'

The two girls settled down on the sofa and Beth pulled the electric fire closer.

'Thanks for the extra ticket Beth, I've given it to Nathan and he's going to meet me there.' Katie paused. 'I don't want to pry, but weren't you going to give it to Bear?'

'I was but not any more. I told you that I'd finished with him and I meant it.'

Katie raised her eyebrows. 'I thought maybe he had persuaded you to give him another chance.'

Beth shook her head. 'What made you think that?'

Katie coloured. 'No particular reason.'

Beth was not convinced she was sure her friend was keeping something from her. 'Katie!'

'Well … Tom did happen to mention that he had seen you with Bear earlier this week so I wondered if you were back together again.'

'No way, Bear and I have definitely parted company for good. When Tom saw us I was telling Bear to get lost.'

'Good for you, you're learning little Beth.'

'Why do you and Tom persist in calling me little?' Beth asked a trifle petulantly.

Katie smiled. 'Because we love you and perhaps because you take the place of that little sister we never had.'

Beth fiddled with her earrings. Katie's statement had taken her by surprise and she had no ready reply.

Katie rummaged in her bag and drew out a small bottle which she held up with a look of triumph.

'What's that?'

'Rum.'

'What's it for?'

'To warm the cockles of our hearts before we venture out into that wet and windy night.'

'I've never had rum before.'

'There has to be a first time for everything,' Katie grinned wickedly. 'Now can you rustle up a couple of glasses?'

Beth went to a cupboard and produced two tumblers.

'My goodness,' Katie laughed. 'I don't usually drink rum from a glass that size but as I said, there has to be a first time for everything.' She poured a generous tot into each glass. 'Cheers!' Katie settled back in her corner of the sofa. 'It was strange the other day my mum telling you about the baby and showing you those baby clothes. I knew there had been another baby after me but I didn't realise she had kept some of her things. Odd thing to do, but then I've not lost a baby so I don't know how I might react in that circumstance.

Beth took a tentative sip of her rum. It wasn't too bad and it did feel warm and tingly as it slipped down her throat. She thought for a moment about Elsie's grief. 'I think it helped her to talk about the baby. She said she'd bottled it up because she hadn't wanted to upset anyone.'

'Well I'm glad she brought out the photo, I was intrigued to see what my little sister looked like.'

'Did she take after Ben or you when you were babies?'

Katie laughed. 'I really couldn't say. I've seen baby pictures of Ben and myself of course but all babies look the same to me. What did interest me though was that my mother had the baby in a maternity home. She's Catholic, as you've probably gathered, so she went into one run by nuns in Cowley. I always presumed she had the baby at home like Ben and me but apparently she had a difficult pregnancy so she went into St. Mary's.'

Beth's ears pricked up. Where had she heard that name before? Katie went on talking but Beth was only listening with half an ear. St. Mary's ... St. Mary's ... the name chased itself round and round in her head. And then it came to her, St. Mary's Maternity Home was the place of birth named on her birth certificate!

Katie broke off mid-sentence. 'What's the matter Beth?

grin.

They turned their attention back to the fireworks but Tom was aware that Beth spent more time looking over her shoulder than she did enjoying the display. He realised that she was worried about more fireworks being let off behind her. Very gently he eased her so that she was standing in front of him and he was therefore protecting her back. A look of thanks from Beth lifted his heart. He placed his hands on her shoulders and stood as close as he dared. He was aware of the sweet smell of shampoo on her hair and it weakened his resolve to treat Beth as a younger sister.

A few moments later a spectacular finale of rockets lit the sky and Beth leaned back to watch their progress across the tree tops. Tom felt her against him; her curls brushed his face and he tightened his grip on her shoulders.

As the last sparks fell from the sky they made their way among the slow moving crowd to the park gates where Katie said goodbye and disappeared into the night in the opposite direction. Tom steered Beth across the road where it was slightly less crowded and they walked briskly until they were on their own. Tom pondered the problem of how and where to tell Beth about Bear and the girl in the fur coat. After walking in silence for some time Beth looked fleetingly at Tom's unsmiling face. 'You're looking very thoughtful, anything the matter?' she remarked.

'No nothing's the matter,' Tom lied, 'I was just wondering, would you like to go for a drink instead of going straight home?'

'That would be nice but don't buy me rum, I've had quite enough of that for one evening.' Beth laughed.

At Tom's suggestion they stopped at the Royal Oak. He knew it would be less busy than a city centre pub and a quiet venue was what he needed for his conversation with Beth. He settled her at a small table in a corner near a crackling fire, and returned with their drinks a few minutes

'Wait there with Katie and Nathan,' he shouted over his shoulder as her raced after the two youths who were pushing their way between groups of onlookers in order to get away from the scene. He followed them as quickly as he could but as they were smaller they found is easier to squeeze in and out of small spaces and Tom momentarily lost sight of them. When he reached the gate he saw with relief that two marshals had the boys firmly by the arms and were marching them towards the local constable who Tom knew would deal with them in an appropriate manner.

Tom turned hurriedly, he needed to check that Beth was ok, but the sight of a couple standing at the back of the crowd halted him. He was pretty sure the boy was Beth's friend Bear but he did not recognise the girl. She was tall and slim with white-blond hair piled on top of her head and she wore a belted overcoat with a fur collar that was pulled up casually around her ears. It looked expensive Tom thought. But the thing that caught his entire attention was seeing Bear's arm around the girl's waist and as Tom watched Bear pulled her towards him and kissed her briefly on the lips.

Tom retraced his steps slowly, thoughts racing through his mind. Should he tell Beth? His instinct told him he must tell her. He couldn't stand by and see her become even more involved with such a deceitful individual. Poor Beth he thought, this is going to upset her terribly. Then he had a happier thought. With Bear out of the way maybe ...

Returning to the others Tom was reassured to find that Beth wasn't hurt. She had been frightened but the damage only amounted to a few holes in her stockings.

'Where's Nathan?' he enquired when he had established that Beth was alright.

'He's gone. He thought he shouldn't stay too long incase anyone saw us and put two and two together. We're meeting up later,' Katie remarked quietly.

'At a secret location.' Tom teased with a wink.

'Something like that.' Katie rejoined with an answering

The park was already filling up when they arrived. They showed their tickets to the marshal on the gate and found a spot behind the ranks of people already there. They were quite some way back from the roped-off area where the fireworks were to be set off but, as Katie remarked, they would be able to see alright from where they were as the action was going to be in the sky. Beth agreed and told them that she enjoyed fireworks from a distance but was not at all keen on being close to them.

The rain had all but stopped and three marshals came forward to drag the tarpaulin off the bonfire. A cheer went up as their torches lit the brushwood at the base and flames licked skyward. As soon as the bonfire was well alight the first fireworks were set off and the show began amid a chorus of oohs and ahhs.

Beth watched the fireworks and Tom watched Beth. He was fascinated by the expressions of delight on her face. The warm glow from the fire flushed her cheeks and accentuated the rich colour of her hair. How he ached to hold her; it felt almost like a physical pain.

During a brief interlude in the show a young bearded man approached them. Beth recognised him immediately, it was Katie's friend Nathan. He shook hands formally with Katie as though they had met quite by accident. 'My brother Tom you know, and this is my friend Beth,' Katie informed him.

'Hello Beth, I believe we have also met before, although very briefly, on the canal path.' Nathan smiled and Beth warmed to him immediately. Introductions made Nathan took up a position next to Katie and the two chatted quietly until the fireworks resumed and the noise was too great for conversation.

The second half of the show was reaching a climax when Beth became aware of activity behind her but before she could turn round to see what caused it, a firecracker went off right behind her. She screamed as she felt hot sparks on her legs. Tom took in the situation in a split second.

You look as though you've seen a ghost.'

'It's the weirdest coincidence,' she said, staring at Katie.

'What is?'

'Did your mother tell you that the baby has the same birthday as me – we were actually born on the same day?'

'Yes she told me. It is a coincidence but stranger things have happened.'

'That's not all.' Beth lowered her voice melodramatically. 'I'm pretty sure we were born in the same maternity home!'

'What!'

'You mentioned St. Mary's maternity home and I'm ninety-nine percent sure that's the place of birth on my birth certificate.'

Katie's eyes opened wide. 'Now that really is a coincidence. But what was your mother doing in St. Mary's she's not catholic is she?'

Beth shook her head. 'That's exactly what I intend to find out.'

She took a large mouthful of her drink and coughed violently as it caught in her throat. Katie was still patting her on the back when Tom arrived.

'On the turps already?'

'It went down the wrong way,' Beth spluttered.

'What is it you're drinking?'

'Rum.' Katie grinned.

'Really Sis you shouldn't have given Beth rum.'

'Why not? I'm not a child.' Beth was indignant.

Tom shrugged. There was nothing he could add to that, he was well aware that Beth was not a child. He decided to change the subject. 'Time we were off.'

Outside Katie tucked her arm into Tom's and he offered his other arm to Beth with a winning smile. She hesitated for a moment remembering the girl in the MG Midget. 'Come on little Sis no time to lose we don't want to miss the start.' Beth found she could not resist Tom's disarming smile and hastily tucked her arm in his.

later.

'This is nice have you been in here before?' Beth asked.

Tom ignored her question. He needed to get on with what he had to say. 'Beth …'

'You've got your somber face on again.'

'Beth please listen to me.' Beth unexpectedly felt a shiver of apprehension. Why was Tom being so serious all of a sudden? 'I need to talk to you … this Bear you're going out with. I saw him tonight … with a girl.'

'Was it Camilla, that small dark-haired girl who brought her red MG to your garage?'

Tom looked startled.' No it was a tall blond.'

'I'm not surprised.'

'You're not? But I thought you and Bear were …' Beth shook her head. 'But I saw you chatting on Little Clarendon Street just the other day.'

Beth laughed grimly. 'That was no friendly chat. I was telling Bear to leave me alone. I already knew about him and Camilla. He told me he had finished with her so I'm not surprised he's found someone else.'

'So you're not going out with Bear?'

'No. He's the type that needs to have several girls at his beck and call and I didn't fancy being one of them.'

Tom was lost for words.

They walked towards Beth's house and Tom tentatively put his arm round Beth's shoulders. He thought he felt her snuggle into him, but there again it could have been wishful thinking, at least she didn't seem to mind so he kept his arm there and enjoyed her closeness. Outside the house Beth turned to him.

'Would you like to come in? I can't offer you a drink but I could make us some hot chocolate.'

Tom shook his head. 'Better not, I don't think your mother approves of me.'

'I couldn't care less what my mother thinks,' Beth replied hotly.

'Beth don't get angry.' Tom put a finger on her lips to

prevent more fury. 'It's better that I don't come in.'

'Why ever not?'

'This is why not.' Tom bent his head and pressed his lips firmly against Beth's. He tightened his hold on her for a few seconds before quickly releasing her. Turning on his heel he was walking briskly away before Beth had time to gather her wits.

Chapter 25

For once winter had lessened its grip on autumn. Gone were the recent freezing cold wet days, instead a yellow-gold sun illuminated the early morning mist with the promise of a fine day to come. Beth blithely bowled along the quiet Saturday streets on her way to work. Today was the Wills girl's wedding day and Beth needed to be at The Flower Basket early to check that the bouquets and buttonholes were perfect before Molly set off to deliver them soon after nine. She was glad the weather had changed for the better and hoped the day would go well for Deirdre. She remembered the disagreement between mother and daughter over the flowers and Deirdre's dress and smiled ruefully. When it came to her wedding she was going to have to handle her mother carefully in order to have things how she wanted. For a few pleasant moments Beth gave herself up to contemplating what kind of a wedding she would have. Winter or summer? Spring or autumn? She asked herself. The choice of flowers would be much better in the summer but a winter wedding might be fun, she could have a train edged in white swansdown … The time of year really didn't matter she told herself, so long as Tom was at her side. Beth wobbled and came close to scraping the side of a parked car. Now where had that thought come from? It had entered her head unannounced and unexpected. Tom was big brother material not husband material, wasn't he?

Beth entered The Flower Basket still wondering about her mental picture of Tom standing at her side at the altar. Ok he had kissed her goodbye last night but that was just to cheer her up because Bear had let her down, wasn't it?

'You on planet earth this morning?' Beth whirled around at the sound of Molly's voice; she hadn't heard her enter the work room.

'Sorry Molly, didn't hear you come in.' Beth smiled a greeting and thrust all thoughts of Tom to the depths of her mind, to be analysed at a later date.

Molly fixed her with a jaundiced eye. 'Who you mooning over now, or shouldn't I ask?'

'I was thinking about my driving,' Beth lied.

'That Tom still helping with the practice?'

Beth flushed at the mention of Tom's name. It was as though Molly could read her mind. 'Yes,' she replied shortly, not wanting to get into a conversation about Tom. Molly saw the colour on Beth's cheeks but decided to let it pass. She had a lot of deliveries to make which didn't leave much time for interesting chats.

Molly set off with the bridal flowers and several other bouquets that required delivery, leaving Beth to manage the shop. Beth loved dealing with customers, well most of them, there were occasionally one or two difficult ones but on the whole most were likeable and friendly. Business this morning was slow. It was November after all Beth reminded herself and people were beginning to think about Christmas preparations rather than floral decorations. She knew things would pick up in a week or two when they stocked up with gift wrapped pot plants and poinsettias and bowls of bulbs specially brought on to bloom on Christmas Day.

Bored with the lack of custom, Beth wandered into the back room. She was carefully checking the day's list to make sure that all the bouquets and arrangements had been made up and sent out when a sharp knock on the back door startled her. Who on earth is that, she wondered? The wholesale delivery man had already called so who else would come to the back of the shop? She opened the door a little way and peered round the narrow gap. A worried looking Tom stood in the back yard.

She opened the door wide. 'Tom what brings you here? Why aren't you at the garage?'

'I'm on top of today's workload so I came to see you but I need to be quick.'

Beth's face lit up. 'Oh Tom, how sweet of you.'

'Beth please can I come inside? I can't talk to you

properly standing on the doorstep like this.'

'Well I'm supposed to be in the shop and it's not my lunch time yet and Molly will be back in a few minutes.'

'Please Beth, it's important.'

'I thought we talked last night. What's so important that you have to rush round here in the middle of the day?' Beth was beginning to worry.

'Let me in and I'll tell you.'

'Alright then, but only for a few minutes and if Molly comes back you'll have to leave.'

Tom stepped inside and Beth hastily closed the door behind him. She led the way into the workroom and glanced into the shop to make certain there were no customers waiting for her attention. 'Well?'

'Beth I must apologise for last night.'

'Apologise … for what?' A puzzled Beth looked at him in consternation. She hadn't the faintest idea what Tom was on about.

'Beth please don't be obtuse. I kissed you and it wasn't a peck on the cheek either.'

'No it wasn't was it.' A wicked grin pulled at the corners of Beth's mouth.

'Well I shouldn't have kissed you like that and it won't happen again I promise.'

'Are you sure?' Her expression was serious but she couldn't suppress the sparkle in her eyes.

'Absolutely. I'm really sorry Beth.'

'Well then I'm really sorry too.' Beth turned her head to hide her smile. 'I rather enjoyed it and I was rather hoping you would do it again,' she spoke quietly.

There was silence for a moment then Tom turned her to face him. 'What did you just say?'

'I'm not in the habit of repeating myself,' Beth could no longer repress the grin that spread across her face.

'You little …' The rest of Ben's words were lost as he tipped up Beth's chin and executed a perfectly placed kiss on her waiting lips.

'So this is what you get up to when I'm out working

my fingers to the bone!' The two sprang apart, neither had heard Molly's entrance. 'I seem to be invisible in my own shop.' Molly attempted a fierce frown.

Beth found her voice. 'Oh Molly I'm so sorry, there were no customers in the shop and I didn't invite him and I told him he'd have to go and …'

Molly held up her hand. 'Ok, ok, save me the spiel. First tell me who I have the pleasure of finding in my workroom in the middle of the day, as if I didn't know!'

'This is Tom.' The colour in Beth's cheeks deepened as she said his name.

'I'm sorry to have taken Beth away from her work Molly, it won't happen again, but I had something important to say to her.'

'So I understand but it didn't look like there was much talking going on from where I stood.' It was Tom's turn to redden. 'I'm glad to meet you Tom. From what Beth has told me you take good care of her. She can be hot-headed at times and needs someone to look out for her.'

'Well I'm not sure I really …'

'Don't argue young man. You walk her home late at night when she shouldn't be out on her own and you give up your time and let her drive your car to make sure that she'll be safe on the road. For that I'm very grateful. Lord knows I'll be glad to hand over the deliveries into her capable hands so it's a load off my mind to know that she's been properly taught and had plenty of practice.' The ringing of the shop bell prevented Molly from continuing. 'I'll go.' She hastily donned her apron and bustled into the shop leaving Beth and Tom alone.

'I'd better go too,' Tom said softly. 'When you've finished work will you call at the garage?' Beth nodded happily. 'I'll take you to the fish restaurant on Walton Street they do the best fish and chips in Oxfordshire.'

'That would be lovely.'

Tom quickly placed the briefest of kisses on Beth's upturned face and left by the back entrance.

Business at The Flower Basket continued to be slow

during the afternoon. By four o'clock both the workroom and shop were tidy and, on Molly's instructions, Beth had fetched in the buckets of flowers from outside the shop.

'There's no point you staying in an empty shop,' Molly told her, 'you get off home.'

'Are you sure Molly? I don't mind staying on 'til five.'

'Quite sure. I'm more than capable of taking care of the odd last minute customer on my own. It's Saturday, you go and see that young man of yours and have a good time.'

A thrill went through Beth as she realised Molly was referring to Tom. Her young man, Tom, it took a bit of getting used to but yes, she was sure now he was her young man and that thought sent waves of happiness through her unlike anything she had ever felt before.

As Tom had suggested, Beth went straight to the garage, taking a short cut that led to a back gate. She flew along, excited at the thought of seeing Tom. But her anticipation was short lived. The garage and office were empty, there was no sign of Tom or Rob. Beth walked back outside onto the forecourt. It was then that she caught sight of Tom by the archway that led out onto the main road. He was squatting in order to talk through the open window to the driver of a small MG Midget. Beth couldn't see the driver clearly but she was sure the car was the same one she had seen Tom in on Little Clarendon Street with the young fair woman driving. She watched as Tom stood up and waved and the car drew away and disappeared from view. As Tom turned to return to the garage Beth could see that he was smiling widely.

Tom was half way across the forecourt when he noticed Beth standing outside the garage doorway. He quickened his footsteps and was rapidly at her side. Putting his arms round her he gave her a brief hug before leading the way inside.

'You're early. Wasn't expecting you for another hour.'

'Sorry. Molly let me off early. I should have waited.'

'There's nothing to be sorry about, the earlier the better. I've finished for today, just a bit of paper work to do, then we can be off. How about you make us a nice cup of tea in the office while I fill in some forms?' Tom was about to turn away when he noticed Beth's solemn face. 'You look glum. Is something the matter?'

'No nothing's the matter,' Beth tried to sound unconcerned but Tom was not to be put off.

He pulled Beth gently to him and encircled her with his arms. 'Come on there is something, I can see it in those beautiful green eyes of yours.'

Beth decided to take the bull by the horns. 'I was wondering who that MG Midget belonged to. The one that just left.'

'That's Sheila.' Tom frowned. 'Why do you ask?'

Beth paused. 'No particular reason,' she mumbled.

'Come on Beth, you don't ask a question like that for nothing there must be a reason behind it.' Tom looked directly at her and waited.

Beth wished she hadn't started this conversation, but she had so there was nothing to do but finish it. She saw the somber look on Tom's face and said helplessly, 'that day in Little Clarendon Street when Bear stopped me …' she glanced down at her fingers twisted together then looked back at Tom's solemn face. 'Bear shouted at the driver of that car and …'

'And?' Tom was still looking intently at her so she had to carry on.

'You were sitting next to her.'

'Does that worry you?'

'Not worry exactly but I did wonder … and she is very pretty.'

Tom pulled Beth closer. 'Now you just listen to me.' He glared sternly into her eyes. 'We've discovered that we like each other a great deal haven't we?' Beth nodded, uncertain what Tom was getting at. 'Well if this relationship is going to stand any chance of surviving and growing we need to trust each other. Am I right?' Beth nodded again. 'You have had a bad experience with Bear lying to you and going with other girls behind your back but I'm not like that, apart from anything else I don't have the time to run a string of girlfriends,' he added with a grin.

'Oh Tom I'm so sorry. I do trust you but I felt so jealous of that girl being with you and then when I saw her again today and you were giving her one of your smiles I felt angry.'

'Well there's no need to be. Sheila is a client. I replaced the clutch on her MG and I was surprised that it was so badly worn considering the age of the car. I suspected that the excess wear could have been due to the way she drove. When I explained this to her she didn't seem to understand what I was getting at so I offered to go with her while she drove through the traffic in Oxford and sure enough she constantly slipped the clutch and had got onto some very bad driving habits. I had to use a great deal of tact to explain to her what she was doing wrong. Anyway, to cut a long story short, she listened carefully to what I said and she came back today to thank me for going that extra mile and to reassure me that she was driving with much more thought than before.' Tom regarded Beth seriously. 'Does that satisfy you Beth or are you still worried that I have a secret stash of girlfriends?'

Beth nodded furiously. 'I'm really, really sorry I doubted you but I'm sure other women find you as attractive as I do, and I'm a lot younger than you and I worry that you think of me as a little sister.' Beth poured out her misgivings then buried her face in Tom's neck.

'Beth there's no way I can go on pretending to myself that you are like a younger sister. I did try but it just didn't work.' His voice softened. 'I love you Beth and have done since that first time I walked you home at my mother's behest.' Tom dropped a kiss onto the top of Beth's bent head. 'Come on, no more doubts, let's get those fish and chips.'

Beth looked at the tall good-looking ginger-haired man before her and happiness swept through her. 'I think I love you too Tom,' she whispered.

'Only *think*. I'll have to do something about that.' Tom pulled her tightly to him and kissed her firmly for a long time. When he released her he looked deep into her eyes. 'Have I convinced you yet or shall I continue?'

'I *do* love you … but you can continue if you like,' she said happily.

***

Elsie greeted them with open arms and a hug each. 'Beth how lovely to see you and Tom you're home early for once.'

'I'm taking Beth out for fish and chips but first you can look after her while I'm getting washed and changed.'

Elsie looked horrified. 'Fish and chips! Surely you can do better than that Tom?'

Beth broke in before Tom could reply. 'No it's alright, I love fish and chips and I hardly ever get them. My mother doesn't like the smell of fish and vinegar. She says it gets into the furnishings and lingers for weeks.'

'Shame. Oh well as long as you're happy m'dear that's all that matters.'

When Tom had left the room Beth settled herself on a kitchen chair, rested her elbows comfortably on the table and sipped the tea that Elsie had poured for her. She glanced up at the dresser shelf and saw that the photograph of baby Angelica was still there. 'Elsie can I ask you something about the nursing home where you had Angelica?'

'It helped a lot to talk to you about the baby m'dear so ask away.'

'Do you remember any of the other women who were having babies there at the same time as you?' Beth asked tentatively.

Elsie shook her head. 'Sorry, can't help you there m'dear.' Elsie drank her tea automatically, a faraway look in her eyes. 'I had a long and difficult labour and when Angelica finally arrived it was late on in the evening so they didn't put me on the ward with the other mothers. Instead, so as not to disturb them, I was put in a small side room.' Elsie's empty cup remained poised above the saucer as the memories of that night came back to her. 'I was awakened during the night by the sister who had delivered Angelica and she took me to the nursery. The babies were all lined up in their cots. Some were sleeping peacefully, others were crying and two nurses were busily giving a couple their night feed.' Elsie's voice cracked. 'Angelica was having difficulty breathing so they had wheeled her cot into an anteroom to the side of the main nursery and they had sent for the doctor.' Beth covered Elsie's hand with her own.

'Sorry Elsie I didn't mean to upset you.'

'No, it does me good to talk about it I've bottled it up inside me too long. The doctor sent for an ambulance,' she continued, 'and while we were waiting the priest came and christened Angelica. They asked me what name I wanted but I couldn't think straight so I asked the Sister what she was called and that's how Angelica got her name.' A tear escaped and ran down the side of Elsie's nose. She brushed it away impatiently. 'I left in the ambulance with Angelica,' Elsie inhaled noisily, 'but she died before we reached the hospital.' She cleared her throat, 'so you see I didn't get to meet any of the other mums.'

'You poor thing, it must have been awful.' Elsie nodded and accepted the fresh cup of tea Beth poured for her. There were a few minutes of silence while the two women thought, each in her own way, about the trauma of losing a child, then Elsie looked up.

'Actually I tell a lie, there was one woman, she was in the same side room as me, I think she'd had a difficult time too.' Elsie mused. 'We spoke very briefly if I remember right. She was very dainty and so pretty, no more than a girl really, lovely long dark hair she had.'

'Do you remember her name?'

'As a matter of a fact I do.' Beth held her breath. 'It was Mary.'

Surprise and disappointment radiated through Beth. 'Are you sure that was her name?'

'Absolutely sure.' Elsie smiled at the memory. 'Sister Angelica asked me my name and I told her it was Elisabeth, although everyone calls me Elsie. She seemed really pleased and she told me that the young woman's name was Mary. Sister Angelica was very taken with the idea that she had a Mary and an Elisabeth in her care who both had babies, like our mother Mary and her relation Elisabeth in the Bible. So that's why the name has stayed in my memory all these years, Mary and Elisabeth, a very easy combination to remember.'

Beth nodded sadly. She had harboured the idea that Elsie and her mother Prudence had met in the maternity home but apparently it was not so. That would have been one more coincidence to add to the fact that she and Elsie's baby had been born on the same day in the same maternity home.

Chapter 26

November progressed in a haze of happiness for Beth. She and Tom spent as much time as their work allowed in each other's company. On a bright frosty Sunday morning Tom collected Beth and they set off out of the city in his MG and headed towards Woodstock. Once past the massive iron gates that guarded the entrance to Blenheim Palace Ben took a sharp left off the main road and pulled up in front of a parade of stone-built houses, some of which had been converted into small bespoke shops. A look of query crossed Beth's face, she hadn't been expecting them to stop in the town.

'It's your turn,'Tom smiled indicating the leather-bound steering wheel. 'I didn't bring you all the way out here for you to sit back and enjoy the scenery,' he told her with mock seriousness. 'Do you want the roof up or down?' he enquired.

Beth stretched, wound down the window and stuck her head out of the small opening. 'It doesn't feel too cold and the wind's not blowing so I think we could put it down,' she remarked, drawing her head back in.

'Right, but before I set to work folding it away I need to talk to you.' Tom looked serious.

'Is something wrong?' Beth still couldn't quite believe that her feelings for Tom were reciprocated and she secretly worried that he would tire of her and find someone older and more sophisticated.

'Now why should there be anything wrong?' Tom smoothed the curls off Beth's forehead. 'You do too much worrying my darling. Nothing is going to go wrong between us if I've got anything to do with it. I stopped because I wanted to talk to you about our future together.' Beth felt reassured and drew a finger gently down Tom's cheek. He caught hold of her wrist and kissed her fingers and then her lips.

Beth surfaced with a smile. 'I hate to sound like Molly,

but there doesn't seem to be much talking going on here,' she chuckled.

Tom grinned in response. 'Right,' he breathed deeply, pausing to find the right words. 'Beth at the moment I don't have a lot to offer you. I'm just a car mechanic with a modest income so there's no way I can provide a home for us. But I am saving hard to go in with Rob at the garage and things should get better in a year or two.'

Beth took his hand and stroked it with her finger tips. 'It doesn't matter Tom so long as we love each other.'

'It matters to me Beth. You come from a privileged background and I'm determined to give you everything you want.'

'All I want is you.'

'You say that now…' Tom looked anxious. 'Beth would you be prepared to wear a ring so that we are committed to each other, no matter how long it takes before we can marry?' Beth, overcome with emotion, remained silent. Tom's formal proposal was so unexpected.

Tom looked at her still face sadly. 'Sorry Beth I have obviously jumped the gun. You're not ready for this yet. I'm so sorry I've rushed you into making a commitment. Please try and forget it.'

Beth sat up straighter in her seat. 'I don't want to forget it Tom. I don't mind how long we have to wait before we can marry and until then I would be proud to wear an engagement ring.'

After a long and lingering kiss Tom hummed as he folded away the canvas roof. He guided Beth out of the parking space and they set off on a pleasant drive towards Chipping Norton.

***

A bulky envelope awaited Beth when she arrived at work. Inside a short note read:

Thank you for my wedding flowers they were great. The

orange roses were perfect and the bridesmaid's flowers were good to. Hope you like wedding cake. Mum said I had to send out bits in little boxes so there's some for you and Mrs Watson with this note. Best wishes, Deirdre Brown (Wills). Beth smiled and tipped up the envelope. Two small silver boxes slid out containing tiny wedges of wedding cake. Beth put them next to the kettle ready to be consumed later. She was glad Deirdre was safely married and that thought turned her mind to contemplating her shopping trip that afternoon. Today was her half day and Tom was going to call after lunch to take her into Oxford where they planned to visit jewellery shops so that Beth could choose a ring.

The third shop they tried was little better than the first two. Beth had decided she wanted a diamond ring and Tom was in agreement. They were shown a tray of rings with tiny stones, some not much bigger than diamond dust, and the settings were universally ugly. Seeing their looks of dismay, the assistant brought out a second tray with larger stones but they turned out to be paste and were dull without the sparkle of real diamonds. Beth examined the rings on the first tray a second time and picked out a small solitaire diamond in a plain setting. 'I quite like this one she announced,' looking hopefully at Tom.

Tom was frustrated. He had savings but it was important to keep them intact. If he started dipping into them he'd never afford to go into partnership with Rob. He was angry with himself for not being able to afford a much better ring for Beth. 'Quite like is not good enough.' He turned away. 'Thank you for your help,' he said coolly to the assistant as he guided Beth to the door.

'Really Tom that ring was …'

'I know *quite* nice, well no girl of mine is going to wear a ring that is *quite nice*.' Tom emphasised the words making them sound like quite nice was the worst thing in the world to be.

Beth felt dejected. How was Tom going to afford a better ring than that? She pulled her coat closer against the cold wind that had sprung up and wished she could help in some way, but in her heart she knew that this was something Tom had to sort out for himself. Tom glanced at Beth's stricken face and pulled her arm through his.

'Cheer up darling, I'll think of something.' He touched her cheek lightly and Beth shivered. She didn't care what the ring was like so long as they were together but she knew that it was a point of pride with Tom that he should give her something beautiful.

She smiled up at him. 'Let's have a coffee in the Kardoma and get warmed up. Perhaps then you'll have an idea.'

***

For once Tom's mind was not completely focused on the sleek Mercedes sports car he was servicing. With a sigh he closed the bonnet, climbed into the driver's seat and slowly drove the finished car out of the garage and into a parking place on the forecourt. Turning off the ignition he remained in the car drumming his fingers on the steering wheel. How was he going to afford the kind of engagement ring that Beth deserved? He could see no other option than using some of his savings, but that would mean an even longer wait before he could buy into the garage and he was so close to having saved enough. A sharp tap on the side window alerted him to Rob bending down to speak to him. He opened the door and unfolded himself from the bucket seat.

'You getting the feel of a Merc then?' Rob grinned broadly.

Tom shook his head gloomily. 'I'll never afford one of these.' He removed the protective cover from the driver's seat and shut the car door firmly. 'I was thinking that's all.'

'Must have been pretty depressing thoughts to have left you looking like that.'

Tom shrugged. 'Just something important I have to sort

out.'

The two men walked in silence back to the garage. Once inside Rob turned to his friend. 'Are you going to tell me or do I have to put up with your miserable face all day?'

Tom considered telling Rob. Over the years they had worked together they had not only become good colleagues but also good mates. It could do no harm to share his problem with Rob and maybe he might come up with an idea. Finally he decided.

'I've asked Beth to marry me and she's agreed.' Tom couldn't keep the pride out of his voice.

'Rob's jaw slackened then he quickly closed his mouth. 'Congratulations!' He slapped Tom enthusiastically on the back. 'You're a dark horse. I never thought you'd quit working long enough to get a steady girlfriend never name a fiancée. Now look at you, a girlfriend and a fiancée in the matter of weeks.' Tom smiled weakly, he wished it was as straight forward as that. 'But why so down in the mouth?' Rob continued, 'you should be over the moon, she's a lovely girl.' He shot Tom a startled look. 'She's not …'

Tom gave a shout. 'No, she's not pregnant. What do you take me for?'

Rob looked indignant. 'Well that's all I could think of that might be a problem. Come on out with it.'

Tom thrust his hands into his overall pockets. 'I can't afford to buy her a decent ring.'

'Mmm …' Rob frowned. 'I can see that is a bit of a hitch. 'Got any savings?'

'Yes but they're earmarked to buy a share in this place. I'm so close to the target I don't want to jeopardise my chance of coming in with you.'

'I'm glad to hear it. I was going to ask you how things were going on that score. No, you mustn't dip into that fund. We really need some investment capital to expand the business and the sooner the better, so your money will be very welcome.' Rob looked serious and Tom turned away to prepare for the next job. 'How about I lend you the money?'

Tom turned shaking his head and glaring at Rob. 'I'm not going to buy Beth a ring with borrowed money,' he said shortly. Seeing the look on Rob's face he added more politely, 'Thanks for the offer though.'

'That's ok, it was just a thought. I'm sure between us we'll think of an answer to the problem.'

'Somebody got problems?' It was Mark the owner of the Mercedes. 'Nothing seriously wrong with my car I hope?' Rob and Tom turned to face the newcomer. He was of mid height but looked shorter due to his roundness. Tom often wondered how he managed to squeeze that bulk behind the wheel of his car. He had a pleasant ruddy complexion caused by the hours spent out of doors shooting and fishing when he wasn't needed on his auctioneer's rostrum.

Tom shook his head. 'No the car's fine, nothing wrong, given it a good check over and changed the oil. It's ready for you.'

'It's Tom that's got the problem,' Rob interrupted. Tom gave him a warning frown but Rob ignored it and carried on. 'He's proposed to a lovely girl and now he can't afford a ring good enough for her.' Tom threw the seat cover he was holding onto the bench and turned away, exasperated that Rob was spreading information that he had parted with in confidence.

Mark rubbed his nose thoughtfully. 'What kind of a ring were you thinking of?' he asked, aiming his question at Tom's stiff back. Tom turned with a frown. 'Sorry, I didn't mean to interfere, but I may be able to help.'

'I would like to buy her a solitaire diamond, but not one of these puny plain little things that pass for stones in the jewellers' shops.' Tom replied grudgingly.

'Mmm …jewellers' shops are not always the best places to buy jewellery their mark up is so high. Have you thought about buying at auction, you're likely to get better value for your money?'

'What a second-hand ring do you mean?' Tom was appalled at the thought. 'There's no way I'm buying Beth someone else's cast off,' he added firmly.

'I was thinking more along the lines of an antique ring,' Mark remarked gently. 'Good quality antique jewellery is quite sought after these days. There are some very nice Victorian and later pieces about, while not all of them are antique in the true sense of the word, they have a certain charm which sets them apart from today's modern stuff.' Tom began to listen with interest. 'And if you buy at auction there are some very good bargains to be had,' Mark concluded.

'Where would I find auctions selling jewellery?' Tom asked with a slightly more eager tone to his voice.

'My auction house in Banbury is one, there are others of course, but we frequently sell a nice selection of rings, brooches, pendants, that sort of thing. In fact we've a sale coming up in a couple of weeks. It comprises the contents of a large country house belonging to an old lady who died recently. Her family has picked over the most expensive stuff of course but there are some good things left for us to auction including some quality jewellery.'

'It'll probably still be out of my reach,' Tom commented unhappily.

'Don't be so sure. If the dealers don't turn up in strength it's quite possible to pick up a bargain,' Mark reassured him. 'Look, we've almost finished cataloging the items and they'll be on view next week. Why don't you and your fiancée come and have a look and if there's anything that takes your fancy then I can give you an idea of what I think it might fetch in the sale.'

'Thanks. I'll have to speak to Beth first of course but we might do just that.' The two men shook hands and Rob gave a pleased smile. His shot in the dark had worked.

'Right I'll settle up what I owe you for the car then I'll be off. Hope to see you at the sale viewing.' Mark flashed a brief smile in Tom's direction as he entered the office with Rob.

***

Beth looked at the bouquet she was arranging with tears in her eyes. She had been interested when Tom had explained about the antique jewellery up for sale at Mark's auction house and on her half day she had gone willingly with him to the viewing at the Banbury auction room. They had been shown the jewellery by a knowledgeable lady by the name of Madge who had told them about the age, provenance and condition of the items.

To Tom's delight and amazement Beth found a ring that she immediately fell in love with. Madge told them that it was Edwardian and that the medium sized solitaire stone was indeed a diamond of a good quality. The stone was in a very pretty setting supported each side with a leaf shape each embellished with tiny diamonds that gave the whole thing a delicious sparkle. When Beth slid it on her finger it fitted perfectly, it was as though it had been made for her. They waited with bated breath while Madge went to find Mark to ask him what he thought the ring might fetch in the sale. He returned with Madge and greeted the two apprehensive faces with a cheery smile. Madge told him the details of the ring and he slowly turned it over on the palm of his hand.

'Mmm ... very pretty,' he commented. Beth could feel the tension rising in her chest as her heart hammered against her ribs. Mark fitted the ring onto the tip of his little finger and looked at it for a few seconds. 'I would put a guide price on it of thirty to fifty pounds,' he said at last. 'A ring of this quality would sell in a good jeweller's for around two hundred,' he added. Tom nodded and Beth broke into a broad smile of relief as she saw Tom was happy with the valuation. Mark looked at their delighted faces. 'If you're interested in bidding for this ring I'll give you some advice.' They both nodded eagerly. 'Get in quickly, make the first bid, then if anyone else is interested they'll have to bid higher. But remember ...' he looked serious, 'always set yourself a limit and don't go over it, you have auction costs to pay on top of the bid price and it's very easy to get carried away so take care.'

They had thanked Mark for his help and had left the auction house feeling excited at the prospect of getting such a pretty ring at a reasonable price. But then things had gone badly wrong. Rob had arranged to be out of Oxford on the day of the auction to buy a dilapidated sports car that was ripe for complete renovation and could bring the garage a nice profit. The seller was not prepared to delay the sale so Tom was not able to leave the garage.

Beth agreed to go on her own and bid for the ring but then she had received a letter giving her the date of her driving test. It was on the same morning as the auction sale! If they had known earlier they could have left a bid with the auctioneer, but it was too late to do that now. Beth was devastated. She had set her hopes on getting the ring and now it had been snatched from her grasp. She tied the ribbon on the completed bouquet and sniffed away her tears. It could be months or even years before another ring she liked as much as that one came onto the market. She would just have to settle for one of the rings they had seen in Oxford, that is if Tom would agree. She was beginning to realise that he had quite a stubborn streak over things he considered important. She couldn't blame him for that, she was the same herself.

Chapter 27

Beth attempted to put the thought of her ring being bought by someone else out of her mind and tried to concentrate on her driving. When the examiner banged his clipboard on the dashboard, as a prearranged signal for her to do an emergency stop, all other thoughts were well and truly banished as she stamped on the brakes. From then on she focused exclusively on her driving and was relieved when the examiner told her she had passed. She tore off the L-plates and flung them into the boot of her father's car as Katie joined her for the ride back to north Oxford.

'Well done, passed first time, that takes a bit of doing,' Katie beamed.

'I can't wait to tell Tom, he'll be over the moon, he's taken so much trouble over my driving practice.'

'Well I hope it cheers him up, something put him in a very bad mood this morning. It's not like him to be snappy but he refused the breakfast mum had prepared and slammed out of the house like a grouchy teenager.'

Beth negotiated a busy roundabout before replying. 'It's because we missed the chance of bidding for an engagement ring that we both had set our hearts on,' she told Katie sadly. 'Tom couldn't go to the sale because he had to manage the garage in Rob's absence and I had my driving test,' she explained.

Katie nodded knowingly. 'That accounts for his frustration this morning. Once Tom has set his mind on achieving something he doesn't like to fail.'

'I know how he feels, I'm the same.' Beth laughed. 'I would have been pretty cheesed off if I'd have failed my test this morning.'

Katie turned to look thoughtfully at Beth's profile as she drove confidently through the busy traffic. 'Yes you and Tom are alike, in more ways than one. It's probably why you get on so well because you understand each other.'

Beth nodded cheerfully and drummed her fingers on the steering wheel as she waited at the traffic lights. The sight of her unadorned fourth finger slightly took the edge off her happiness but she told herself that the important thing was that she and Tom loved each other and that's what really mattered.

Katie saw the happiness and thoughtfulness on her friend's face and was pleased for her. It will be great to have Beth as a sister-in-law she thought. 'Don't worry about the ring Beth,' she told her. 'It will sort itself out eventually. In the mean time perhaps you could wear a dress ring on your engagement finger to show the world that you are spoken for.'

'Mmm … it's a thought. I'll put it past Tom when I see him tonight, although I rather think he won't like the idea.'

'Well at least when you've found one you like you'll be able to wear it straight away. I can't wear Nathan's ring until after he has resigned his job.'

'Oh Katie I'm sorry, I should count my blessings shouldn't I? Now, to change the subject, how are your applications going to study accountancy?'

***

Beth parked the car on the drive and hurried inside to tell her mother that she had passed her driving test. Having accomplished that, she mounted her bicycle and pedalled furiously to The Flower Basket, eager to tell Molly the good news that she would now be able to take over the van deliveries.

Molly was pleased. 'I knew you'd pass,' she declared with a knowing nod of her head. 'That Tom of yours did right to take over teaching you. Didn't like the sound of that driving instructor you had, far too easy going if you ask me.'

Beth smiled. Molly never beat about the bush, she was always forthright, and in this instance she was correct in her summing up of the situation. 'He was a bit too laid back, kept telling me I was a fantastic driver, which was patently not true,' Beth agreed. 'Unlike Tom who made me practice and practice until it became second nature.' Beth's eyes took on a faraway look as she remembered the practice sessions with Tom. Despite the fact that he had criticised her driving and had made her repeat manoeuvres over and over again until she could do them in her sleep, she surprisingly hadn't lost her temper once. She had looked forward to the time spent with him in eager anticipation and now she couldn't wait to tell him that his hard work had paid off.

'Deliveries.' Molly brought her back to reality with an abrupt change of topic. 'There's no time like the present so you might as well do today's lot, they're all laid out on the bench.' She inclined her head towards the workroom. Beth turned eagerly. 'Not so quick,' Molly admonished. 'Before you leave, check all the addresses against the map and make sure that you know where you're going. I don't want you wasting time and petrol driving round Oxford looking for places.' Beth grinned to herself, she was quite used to Molly giving a string of instructions and it didn't bother her, she knew Molly had a heart of gold beneath her gruff exterior. 'And another thing …' Beth waited patiently. 'When you get back I want you to take over the shop for the afternoon. There's something I need to do.' Beth raised an eyebrow but Molly turned away and busied herself rearranging a perfectly arranged bucket of cut flowers. The conversation was definitely at an end.

Beth returned, exhilarated with achieving her first round of deliveries. The minute she entered the shop Molly acknowledged her arrival, hung up her apron and climbed the stairs to her flat. Ten minutes later she was back downstairs and Beth could hear her moving around and muttering irritably to herself in the workroom. Beth finished serving her customer then went to see what was annoying Molly so much. A remarkable sight met her eyes. Molly was all dressed up, something Beth had not witnessed before. She wore a cherry red overcoat with a large paisley scarf in shades of reds and blues draped over her shoulders. It was fastened at the front with a large ornate silver brooch that Beth had not seen Molly wear before. In fact, when she thought about it, Molly never wore jewellery of any kind. Her hair had been coaxed into the tightest bun Beth had ever seen and on top perched a small neat felt hat in the same shade as the coat.

'Well don't stand there gawping, help me find something. 'Molly's face was flushed.

'What exactly have you lost?'

'I don't lose things,' Molly retorted vigorously. 'I have *mislaid* my tape measure.'

'You usually keep it in your apron pocket,' Beth replied keeping a straight face. Molly puffed and looked slightly embarrassed as she dug her hand into the apron pocket and took out the missing tape measure.

'There, I told you it wasn't lost,' she said, thrusting it into a large brown leather handbag that had seen better days. Beth couldn't help noticing the bag contained a sheaf of papers and she wondered what they were for.

'Going somewhere nice?' Beth enquired hopefully.

'That's as maybe,' Molly replied vaguely and with a cursory glance in the small mirror above the work surface and a brief wave for Beth, she left by the back door.

Beth returned to the shop considerably puzzled at Molly's uncharacteristic behaviour. Never before had she seen her so neat *and* wearing a hat! And what did she want a tape measure for? No doubt Molly would tell her in her own good time, in the meantime there was plenty to keep her busy in the shop.

At five o'clock Molly still hadn't returned so Beth closed the shop, left a note regarding flowers that were needed for an urgent order the next day, and set off for the garage to tell Tom the good news of her successful driving test.

Unusually the main doors of the garage workshop were closed and all was ominously quiet. There were a couple of cars parked on the forecourt awaiting collection but other than that there was little sign that the garage was open for business. Beth went round to the back and tried the door to the office. It opened and she peered in cautiously. The air was thick with cigarette smoke and through the haze she could see Rob sitting at his desk engrossed in paperwork, but of Tom there was no sign. Beth coughed and Rob spun round.

'Oh Beth it's you … Tom's not here I'm afraid.'

'Has he gone home early?' Beth's voice showed the surprise she felt. Tom never left work early.

'I don't think so.' Rob stubbed out his cigarette into an overflowing ash tray, stood up and stretched. 'He didn't say where he was going, just that he had some urgent business to see to … and he went off at speed in his car,' he added.

'What's the matter with everyone today?' Beth asked with a frown. 'First Molly disappears for the afternoon without an explanation and then Tom does a vanishing act.'

Rob shrugged, not knowing what to say in answer to Beth's question. 'You could wait here until he gets back, he shouldn't be too much longer,' he said helpfully.

Beth shook her head. 'Thanks but I think I'll go home. He might not want me waiting about for him when he gets back.'

'Ok I'll tell him you called in.' Rob turned back to his papers and Beth left quietly closing the door behind her.

***

Tom was frustrated. He had found a ring that Beth loved at a valuation that he could afford but he was unable to get it for her. He tried to put the disappointment out of his mind by working at double speed and when Rob returned after lunch he had almost finished the day's workload.

Rob had had a successful day. He had managed to get the car for a good price and was pleased with his purchase. The two admired the smooth lines of the rusting MGA perched on the long trailer behind Rob's car. Together they unloaded it and rolled it into the garage so that Tom could look it over. Tom loved the restoration side of the business. It gave him enormous pleasure to breathe new life into an old sports car and he forgot about everything else as he lifted the bonnet and began to asses the amount of work needed.

'Tom!' Rob was poking him painfully in the side. 'I've been calling you from the office but you seem oblivious once you get your head under a bonnet.'

'What's so urgent …?'

'You're wanted on the phone.'

'Who?'

'Don't know, didn't say, woman's voice. Now get a move on before she rings off.'

Tom picked up the receiver with a clean piece of rag. 'Hello.'

'Tom I've got Mark here for you from the Banbury auction rooms.' It was Madge's voice at the other end. There was a brief pause then …

'Tom, Mark here. The sale's just ended and I thought I'd let you know the result.'

'Thank you.' Needn't have bothered Tom thought, don't really want to know who bought the ring. But he didn't voice his thoughts.

'That ring you were interested in.'

'Yes.'

'It didn't sell.'

'What?'

'It didn't sell. Didn't reach the reserve price of thirty pounds.'

Tom was not sure of how to respond to this news. 'Oh that's a shame.'

'Not really. I was sorry that you were unable to get to the sale but this is good news for you if you are still interested in the ring.'

Tom's heart did a flip. 'I certainly am interested,' he spoke quickly down the phone.

'I thought you might be, so I took the liberty of speaking to the vendor and he is happy to let you have it for thirty pounds.' There was silence on the line while Tom gathered his thoughts. This was amazing, he couldn't believe his luck. 'Tom?'

'Sorry Mark. That is fantastic. I'll certainly buy it for that price. When can I collect it?'

'You can come now if you want. I'll be here until five, possibly later.'

'Ok. I'll be right over.' Tom replaced the receiver and punched the air. What an unexpected result! He couldn't wait to see Beth's face when he showed her the ring.

***

The magazine was not very inspiring. Beth flipped through the pages barely registering the contents. A pretty face here, a smart dress there, a short story she couldn't be bothered to read and some recipes for food she had no appetite for. With a sigh she tossed it onto the coffee table and, tucking her legs under her, she pulled the electric fire closer and snuggled into the squashy armchair. Where had Tom gone this afternoon and why hadn't he contacted her? Why had Molly behaved so strangely and been so secretive? Should she go round to Tom's and see if he was home yet? Questions without answers chased each other around in her head. If only Tom would call and set her mind at rest. Unable to sit still any longer Beth jumped up and paced the room. Her little basement sitting room that she had been so pleased with, now it suddenly seemed stuffy and confining. There was nothing she could do but stay here and wait for Tom to contact her. Perhaps she should put on a clean sweater and brush her hair, yes that's what she would do.

Beth took the two flights of stairs two at a time, arriving breathless at her bedroom on the top floor. She splashed cold water onto her face, powdered her nose, applied a little light pink lipstick and brushed her titian curls into some semblance of order. It was while she was thus busily occupied that the door bell rang. Normally she ignored the bell and sometimes didn't even hear it when she was in her room but tonight she was attuned to its ring and responded with a headlong dash down the stairs. Before she had reached the hall she could see Prudence had already opened the front door to reveal Tom standing in the porch. Beth stopped half way down the final flight, ready to intervene if her mother decided to turn Tom away.

Tom had changed from his work clothes into slim beige trousers, a cream open-necked shirt and a navy sweater. His ginger curls were still damp from his recent shower and were stuck close to his head. A neatly wrapped bunch of flowers were held loosely in one hand. Beth's stomach tightened as she looked at him and she slowly began to descend the last few stairs.

'Mrs. Burnett I'm Thomas, we met once before. I've come to see Beth, is she in?'

Prudence briefly looked Tom up and down. She noted his smart appearance and particularly his grease-free finger nails. This was a very different boy from the one she had met previously. She smiled and held the door wider open.

'Come in Timothy and I'll fetch Beth for you.'

'Actually my name's Thomas but I prefer to be called Tom.'

Prudence ignored this remark and, seeing Beth coming towards them, she called out. 'Beth, someone to see you and he's brought you some beautiful flowers.'

Tom looked directly at Prudence. 'The flowers aren't for Beth Mrs. Burnett, they're for you.'

Prudence coloured slightly then, regaining her composure, she held out her hands to receive the bouquet. 'How very thoughtful of you … err … Tom, thank you they're lovely.' As Beth reached the door Prudence, her face still pink, turned away towards the kitchen. As soon as the door closed behind her Tom took Beth into his arms and held her close. She looked up at him, their eyes met and the look in his made her pulse quicken.

'I came to find you,' she whispered, 'but you had disappeared and Rob didn't know where you were.'

'I know, I'm sorry, something very important came up and there wasn't time to contact you. Let's go and sit down and I'll tell you all about it.'

She took Tom's hand and led the way down to her sitting room. He settled himself on the sofa and Beth cuddled up next to him.

'Right, now tell me what you've been up to,' she demanded.

'Before I tell you what I've been doing I've got something to ask you.' Tom looked into Beth's expectant eyes.

'Go on,' she nodded.

'Beth … will you marry me?'

The question surprised Beth. Her green eyes opened wide and she smiled. 'Yes Tom I would like nothing better than to marry you … but I thought you already knew that.' She looked puzzled.

Tom gave her shoulders a squeeze. 'I just wanted to hear you say it.' He kissed the tip of her nose. 'And now I've got something to show you.' He reached into his pocket and withdrew his hand, opening it to show a small brown leather covered ring box nestling in his palm.

'Oh Tom, you've bought a ring!' she cried in delight.

Tom could hardly contain his enthusiasm. 'Not just any old ring. Open it.' He held out the box and Beth, picking it up between forefinger and thumb, loosened the tiny gold catch and raised the lid. She gazed from the ring to Tom's face and back to the ring, unable to believe her eyes.

'It's … '

Tom glowed in the surprise and delight that radiated from Beth. 'Yes, it's the ring you really wanted, the one in the auction sale.'

'But how did you manage to get it?' Beth was still in a state of shock.

'I will explain all, but first …' Tom gently removed the ring from its protective box and, taking Beth's hand, he slid it smoothly onto the fourth finger of her left hand. His lips found hers and the little box dropped unnoticed to the floor as they fell into each other's arms.

Some time later Tom explained how he had come by the ring while Beth sat next to him, her hand outstretched. She turned it slowly from side to side to catch the light so that tiny flashes of colour gleamed from the stone. It was the most beautiful thing she had ever owned and all the more so because Tom had given it to her.

Tom cupped her chin in his hand and turned her to face him. 'We need to talk to your parents Beth,' he told her gravely.

'Suppose so.' Beth looked worried. 'I don't care if they say I'm too young. It won't make any difference,' she announced rather belligerently. 'We'll just wait to marry until I'm twenty-one then there will be nothing they can do about it.'

'It shouldn't come to that,' Tom told her quietly, stroking her unruly curls. 'I'll talk to your father. I'm sure if I tackle him carefully there won't be a problem. How do you think your mother will react? She didn't take to me the first time we met'

Beth smiled. 'You've already crossed the first barrier with the flowers, carry on like that and she'll be eating out of your hand. And anyway if Daddy is happy with our engagement then Mum will go along with whatever he says.'

'Good. Let's get it over then.'

Chapter 28

Beth sat uncomfortably in the drawing room making small talk with her mother. She had taken the precaution of slipping the ring into her pocket so that Prudence was not aware of their plans.

'Has Timothy gone then?' Prudence looked enquiringly in Beth's direction.

'If you must call him by his full name its *Thomas* mother but he much prefers to be called Tom,' Beth replied irritably.

Prudence ignored the rebuke. 'You haven't answered my question.'

'No he's still here.'

'Then why isn't he here with us?'

Beth fiddled with the fringe on the edge of a cushion. 'Because he wanted a word with Dad.'

'Oh?' Prudence raised an elegantly arched eyebrow. 'Anything I should know about?'

Oh God, how long am I going to be able to keep this up? Beth thought. Aloud she remarked calmly, 'Something about the car I think, probably to do with the servicing.'

'Of course Thomas is a car mechanic. I'd forgotten.' Beth glowered. She thought it was highly unlikely that her mother had forgotten Tom's occupation. Her mother was apt to categorise people according to the work they did. 'Have you seen anything of that nice young medical student lately Rupert I believe he was called.' Prudence continued blithely.

Beth felt anger rise up. She bit her lip and breathed deeply before replying. 'Mother, I told you, Bear was *not* a nice young man. He was an arrogant liar who had a string of girlfriends and he tried it on with all of them, including me, and I am never going to see him again. Now can we forget about him?'

'Oh my dear, sorry, I must have forgotten …' Prudence's pale cheeks flushed. She swept her hands over her neat chignon, tucking in imaginary stray strands of hair. 'You should have told us Bethany your father would have had strong words with him.'

Beth smiled despite her irritation. 'There was no need for that. Tom dealt with the situation and looked after me.'

'Well I'm very glad someone did.' Prudence leant over and patted Beth's hand. 'You're very young still my dear, you must be careful that people, men in particular, don't take advantage of your inexperience.'

That remark was just what Beth did not want to hear. 'Mother I'm ...' she began but at that moment her father, accompanied by Tom, entered the room.

Prudence looked up cheerfully. 'Have you two had a good chat about the car?' she asked brightly. A puzzled frown crossed Desmond's face and he glanced at Tom for clarification. Tom raised his eyebrows and shrugged slightly.

Beth gave Tom a piercing look and opened her eyes wide. 'I was telling Mother that you had gone to talk to Dad about the car,' she interjected quickly.

Desmond caught on to the situation. 'Oh yes, the car was mentioned, but Tom and I had more important things to discuss.' Prudence looked surprised but did not comment. 'Tom informs me that he and Beth intend to get married and he has asked for our blessing on their engagement.'

Prudence jumped up and brushed the palms of her hands down either side of her skirt. 'Engagement!' she exclaimed, looking from her husband to Beth and back to Desmond. 'But she's so young.' she wrung her hands.

Desmond put a calming arm round his wife's shoulders. 'Beth is over eighteen so age doesn't come into it my dear as you should know,' he told her gently. Prudence coloured slightly and nodded, knowing that Desmond referred to her young age when they were married. 'What does concern us is whether Tom is able to look after Beth properly and,' he paused, 'I am happy that in a year or so, when they plan to wed, he will be able to do so. Tom has a useful trade and together with his admirable ambitions he should do very well. The car industry, in my opinion, is ripe for expansion. I can see the time coming when it will be commonplace for families to own a car and possibly two, so that can only be good for Tom's plans to own a share in a thriving garage.' Desmond paused again and looked fondly at his daughter. 'We are happy for you both to marry when Tom has acquired his share in the garage and we wish you every happiness my dear.'

Beth leapt to her feet and flung her arms round her father. She then kissed her mother and twirled her round the room.

'Oh my goodness,' Prudence exclaimed breathlessly when Beth finally let go of her. 'This is all so sudden.' She looked towards her husband with a smile and he nodded in return.

Tom gave Beth a hug and bent his head to her ear. 'You see I said it would be alright,' he whispered quietly. Beth felt into her pocket and produced the ring. She passed it to Tom and he slipped it quickly onto her finger. She stretched her fingers and held out her hand towards her parents.

'Very nice indeed,' was Desmond's measured reaction.

Prudence was visibly impressed. 'It's beautiful,' she whispered, holding Beth's hand to get a closer look. She looked up at Tom with a new expression in her eyes. 'You chose very well Tom,' she told him with a smile.

'I know I did,' Tom replied giving Beth a squeeze, 'she's the best and most beautiful girl in the world.' It hadn't been quite what Prudence had meant but she smiled and nodded.

Beth gave a deep heartfelt sigh of happiness. 'All we need to do now is to start saving for somewhere to live when we are married.'

Prudence looked startled. 'But you'll live here to start with, you won't be able to afford a home of your own straight away surely,' she exclaimed.

Beth shook her head. 'We want a place of own right

from the start,' she told her firmly. 'We'll find something, even if it's tiny,' she added less positively and a worried frown clouded her eyes.

'She's right,' Desmond said. 'Starting married life with in-laws is not the best idea.'

'But …' Prudence began.

'If you remember when we were married your parents kindly offered to house us here with them but we refused, much as Beth and Tom have refused our offer. We managed to find a place of our own and it was a good decision.'

Prudence thought back to that difficult time at the end of the war and she knew that Desmond was right. They had asserted their independence and had made a cosy little home for themselves. But all the same she was concerned for Beth. The cost of property was going up fast. How were they going to afford anything half decent?

***

Beth woke and stretched lazily. She switched on her bedside light and reached for her ring. Slipping it onto her finger she held it up to the light and admired its simple beauty. How her life had changed in the last few months. First there had been Bear with his shallow lies and callous behaviour. She didn't hate him for it; dealing with him had made her grow up fast. And then there was Tom the big brother and now there was Tom the lover and an engagement to celebrate. Beth threw back the bedclothes, eager to get to work and tell Molly her news and show her the ring.

'Morning Molly.' Beth tied the strings of her apron and smoothed the front of it with her left hand.

'Morning.' Molly replied with a brief glance in Beth's direction before returning to her perusal of the day's orders.

Beth had hoped Molly would notice the ring straight away to save her having to start the conversation. She leant across and took the sheaf of papers from Molly with her left hand. 'Let me deal with those Molly, after all I'll be doing the deliveries.'

'Please yourself.' Molly shrugged and made her way into the shop. A short time later Beth followed with a list of the blooms she needed to make up the first order. She put the list down on the counter next to where Molly was busy organising the till and put her left hand on top of it.

'What's all this then?' Molly remarked without raising her head. 'You want to be careful it don't get rusty with your hands in and out of water when you're conditioning the flowers.'

'Oh Molly you did notice then!'

Molly turned to face Beth with a mischievous smile crinkling the corners of her eyes. 'Course I did m'dear. Just thought a bit of teasing might brighten the morning.' She took hold of Beth's hand. 'Mmm ... done you proud has that young Tom and I'm very happy for the both of you, you're right for each other I can tell.' Beth opened her mouth to speak but Molly looked up sharply. 'And don't you tell me I know nothing about romance my girl. I know a great deal more than you give me credit for.'

'I wasn't going to say anything of the sort,' Beth retorted. 'But Molly you did say ages ago that you would tell me how you know about men and marriage when you're not married yourself.' Beth looked hopefully at Molly who was now busily tidying the containers of flowers.

Molly straightened up. 'As I said before, it's a long story, so now's not the time.' Beth could barely hide her disappointment. 'But if you care to join me for a cuppa after we close the shop I'll enlighten you. Now you'd better start on those orders you were so keen to do, they won't be ready before midnight at this rate.'

***

Beth settled herself in a blue velvet-covered armchair in

Molly's comfortable sitting room and held out her hands to the warm glow from the gas fire set in the cream-painted fireplace.

'I love your flat Molly, it's so comfortable and cosy,' Beth remarked as Molly placed the tea tray on a low table between them.

'You'd better see the rest of it when you've finished your tea, then you can make a proper judgment.'

Beth was surprised. She had been in the kitchen before but Molly had never offered to show her around the rest of the flat and she had not liked to ask. 'I'd love that Molly,' she replied with a smile.

'Drink up then, we haven't got all night, you'll need to get home to your supper before long.'

Beth obediently drained her cup and replaced it quickly on the tray. There was no way she was going to miss a look round Molly's home. She followed Molly out onto the landing and peeped into the kitchen. It was much as she remembered it, a gas cooker, a cream kitchen cabinet, a small table and two chairs with red gingham cushions, and a white pot sink set between wooden draining boards from which hung matching red gingham curtains. It was small but neat and functional.

Molly led the way up a narrow flight of stairs to the rooms at the top of the building. Two bedrooms sat either side of a tiny bathroom. The larger room was obviously Molly's bedroom. The walls were painted a restful pale turquoise and the large brass bed was covered with a beautiful quilt made up from many different fabrics sewn together in an intricate patchwork design. The patches blended together in a harmonious mixture of blues and greens.

When she saw it Beth exclaimed in delight. 'Molly did you make this?'

Molly nodded, a small smile playing across her face. 'Like a bit of sewing,' she replied. This fact became obvious when Beth peered into the small bedroom. There was no bed in this room; instead a table, set with a black and gold Singer sewing machine, took up centre stage with various pieces of fabric piled on chairs and the top of a mahogany chest.

'I didn't know you sewed Molly.' Beth said surprised.

'There's a lot you don't know about me m'dear.' Molly replied darkly.

They retraced their steps and at the bottom of the narrow stairs Molly opened a door next to the kitchen. The size of the room matched that of the small bedroom above. It was sparsely furnished as a dining room. Beth shivered, the room was cold and smelled rather dank.

'Don't get much cause to use this room now, usually eat in the kitchen or have something on a tray.' Molly paused and looked around the room morosely. 'Used to have some jolly times in here, specially when we had friends round for a meal.'

Beth couldn't help noticing the use of "we" as Molly closed the door firmly and led the way back to the warm and cosy sitting room.

Chapter 29

Molly's Story

Beth looked expectantly at Molly as they settled themselves in the comfortable armchairs on either side of the gently hissing gas fire. Molly shifted herself in her chair for a moment or two then linked her hands across her middle and crossed her ankles.

'I had a fiancé once,' she began. Beth leaned forward, her green eyes like saucers, waiting for Molly to elaborate. But Molly closed her eyes and was quite still. Beth was dismayed. Molly couldn't possibly have dropped asleep just as she was about to unfold the secrets of her past, could she? But Beth need not have fretted. Molly opened her eyes and continued. 'George his name was. We lived in the same small town and had known each other since we were children at school together. He was in a higher class than me but we always sought each other out at play times; we loved each other even at that young age.' Molly uncrossed and re-crossed her ankles while Beth sat back in her chair and waited, she knew better than to interrupt. 'Well, we grew up and everyone expected us to marry eventually but then came the Great War. It wasn't *great* at all in my opinion, it was a travesty, but that's all in the past now, doesn't do any good to dwell on what might have been.' Molly sighed deeply. 'George was called up in the summer of nineteen-fifteen, he was just seventeen and I was a year younger. With our parents' blessing we declared our love for each other and got engaged and before we had time to think what was happening George had gone.'

Beth was transfixed. 'What happened then?' she whispered.

Molly scratched her head as if trying to remember the sequence of events. 'I had several letters from him but they never said where he was or what he was doing. Some of what he wrote was blacked out so I presume they were censored. Anyway he seemed cheerful enough and I just hung onto the thought that he would be home soon and then we would get married and start a family. But the wait was longer than anyone expected.' Molly's eyes bore a faraway look. 'Two years later in nineteen-seventeen his letters stopped and then, after a while, another letter arrived. It wasn't from George, it was from the Home Office ... it said that George was missing in action and was presumed dead.'

'Oh no!' Beth leaped from her chair and knelt beside her employer, taking hold of her cold hands. 'Oh Molly ...' she searched for words of comfort and as she looked up at Molly she could see a lifetime of pain in her old eyes.

'Don't you fret yourself m'dear. It was a long time ago and I eventually got over my loss.' Beth knew this was not entirely true, she had seen the distress in Molly's eyes.

'What did you do then?' Beth asked quietly.

'For a while I refused to believe that he was dead. I clung to the words *presumed dead* and thought that he would return one day. I made up all sorts of fantasies about him lying in a hospital in some foreign town, or he had lost his memory and no one knew who he was. But eventually, after several years of deluding myself, I had to face reality and come to terms with the fact that he really was dead.'

'Poor you, it must have been terrible.' Beth's eyes filled with tears of sympathy.

'Don't you upset yourself m'dear, time is a great healer.' Molly patted Beth's hand. 'It was during this time,' she continued, 'that I came to Oxford. There were many young women in the same boat as me, young men were scarce, and so we had to get on with our lives as spinsters. I took a job doing alterations at a men's outfitters here in Oxford and occasionally if a gentleman came in for something simple, like a necktie, I was allowed to serve him. That is how I met John.'

Beth sat up straight. She thought the story had ended but here were more surprising revelations! 'John?' she repeated.

Molly grinned. 'Get's interesting doesn't it? You'd better sit back on your chair it can't be too comfortable down there.' Beth did as she was bid and settled herself expectantly. She wasn't disappointed as Molly continued her tale.

'John was a travelling salesman in menswear. He had his own car and travelled all over the Midlands making regular visits to high-class men's outfitters like the one where I worked. Well, he visited our shop every month and we got to know each other quite well. He would sometimes take me out for lunch if he had the time. To begin with I thought he wasn't my type, he was loud and outspoken, not at all like George, but he was kind and he had a good sense of humour so after about two years of him coming to the shop regularly and taking me out whenever he could, I agreed to marry him. I thought it didn't matter that I didn't love him. Being looked after by a kind and cheerful man was better I thought than living a lonely life as a spinster.'

'And did you marry him?'

Molly nodded slowly. 'Yes we married in the spring of nineteen twenty-four, took on the lease of this flat and lived here reasonably happily for several years.'

'Molly I didn't realise …'

Molly held up her hand. 'I haven't finished yet,' she smiled sadly. What else could there possibly be Beth wondered? She was soon to find out. 'As I said John travelled all over the Midlands which meant that he was away a great deal of the time. It didn't bother me too much, I liked his company when he was at home but I didn't miss it when he was away, I could always find things to busy myself with.'

'And you had your job to go to every day,' Beth broke in.

Molly gave a rueful smile and shook her head. 'In those

days married women were still expected to stay at home and look after their husbands. When I got married to John my service with the shop was ended.'

'How unfair!' Beth cried.

Molly shrugged. 'I didn't mind too much. I had time to make friends and do my sewing and we lived quite well, despite the fact that John was very careful with his money. There was only one regret in my life.'

'What was that?'

'I would have liked a child, particularly a little girl. I could have taught her to read and sew and knit and she would have been a human being to love and who I hoped would love me in return.' Molly blew out her cheeks. 'But it was not to be so ... thank goodness.'

'Thank goodness?' Beth queried, perplexed. 'You said you wanted a child.'

'I did but John was not what he appeared to be. He wouldn't have made a good father.' Beth was even more intrigued. What ever could be coming next? 'One day,' Molly carried on, 'John was grumbling about having a hole in the pocket of his best suit so while he was away working I mended it for him and then I checked all of the other pockets to make sure that was the only hole. I didn't find another hole but I did find a photograph of a young woman holding a baby and with a toddler at her side. When John returned I asked him who they were.' A look of anger passed across Molly's face. 'At first he lied to me and said it was his sister, but I persisted. Who carries a picture of their sister in their inside pocket for goodness sake? And eventually he admitted that the children were his.

'And the woman?' Beth held her breath.

'His wife.'

'His wife ... but he was married to you!'

Molly shook her head.' He was married to her when we met and remained so.'

'So he was a bigamist!' Beth could hardly believe she was hearing this. 'So you reported him to the police?'

Once again Molly shook her head. 'He begged me not to tell and I thought about it and then decided to keep quiet. He would get sent to jail and his wife and children would suffer unnecessarily, what was the point in ruining their lives as well? He was more than grateful when I told him of my decision and put the lease of this place into my name. He left and I never saw him again. Presumably he went back to his wife and she was none the wiser. I told anyone that asked that he had gone off with another woman, which was true in a manner of speaking, and that we had divorced, which wasn't. I kept the Mrs. But reverted to my maiden name of Watson, took a job in a department store and began life all over again as a single divorcee.'

Beth was wide-eyed as Molly finished her story. 'So you never heard from him again?'

'Not from him directly, but a few years later I got a letter from a solicitor telling me that John had left me a considerable sum in his will. I was surprised because he would have been in his late forties then ... young to die. Anyway the solicitor's letter gave no indication as to the cause of his death and I didn't like to ask, so I accepted the money. Goodness knows what his wife thought about him leaving a large sum to some unknown woman but it wasn't my problem. I'd done what I could to keep his secret from her.'

'So you didn't need to work.'

'I didn't need to but I wanted to. It was a difficult time in the thirties for people, the depression had left many without work and those with businesses found themselves in debt and unable to carry on. I was in the fortunate position of having money and I didn't want to see it dwindle away so I negotiated a longer lease on this flat, obtained some nice pieces of furniture, and bought the shop downstairs.'

Beth was enthralled with Molly's tale. 'Go on,' she urged.

'There's not much more to tell. The next war came

quite soon after and that was a hard time for everyone. I survived by opening the shop as a green grocery and I also sold seeds and garden implements, both new and second-hand. Those that had gardens turned them over to vegetables to feed themselves and their families and others got allotments to do the same. When the war finished I started stocking flower seeds and pots of flowering plants; people were desperate for a little colour in their lives once more. Gradually the flowers took over and I stopped selling vegetables, and the rest you know.'

'Molly I never imagined you had such an exciting life!'

'I'm not sure exciting is quite the right word m'dear, extraordinary might be a better one. But there's one more thing before you rush off home for your long overdue supper, please don't breathe a word of this to anyone, not even Tom. I've told you all this because I wanted you to know that it's best never to trust someone like Bear who found it so easy to lie to you. I knew I loved George and I'm pretty sue you feel the same way about Tom, so trust your instincts and grasp happiness when it comes along.'

'I will, and Molly …'

'What?'

'Thank you for sharing it with me. I think you've been very brave and you deserve to be happy too.' Molly's story had taught Beth not to underestimate anyone. Even in the most ordinary of lives she realised, there could be periods of great sadness.

Molly looked thoughtfully at the beautiful red haired girl sitting opposite and her eyes glittered with unshed tears. 'I am happy Beth,' she said gently as she got up from her chair. 'Especially since you came to work for me when you were little more than sixteen. It's been like having the daughter that I longed for.'

Beth stepped forward and put her arms round Molly's thin frame and gave her a hug.

'Molly gently pushed her away. 'That's enough of that m'girl, your mother will be wondering what's become of you and I'm exhausted, never talked so much in all my life, now off home with you.'

Chapter 30

That night a storm blew up and it began to snow. In the morning, when the wind had dropped, the ground was covered with a layer of soft wet snow.

'Goodness me,' Desmond exclaimed, peering through the kitchen window at the white landscape of the garden. 'It's only the beginning of December. Hope we're not in for a snow-bound winter.'

Prudence nodded. 'I'd planned to go up to town today. I really need something new to wear for the Christmas season. I hope the trains are running alright.'

'Shouldn't be a problem,' Desmond told her. 'It's wet snow, should melt fairly soon, probably cause a few delays at worst. I'll phone for a taxi to take you to the station.'

Prudence shot him a grateful look and passed him a plate of bacon and eggs.

Beth breezed into the kitchen, excited as a small child. 'Snow, have you seen it? Lots of lovely snow.'

'I'm not sure how lovely it is,' Desmond grumbled. 'I've got to get to work in that lot and so have you Beth, no riding your bicycle, you'll have to walk.'

Beth was irrepressible. 'I don't mind, it'll be fun.'

After a hasty breakfast she donned wellingtons and her warm duffle coat and pulled a knitted hat well down over her copper curls to cover her ears. Outside the smell of the snow tickled her nose as she crunched her way along the snow-covered footpath. On the spur of the moment she decided to take a short detour via the garage to say hello to Tom.

Tom was already at work on the MGA restoration and greeted her with an oily kiss,

'It's been snowing.' Beth announced unnecessarily.

Tom grinned at her enthusiasm. 'So it has,' he said in mock surprise.

'I was wondering.' Beth ran her fingers through his tight curls and planted a light kiss on his oil-smudged cheek. 'The Flower Basket is likely to be fairly quiet today and anyway it's my half day, so how about we take a walk in the snow this afternoon?'

'Don't see why not.' Tom returned her kiss. 'Two of our booked-in services have cancelled already this morning so, apart from working on the restoration, there's not much on today. An hour off after lunch shouldn't be a problem.'

'Good. Call at the shop at lunch time if you can and we'll take it from there.' Beth gave Tom a hug and, with a cheery wave, she continued on her way to work.

***

After a hurried lunch the two set off at Beth's request for Port Meadow, a stretch of grassland adjoining the Thames and stretching from Oxford, close to Tom's home, to the village of Wolvercote on the outskirts of the city. They crossed the canal and headed for the river's edge on a snow-covered footpath. Beth took Tom's hand and they swung along with Beth chatting non-stop. Tom felt light-headed. It had been a long time since he had allowed himself time off from the daily grind of earning money.

They continued for some time with Beth commenting on any and everything she saw and with Tom enjoying her youthful enthusiasm and thinking how much he loved her. Suddenly Beth released his hand and dived off the path. Picking up a pile of wet snow in her gloves hands, she ran and tossed it at Tom with a whoop of delight. For a moment he was transfixed, as the melting snow trickled down his neck and wetted his shirt, then he was galvanised into action.

'Right, if it's war you want,' he cried, picking up two handfuls of snow and squeezing them into a wicked snowball that he lobbed accurately in Beth's direction. She squealed as the missile reached its target and she was covered in wet snow. The snowball fight continued with shouts and squeals until, wet and tired, they landed up in each other's arms. Tom kissed the tip of Beth's nose and then his lips found hers and they clung together until Beth pulled away.

'Just one more,' she cried as she ran towards the river where the snow was deeper. She bent to gather an armful. Tom was not sure what happened next but he was sure that Beth had disappeared from sight. He ran towards where she had been gathering snow and was concerned to find her half way down the river bank with her legs immersed in the river and gradually slipping further into the icy water.

'I slipped!' she announced.

'That much is obvious. Here take my hand.' A worried Tom braced himself against the snow-covered bank and reached for Beth's outstretched hand. He grasped it firmly and pulled her up the slushy bank. Safely out of the water Beth looked down at her dripping coat and sodden legs and began to laugh.

'I'm wet,' she giggled.

'Come on, let's get you back in the warm before you get pneumonia. My house is the nearest, we'll go there.'

Beth shook her head. 'My house is not much further and I'll need clean clothes, we'll go there.'

Tom acquiesced and, with his arm firmly round Beth he hurried her home.

By the time they reached the house Beth was shivering violently and Tom was worried. He half carried her down to the basement sitting room, put her down on the sofa and switched on the electric fire.

'You need dry things. Where's your mother?' he asked.

'She gone up to London shopping,' Beth replied with chattering teeth.

Tom knew he needed to get Beth warmed up quickly. 'Where can I find dry things for you?'

'Upstairs in my bedroom on the top floor,' she pulled her wet coat closer in an attempt to warm up.

'Right.' Tom raced up the three flights of stairs. He looked around Beth's room. Her clothes were all tidied away and he didn't want to go searching through drawers so he grabbed a warm dressing gown hanging on the back of the door and pulled the eiderdown from her bed. Armed with these he dashed back to the basement, which was now feeling a little warmer.

'Here, get your wet things off,' he ordered, handing Beth the dressing gown and eiderdown. He turned away as Beth obediently shed her sodden clothes and left them in a wet heap on the floor. She wrapped herself in the warm comfort of the fleecy gown and felt better.

'There's some rum over there,' she pointed to a cupboard in the corner.

'Rum!' Tom was surprised.

'Blame your sister,' Beth laughed, 'and please make mine a large one.'

Tom poured the drinks and carried them to the sofa where Beth had wrapped the eiderdown round her shoulders. She still felt a bit shivery and took the drink thankfully. They drank silently for a while.

'Well that didn't end too well,' Beth commented with a smile.

'How are you feeling now?' Tom was still concerned.

'Much better, just a bit cold still.'

Tom put the remains of his drink down and pulled the fire closer. He felt Beth's cold hands clasped around her glass and, taking her glass away, he pulled her closer and wrapped his warm arms around her shivering body. They remained like that for some time then Tom became aware that Beth's dressing gown had loosened and he was conscious that she wore nothing beneath it. He slid a warm hand inside and stroked her firm breasts. Beth moaned and moved even closer. She raised her arms and his hands slid down her torso and felt the round contours of her belly. She moaned again and this time the sound brought Tom to his senses. What was he doing? He had to stop before things went too far. He reluctantly removed his hands and gently pulled Beth's dressing gown around her desirable body.

Beth opened her eyes. 'Tom I don't mind,' she whispered.

'But I do,' Tom replied fiercely. When we make love it won't be because you're vulnerable. That's no way to start our life together. I love you Beth and I'll not compromise that by getting you pregnant.'

'I love you too Tom, more than I can tell you, and I want you to make love to me.'

'Not now, not like this,' Tom moved away from the temptation of her body and stood up. 'We need to talk Beth … it's going to be a while before we can get married, we can't go on like this for months and possibly years, we need to do something.'

Beth looked up at his serious face. 'I'll go on the pill,' she said firmly.

'Only if you really want to.'

Beth nodded. 'It's the safest solution. The surgery holds a family planning clinic, I've seen posters up advertising it, I'll find out when the next one is and see if they'll put me on the pill. They might not, as I'm not married, but if they won't I'll persuade my GP somehow that I need it.'

Tom bent and kissed her forehead. 'Don't rush into it. Think about it carefully and make sure in your mind that you're happy with the idea before you do anything.' He straightened up. 'Better get back to work. Sure you feel ok now?'

'Absolutely fine.' Beth gathered up her wet things. 'I'll go and get dressed. See you tomorrow Tom?'

'Probably better if we leave it until the weekend. There's a lot on at work at the moment.' Tom kissed her lips and quickly left the room.

Beth watched his retreating back with a troubled frown. She thought the garage wasn't very busy at the moment.

***

Prudence paid off the taxi and gathered up the bags

containing the spoils of her shopping trip. Seeing the light shining out from the basement, she decided to show her purchases to Beth straight away.

Beth turned at the delicate tap on her door. 'You've had your hair cut!' she exclaimed. 'It's lovely, makes you look ten years younger.'

Prudence flushed, pleased at Beth's reaction, and putting down her shopping she lightly touched her new shorter style that curled gently round her face. 'Well I thought I might as well while I was up in town. But what do you mean ten years younger? You must have thought I looked ancient before,' she said jokingly.

'Mum, you know I didn't mean that. Now let's see what you've been buying.'

Prudence needed no more encouragement and the contents of the carrier bags were soon spread out across Beth's sofa. Prudence paraded up and down the room holding first one garment then another to her chest. There was a long sapphire-blue gown for the Rotary club dinner dance and, Beth's favourite, a short black cocktail dress for Desmond's office Christmas party.

'We ought to get you something new to wear you know your father likes family members to join the party.'

Beth grinned. 'So long as it's bright pink,' she laughed.

'But my dear, your hair! It won't …' Prudence's hand flew to her mouth. 'There I go again treating you like a child. Pink it will be then.'

They collected up the dresses and Beth helped her mother carry them upstairs to her bedroom where she sat on the satin-covered bedspread and chatted while Prudence carefully hung up the new clothes. Closing the wardrobe door, Prudence briefly contemplated her daughter in the full-length mirror before sitting beside her on the bed.

'Bethany … the other day … when you brought Thomas to see us and told us you and he were engaged …'

'Tom,' Beth automatically corrected her.

'I'm afraid I might have been a little less than welcoming to … Tom. Your engagement was such a surprise, I wasn't expecting it. But now your father has told me what a hard working and ambitious young man he is and I just want to say that I'm very pleased for you both and I think he'll make you a good husband.' Beth was overcome. She brushed away a happy tear and hugged her mother. 'There's only one thing that bothers me.' Prudence held Beth at arm's length. What's coming now? Beth thought, worried. 'Where will you find somewhere to live that you can afford? Desmond tells me that Ben refused his offer of help with a loan. It's admirable that he wants to provide for you by himself but how will you manage?'

Beth knew her mother had a valid point and a frown creased her forehead. 'At the moment Mum I don't know when or where we'll be able to get a place but there's lots of time yet before we can get married, something will turn up,' she added more bravely than she felt. 'You and Dad managed it after all.'

'I suppose we were in a similar situation,' Prudence admitted.

I didn't know you lived in a flat when you were first married. I don't remember it and I always presumed you lived here with Grandma and Granddad. Why didn't you tell me?'

'There didn't seem any point. You were barely three years old when we moved in here, too young to be bothered with where you had lived before.'

Beth rested her clasped hands on her chin. 'Mum, can I ask you something?'

'Of course.'

'Why do you never talk about the past, when I was a baby for instance?'

Prudence looked startled. 'I don't know,' she admitted after a pause. 'I probably thought you wouldn't be interested.'

'Of course I'm interested.'

'What did you want to know?'

'Why didn't I have any brothers or sisters, didn't you

want any more children?'

Prudence felt flustered at Beth's outspoken question. She didn't know how to reply but Beth was staring at her waiting for an answer. 'You were all I needed, one beautiful little daughter,' she said at last.

'I wasn't that beautiful I had, and still have, a foul temper.'

'It wasn't that bad,' Prudence assured her, 'and in all other ways you were delightful.'

'All the more reason to have another delightful child,' Beth persisted.

Prudence felt cornered. What should she tell Beth? Finally she made up her mind. 'There was another reason.' The words were so quiet that Beth had to move closer to hear what her mother said. She waited expectantly. 'Your birth was difficult and ... frightening. You were born before your due date and it all came as a shock. I hadn't expected to go into labour and things happened so quickly I was terrified.'

'Is that why I was born at a Catholic nursing home?'

'How do you know that?' Prudence said, taken aback.

'It was on my birth certificate.'

'Oh yes, it would have been.' Prudence took a deep breath, determined now to finish what she had started. 'When you were safely delivered I decided I couldn't go through that trauma again.'

'Why haven't you told me about this before?'

'Because, my dear, I hoped one day you would have children and I didn't want to put you off or frighten you by telling you about my ordeal.'

'It wouldn't do that,' Beth assured her. 'I'm much bigger than you, I'll probably have no trouble at all giving birth.'

Spoken with the optimism of youth, Prudence thought, but she did not voice her thoughts. She smiled encouragingly, 'of course you won't,' she agreed.

'Tell me about it,' Beth pleaded. 'I really want to know how I came into this world. I don't mind if it is frightening, I want to know.' She covered her mother's cold hand with hers. 'Sharing it will bring us closer and one day I hope I'll be able to share my children's births with you.'

Prudence was touched by Beth's passion. 'Right ... it's cold up here, let's go downstairs and make a cup of tea and then I'll tell what I can remember.'

Chapter 31

Prudence's story

Prudence was tired. Nearly eight months pregnant and she was very, very tired. A whole month or more to go! The flat was claustrophobic. She wanted space to walk about but she didn't have the energy to go outside. She had knitted baby clothes until her hands were tired of holding the needles. She wanted something different to do, something exciting. But there was nothing, just interminable waiting.

Desmond was worried about her. He could see her discomfort and the impatience in her eyes. 'Why don't we visit Paul and Jane on Saturday,' he suggested. 'They're not far away at Kennington and they're always asking us over for a meal.'

Prudence shook her head. 'Don't feel like eating, still feel sick at times.'

'Well you don't have to eat much, Jane will understand. It will do you good to get dressed up and have a change of scene.'

Prudence gave a hollow laugh. 'And what do you suggest I get dressed up in?' she snapped. 'This old smock is the only thing I can get into and I look like a sack of potatoes in it.'

Desmond tried again. 'You have never looked more beautiful my darling,' he told her, putting his arms around her and stroking the burgeoning bump that was their baby.

'You're just saying that to satisfy me,' Prudence replied petulantly.

'Yes,' Desmond sighed, 'but I mean it.'

After two more days of total boredom and Desmond's gentle persuasion, Prudence agreed to visit Paul and Jane. Having received a delighted reply to their request, they boarded the bus for Kennington and twenty minutes later they alighted close to their friends' small red-brick house.

Despite her misgivings, Prudence enjoyed the change of scene and it was good to have Jane to chat to. It was while she was taking a gentle stroll round their small garden and admiring the flower borders and vegetable plot, that she felt a tightening in her abdomen. After her initial shock she regained her composure. "Branson Hicks contraction" she told herself. The midwife at the clinic had told her to expect these mild contractions during the final few weeks. As the afternoon wore on the mild contractions were repeated several times and Prudence thought they were getting slightly stronger. She began to wish she had remained at home, but they had come for dinner and Desmond was relaxed and obviously enjoying himself so she didn't want to make a fuss. Jane had gone to a lot of trouble to make a chicken casserole and a special trifle for pudding. Prudence managed to eat a little casserole, although she had no appetite, but felt quite sick after a small helping of trifle.

After dinner Desmond and Paul went into the garden to enjoy a cigar and Jane settled Prudence into a comfortable armchair while she cleared away the dishes. While Jane was in the kitchen Prudence felt another contraction coming on. This time it built slowly and painfully and she had to dig her fingers into the arms of the chair until it had passed.

'My goodness you look pale.' Jane returned and laid a cool hand on Prudence's forehead. 'Are you feeling alright?'

Prudence shook her head. 'I feel a bit sick and I've been having Branson Hicks contractions all afternoon,' she admitted tearfully.

'Are you sure they're not the real thing?' Jane looked worried.

'Quite sure, the baby's not due for another month yet.'

'All the same I think Desmond should take you home, you look worn out, and I shouldn't like you to give birth here.'

Prudence attempted a smile. 'No chance of that,' she

assured her friend as Jane hurried off to get Desmond.

Desmond took one look at Prudence's pallor. 'I need to get a taxi,' he announced. 'Where's your telephone?'

Paul scratched his head. 'We don't have one,' he admitted but there's a phone box about ten minutes walk away.

'That is if it hasn't been vandalised again,' Jane put in with a worried frown.

'Please stop fussing all of you. There's a bus due soon it'll be quicker to get that.' Prudence held onto the edge of the table as another contraction took her breath away.'

Paul looked worried. 'Ambulance?' he mouthed at Desmond.

Prudence caught sight of the message. 'I do *not* need an ambulance,' she asserted vehemently. 'I just need to get home. Now will someone get my coat before we miss the bus and have to stay the night here!' The three exchanged glances. Prudence was usually so polite they were quite shocked at her outburst.

On the bus Prudence had another strong contraction. She held her distended stomach and tried to breathe normally.

Desmond put his arm round her but she shrugged it off. 'Everything alright love?'

She nodded. 'Bad indigestion, must have been that chicken casserole, Jane's not much of a cook.' Desmond was surprised; he had always enjoyed Jane's cooking and the diner hadn't given him stomach ache.

Five minutes later a pain came that made Prudence cry out.

When it had passed Desmond looked her in the eye. 'How long have you been having these pains?' he asked urgently.

'All afternoon but they're just Branson Hicks,' she insisted.

'I don't think so. I think you're in labour.' Desmond ran a hand through his hair.

'And what would you know about it?' Prudence asked

nastily.

'More than you think.' Desmond stared hard at his wife. 'Do you think you can get home?'

Prudence was saved having to answer his question by the onset of another strong contraction. By the time it was over she was convinced that Desmond was right. 'I'm scared,' she whimpered.

'It's alright, we're nearly home.'

The bus pulled up in Oxford to let passengers get off and Desmond ran forward to speak to the driver. 'My wife's gone into labour,' he breathed, 'and I need to phone for an ambulance.'

The driver looked dismayed. 'There's a call box near the next stop. I could drop you off there.' He started up the bus and they moved forward.

'I don't want to be dropped off anywhere. I want you to wait while I phone for an ambulance and then stay until it arrives.' Desmond was adamant.

'Sorry mate, no can do. I've got to get this bus back to the depot before nine, otherwise I'm for the chop.'

'But you can't leave us on the street. My wife might give birth at any moment!' Desmond was distraught.

'Look mate, babies don't come that quickly, they take their time. I've got six nippers at home, I should know.' The driver pulled up and pointed to a phone box a few yards down the road. 'There's a bench in front of the catholic church where your missus can sit while you're phoning,' he said firmly.

Desmond helped Prudence to the bench and sat with her until the next contraction passed then ran to the phone box. He quickly emerged from the kiosk and looked around frantically, before returning to Prudence's side.

'What's the matter?' she groaned as another pain had her in its grasp.

'The phone's out of order. Can you wait here while I run to find another one?'

Prudence nodded. 'But please be quick,' she implored.

'Is anything the matter? Can I help?' A quiet voice

spoke behind them. They turned to see a nun in a blue habit approaching along the path from the church.

'It's my wife, she's expecting a baby.' Desmond's voice sounded loud in the quiet street.

'I can see that, how often are her contractions coming?'

'About every five minutes,' Desmond replied urgently, 'I tried to phone for an ambulance but the phone's out of order.'

'I'm a midwife,' the nun told him soothingly. 'I work at St. Mary's maternity home just a few minutes walk from here.' Prudence gave another deep groan and grasped the edge of the seat as another contraction wracked her body. The nun took hold or Prudence's hands and urged her quietly to breathe through the pain. When Prudence finally relaxed the nun looked at Desmond, concern in her eyes. 'I think the best plan is to get your wife to St. Mary's. It's only a few minutes from here and once there you can telephone while I look after her.'

'Thank you so much.' Desmond was more than relieved that someone responsible was taking charge of the situation. 'I'm Desmond Burnett,' he told her thankfully.

'I'm sister Angelica,' she responded as she lifted Prudence to her feet and with Desmond's help the three crossed the road. They made their way slowly down a side street, supporting Prudence between them.

After a short while Prudence stopped. 'Oh God!' she exclaimed, as she felt warm liquid soaking her legs.

'Her waters have broken,' Sister Angelica told Desmond. 'Wait here. We're nearly there. I'll run on and get a wheelchair.'

In a flurry of robes the sister disappeared into the darkness and Desmond was left alone on the deserted street with his wife who was about to give birth. Prudence cried out and Desmond gathered her up in his arms and struggled forward towards the forbidding grey walls of St. Mary's maternity home. As he entered through the tall iron gates he was met by sister Angelica pushing a rattling wheelchair.

Inside the building all was quiet. Hushed carbolic-odoured corridors led off to left and right. Without warning a long agonised cry broke the silence. Prudence gripped the arms of the wheelchair and looked up at Desmond with anguish and he felt the hairs rise on the back of his neck. A nurse hurried towards them.

'This is the woman I told you about,' Sister Angelica told her as she skilfully turned the wheelchair and set off towards a pair of swing doors. 'Please wait here Mr. Burnett,' she called over her shoulder. 'There's no time to call an ambulance, but don't worry, your wife is in good hands, we'll take care of her.'

Two hours later Prudence lay in a fresh bed in a small side room. Sister Angelica took her temperature and, at the same time, smoothed her hair from her forehead. 'You have a beautiful wee daughter,' she told Prudence. But you've had a difficult time and need to sleep now. The other mothers on the ward have been settled down for the night so you'll stay here in this side room tonight and we'll move you onto the ward tomorrow. She removed the thermometer from Prudence's mouth. 'What do I call you while you are staying with us,' she asked brightly.

'Prudence.'

The sister's cheerful face fell. 'That's a very … puritan … name,' she commented. 'Do you have another name?'

'My second name's Mary,' Prudence told her tiredly.

'That's wonderful! Do you mind if I call you Mary?'

Prudence shook her head. She didn't mind what the sister called her so long as she let her sleep.

'I'll bring the wee one in to say goodnight to you shortly, in the meantime your husband is here.' Sister Angelica left in a rustle of her stiff white cotton pinafore.

When Desmond had been dispatched with instructions to bring Prudence all the things she needed in the morning, she closed her eyes. The memories of the final stages of her labour were hazy. Pain, bright lights, loud voices urging her on, and yet more pain, merged together in her tired mind. She heard the first cry of her child, like the mew of a frightened kitten, before they took her away to be cleaned, weighed and dressed. She stretched in the crisp stiff sheets and was glad it was all over at last ; now she could sleep. Her eyelids closed.

Prudence didn't know how long she slept, it could have been minutes or hours, but she did know that she had been aroused by people entering the room. A ward orderly bumped the door open with her bottom as she entered backwards, pulling a wheelchair in which sat a fair-haired young woman wearing a hospital gown.

'This is Elisabeth,' Sister Angelica informed Prudence as she helped the fair woman into the only other bed in the room. 'She's had a little girl too and will be joining you in here for tonight. The two of you should get a better night's sleep away from the snoring of the other mothers on the ward,' she told them with a laugh. She turned to the fair-haired young woman in the other bed. 'This is Mary,' she told her, pointing to Prudence. 'Now aren't I the luckiest to have a Mary and an Elisabeth in my care, just like our mother Mary and her sister Elisabeth in the holy bible,' she announced happily. Prudence gave a wry smile. The only difference being, she thought, was that one had a virgin birth and they both gave birth to boys, but she hadn't the energy to argue, and what did it matter anyway if it made Sister Angelica happy?

'I'll be back in a jiffy with your wee babes,' Sister Angelica told them merrily, ushering the ward orderly and the wheelchair out of the room in front of her. True to her word Sister Angelica returned with two identically swaddled babies, one in the crook of each arm. 'Here are your lovely girls,' she told them, handing each a baby tightly wrapped in a white hospital baby blanket. 'Now I'll leave you for a few minutes to have a little chat then I'll be back to take the wee ones to the nursery for the night so that you mothers can get a good night's sleep after all your hard work.'

Prudence gazed at the tiny form in her arms. A little creased face with closed eyes was the only part that could be seen among the folds of the swaddling blanket. Prudence loosened the tight layers and slipped her hand inside until she felt a minute hand. She stroked it and the tiny fingers fastened round her forefinger with a limpet-like grip. Elisabeth grinned at her from the next bed. 'Nothing like a newborn is there?' she commented.

'I'm not sure. This is my first,' Prudence replied. 'Have you other children?'

'Yes a boy and a girl, this little one is my third.'

'Goodness, you've been through this three times?' Prudence exclaimed.

'It's not so bad. This time was the worst, I must admit, but nature has a way of fading the bad bits quite quickly and when you look at the miracle of a healthy child it all seem worth while somehow.' Elisabeth stroked the tiny face in her arms and kissed the little button nose. The two young women chatted for a while until Sister Angelica breezed into the room and scooped up the two tightly wrapped bundles. 'Come on girls,' she crooned,' it's time your mums had a nice sleep.' At the door she wished Elisabeth and "Mary" goodnight and, putting out the light with her elbow, she left them to the only full night's sleep they were likely to get for some months.

Once again Prudence was disturbed by activity in the room. She opened her eyes and turned slowly onto her side. Elisabeth was being helped out of bed and into a dressing gown by Sister Angelica and another nurse. They each took hold of an arm and hurried the sleep-dazed woman from the dim room and out into the brightly lit corridor. Prudence was worried. She hoped Elisabeth was alright. She tossed and turned for what seemed like hours but Elisabeth did not return. Eventually Prudence fell into a fitful sleep from which she was awakened by a nurse carrying a tray containing a cup of tea and a bowl of steaming porridge.

'Good morning Mrs. Burnett,' the nurse said solemnly. 'When you've had your breakfast I'll help you move onto the ward.'

'Where's Sister Angelica?' Prudence asked the nurse.

'Gone home to sleep I should think, she's been on duty all night.'

'Oh.' Prudence sipped her tea. 'Where's Elisabeth?' she asked indicating the empty bed next to her.

The nurse looked away. 'Nothing to worry your head about,' she replied.

Prudence was angry at the nurse's abrupt reply. 'But I am worried,' she said. 'She seemed perfectly alright last night and we were both due to be moved onto the ward today.' The nurse gave Prudence a sidelong glance. 'I'll see what I can find out,' she said grudgingly as she left the room. But some time later the nurse had not reappeared and an auxiliary nurse came to escort Prudence to the ward. Prudence asked her about Elisabeth but she only shook her head and said nothing.

On the ward five other mothers were chatting, feeding their babies and changing nappies. Prudence felt overwhelmed with the hum of activity. Her baby was brought in and the Moses basket was placed next to her bed. She leaned over and gingerly picked up the swaddled bundle. This morning the face seemed less creased and as Prudence watched the eyes opened and a pair of dark blue-green eyes regarded her solemnly. Prudence was captivated.

At the end of the day Prudence took her baby to the nursery to settle her down for the night. In a corner of the room Sister Angelica was talking ardently to a white-coated doctor. When he left Prudence hurried across to the sister's side.

'Sister, where is Elisabeth?' she asked urgently. 'She left during the night and no one will tell me where she's gone.'

Sister Angelica looked sadly at Prudence. 'I shouldn't really be telling you about another patient,' she said quietly, 'but I can see that you are upset by her sudden departure.' She dropped her voice. 'Elisabeth's baby turned blue in the night. We were extremely worried so we fetched Elisabeth quickly so that she could be with her child.' Sister Angelica paused and Prudence could see from the expression on her face that the nun was reliving the happenings of the night. She took a breath and continued. 'The wee soul was so poorly we sent for the priest and he christened her before the ambulance came to take mother and baby to the hospital.'

'Do you know what happened?' Prudence held her breath.

Sister Angelica put a restraining hand on Prudence's arm. 'Please don't breathe a word of this, I shouldn't be telling you really, but you and Elisabeth did share a room and seemed to be getting along well.' Prudence nodded on both counts. 'The doctor has just told me that the poor wee girl joined the angels before they reached the hospital.'

'Oh no!' Prudence felt her eyes fill with tears. 'Poor Elisabeth.'

'There's one consolation,' the sister smiled gently. 'She has the joy of two other children.'

Prudence nodded sadly. 'Could you tell me where she lives. I'd like to send her some flowers and a note?'

'I'm sorry,' Sister Angelica shook her head. 'I'm not allowed to give out patients' addresses.' She glanced round to make sure they were not overheard. 'But if you get your husband to bring in some flowers I'll see that she gets them.'

'Thank you,' Prudence turned away. 'What did they christen the baby?' she asked over her shoulder.

'Angelica.' The sister's face was filled with pleasure.

Beth put her cup of tea down on the low table. She had been so engrossed in her mother's story that she had forgotten to drink it and now it was cold.

Her green eyes were saucer-wide as she squeezed her mother's hand. 'You poor thing, I'm sorry you had such an awful time having me.'

Prudence felt guilty. 'It really wasn't that bad and

having you at the end of it made it all worthwhile, and things have improved enormously for mothers since then,' she added.

Beth nodded. 'It was so sad, about Elisabeth's baby I mean, dying like that.'

'Yes. I never saw her again. I often wondered how she got on and whether she had any more children since.'

Beth looked at her mother oddly and shook her head. 'She didn't have any more and she grieved for that baby for a long time.'

Prudence looked up startled.' Don't be silly Bethany, how could you possibly know that?'

'Because ... from what you have told me I am absolutely sure that your Elisabeth is Tom's mother.' Prudence's lips parted and she stared at her daughter. 'She calls herself Elsie but she told me that her real name is Elisabeth and she also told me that she had a baby called Angelica in St. Mary's on the same day I was born. The baby died and is buried at St. Luke's's just down the road from here. So you see it has to be true. The dates fit, the place is the same and Angelica is an unusual name.'

'Goodness me ...' Prudence could hardly take in what Bethany was saying. 'All these years and she lives a short walk from here!'

'And now you can visit her and get to know her properly,' Bethany added happily.

Prudence looked stricken. 'Maybe that's not such a good idea after such a long time,' she said, twisting her hands in her lap. 'It's nineteen years ago and we hardly knew each other.'

'But Mum, you have to meet her. When Tom and I marry she'll be my mother-in-law. You two will have to see each other then and I hope you'll become friends.' Beth blurted out, upset at her mother's obvious reluctance to get to know Elsie.

'I don't expect she even remembers me. It would be embarrassing to bring up what happened in the past only to find she had no recollection of our meeting.'

'Well you will have to meet her eventually and I'm sure she'll remember you.'

'Maybe, we'll see, it's a long way off … Now let's forget about the past and think about the future.' Prudence returned to her usual brisk self. 'Would you and Tom like a party to celebrate your engagement? It's already December so I thought it might be quite nice to have a family get together near Christmas.'

'I suppose so. I hadn't really thought about it.' Beth couldn't take her mind off the story her mother had unfolded.

'Well I'd like you to think about it now and let me know soon what you would like to do so that I can prepare things in good time.' Prudence stood up and glanced at the tiny gold watch on her wrist. 'Goodness, look at the time, I'd better get on with the dinner your father will be home in no time.' She left carrying the tea cups and Beth remained on the sofa deep in thought.

Beth stared unseeingly at the pictures on the wall facing her but it was the pictures in her mind that troubled her at this moment. She carefully revisited the incidents that her mother had described and then went over them several times more.

Something bothered her but she could not quite pin point what it was that disturbed her. She imagined the midwife carrying two identically swaddled babies into her mother's room in the nursing home and the two mothers holding their babies for the first time. She pictured Sister Angelica collecting them and having to put out the light with her elbow because both arms held an infant. Back in the nursery she would have had to give one baby to a nurse to hold while she put the other in its cot. The second baby would have then been lowered into its cot … its cot … its cot? The two small words repeated themselves several times until a terrible thought entered Beth's mind. An idea that, if true, could ruin her life. Her head pounded and her heart beat so loudly she could hear its drumming.

Chapter 32

At dinner Beth picked at her food.

Prudence turned from describing her day to Desmond and regarded her silent daughter. 'My dear you haven't eaten anything and you're looking rather pale. Are you feeling alright?'

Beth nodded unhappily and put down her knife and fork. 'I do feel shivery,' she told them. 'I fell over in the snow this afternoon and got very wet. I think I might have caught a chill. If you don't mind I think I'll have an early night.'

'My dear, why didn't you tell me?' Prudence was concerned. 'Of course you should go to bed and when I've cleared away I'll bring you a hot water bottle and an aspirin.'

Desmond nodded his agreement and resumed his meal. As Beth pushed back her chair she looked at Prudence across the table. 'Mum, when I was born did I have one of those bands round my wrist with my details on, like the one you had when you were in the infirmary after your fall?'

Prudence shook her head. 'They weren't around then, but your cot was labelled with your name. Why do you ask?'

Beth shrugged. 'Just thought it might be nice to keep it if I had one.' She quietly left the dining room and trudged up the stairs to the quiet sanctuary of her bedroom.

***

Next morning Beth dressed automatically and stared out at the damp grey day. The snow had melted leaving only small mud-splattered patches as a reminder of yesterday's brightness. Beth sighed, she wished she could turn the clock back twenty-four hours, but she knew that was impossible. She would have to deal with the events that now threatened to overwhelm her.

She badly needed someone to talk things over with. Her mother? That would only complicate things. Tom? Impossible. The thought of telling Tom about the idea that was making her head reel brought tears to her eyes and a sob built up in her chest that felt like an immoveable boulder. Elsie? She was just beginning to come to terms with the death of her baby. Raking over the past would be cruel.

Downstairs Beth managed to swallow a piece of toast and a cup of tea, despite the huge lump in her throat that threatened to choke her with every mouthful.

'Don't you think you should stay in bed today?' Prudence asked, noting Beth's pale face and black smudges under her eyes. Beth shook her head and switched on a wan smile, 'I'll be fine, I'm feeling a bit better this morning,' she lied.

At The Flower Basket Beth worked mechanically, serving customers with a pasted-on smile and quietly helping Molly in the workroom when the shop was empty. The morning dragged slowly until at last lunch time arrived. Beth unwrapped her unappetising sandwiches and helped herself to a glass of water. She and Molly both looked up as a knock at the back door rang through the workroom. 'I'll go.' Beth was glad of any small occurrence to break up the interminable length of the day. But what met her eyes when she opened the door did nothing to relieve her mood. Tom stood there smiling.

'Hi darling. Can't stay, just popped round quickly to see how you were after yesterday and to ask if you would like to go for a drink after work.'

Beth stared silently, trying to collect her thoughts. 'I'm ok,' she said at last, 'but I think I've got a bit of a chill so I'll go straight home after work if you don't mind.'

''Course not, sensible thing to do. I'll call tomorrow and see how you are.' Tom bent to place a kiss on Beth's upturned lips but she turned her head quickly and it landed on her ear.

'Ok see you,' she nodded and quietly closed the door. The tears she had been holding back trickled down her cheeks. She scrubbed at them with a damp tissue and returned miserably to her lunch in the work room. Molly had already finished and was busily making a pot of tea. She poured out two cups, sugared them both liberally and pushed one across the table towards a silent Beth.

'You going to tell me what's up? Or is this place going to resemble a morgue for the rest of the week?'

Beth stared at Molly as though she was seeing her for the first time, and then the tears began in earnest. They poured down her cheeks and dripped off the end of her nose and were accompanied by sobs that began life deep down in her chest.

'M'dear I didn't mean to upset you.' Molly was distraught. 'Here.' She pushed the tea nearer to Beth. When that was ignored she resorted to patting Beth's back as though she was comforting a windy baby. The sobs slowly subsided and were replaced by hiccoughs. Beth twisted half a dozen drenched tissues into a tight ball and spasmodically dabbed her eyes. Molly ceased her patting and sat down. 'Now what was that all about?' she asked kindly. 'It must be something terrible to make a cheerful girl like you cry like that.' She looked at the beautiful girl beside her, whose head was bent and shoulders sagged in abject misery, and Molly was worried. Beth sometimes got in a stew about things that weren't going right and sometimes got downright angry, but this was completely out of character.

Beth gave her red-rimmed eyes another rub with the ball of tissues. 'You're right it is something terrible,' she whispered between hiccoughs, 'and I can't tell you.'

'Well it's obvious to me that you need to talk to someone what about your mother?'

'She's the last person I can tell,' Beth replied miserably.

'Tom then. You're going to get married so there should

be no secrets between you.'

A cry escaped Beth's lips. 'I can't possibly tell Tom.' She rubbed her temples with her finger tips.

'Is it something to do with him then?' Molly gently probed.

Beth nodded. 'I can't marry him now,' she whispered and put her head down onto her arms on the work bench.

Molly was astounded. What on earth had brought this state of affairs about? It was obvious that Beth needed help, but how was she going to get the girl to talk? She rested a hand on Beth's arm. 'This really is a pickle and no mistake,' she said gently. 'If that is the case you're going to have to talk to him.'

Beth raised her head. 'I don't know how to tell him,' she wailed.

'Beth, I've been through some difficult times as you know and I might be able to help, please let me, whatever you tell me will go no further than these four walls.'

Beth rested her heavy head on her hand and regarded Molly forlornly. She knew she could not go on like this, she needed to share her misery, and who better than Molly to share it with? She straightened up and took a deep breath. 'I do need to tell someone what I've found out otherwise I think I'll go mad, but you mustn't tell anyone.'

Molly gave her arm a squeeze. 'You can rely on me m'dear. Now, it's almost time to open up for the afternoon so what I suggest is that I serve in the shop, we don't want customers seeing you looking as though you've the cares of the world on your shoulders, not to mention having puffy eyes and a red nose, and you get some fresh air. There's three deliveries to make and being busy will keep your mind off your troubles.' Beth gave her eyes a final wipe and managed a watery smile. Molly's down to earth approach was infectious and the thought of sharing her worries with her made her feel marginally better. Her heart was still heavy but perhaps Molly could, by some unimaginable means, help to solve her predicament? 'We'll shut the shop promptly at five then I'll make tea and we can talk in the peace and quiet of the flat.' Molly bustled away to answer the ring of the shop bell.

Beth nodded her agreement to this plan and went to load the van with the beautiful bouquets they had made earlier.

***

Beth curled up in her favourite chair and listened to the comforting sounds of Molly making tea in the kitchen.

Molly put down a tray laden with tea and a rich fruit cake. She poured tea for them both and placed a large slice of cake in front of Beth. She sat in the chair opposite, folded her hands across her stomach and looked at Beth. 'Now m'dear it's high time you shared whatever is worrying you so much.'

Beth crumbled the cake and ate some of the fruit. Looking up at Molly's kind face she began. 'Molly you remember me telling you that I was worried about being the only person in my family with red hair and I had the silly idea that I was adopted?'

Molly nodded. 'But I thought you sorted that out.'

'I did. I looked at my birth certificate and my parents were on there so there was no way I was adopted.'

'So?'

'Well I decided that I must have inherited my hair from some distant relative so I wrote to Great Aunt Edith, whom my father thought might possibly have auburn hair like mine. Anyway I didn't get a reply and then I met Tom and when I fell in love with him nothing else seemed to matter so I put it out of my mind … until now.'

'What's so special about now?'

Beth broke more pieces of cake into crumbs and pushed them around her plate. She breathed deeply before replying. 'When I was born I believe I was given to the wrong mother!'

There was silence in the room, apart from the brass clock on the mantelpiece that noisily ticked away the seconds.

'That is ridiculous!' Molly exploded. 'You're flying into the realms of fantasy m'dear. Things like that don't happen any more.'

Beth regarded her angrily. 'That's just the reaction I expected. That's why I can't tell anyone,' she cried. 'No one will believe me.'

'What proof do you have?' Molly was calmer now.

'None, but the circumstances surrounding my birth and that of another baby are so compelling that I'm convinced that we were swapped.' The look of utter misery on Beth's face moved Molly.

'Why can't you share this with Tom? He strikes me as being a kind and sympathetic boy. I'm sure he wouldn't dismiss your fears out of hand.'

'Because if it's true …' Beth swallowed … 'he's my brother.'

A look of horror spread across Molly's face. 'You'd better tell me all about it,' she said.

So Beth recounted how Prudence and Elsie had ended up in the same maternity home and had given birth at the same time. She described how Sister Angelica had carried both babies, each wrapped identically, into the room and given them to the mothers. 'She could have given them to the wrong mother then,' Beth explained, 'or, when she took them back to the nursery that night, she could easily have put them into the wrong cots.'

'That's highly unlikely.' Molly endeavoured to calm Beth's fears. 'She was an experienced midwife, used to dealing with newborn babies.'

Beth continued. 'My mother said that the babies were tightly swaddled. Only their faces were peeping out from the covers and they were both sleeping so differences in their eyes would not have been apparent. Also the babies didn't wear wrist bands with their names on, the nurses relied on their cots being labelled. But what if they were put in the wrong cot?'

'M'dear this is a problem that you've dreamed up.

There's no proof that the midwife muddled up the two babies, it's highly unlikely, as I said before.'

Beth was unconvinced. 'Then there's the added proof of my red hair,' she went on. 'Tom and his father both have ginger hair and they're both tall like me, unlike the members of my family, and … I feel happy and at home when I'm with them. I feel I belong with Tom's family more than I do with my parents.'

Molly was extremely bothered. Beth had made a good case for having been swapped at birth and, much as she didn't want to believe it, the story rang true, particularly with the added fact that Beth strongly resembled Elsie's husband and son and looked nothing like her own parents. But she was not going to let Beth know how she felt. 'Beth, I think your mother's story has upset you more than you think and you're seeing more in it than there is. You have no proof at all that anything untoward happened at that maternity home.'

'But I can't be sure can I? And what if it is true, how can I go ahead and marry Tom with the possibility that he's my brother? It just can't happen.'

Molly acknowledged that Beth had a point. The whole matter needed clearing up once and for all.

'But how am I going to do that?' Beth wailed. 'Elsie is convinced that the baby that died was hers and my mother happily accepted the baby that was given to her. But what if she realised I was not her baby and said nothing? She told me she didn't want to go through the trauma of giving birth a second time so there was no chance of her having another child and she knew that Elsie already had two other children. What if she decided to keep the wrong child?'

'I don't know your mother very well but she doesn't strike me as the sort of person to do a thing like that.'

'Then why is she so reluctant to meet up with Elsie now that we know she was the other mother in the same room as my mother at the maternity home?'

Molly had no answer to that so she changed the subject.

'The maternity home must have had procedures to prevent the identity of babies being muddled. There should be some way of finding out what they were,' she mused. They drank their tea in silence, each deep in their own thoughts. 'Does the maternity home still exist?' The question hovered in the stillness.

'I don't know but I'll find out.' Why hadn't she thought of that?

'If it does there's a faint chance that the midwife, Sister Angelica, might still be around. She's a nun so it's unlikely she's moved away or got married or anything like that.' Molly smiled at the thought.

'I wonder how old she was when I was born.' Beth pondered. 'If she was near retirement age then she could be very old now and even dead.'

'That's as maybe but it's worth finding out.'

Chapter 33

Beth cycled the short journey home in a haze of misery and uncertainty. Her conviction that there had been a mix up at the maternity home when she was born and the repercussions of this on her future with Tom weighed down on her so that her legs felt like lead and she could barely turn the pedals. She could not go on like this, she had to do something, but what? The only prospect open to her was to visit the site of the maternity home and see what she could find out. She made up her mind, there way no use putting it off, delay would only intensify her fears, she would go this evening.

She quietly stowed her bicycle in the shed at the side of the house and walked stealthily back to the front gate. The drawing room window was in darkness so she hoped her mother was busy in the kitchen and therefore would not have heard her arrive home.

Beth took a bus across town and alighted on Iffley Road opposite the Catholic Church. She had worked out from what her mother had told her that this must be the place where her mother had first met Sister Angelica when she was in labour. Taking a left turn she made her way down a narrow street of terraced houses. It didn't look a likely place for a maternity home but at a T junction the road was intercepted by a wider road and Beth read the name, St. Mary's Road, with relief. That was more like it. A short walk brought her to a high grey wall, behind which was an equally forbidding large grey building. She followed the wall for a considerable distance until it ended in a pair of heavy iron gates. The sign on the rusty gates read *St. Mary's Rest Home*. Disappointed but undaunted by the change of use Beth pushed open one of the gates a few inches and squeezed through the gap.

A weed-encrusted gravelled drive led up to an unwelcoming stone house of a considerable size. Its many windows were small and shrouded with dark curtains that made it peer blindly onto the outside world. Beth apprehensively climbed a flight of worn steps and approached the heavy front door. She found a metal bell-pull and tugged it eagerly. The sound of the bell reverberated hollowly through the interior but there was no answer to its jangled sound. Beth knocked on the peeling paint of the front door and waited. When no one answered, she tried the handle. It was well and truly locked. She retraced her steps down the stone steps and went round to the side of the building where she found a smaller door. Once again her knock was unanswered but this time the door opened when she pushed it and she let herself in. A long narrow passage led into the building and Beth wrinkled her nose at the rank small of boiled cabbage. She soon found the origin of the smell. Further down the passage a door on her left opened onto a noisy kitchen. She stood just inside the door, uncertain what to do next.

A fat woman in a green overall, her hair tied up in a scarf, was scraping out the remains of some kind of minced meat from a blackened dish onto a chipped plate. She ladled on a scoop of mashed potato and a spoonful of the pungent cabbage and handed the filled plate to another similarly dressed woman who stood in attendance at a trolley laden with similar plates of food.

'Yes?' She fixed Beth with an impatient eye.

'Was this once a maternity home?' Beth raised her voice above the racket of the busy kitchen.

The woman shrugged. 'Dunno ... Flo did this used to be a maternity home?' she bellowed across the kitchen.

Flo stopped filling a jug with thick brown gravy. 'Yes,' she shouted back over the noise. Flo passed the gravy jug to a waiting server and turned her attention to Beth. 'The church closed it some years ago when the new hospital opened. No call for a maternity home after that, the mothers preferred the facilities of the Radcliffe maternity hospital.' She looked at Beth and wondered why a pretty young girl would be interested in the fortunes of a catholic nunnery. 'The church decided the time was right to look after the other end of humanity, the old and infirm. That's when we took over and started this geriatric rest home.'

'I see.' Beth was unsure how to proceed.

'What brings you here?' the woman asked as she began doling out slices of jam roll which she covered with a splodge of thick custard.

'I was born here,' Beth told her breathlessly, 'and I wondered if any of the maternity staff that attended my mother were still about.' Flo looked at the beautiful girl before her in surprise. 'I would like to say thank you to the midwife who brought me into the world,' Beth added, thinking fast.

Flo shook her head. 'Don't think so ducks. They're all long gone by now.'

The first woman, listening to the conversation, broke in. 'Not all of 'em Flo, there's that old 'un upstairs. She's always telling me how different it was in 'er day.'

'Do you know her name?' Beth held her breath.

The woman shrugged. 'Sister, that what we call her, just Sister. She's the only nun in the 'ome at the moment so Sister is good enough.'

Flo laughed. 'Not much good speaking to her. She's asleep most of the time and when she's awake she's away with the fairies. Always mumbling about what happened in the past and most of it makes no sense.'

'All the same I would like to talk to her please.' This was the nearest Beth had come to a lead and she wasn't going to let it slip between her fingers.

'Now's not a good time.' Flo dolloped another slice of pudding onto yet another waiting plate. 'We've got to get these dinners to the residents, feed those who can't manage on their own and then get cleared away before their bed time at eight. And anyway,' she added, 'even if you waited until they've been fed, the old lady would be fast asleep, she rarely stays awake long enough to finish her dinner.'

The fat woman joined in. 'The best time to see 'er is on Sunday, early afternoon. She always a bit perkier then when she's been taken to church and confessed 'er sins.'

A young girl, up to her elbows in a sink full of greasy water, giggled. 'Pretty boring confession she'd make,' she volunteered.

'Get on with your work Grace,' Flo admonished. 'You can confess bad thoughts as well as bad deeds you know and I'm sure you have plenty of both.' Grace stuck her tongue out at Flo's back before returning to her sink of washing up. Normally Beth would have smiled at her behaviour but today she was weighed down with worries. Was the old lady upstairs Sister Angelica? And if so, was she in control of her faculties sufficiently to understand the questions Beth needed answering?

'Are you sure I can't see her now, just for a few minutes?' Beth pleaded.

Flo shook her net-covered head. 'Sorry ducks, it's more than my life's worth to take you to see her at this time. If the supervisor sees us I'd lose my job and no mistake. Come back on Sunday, visiting's between two and four,' she added helpfully.

Beth knew when she was beaten. She thanked Flo and nodded towards the fat green-overalled helper. She would just have to come back on Sunday and find out if the old nun upstairs remembered anything about the workings of the maternity home nineteen years ago.

It was late when Beth arrived home and, no sooner had she had taken off her coat, than Prudence's concerned face appeared round the basement room door.

'You're late home. Have you had some supper?'

Beth shook her head. 'Not hungry,' she replied bluntly.

'Molly shouldn't keep you this late at the shop, particularly when you're not feeling well. Would you like me to have a word with her?'

'Mum, I haven't been at the shop, I've been to Cowley to see ... a friend.'

Prudence raised an eyebrow. 'I didn't know you knew anyone in Cowley.'

'More an acquaintance really,' Beth improvised, 'but

I've been meaning to call on her for ages so I went after work.'

'Thomas called round while you were out.'

Beth's heart sank. 'Did he say what he wanted?'

'No, but he did say that he would call back in an hour.' Prudence looked at her watch, 'so he could be here at any time.'

True to his word Tom appeared ten minutes later. Prudence let him in with a smile. 'Bethany's in the basement she told him,' then added, 'I don't think she's feeling well, she's not at all her usual self.' Tom nodded. He had the same impression. It was not like Beth to be so quiet and so short of things to say.

He greeted Beth with a hug and a kiss but Beth pulled away from his encircling arms and once again his embrace was not returned.

'Is something the matter Beth?' he asked, perplexed at the sudden change in her.

Beth couldn't look him in the eye. She hung her head and nodded. 'Yes,' she whispered.

'What is it Beth, what's the matter?' Tom reached out to take hold of her but Beth quickly moved out of the way.

'I can't tell you Tom, it's something I have to sort out before we can get married and in the meantime …' she slid her engagement ring off her finger and held it out to Tom, 'I want you to look after this.'

Tom stood transfixed. What was going on? His new-found happiness with Beth was seeping away and he had no idea why. 'Beth, tell me what's going on,' he pleaded.

Beth shook her head wretchedly. 'I can't Tom, you'll have to trust me. As soon as I have things sorted out I'll tell you, but until then it'll be better if we don't see each other.'

Tom could hardly believe what he was hearing. 'Beth!' he cried out in anguish and Beth could see the hurt in his eyes.

'Here, take it.' The ring lay in the palm of her upturned hand.

Colour diffused Tom's pale skin as anger and frustration took over. 'What are you trying to tell me, that we're finished?' Beth had no reply. She hung her head and refused to meet his eyes. If her fears were proved true then their relationship would have to end. Tom looked from the ring resting on the palm of her open hand to Beth's resolute face. He was shaking with a mixture of fear and passion. 'It's yours, I don't want it back. You can do what the hell you like with it.' He crossed the room and was taking the stairs two at a time before Beth could respond.

Beth put the ring in her pocket and closed the door gently behind Tom. When the sound of the front door slamming reached her ears she threw herself onto the sofa and cried as she had never cried before.

Chapter 34

On Sunday afternoon Beth once more approached the iron gates of St. Mary's rest home and was surprised to see that they were propped wide open. The heavy front door also stood ajar. She pushed it wider and peered into a dark panelled hallway from which rose a flight of wide uncarpeted stairs. Beth entered tentatively, looking around for someone who could help her find the nun that Flo had told her about, but the place appeared to be deserted. She took a few steps forward then turned at the sound of voices behind her. A middle-aged couple were shaking the rain off their umbrella and complaining about the weather. The woman held a bedraggled pot plant which she gave to her husband as soon as he had stowed the umbrella in a corner with several others. Must be visitors, Beth thought, which was good, but she still had no idea of where to find the old nun, which was bad. She shot the couple a quick smile and began to ask them if they knew the whereabouts of an elderly nun but the clatter their shoes made on the bare stairs drowned out her words and they did not respond.

Beth decided to try the ground floor first and made her way hesitantly along a wide corridor. The squeak of rubber-soled shoes signalled someone's approach and Beth was relieved to see Flo come into view carrying a tray of tea things.

'You've come to see the Sister then,' Flo smiled a greeting. Beth nodded, relieved. 'Hang on a mo while I get rid of this tray then I'll show you to her room.'

Flo led the way up the broad staircase to the first floor and then across the landing to a narrower flight of stairs. Beth was thankful that Flo had turned up when she had, starting on the ground floor it would have taken her the whole of visiting time to get to the top of the building. On the second floor Flo knocked loudly on a door numbered twelve. 'It's a pity she has to be up here,' she commented. 'If she was on the ground floor we could wheel her outside for some fresh air on warm days.' She knocked again and put her ear to the door. 'Must be asleep,' she grinned at Beth. 'She does a lot of sleeping does Sister.' Flo opened the door. 'Visitor for you!' she shouted, making Beth jump.

The room was sparsely furnished. A table and upright chair, a low bookcase containing a few faded and dusty volumes, an iron bedstead and an armchair with its back to the door made up the furniture. On the mantelpiece stood a large wooden cross, a small crucifix on a stand and a painted porcelain figure of a saint. Beth walked round the chair to face the occupant.

She was very old and very thin. Her lined face was enclosed in a once white wimple which in turn was covered by a black veil that rested on her bony shoulders. The rest of her, apart from two large feet clad in checked slippers with bobbles on the front, was covered with a blanket made up from knitted squares.

Beth crossed her fingers so tightly it hurt. 'Sister Angelica?' she whispered.

The creased eyelids flew open and Beth was surveyed by two deep-set dark eyes that reminded her of the jet buttons on her childhood teddy bear. 'Who are you?' The voice was strong despite the apparent frailty of the chair's occupant. 'I don't know you do I?' The nun clutched the blanket and drew it up to her chin. Her eyes briskly scanned Beth's appearance from top to toe.

Beth dragged over the upright chair and sat down opposite the old woman. 'My name's Bethany and I do hope you don't mind me coming to see you.'

'I suppose you're one of those interfering social workers.' The beady eyes regarded Beth belligerently. 'Well if you've come to tell me I can't stay here you can clear off because the only way I'm going to leave is feet first in a box.' The old lady's arthritic hands picked at the woollen blanket.

Beth had to smile at the Sister's robust hostility. 'I'm not a social worker,' she told her. 'I came to see you because I was born here.'

'I can't see what that has to do with me but you can stay if you like, I don't get any visitors these days and with a bit of luck they'll bring us some tea. What day is it?'

'Sunday.'

'Ah, visiting day that's why you're here.'

Beth sighed. If the old woman couldn't even remember what day it was, what chance was there of her remembering her birth nineteen years ago? Well she had come this far so she might as well give it a go. 'You were the midwife who brought me into the world.' Beth paused to judge the effect of her words.

'Brought a lot of babies into the world. What did you say your name was?'

'Bethany.'

Sister Angelica shook her head. 'Don't remember one called that.'

'My mother was called Mary when she was here and she shared a room with another mother called Elisabeth. It was a long time ago, I'm nineteen now.'

The nun closed her eyes and didn't reply. She remained very still. Beth touched the old woman's hand. She did not stir at Beth's touch and her hand felt icy cold. Beth waited a few seconds longer but still there was no response. Oh well, that's that, she thought. She's not heard what I said and has gone to sleep. Beth resignedly gathered up her handbag from the floor beside the chair and rose to leave.

'You can sit down,' the voice from the armchair ordered, 'I'm not asleep, just thinking.' Beth sat down heavily, surprised at the sudden command. The lively eyes opened and fixed Beth with a spirited stare. 'You may think I'm a silly old woman because I can't remember your name after five minutes or what day of the week it is but that's what happens when you get old and have no one to talk to, the brain atrophies. But I can remember clearly what happened a long time ago.' Beth nodded encouragingly. This was looking more hopeful. The nun picked some pieces of fluff off the blanket and Beth silently urged her to continue. 'I do remember a Mary and an Elisabeth.' Beth's heart speeded up. 'Their names reminded me of how in the bible our Mother Mary and her relation Elisabeth gave birth at around the same time.'

'Do you remember their babies?' Beth asked breathlessly.

Sister Angelica nodded slowly. 'I remember Elisabeth's baby.' A look of sadness crossed her face. 'The poor wee thing died in the night. I can see now the look of horror on that mother's face when the priest came to baptise the child.' The nun had a faraway look as she recalled the events of that fateful night, but then she smiled at Beth. 'She was christened Angelica after me, which is why I have never forgotten the wee mite.'

'How did you know which baby belonged to which mother?' Beth asked in trepidation.

Sister Angelica looked surprised at the question. 'No two babies look exactly alike unless they are identical twins and even then there are often small differences,' she answered, puzzled.

'But nowadays babies wear wrist bands with their details on so there can be no mistake to whom they belong.'

'Each cot was labelled with the baby's surname,' sister Angelica replied quickly.

'But ... what if the babies were put back in the wrong cot? You carried both of them together to the nursery. Could you have put my mother's baby in Elisabeth's baby's cot?'

The nun glared at Beth. 'What are you suggesting?' she croaked, 'that I muddled up Elisabeth's baby with another one? That's ridiculous!' She let go of the blanket and sat up straight in her chair. 'If you're going to make insinuations like that you'd better leave.'

Beth ignored the threat. She had got this far and wasn't going to give up now. 'Why is it so unlikely?' she persisted

Sister Angelica was silent. She plucked nervously at the

multi coloured blanket then shook her head. 'I can't remember why, but I'm sure there was a reason,' she replied.

'Please try to remember,' Beth urged.

The nun pointed a gnarled finger at Beth. 'Well I can't so that's that,' she shouted, frustrated that her memory had let her down.

At that moment the door banged open and Flo walked in bearing two cups of tea on a plastic tray. 'I hope you're not upsetting Sister.' She frowned at Beth.

'Well she is. She's suggesting I muddled up the babies in my care.' Sister Angelica glared over the rim of her cup.

'Perhaps you'd better go. I think the Sister has had enough excitement for one day, she has a weak heart you know.'

'Oh no, please, I didn't mean to upset her.' Beth was distraught. She was just beginning to get somewhere.

'Let her stay,' the old woman insisted. 'I haven't had a visitor in weeks.'

Flo shrugged. 'It's up to you, but I'll be back in fifteen minutes at the end of visiting time, then she'll have to go.'

Sister Angelica slurped her tea noisily. 'Why are you suggesting these things about Elisabeth's baby?' she demanded.

Beth decided to take the bull by the horns. 'I have got red hair,' she began.

'So I noticed, I'm not blind you know.'

Beth ignored the interruption. 'I can find no one in my family with red hair like mine.' Sister Angelica opened her mouth but Beth raised her hand and continued, 'I'm not at all like my father or mother in appearance or temperament ... on the other hand Elisabeth's husband and son are tall like me and they both have ginger hair.' Once again the nun went to speak but Beth hadn't finished her speech. 'And,' she leant forward to emphasise her words, 'I feel more at home with Elisabeth's family than my own ... so I wondered if I am Elisabeth's child and the baby that died belonged to my mother.' Her tea slopped over into the saucer and she hastily put it down on the floor. When she looked up sister Angelica once again had her eyes closed. This time the heavy breathing told Beth that the old lady was in fact asleep. Had she heard Beth's words? When she woke up would she remember what Beth had told her? Beth gently tapped the sister's knee but this only had the effect of making her shift her position and her mouth dropped open as she drifted into an even deeper sleep.

Beth placed her handbag on her knee and waited, hoping that the nap would be short and she would be able to resume her conversation with Sister Angelica. But it was not to be so. Flo popped her head round the door. 'Oh good, she's asleep. Time for you to go now, visiting is over.'

As she followed Flo from the room Beth glanced at the sleeping figure. She was convinced that sister Angelica held the key to her future happiness, but how was she going to find out?

Chapter 35

At work the next day Molly noticed the lack of a ring on Beth's finger and felt extremely uneasy but she didn't like to pry. She hoped Beth would tell her what had happened in her own good time. Beth was more pale than usual and the dark smudges under her eyes were testament to her lack of sleep. She went about her tasks with neither a smile nor her usual chat. At last Molly could no longer bear Beth's distress.

During a lull in business she enquired.' Did you find the maternity home Beth?'

'It's an old person's rest home now, 'she replied flatly.

'What about Sister Angelica?'

'She's there, tucked away in an upstairs room with no one to talk to.'

'Did you get to see her?'

Beth nodded. 'For all the good it did,' she answered sourly.

'Well?'

'Well what?'

'Oh my lord, this is like trying to get blood out of a stone. What happened for goodness sake?'

The shop bell jangled. 'I'll tell you at lunch time Beth promised.' Molly gave an impatient sigh and retreated to the work room.

As they ate their sandwiches Beth described her visit to St. Mary's rest home.

'So you see,' she finished, 'it was all a waste of time. Sister Angelica remembered my mother and Elisabeth but she was adamant that she did not swap the babies over. She thought there was a reason why that was but she couldn't remember what it was … so it looks as though I'll never know for certain one way or the other.'

Molly listened carefully. 'But that doesn't mean you and Tom can't marry.'

'It does,' Beth was adamant. 'We could never run the

risk of having children and that wouldn't be fair on Tom. I have to let him go.' Her young face was pinched and tired and Molly's heart went out to her.

'Give it one more chance Beth,' she urged. 'Go and see Sister Angelica one more time, she might have remembered something.'

Beth shrugged. 'I doubt it, but if you think it's worth it I might go and see her again next Sunday.' She put away her half-eaten sandwiches and went back into the shop, leaving Molly to finish her lunch alone.

***

That week Beth saw nothing of Tom. She had half hoped he would try to contact her but then again nothing had changed so it was probably better that he had not.

A cold mist swept up the Thames valley on Sunday morning. After lunch Beth looked out at the forbidding weather; she didn't fancy riding her bicycle or waiting around for buses in such conditions. She'd ask her father if she could borrow his car.

Desmond was reluctant. 'You haven't had any experience of driving in foggy conditions,' he told her.

'And how am I going to get experience if you won't let me have the car?' Beth retorted. 'It's not foggy, just a bit misty,' she added hopefully.

'Well ... I don't know,' Desmond hedged.

Bethany, feeling she had the advantage, persisted. 'It's not as though I'm going far, only across town, and I did promise this friend ...' She blushed and couldn't quite meet her father's eye.

Desmond looked out of the window. 'It doesn't look too bad I suppose.'

Beth took that as capitulation and gave her father a hug. 'Thank you, thank you. I will be careful,' she assured him.

'Be sure you are back before it gets dark,' Desmond instructed, handing her the keys. 'It's no weather to be out in on your own.'

'I'll be fine,' Beth assured him and with a jangle of the keys she sped off to get her coat.

As Beth approached the river the mist thickened into full-blown fog and she had to slow down to a crawl. Luckily there were few other vehicles on the road so she was able to edge her way along by the kerb. At last the forbidding grey walls of St. Mary's loomed out of the fog and she parked the car carefully near the entrance gates. She had brought a small bouquet for Sister Angelica from the shop and she reached across to the passenger seat for the cellophane-wrapped posy.

This time she slipped upstairs unseen and knocked on the door of number twelve. There was no answer. Beth waited and knocked again, with the same result. Must be asleep she smiled and opened the door.

The sight that met her eyes was unexpected. Sister Angelica's personal possessions had gone, the armchair was covered with a dust sheet and the bed had been stripped. The air smelt strongly of pine disinfectant which made Beth feel slightly nauseous. She checked the number on the door, twelve, there was no mistake. Beth returned to the landing and looked around. They must have moved Sister Angelica to a downstairs room, as Flo had suggested, but which one? How was she going to find her in this rambling building? She could hardly open every door and peer inside.

After a moment's thought Beth decided that the only option was to make her way down to the kitchen. Hopefully Flo might be there or failing that someone else might know where Sister Angelica was. She found her way downstairs but all the corridors leading off the central hall looked the same. She had no idea which one would lead her to the kitchen. There was only one thing to do, make a random choice and explore. The corridor seemed never ending. Beth turned a corner and nearly bumped into a helper carrying a tea tray.

'I'm lost,' Beth told her plaintively.

The woman straightened the contents of her tray.

'Where do you want to go?' she asked pleasantly.

'The kitchen.'

'Follow me.' She set off at speed and Beth had to trot to keep up with her. Finally they reached the clatter of the kitchen. 'Who exactly did you want?'

'Flo,' Beth replied uneasily.

'Flo, someone to see you!' the woman shouted over the noise of the kitchen.

Flo and the fat woman in the green overall were busily setting out tea cups ready to be filled for the residents and their visitors. They looked at Beth with strained expressions.

'Sorry to bother you when you're so busy, but could you tell me where Sister Angelica has been moved to?'

Flo put her hand to her mouth. 'I'm so sorry, sister Angelica is no longer with us.'

'Where has she gone?' Beth enquired again.

'To meet her maker!' the fat one replied bluntly.

'Dot!' Flo admonished, 'there's no need for that.' She turned to Beth. 'Sister Angelica passed away on Thursday. A heart attack they said.'

'Right after she'd had her tea.'

Flo shot Dot another reproving look.

Beth stood rooted to the spot. Now she would never know whether she was Prudence's child or Elisabeth's! She left the flowers intended for Sister Angelica on the kitchen surface and turned away blindly.

Outside Beth climbed into the car and rested her head on the steering wheel. She felt let down. How could sister Angelica have left her with this awful decision? Why did she have to die just when she might have remembered something that would settle Beth's questions once and for all? Beth knew there was nothing more to be done. The one person who might have helped was dead. There was nothing left but to face Tom and see the anger and misery on his face when she told him finally that their relationship was finished. She rubbed her temples to try and ease the beginnings of a headache, started the engine and pulled slowly away from the kerb.

The fog had thickened and Beth inched her way along the deserted side street to the main road where she needed to turn right and head towards Magdalene Bridge. At first she was afraid to pull out incase another car was approaching in the murk. After a brief thought she wound down her window, stuck her head out and listened intently. When she was sure no other car was coming she thankfully turned right into the main road. There was very little traffic about and the few cars that had ventured out were slowly creeping along, hugging the edge of the road.

Beth was concentrating on following the kerb when suddenly a van loomed out of the fog in the middle of the road right in front of her. Beth swerved to her left to avoid a collision, mounted the pavement and came to rest with the front of the car imbedded in a lamppost. The jolt shook her and she sat dazed for a few minutes before climbing out to inspect the damage. Water poured from the radiator and Beth knew that she was not going to be able to drive the rest of the way home. What should she do? She couldn't leave the car half on the road and half on the pavement it would be a hazard to other road users. The van driver was nowhere to be seen. This was turning out to be the worst day of her life.

'You in a spot of bother Miss?' Beth turned to see a policeman pushing his bicycle along the pavement. She nodded miserably and explained what had happened. 'You'll not be driving that tonight,' the constable shook his head knowingly. 'You need a breakdown truck. I'll radio through to the station and see what can be done, they should be able to contact the nearest one for you.' He switched on his radio, held it close to his mouth and spoke into it. 'Yes … young lady … crashed her car on Iffley Road … yes she is,' the constable smiled, 'lots of lovely red hair.' He replaced his radio. 'They're phoning a garage, shouldn't be long.'

Tom was working late. Since his last conversation with Beth he had thrown himself into the renovation of the

MGA that Rob had bought some weeks earlier. It was the only thing that took his mind off worrying about Beth's change of heart.

'Tom!' Rob bellowed from the office.

What's he want now? Tom thought grumpily. 'Ok, ok, I'm coming.' He tossed the spanner he was holding onto the bench and wiped his hands on a rag.

'Call from the police. Some wench has crashed her car on Iffley Road and needs a tow truck. Said we'd oblige.'

'You mean me, you don't know how to operate the thing.'

'True,' Rob grinned. 'You're the mechanic round here so you'd better get a move on.'

'She hurt ... the girl?'

'Don't think so. The constable said she was gorgeous with lots of lovely red hair.' As soon as the words were out of his mouth Rob realised the importance of what he had said. Tom stared at him for a split second before running from the office and a moment later Rob heard the roar of the tow truck's engine.

The thickening fog prevented Tom from driving fast. He was frustrated at having to move at a crawl and look out for approaching vehicles. Eventually he spotted Desmond's car and Beth standing on the pavement talking to a policeman. He parked the truck, jumped down from the cab and ran to Beth.

'Are you hurt?' he asked anxiously.

Beth shook her head. 'No, but my father's car is a mess,' she answered dejectedly.

Tom took a quick look at the damage. 'It's not as bad as it looks, soon have it sorted out.'

The constable wished Beth well. 'You're in good hands now,' he said as he wheeled his bicycle away.

When the car was hitched up Tom turned to Beth. 'Hop up,' he indicated the passenger door of the cab.

'I can walk from here,' she insisted stubbornly.

Tom folded his arms across his broad chest and glared angrily at Beth. 'I've just about had enough of this Beth,' he told her furiously. 'Now get in the cab, otherwise I'll put you in myself.' Beth knew when she was beaten and climbed reluctantly into the truck. Tom switched on the ignition, then turned to her with sadness in his eyes.

'We cannot go on like this Beth, we have to talk. I'll take the car to the garage then we'll go and have a word with your Dad to set his mind at rest. After that you and I are going to sort things out.'

Beth hung her head. She knew Tom was right. The time had come to tell him what she suspected.

Beth settled nervously on the sofa but Tom paced the room.

'Sit down please Tom.'

With a grunt Tom threw himself into the chair opposite and leaned forward, his hands clasped between his knees.

'Right, fire away.'

'Tom please, this isn't easy for me.'

'Do you think it's any easier for me,' he demanded. 'You say you love me, we get engaged and then in a matter of days you have changed your mind and offer me the ring back. What do you expect me to think?'

'Tom please,' Beth implored. 'Listen to me.'

'I'm listening and this better be good.'

Beth briefly recounted the events surrounding her birth and that of Tom's dead sister. He was surprised that his mother and Beth's mother had given birth at the same time and in the same maternity home and even shared a room but he couldn't see the significance of it, it was just a coincidence, wasn't it?

Beth spoke earnestly. 'As you know I've been worried for some time because I don't take after my parents, or any other member of my family for that matter.'

'Yes, you had the daft idea that you were adopted but that was disproved.' Tom's impatience got the better of him. 'It's time you grew up Beth.'

Beth was infuriated by Tom's remark. 'You wouldn't think it daft if you felt like I do. Now please listen.' She resumed her account of the events of that night nineteen years ago. 'In the maternity home the midwife took both of our mothers' babies together to settle them down in the nursery. Neither baby had an identity bracelet so how do we know that she put them in the right cots?'

'You're suggesting she muddled them up?'

'It's a possibility.'

Tom considered Beth's words. 'That would mean ... if that was the case ... it was your mother's baby that died and ...'

'And I could be your sister,' Beth finished for him.

Tom stared as Beth's words sank in. 'That's preposterous!' He gave a shout of mirthless laughter. 'My mother would have realised the baby wasn't hers.'

'Not necessarily,' Beth informed him. 'Both mothers had difficult births and only saw their babies for a few minutes that first night. Both the babies were tightly swaddled and were asleep. An exhausted mother would not necessarily have taken in the details of her baby's face in the short time they had together.'

'Beth this is all supposition on your part. It's a figment of your imagination.'

'I wish it were,' Beth answered sadly. 'All the evidence points to the fact that I'm right. I'm tall like you and your father and you both have ginger hair. No one in my family has the red gene that I know of.'

'No,no,no.' Tom punched the arm of the chair. 'You can't possibly be my sister, the idea is ridiculous.'

'You didn't think so when we first met, you treated me just like a little sister.'

Tom was grim faced. 'I can assure you I didn't think of you as a sister. I tried the big brother act because I thought I had no chance with you and that way I could at least keep on seeing you. I was afraid that if I made my feelings clear you would disappear from my life.' Tom looked shaken.

Beth saw the look on Tom's face and said helplessly, 'I have been to visit the midwife that brought me into the world. She was angry when I suggested that she might have inadvertently swapped the two babies but she could give me no guarantee that it didn't happen. She mumbled something about it not being possible but she couldn't tell me why.'

'You must ask her again she might remember something important.' Tom eagerly grasped at a possible solution.

'That's what I was going to do this afternoon. I went to St. Mary's to talk to her but ... she's dead Tom. We'll never know the truth.' Beth's words were little more than a whisper and Tom had to strain to hear what she said.

The two remained wrapped in their own thoughts. The silence grew oppressive and Tom was overwhelmed with foreboding.

'What do we do now?' Tom's looked at Beth bleakly.

'There's only one thing we can do,' she replied with resignation. 'We have to call off the engagement and I think it would be better if we didn't see each other for a while.'

Tom ran his hands through his hair. 'Why don't we forget this ever happened and go ahead with our lives as before? No one else suspects we could be related.'

'Don't think I haven't thought of that,' Beth replied grimly. 'But it wouldn't work Tom. It would always be hanging over us and, more importantly, we could run the risk of having children.'

Tom stood up and kicked at the edge of the rug. 'So that's it, we part, just like that! All on the basis of your unfounded suspicions. Hell, I wish you hadn't started all this.' His voice was harsh. 'Why couldn't you leave well alone for God's sake?'

'I'm so sorry Tom.' Beth was filled with a desperate resignation. She wanted to cry but tears eluded her. She rubbed her dry eyes. 'Perhaps ...'

She was interrupted by a sharp knock as Prudence popped her head round the door. 'Oh good I've caught you, I was hoping you'd both still be here.' Beth and Tom stared, and waited for her to continue. 'Time is marching on and you haven't yet let me know when you would like the engagement party to be.' Beth opened her mouth but Prudence was not to be forestalled. 'I thought, as Christmas is getting close, Christmas Eve might be a good time, or perhaps …'

'Mum,' Beth tried again but Prudence was on a mission. 'If that is too soon I thought New Year's Eve might be rather fun.'

'Mum!' Beth raised her voice several decibels and it was Prudence's turn to stare. 'There is not going to be a party!'

'But we agreed,' Prudence was taken aback by the vehemence of Beth's assertion.

'Things have changed. There's no engagement so there's no need for a party,' Beth told her a little more quietly.

'No engagement?' Prudence looked from Beth to Tom and back to Beth.

'That's what I said.' Beth stood up. 'You can have a bloody party if you want but I shan't be there and neither will Tom.' Her voice cracked. 'And now Tom's leaving.'

'Beth!' Tom took a step towards her.

'I said you were leaving.'

'Beth we can't leave it like this.' His eyes were filled with anguish.

'Well if you won't leave then I will.' Beth ran from the room. The tears that had evaded her earlier now threatened to drown her as she flew upstairs to the sanctuary of her room.

Chapter 36

Grey day followed grey day. Beth existed on autopilot. At home, avoiding eye contact with her mother, in the shop, serving customers, making up orders, and avoiding Molly whenever possible.

Beth was drained of emotion. She hadn't apologised or explained matters to her mother, nor had she apologised to Tom for her outburst at the weekend. She knew she couldn't leave things as they were, she had to smooth over the cracks before she could move on. She would tackle Tom first, she decided. She needed to apologise properly so that they could part friends. With that thought uppermost in her mind she resolved to talk to Tom that evening after work.

Five o'clock eventually arrived and Beth thankfully locked the shop door and pulled down the blind. Molly had disappeared earlier in the afternoon to attend an appointment, the purpose of which she hadn't shared with Beth. Why should she? Beth thought. I don't tell my problems to Molly anymore, so why should she share her secrets with me?

Beth hung her green cotton apron on its hook in the workroom and left by the back door. She wheeled her bicycle past Molly's small green Austin van and proceeded to ride towards the garage. She didn't know exactly what she was going to say to Tom, she only knew that she had to make it right between them so that they both could move on with their lives.

Her legs felt even heavier than her heart as she struggled on towards the garage. She propped her bicycle against the open doors and stepped inside with trepidation.

The garage was deserted. Where she had expected to see Tom busy working there was a Wolsey car abandoned with its bonnet up and a few tools spread around on the oily concrete floor. Beth tiptoed past the car. It gave her a bad feeling, as though some catastrophic action had taken place and it alone remained to bear witness. She shivered as she pushed open the door into the office. The air in here was rank with cigarette smoke. She rubbed her smarting eyes and could just make out Rob sitting at his desk, a lighted cigarette between his fingers. His back was turned as he carefully scrutinising the papers in front of him.

'Rob.' Beth spoke the word quietly but Rob spun round as though a shot had been fired.

'Oh Beth it's you.' He stubbed out the cigarette that threatened to burn his fingers.

'Do you know where Tom is?' Beth asked, clutching the ends of her scarf tightly.

Rob was bothered. He sensed there was something bad going on between Tom and Beth but he didn't know what. He lit another cigarette. How much should he tell her? He decided in favour of caution. 'He had to rush off suddenly, not sure where,' he told her.

Beth was not one to be put off. 'When did he go?'

'This afternoon, I think.'

Beth had had enough of Rob's prevarication. 'Rob will you please tell me what's going on. Tom works here every afternoon and yet this afternoon, when I badly need to speak to him, he's not here and you don't know where he is despite the fact that he's left a job half finished out there.'

Rob scratched the back of his neck. 'To tell you the truth Beth, I don't know much more than you do. I'm worried about Tom, he's been behaving very strangely lately.'

Beth was worried too. 'Tell me what you know Rob,' she commanded. Rob lit another cigarette from the stub of the previous one and threw the dead end into an overflowing ashtray. The sight of Beth's concerned face decided him to tell her what he knew.

'Tom's been behaving very oddly lately,' he repeated. 'He's been making a lot of telephone calls, something he never used to do. Then a woman phoned to speak to him. I took the call and passed the phone to Tom. When he heard who was on the other end he covered the receiver with his hand and glared at me and nodded towards the door. I took the hint that he wanted to speak privately with the woman so I went outside for a cigarette while he spoke to her.'

Beth listened to Rob's words with foreboding. So Tom had wasted no time in finding someone else. She could hardly blame him but that didn't make the pain any easier to bear. 'And you don't know where he's gone this afternoon?'

Rob shook his head. 'He jumped into that sports car of his and called out that he had someone to see and wouldn't be back at work today. I was more than a bit aggrieved I can tell you. I was supposed to deliver that Wolsey this evening with a full service under its bonnet.'

'Thanks Rob.' Beth turned miserably away.

Tom's MG turned left off the main road and roared through the archway leading to the garage at the precise moment that Beth cycled through in the opposite direction. She braked and swerved to one side, grazing her knuckles on the wall as she did so.

Tom's car screeched to a halt and he leaped out and ran to where Beth was wiping the blood from the back of her hand. His face was drawn and white.

'Beth! I'm sorry I only saw you at the last minute. Are you hurt?'

Beth shook her head. 'Nothing much, I've grazed my hand that's all but you could have killed me driving like that.' She fixed Tom with an accusing stare.

'I'm so sorry, I wasn't concentrating, I had things on my mind and I was in a hurry.'

'That was obvious.' Beth righted her bicycle and took a step forward.

'I was in a hurry to see you Beth. There's something important I need to tell you.'

'It's alright Rob has already told me,' Beth answered sadly.

A look of alarmed puzzlement crossed Tom's face. 'What exactly had Rob told you?' His eyes searched

Beth's face.

'That you have met someone, that you talk a lot to her on the telephone and that you rushed off today to see her,' Beth improvised.

'Rob told you that?'

'Well not in so many words but it was obvious what he meant.' Beth eased herself onto the saddle and prepared to leave.

'Beth some of what you say is true but you have reached quite the wrong conclusion. Now get off that bike, we need to talk.'

'Don't speak to me like that Tom. We've done all the talking necessary there's nothing left to say.' Beth turned away angrily, pushed on the pedals and began to ride away.

'Beth damn you, stop being so pig headed!' Tom took two strides after her and caught hold of the handlebars. 'Get off that bike. I'm going to talk to you whether you like it or not. It's time you curbed that temper of yours and listened to other people for once.'

Beth was shocked. Tom had never before spoken to her in that angry way and his mention of her temper caused her to hesitate. Perhaps she was being unreasonable? 'Alright we'll talk but this is the very last time,' she stipulated. 'We have to move on Tom, we can't keep going over the situation.'

Tom wheeled her bike towards the garage. 'Get in the car,' he ordered as he disappeared inside. 'I've had a word with Rob,' he said darkly when he returned, 'and he's going to lock up tonight.' He pressed the starter and rapidly turned the car.

Beth was startled, she thought they would sit in the car and talk. 'Where are we going?'

'You'll see.' Tom fell silent and concentrated on driving. Beth took in the set line of his jaw and decided to say no more.

Fifteen minutes later they had left the city by-pass and were motoring uphill. Beth looked out at the dark unlit road and tried to make out where they were but the hedges and trees they passed could be anywhere. A few minutes later Tom turned right and pulled off the road into a deserted lay by. He turned to Beth.

'We'll not be disturbed here,' he told her. 'Now I've important things to tell you and I would be grateful if, for once, you did not interrupt and let me finish what I've got to say.' Beth opened her mouth and Tom laid a finger on her lips. 'I meant what I said Beth, no interruptions.' Beth huddled back in her seat and Tom began.

'You were right about me speaking on the phone to a woman and she did indeed phone me back but you were entirely wrong in your assumption that there was a romantic element to our conversation. She is a research scientist working in London University. I made a lot of phone calls to people in Oxford that I thought might be able to help and eventually her name came up, she's called Susan Taylor by the way.' Beth could not see for the life of her what Tom was getting at but he had asked her to listen so she kept quiet. 'After we last talked I thought very hard about our situation,' Tom continued. 'I was not prepared to leave things as they were, there had to be something we could do, and then it came to me. Paternity testing!' He looked at Beth with a gleam of triumph. 'For years there have been cases where the paternity of a child has been in question and tests have been used in an effort to establish who was or was not the father. Well, I thought that if these tests could establish who the father was then they could also be used to find out if a particular person was the mother of a child.' Tom paused to take breath and Beth sat up straighter in her seat. She now had an inkling of what Tom was getting at.

Tom continued. 'Well it turns out that the paternity tests mainly consisted of simple blood tests to find out the blood groups involved. While this could in some circumstances rule out the possibility of a particular person being the father it couldn't always prove that a particular man was the father.'

'What's the use of that then,' Beth exclaimed disappointedly.

Tom held up his hand. 'Hang on I've not finished yet. It appears that recently a new test has been devised that has a high degree of accuracy and Susan Taylor is one of the scientists working on it. When I spoke to Susan she said the test had been devised to prove or disprove paternity but the idea that it could be used to find out whether or not two children had the same mother had not occurred to her. She was very interested in our situation and said she would like to help if she could. The test was still quite new and she would have to get permission for it to be used it in our case.'

'And?' Beth looked eagerly at Tom.

'Well the upshot was that she asked me to come to London to make our case to her boss, which is what I did today, and he's given the go ahead, provided we pay for the test and the time involved in analysing the results.'

'How much will that be?'

'I'm not sure of the exact amount yet but they did intimate it would be a considerable sum.'

'Well that's that then!' Beth sank into her seat.

'I've got money.' Tom declared easily.

The realisation of what Tom was saying dawned on Beth. 'You can't use you partnership money!' she squealed.

'And why not?' he demanded. 'Being able to marry you Beth is far more important than being able to buy a share in the garage. It will probably mean we'll be poor for some years but something else will turn up, I'm not afraid of hard work. Will you mind not having all the luxuries you've been used to?' Tom added fearfully.

Beth squeezed his arm. 'All I want is you Tom, nothing else matters. But you realise that this test might confirm our worst fears by proving that I am Elsie's child and therefore your sister?'

Tom nodded. 'At least we'd know one way or the other and wouldn't have to spend the rest of our lives wondering. And anyway I love you Beth and I don't believe you are my sister so I'm prepared to go ahead to prove it.'

Beth gave him a gentle smile. 'I love you too Tom.' They lapsed into silence for a while then Beth added. 'There's one thing we haven't considered.'

'What's that?'

'I don't mind undergoing this test whatever it involves but your mother might think differently. She might be upset by the suggestion that I could be her daughter and not the baby Angelica that she has mourned all these years. It's bound to come as a shock to her and she might not want to take the test.'

'Mum will be ok with it.' Tom was adamant. 'Now come and look at the view and stop making problems where non exist.'

Beth followed Tom out of the car. The clouds were clearing and patches of night sky, bright with stars, shone out. Tom led the way along the road and stopped by a fence bordering a field that fell away steeply. It was then that Beth recognised where she was, Boars Hill, where Tom had brought her once before when he had been teaching her to drive. Tom leaned on the fence and surveyed the lights of Oxford spread out along the valley of the Thames in the distance. He put his arm lightly round Beth's shoulders. 'That's where we belong,' he told her. 'That's where our future lies ... together.'

Beth did not have Tom's conviction. Doubt still raised its worrying head in her mind. But she said nothing.

Chapter 37

Tom had decided that after work was not a good time to talk to Elsie. 'Katie and Dad are likely to be around so we wouldn't be able to talk to Mum privately,' he had told Beth. She had agreed and they had settled on lunch time. That morning Tom informed his Mother that he would be home for lunch to make sure that she was there when they called.

'I'll look forward to it, it'll be a rare treat,' she had happily replied.

Tom and Beth hung up their coats in the hall and Tom pushed open the kitchen door.

'Both of you!' A delighted Elsie came forward with arms akimbo to envelop first one and then the other in a welcoming hug. 'Good thing I made a large pot of soup,' she exclaimed cheerfully. 'There'll be plenty.' She looked closely at Beth. 'And you look as though you need feeding up my dear, you're so pale, whatever have you been doing?'

'Mum we haven't come for lunch,'

'But you said …'

'I know I did but that was just to make sure that you would be in. We have something important to tell you.'

Elsie looked from one to the other. She looked at their long faces. 'I'm not sure I want to hear it,' she commented, putting on the kettle.

'Mum please come and sit down and listen,' Tom said gently. 'What we have to tell you is bizarre to say the least but it is very important to Beth and me and you might be able to help us to sort it out.'

'Well if I can help …' Elsie slid her ample frame back onto her chair and looked expectantly at Tom.

Tom nudged Beth. 'You start.'

'Elsie,' she began nervously, 'do you remember when you told me about Angelica's birth in the nursing home?'

'Indeed I do.'

'Well the person you shared a room with on the night that Angelica was taken ill was my mother.'

Elsie shook her head. 'I can't have been, I distinctly remember the woman's name was Mary and you told me that your mother is called Prudence.'

'It is, but her second name is Mary and that is what Sister Angelica insisted on calling her.'

Elsie's eyes opened wide. 'Are you sure of this?'

'Quite sure. My mother remembers an Elisabeth in the bed next to hers who had a sick baby that was christened Angelica.'

'Well I'm blowed!' Elsie beamed. 'So that pretty little slip of a thing that had such a hard time having her first was your mother. Well what a lovely coincidence.'

'That's as maybe Mum,' Tom took up the story. 'But what Beth hasn't told you is that she thinks the baby, Angelica, might have been her mother's child and not yours.'

Elsie stared then brought the flat of her hand down noisily on the table. 'Don't be so ridiculous Tom. What are you suggesting, that I didn't know my own baby?' Tom nodded and Elsie gave him a horrified look. 'If that was true, which it's not, and Angelica was Prudence's baby then that would mean that Beth here was mine and …'

'That would make her my sister.' Tom finished grimly.

The kettle whistled shrilly but Elsie ignored it. 'Now you can see why we are worried,' Tom said, rising to silence the kettle. 'Beth has been concerned for some time because she doesn't resemble anyone in her family and yet she has the height and red hair that are common in ours.' Elsie continued to stare at her son.

'I'm sure that baby was mine,' she repeated dully.

'Well we need to prove it, and the only way to do that is to establish that Beth is not your daughter.'

'And how can we possibly do that?'

Beth put her hand on Elsie's arm. 'Tom has found out that there is a test that can be carried out that might give us the proof we need. I'm not sure of how it works but I think they need a blood sample from you and one from me and they examine the white blood cells for similarities.'

Tom leant forward. 'Would you be prepared to do that for us Mum?'

Elsie didn't reply immediately. 'I'm not sure,' she said at last.

'Mum! Why not?' Tom couldn't believe what he was hearing.

Elsie's brow creased with unease. 'What if the test isn't definite one way or the other?'

'Then we're no worse off than we are now.' Tom said positively. 'And it's more than likely we'll get a result. The researchers told me it is the latest genetic testing and it is highly accurate.'

Elsie covered Beth's hand with hers. 'It's not that I don't want to help pet, it's just that you've given me so much to think about. I need time to get my head around what you've come up with.'

'What's there to think about?' Tom said impatiently. 'It's either a yes or a no.'

Beth frowned. 'Tom we must give your mum time to think, it's only fair after what we've told her.'

Tom shrugged. How long was he going to have to wait before he knew for certain?

***

Monday morning came round and still Beth hadn't heard anything from Tom regarding his mother's decision. They had agreed to stay apart once more, until such time as they had a result from the test. That is if there was going to be a test, Beth thought. The longer Elsie put off making a decision the more likely, Beth thought, she would say no.

Beth rearranged the few remaining poinsettias into an attractive display in the shop window. It would be Christmas next week and they had been selling like the proverbial hot cakes but she needed to sell the remaining ones this week otherwise they would go to waste over the

Christmas holiday. Because the shop was quiet Molly had returned to the flat. Beth could hear her footsteps above her head and every now and then loud scrapings and bumping. Whatever's she doing up there? Beth questioned. Sounds like she's rearranging the furniture.

Beth had just finished serving the first customer of the day when a deafening bang erupted from the work room. She rushed through the adjoining arch to be faced with a disheveled Molly heaving a tatty old trunk that was obviously heavily laden.

'Molly what ever are you doing with that? You'll do yourself an injury trying to move that old thing on your own.'

'Got too much rubbish, need to have a sort out,' Molly panted, tucking stray strands of wiry hair back where they belonged. 'There's a chap on the market will take this lot for me, said he'd call today and I hope he comes soon, there's little enough room in here without that taking up most of it.' She pointed to the bulging trunk. Beth agreed and wondered how she was going to manage to have sufficient space to make up the twenty table decorations which were needed by a local hotel for tomorrow.

'Let's see if we can move it behind the counter Molly then the work room will be usable,' Beth suggested. The two of them heaved and pushed the trunk along the floor until at last it lay dustily behind the shop counter.

The shop bell rang and a customer entered who wanted several pot plants to give as Christmas presents. While Beth was helping her make her choices another customer slipped quietly into the shop and waited by the poinsettia display. Beth glanced in her direction. There was something familiar about the woman but Beth could not put her finger on what it was. After considerable deliberation the first woman finally made her selection and left the shop.

Beth turned to the other customer who now moved towards to the counter. Her coat was buttoned up against the cold December weather but it was several sizes too small to fit over the woman's large size and the fabric strained back from the buttons revealing a dark green garment underneath. It was seeing this that jolted Beth's memory and she recalled where she had seen this person before. She was Dot, the outspoken fat woman, Flo's assistant, who worked in the kitchen of St. Mary's rest home.

Beth smiled politely. 'What can I do for you?' she asked.

'It's more what I can do for you,' the woman replied nervously. 'I haven't come to buy anything,' she added quickly. 'I have something for you.' She unbuttoned her coat and reached into the pocket of her green pinafore, bringing out a crumpled envelope. 'I found it in the Sister's room when I cleaned it out after she died. It was meant for you but we didn't know how to find you. Then the next time you came you left so quickly that I didn't have chance to give it to you. The only thing we had were the flowers you left behind with the name of this shop on the wrapper, so I thought I'd come here and see if they knew who you were, but luckily you work here.' The woman took a deep breath and held out the envelope to Beth. 'I'm sorry it's taken me so long to call but what with Christmas preparations and all that …' she tailed off. 'I hope it's not important,' she added with an apologetic smile.

I don't expect so,' Beth told her. 'Thank you so much for taking the trouble to find me.'

'No trouble. The Sister talked a lot about you after you visited her. I think she took to you.'

'I'm glad.' Beth felt sad that she hadn't been able to visit the old lady again. Things might now be very different for her and Tom had she been able to do so.

The woman buttoned up her tight coat. 'Have a nice Christmas.'

'And you.' Beth picked up the envelope from the counter and watched the woman hurry across the road.

'Who was that?' Molly entered the shop with a can full

of water to refresh the flower containers.

'She works at the old people's home where I visited Sister Angelica. She brought me something from her.' Beth looked at the envelope. The message on the front was penned in a delicate cursive style. It read:

For the red-haired girl who visited me this week

Molly watched with interest as Beth carefully removed a single sheet of paper and read the enclosed letter. She then re-read it before looking up. The look on Beth's face frightened Molly. She was deathly pale as though she was about to faint and the hand that held the letter was shaking. Molly grabbed both arms and forced Beth down until she was sitting on the old trunk.

'Put your head between your knees,' she commanded.

'It's alright Molly I'm not going to faint. I've just had a shock that's all.' Beth looked at the letter in her hand and tears trickled down her pale cheeks. She wiped them away on the cuff of her jumper.

'Here.' Molly handed her a box of tissues. 'Whatever is it now m'dear? You do seem to be having more than you fair share of troubles lately.'

Beth wiped her eyes and blew her nose noisily. She gave Molly a watery smile. 'This isn't trouble Molly, it's good news, very good news.' She passed the letter to Molly. 'Read it,' she instructed, 'and you'll see why.'

Molly read:

Dear young Lady with the beautiful red hair (I'm sorry I can't remember your name),

You came to see me yesterday and you were worried. You thought that when you were born under my care you might have been given to the wrong mother. At the time I was angry at such a suggestion and told you that no such thing could have happened. But that wasn't sufficient, you wanted proof, and I wasn't able to provide you with such. On reflection I understood your anxiety and searched my poor old brains to come up with something that was hiding at the back of my mind, and at last I have remembered what it was.

Immediately after Elisabeth's baby was born I bathed it and dressed it in the baby clothes that she had brought with her. There was a little hand-knitted vest, a beautifully embroidered nightgown and a crochet matinee jacket. I remember admiring the clothes and Elisabeth proudly told me that she had made them herself. Well. I'm sure you know what I'm now going to say. The baby that died that night was wearing those clothes so there is no mistaking the fact that poor little Angelica was indeed Elisabeth's baby.

I do hope this sets your mind at rest and please visit again soon.

Yours in Christ,

Sister Angelica.

Beth rose unsteadily from the trunk and held out her hand for the letter.

'At last! Now perhaps we can get back to normal and get some work done around here,' Molly grinned.

Beth hugged her and for the first time Molly did not shrug her off but returned the embrace. 'Oh Molly, I'm so sorry you've had to put up with me these last few weeks. It must have been awful for you.'

'It certainly has and from now on I'll expect you to work doubly hard to make up for it,' Molly replied with a twinkle.

'I just need to ask one more thing of you please Molly.'

'And what might that be, as if I can't guess?'

'I need to tell Tom right away.'

Molly grinned. 'Be off with you, it's nearly lunchtime anyway.'

Beth covered the short distance between The Flower Basket and the garage in record time. She threw her bicycle to the ground and ran in through the big double doors. Rob appeared from the office and greeted her with a scowl.

'Before you ask – he's not here.'

'What do you mean, not here?'

'I mean he's not present, missing, gone out, absent without leave, yet again.' An irate Rob returned to his office and Beth quickly followed him.

'Where's he gone to?' she asked.

'You're not going to believe this.'

'Try me.' Beth replied bluntly; she was becoming more and more agitated with Rob's attitude.

'He's gone to see his mother!'

'His mother?'

'Is there something the matter with your hearing Beth or is it me? I seem to be repeating myself rather a lot. Yes, his mother for goodness sake. He must have seen her before he left this morning and presumably will be seeing her again this evening but …' Rob paused to light a cigarette, 'he has to see her in the middle of the day too!'

At that moment the sound of Tom's car filled the air and Beth ran out of the garage to meet him. Tom unfolded his tall frame from the driver's seat and entered the work room with a grim look on his face.

'She won't do it Beth.'

'What?'

'The test, she won't go through with it. She's convinced the baby was hers.'

Beth saw the deeply troubled look in his eyes. 'It doesn't matter Tom. She's right.'

'How can you say that? Of course it matters.' He ran a distracted hand through his hair. 'What are we going to do Beth?' he asked in a whisper.

'We don't need to do anything Tom. It really doesn't

matter anymore. Your mother's right, the baby that died, Angelica, was her baby and your little sister.'

Tom was unconvinced. 'How do you know this all of a sudden?' he asked tersely.

Beth gave him the letter. 'Read it Tom,' she urged.

Tom scanned the letter's contents then dropped it as he swept Beth up into his arms and kissed her powerfully.

'Don't mind me. I only own the place.' Rob retreated to his office but his words belied the smile on his face.

Chapter 38

New Year's Eve

Beth surveyed the drawing room with a critical eye. Everything had to be perfect for tonight's party.

Desmond had rolled up the carpet, moved the furniture to the edge of the room and set up a trestle table covered with a white damask cloth ready to receive the food that Prudence had been industriously preparing. The Christmas tree that Beth and Prudence had decorated last week looked bright and cheerful with its tiny lights, tinsel and multicoloured glass baubles but there was a scattering of needles round its base that spoiled the effect. Beth hastily swept them up before straightening the cards on the mantelpiece. She picked one up. It didn't look like a Christmas card, there was no snow or robins or nativity scene, but instead it displayed a picture of Sydney Harbour Bridge. The card had arrived a few days earlier and it contained a letter which Beth had carefully stowed in the pocket of her skirt. It was from her Great Uncle, Great Aunt Edith's husband, in Australia. She knew the contents of the letter by heart but nevertheless she took it out and re-read it.

Dear Bethany,

Please forgive the length of time it has taken to reply to your letter. It was eventually forwarded on to me as I no longer live at the address in Melbourne to which you sent it, the reason why I will explain.

My dear wife Edith sadly died a year ago and last summer I moved in with my daughter and her family here in Sydney.

You asked about Edith and her hair and I'm pleased to tell you that she had the most glorious bright auburn hair. I was so delighted to read that you have the same colouring. You are, as far as I know, the only one in her family who has inherited her beautiful red hair. I do have to tell you that she also had the quick temper that is supposed to be allied with red hair. Don't get me wrong – I loved her for it – it was part of her character and I would not have had it any other way and she was always full of remorse when her anger subsided.

I'm enclosing a copy I have had made of a studio photograph of Edith, taken when she was about your age. The picture was of course taken in black and white but it was such a good likeness that we had it professionally tinted. The colours have faded somewhat but you will get the impression of what a beauty she was. Do you think you could send a photograph of yourself? I would love to see if you resemble her in looks as well as in colouring.

Yours truly,

Edmund Trent (your Great Uncle)

P.S. My daughter says you would be more than welcome to visit us here in Sydney at any time.

Beth refolded the letter and returned it to her pocket. She touched the photograph of the red-haired girl which she had placed next to the card and smiled happily. Her parents told her that she bore an uncanny resemblance to the young woman in the picture.

She popped her head round the kitchen door. Prudence was putting the finishing touches to numerous plates of canapés and beautifully decorated petits fours.

'Want any help?'

Prudence flapped her hand in Beth's direction. 'Just about finished here. You go and get changed your guests will be arriving in half an hour.'

Beth unzipped the dust cover from her latest acquisition, took the dress from its hanger and laid it on the bed. It was a plain short shift in a soft wool fabric. The only embellishment was two large patch pockets at hip level. It had a v-neck, short sleeves and ended well above her knees. But the thing that Beth loved the most was the colour. It was a vibrant shocking pink. She held it against herself and looked in the full-length mirror. The dress and her hair both screamed for attention, the effect was electrifying, and Beth loved it. She washed and dressed and did her make-up. Pale foundation, green eye shadow, the palest pink lipstick she could find, and thick dark eyeliner and mascara to accentuate her beautiful green eyes. She brushed her hair vigorously until it formed a mass of titian curls surrounding her face. Satisfied with her appearance, Beth went downstairs.

Desmond, dressed in a smart grey suit, was arranging a bottle of champagne on a tray with a dozen glasses.

'Anything I can do to help Dad?'

Desmond shook his head. 'All ship-shape and Bristol fashion,' he said. 'All we need now are the guests.'

Prudence entered wearing her latest black cocktail dress with a stunning diamond brooch gleaming on the shoulder.

Beth bent to examine it. 'Mum it's beautiful, why I haven't seen it before?'

Prudence coloured with pleasure. 'My mother left me a few very nice pieces of jewellery.' She told Beth. 'Some of them are quite valuable so I generally keep them in your father's safe deposit box, but I thought, as tonight was a very special occasion, perhaps it was a good time to air them.'

Prudence turned her attention to Beth's dress. 'Beth, that dress …'

'I know, I know it's doesn't go with my hair, but I love it.'

'I was about to say how much it suits you,' Prudence said with a smile.

Beth was, for once, lost for words. 'Thank you,' was the best she could do.

Their conversation was interrupted by the roar of a sports car and Beth ran to the front door to greet Tom. He lifted her feet off the ground and spun her around and Beth noted with pleasure that he was wearing the expensive navy sweater she had bought him for Christmas. Behind him stood Elsie holding a large iced fruit cake on a silver board. It was decorated with "Tom" and "Beth" intertwined with hearts in pink and blue icing. She passed the cake into Prudence's waiting hands and gave her coat to Desmond.

Under the coat Elsie wore a multi-coloured silk caftan that reached to her ankles. 'Tom gave me a lift because of the cake, the others will be here shortly,' she told Beth, smoothing the bright garment that flowed over her ample frame and tucking back a stray strand of hair that had already escaped from its restraining band.

'Elsie what a fantastic dress, where did you get it?'

'Made it myself.' Elsie said proudly, doing a twirl for Beth's benefit.

They moved to the drawing room where they were soon joined by Elsie's husband Jack, and Katie and Nathan and shortly afterwards by Molly and Rob and his wife Jean. Desmond hurriedly dispensed champagne and the party was underway.

When everyone had a drink in their hand Desmond rapped his glass with a teaspoon to attract their attention.

'Please raise your glasses to wish Tom and Beth all the best in their future life together.' Glasses were raised and "Tom and Beth" echoed round the room.

Everyone, apart from Molly, had brought presents to mark Beth and Tom's engagement. Katie and Nathan gave a fondue set. 'It's the very latest thing,' she told them eagerly. Katie then went on to shyly inform everybody that she had been accepted as a trainee accountant by a London firm and Nathan had been offered a post as a maths lecturer at UCL. She held on tightly to Nathan's hand. 'We should be able to marry in the summer and you are all invited to the wedding,' she announced happily.

When the applause died down Elsie presented Beth and Tom with half a dozen napkins, hand embroidered with their initials, and Rob gave them a cut glass ash tray and a set of coasters bearing pictures of vintage cars.

'Here you are partner,' Rob said as he gave the hastily wrapped gift to Tom.

'What did you call him?' Beth cried.

'You heard,' Rob answered bluntly, grinning. Beth turned to Tom and he nodded in agreement. 'As from tomorrow, January the first, Tom is officially a joint owner of the garage.' Rob told the gathering.

Another round of applause greeted Rob's announcement.

When the congratulations were finished Prudence stepped forward. She felt a trifle embarrassed. The presents so far had been modest and useful. Her gift was neither of those things and was specifically for Beth. She hoped it wouldn't seem too ostentatious. She handed Beth a flat leather-covered box.

'This present really comes from your grandmother,' she told Beth. 'I was going to keep it for your twenty-first but, with your wedding on the horizon, I thought now was a more appropriate moment.'

Beth slowly opened the box to reveal a choker of beautifully matched creamy pearls fastened with a striking pave-set diamond clasp. Her eyes filled as she hugged her mother. 'Thank you, it's beautiful and I'll be proud to wear it on my wedding day.'

'They're real pearls,' Prudence whispered in her ear and Beth laughed. It was so like her mother to mention that fact. She held up her hair and motioned to Tom to fasten the pearls around her neck.

Molly flushed and fidgeted from foot to foot. 'I haven't brought a present ...' she said quietly.

Beth was upset. 'Molly, please, we didn't expect any presents. It's enough that you're here celebrating with us.'

'... but I do have some news to share with you,' Molly continued. 'I've bought myself a bungalow.' That caught everyone's attention and all eyes were on Molly.

'Where?' Beth was shocked.

'Don't you fret m'girl, you're not going to get rid of me that easily. It's in Wolvercote, not far away, so I'll still be coming into the shop every day.' Beth breathed a sigh of relief. 'There's four bungalows being built and I went to have a look at them last month and when I'd measured up I decided one would be just the job so I went to see Desmond here and he undertook to do the conveyancing for me.' A memory stirred in Beth's mind. That day when Molly couldn't find her tape measure and went out wearing a hat, now she understood.

Beth was a little concerned. Molly had lived in the flat for so many years, why did she want to move now and would she be happy on her own in a bungalow? She voiced her fears.

Molly patted her arm. 'Solitude and me have been neighbours for a very long time m'dear. Until you came along I was on my own for more years than I can remember, and I survived quite well. As to a bungalow, well I know it's the opposite of an upstairs flat but I'm sure my old knees will be glad of a rest from all those stairs. And,' she continued happily, 'It's got a nice little plot of land so I'll be able to grow flowers as well as sell them.'

Beth was satisfied and gave Molly a hug. 'So long as you'll be happy,' she told her.

'There's just one more thing ...' Beth wondered what more Molly could possibly have to tell. 'For the last three years you've been the nearest thing I'll ever have to a daughter ...' Molly paused and Beth fiddled with her pearls. 'I would like you and Tom to have the flat. It would make me really happy to think of you there ... and possibly some little 'uns too.' She added with a smirk.

Molly's words brought a flush to Beth's cheeks and her eyes opened wide.

'Molly are you quite sure of this?'

'Never been surer. The bungalow will be ready in four months so I'm hoping to be invited to a spring wedding, the flowers will be at their best then!'

The party gathered momentum. The canapés and petits fours were soon consumed with many a compliment to Prudence who's stock reply was,' It's nothing, they're really very easy to make took no time at all.' And Desmond smiled and refrained from saying that he had been banned from the kitchen for the past two days. Beth and Tom cut their cake and the approval was extended to Elsie who coloured and flapped her hand at the praise.

A record was put on the gramophone and Katie and Nathan, and Rob and his pretty wife Jean began to dance. Tom was not fond of dancing but eventually Beth persuaded him to join the others. Out of the corner of her eye Beth noticed her mother, Elsie and Molly sitting together on one of the big sofas. Their heads were together and the three were deep in conversation. Who would have thought it, three such different people and yet they are chatting away as though they've know each other for years? Beth felt a lump in her throat. How much better could life get? Then she looked up at the handsome man next to her, doing his best to keep in time with the music to please her, and she thought her heart would burst with happiness.

Desmond and Jack were chatting over a couple of pints. Beth was surprised, she had not seen her father drink beer before but he seemed to be enjoying it. He caught her eye and beckoned her over. 'Beth, a brief word in your ear,' he said quietly. Beth left Tom talking to his father and followed Desmond to the corner of the room furthest away from the noise of the music.

'There's something else you need to know Beth, but I didn't wish to announce it earlier as it's a private family matter.' What on earth is coming now? Beth thought.

'I was worried that without money from the flat, Molly might, in future years, be a little strapped for cash,' Desmond looked concerned and Beth echoed his fear. 'So I made a suggestion to her that she was pleased to accept.' Desmond took a sip of his beer and Beth waited patiently for her father to continue. 'I have bought the shop and

Molly's interest in the business,' he announced. 'The money raised from that should, if invested wisely, keep Molly very comfortably when she retires.'

'But how will you manage to run the business, you're a solicitor, you don't know anything about floristry,' Beth burst out bluntly.

Desmond smiled. Nothing would curb Bethany's outspoken manner he realised and he hoped she wouldn't change, he loved her just as she was. 'I'm not going to run the business. You are, with Molly's blessing. I have put The Flower Basket in trust for you until you are twenty-one, after that it becomes yours to do will as you will.'

Bethany felt for the chair behind her and sat down heavily. 'Thank you Dad,' she whispered and her green eyes shone with unshed tears.

Desmond squeezed her shoulder. 'I think your young man is trying to attract your attention,' he said and returned to his conversation with Jack.

Tom put his arm round Beth's shoulders and his eyes were shining. 'It's marvellous news about the flat.' Beth nodded happily. 'Now we can marry much sooner than we thought and ... there are two bedrooms'

Beth coloured. 'Just what are you suggesting?' she asked with a grin. Tom raised an eyebrow. 'You can think again,' Beth told him robustly. 'In a few years time maybe, but just now I've got a business to run!' Tom bent and kissed her upturned face, he loved Beth for her energy and ambition. Having a family mattered to him but there was plenty of time for that, after all Beth was only nineteen.

It was close to midnight. Desmond switched on the radio and began filling fresh glasses with champagne.

As Big Ben sounded the first stroke of midnight, glasses were raised, kisses and hugs were exchanged, and cries of 'Happy New Year!' filled the room.

'Could do with more champagne,' Desmond muttered, holding up a half empty bottle.

'I'll go, you start circulating that.' Tom took hold of Beth's hand and towed her after him to the kitchen.

Once there he pulled her into his arms and his lips found hers.

'I love you Beth,' he told her tenderly.

'I love you too,' Beth replied with a gentle smile.

She buried her face in the rough wool of his sweater and Tom put his arms around her and tightened his grasp as he felt her sobs. He stroked her copper curls and when her crying ceased he lifted her chin and kissed her salty face.

'Feeling better?'

Beth nodded. She had wept for the ending of an age, but they were tears of joy, her childish fears had been laid to rest and she was ready to face the future with Tom by her side.

Lightning Source UK Ltd.
Milton Keynes UK
UKOW04f1156050315

247324UK00002B/16/P